The

Darkest

Clearing

THE DARKEST CLEARING

A Novel By

Brian Railsback

High Sierra Books π Gold Beach, Oregon

ISBN: 0-9715482-5-0

LCCN: 2003108450

First Edition: January 2004

High Sierra Books
P.O. Box 489
Gold Beach, OR 97444
www.highsierrabooks.com

For Cadence Alexandra,
who plays at the edge of the woods.

"Some of those redwoods are older than god," he said. "And they are clearing them out, sawing down the centuries."

"What can we do?" she asked.

"Spike the trees," the other replied.

"But what about the lumberjack?" she whispered, leaning forward. "His arm might be lopped off when the chainsaw bucks."

"Ah," he smiled. "That's the chance he takes, isn't it?"

ONE

I

The line of delicate blue tracks in the snow disappeared upward into thunder.

Eli Ware followed them. She ran against the slope, legs pumping, snowshoes plodding, losing ground behind the two dogs as they leapt through the drifts toward the high probability area. She ran with the SAR team and they broke through a line of bent pines at the top of a hill. The small group of Park rangers and ski patrollers quickened as the wide, white avalanche path spread into view before them—they scrambled down the ridge to where the woman's tracks were abruptly erased by a wall of snow that had just tumbled down from the mountain above. The team, tiny specks blown across the great white sheet, moved under a wall of sharp Sierra peaks that cut into the cold blue sky. Had they not been on search and rescue, the rangers would have found it to be another familiar, beautiful scene in the Park.

Eli kept pace on the soft, broken snow while somewhere, unattached to the strain and movement, an image of her daughter's face of a few moments before came again and again. Sarah's face, blank in nonchalance somehow wrong for a nine-year-old, had watched as her mother jumped in a Park truck and raced after another wanderer.

Early that morning Eli had awakened, put on her ranger's uniform, and lingered over coffee. The quiet hour, the sun breaking over the white ridges, and the seductive steam snaking out of her cup—these things lulled her into thinking she could take the day off. Call in sick, spend a day at home with her daughter and husband. Sarah and Karol had stolen out for an early hike, to track the winter stars and watch the dawn. After she had answered the phone and pulled on the gear needed for the rescue, Eli opened the cabin door and saw Sarah and Karol walking from under the huge shadow of White House Mountain. She waited, not moving, wanting to see them step out of the shadow onto the new glare of the early sun, but the Park jeep arrived. It blotted them from her view. Eli jumped in and sped off with the SAR team. For a second Eli saw Sarah; the small girl waved and looked away. Father and daughter walked on, hand in hand, never looking back. They were too used to seeing her whisked off, by truck or helicopter, but she was becoming less numb to watching them—often from a rearview mirror. In her mind she saw her family, always receding, so often lately that no one bothered with goodbyes when work tore her away.

Blackie and Buck, the dark labs just ahead, pushed through the snow with backs humped like dolphins. Lars, the handler, pulled at them as the nearest man from the ski patrol threw down his ten-foot avalanche probe and hacked at the ice with a shovel. Now Eli joined in, breathing hard, working her shovel so heaps of snow flew into the air.

"Here!" A ski patroller yelled, exposing a swath of bright orange pant leg under a few feet of snow. They dug hard and fast, clearing ice away from the body. A delicate balance of power: the urge to push away snow, the need to miss flesh and bone. The skier had fallen under face up, and he squinted in the light. He wasn't the one they were looking for.

Eli threw down her shovel and looked close into his face. "Are you in pain?"

"No," the man said.

"How many others were with you?"

"One."

"Another skier?"

"Yeah."

They had not come to find skiers.

Eli rose up and yelled to Lars. "He says there's one more! Another skier!"

"Not the woman we're tracking?"

"No!"

"This area is off-limits. Why in the hell were they skiing up here?"

Twenty feet away, the dogs dug into the snow again. Lars chased them. "Trading lives for fresh powder," he muttered.

A medic skied down to the first man. "He's been under for how long?"

"Maybe twenty minutes," Eli said. "He had an air pocket."

"Lucky," the medic said, opening his backpack, looking at the stunned man. "You feel anything?"

The man stared up.

"He said he felt no pain," Eli said.

"We'll take C-spine precaution—cervical collar and a backboard."

The man closed his eyes, turning blue.

"Oxygen."

Another medic had skied in.

"Ware, bring your shovel," Olivos, the Park's chief of protection, yelled.

He had moved to the next site with a ski patroller. Eli thought he didn't need her.

"Ware!"

She ran to Olivos, stopped where he worked, and plunged her shovel into the snow. Her blade just missed a crop of grey hair; this skier had landed facedown. The three dug a bowl around him and very gently turned him up.

"Unconscious, but breathing on his own," Olivos said.

Two medics skied down to this man; Olivos already had an oxygen mask on him. He started to place a heart monitor when a medic took over.

"You've got another one," the medic said. "Might be her."

"Shit!" Olivos stood up, towering over Eli. "I hoped maybe she walked past this."

Lars ran toward the dogs, at the base of the avalanche, where they were digging again. A ranger at the base, looking for tracks on the perimeter, joined Lars.

"Ware—let's go," Olivos said.

She followed him down into the shadow of pines, into a field of blue ice and crumbled snow.

"Stay with me, Ware!" Olivos huffed.

"Right here," she grunted.

"You sound breathless," he said.

"Go figure."

"I like that sound, so close to me."

"Enjoy it while you can," she told him.

"Ah, my child."

As she watched his broad back heave against the ice, she could imagine his big white smile. What an ass, she thought, even now. In the middle of a rescue.

They dug a few feet and found nothing. The dogs scratched at the snow just to the left, at the foot of a big tree, and Lars pulled them back. "Here," he said.

Two feet down they uncovered a leg.

"Snowshoer," Olivos said. "Small person."

They uncovered more.

"Is this her?" Eli said. "It's a young woman, and not dressed for the snow."

"We're too close to the damn tree," Olivos said, all the sass gone from his voice.

They dug out her shoulders and then red snow. Carefully they worked around her head, the blonde hair soaked with blood.

Lars dug with his hands while the dogs whined. Eli and Olivos slowly turned the woman over–her forehead had been driven down over the bridge of her nose. Her eyes were hidden under a broken helmet of exposed pink bone.

"The snow slammed her headfirst into the tree," Lars said, standing back. "Like she was a torpedo."

"Nothing." Eli checked for vital signs. "We have nothing here."

She pulled off her Polartex gloves and began to work; a medic who skied down offered her surgical gloves but she ignored him, working the woman's chest.

"You put on the gloves," Olivos said. "Lot of blood here—you gotta wear them."

She kept on, and he was too busy administering an I.V. to persist. Lars radioed operations, which had been set up near one of the medevac helicopters a half mile away. Soon the best medic for head trauma skied down. Eli kept pumping the woman's chest, puffing breaths into the cold blue lips. She ignored the jiggling, exposed forehead plate.

After eighteen minutes, the medic and Olivos agreed.

"We lost her, Eli," Olivos said.

"She was probably dead a few minutes after hitting the tree," the medic stood up, looking down on the head he had covered. "Operations says the conscious skier has a broken neck, but the other one is coming around and should be fine."

Eli sat back, exhausted, hurt, and relieved that she could stop. She looked up the slope. In the still moment, Eli, Olivos, and the medic sat on the snow. Lars stood nearby. This calm few seconds came before the routine investigation, the reports, and the autopsy.

Quietly, Olivos slid his hand under the woman's buttocks, searching until he found a pocket. He fished out a license.

"No doubt about it," he said. "We found Ellen Cheltingham."

"We're in for it," Lars said, rubbing the backs of his panting, grinning dogs.

"What's that mean, Lars?" Olivos stared at the license.

No one answered.

Eli noticed that the woman had stuffed an expensive woolen nightshirt into her jeans. As they tracked Cheltingham, Olivos had told Eli all that he knew. And what he did not say, Eli filled in. As she watched the dead woman in the snow, she could picture Ellen Cheltingham pulling on jeans and the fur-lined boots in her room at the Muir Hotel, perhaps leaving a lover sleeping or perhaps alone. She had been drinking, maybe taken too many pills. By 3 a.m. Cheltingham had wandered the long, dark halls in the hotel long enough that the night clerk noticed her. She wanted to hike to a place she knew, but could not seem to find her way out of the Muir Hotel. She would not say what room she had come from, nor what was the name of the man who had checked the room.

But she said there was a place in the Valley that waited for her.

By 4 a.m. two rangers took her to the Park infirmary; Cheltingham seemed to pass out on the bed the night nurse offered her. The nurse smelled alcohol but the vital signs were good and she felt the young woman would sleep it off. She checked on Ellen on the half hour. Maybe the last time around it was closer to an hour. But by 6:30 a.m., Cheltingham was gone. She had found snowshoes at the back landing of the infirmary and broke into a remarkable stride across the Valley floor.

Within an hour Eli and the SAR team were closing in on her nearly four miles away from the infirmary. "Not so drugged up," Lars had said. "She's picking up speed and seems to know exactly where she's going. This is a hellava strong woman, and she's knows we're after her."

And we chased her to this place, Eli thought, as she looked at the body. I chased her here. I came to this Valley to be an interpreter, I was going to be the kind of Park ranger who leads nature hikes. I'm not a damned protection ranger, not a search and rescue expert, not a police woman.

But here we are, she thought. Here I am. She stared at Ellen's body. One spring Eli had taken Sarah here, and when they came to the rock face she took her daughter's hand, rubbed it gently across the pattern of granite and explained how the rock had been laid bare by an ancient glacier. The same ridge, running north south, leeward to west winds, so on the east side, above, the snow piled into an overhang, backed by thousands of feet of soft slab; below it two skiers had come, traveling out of bounds, illegally, sliding along until the slab broke loose, a hundred yards wide and four feet deep, crashing down upon them, crowding down in a roar to Ellen Cheltingham who stood at the bottom in her snowshoes, waiting for the ice to tap her with a thumb of snow and bring down her forehead like a tiny pink shell.

"What you think about," Lars broke the silence. "You think about who's on the other end of this woman, who will come to claim her and who will care that she is dead. Who will come after us."

"Damn it, Lars." Olivos shoved back his black hair and covered his small brown eyes with his sunglasses. "Don't be so gloomy. We just did our job—tried to save her."

"I get gloomy around mangled bodies."

"Right." Olivos was ready to move on, tend to the task at hand.

"I got a feeling," Lars pulled one of the dogs close to him. "It's like I'm following tracks that go outside this Valley. This is trouble."

"Bullshit, Lars."

"I bet Eli feels it, too." Lars said.

Eli looked up from the body, past Lars and his dogs. She watched the crest face, where the slab had broken loose. It stretched wide across the ridge, smiling majestically in the harsh morning sun while Eli was not sure what she felt beyond the winter chill.

II

A heavy shudder moved up the steel rib cage in his tower at the World Trade Center. As the floor and ceiling of his office rocked, he watched the room move, inhale and exhale. Lights flickered and his computer screen cut out. Then everything wobbled back into shape, and Eldred Spell realized how flimsy the floors were; the offices of Whitston Harris were housed between thin membranes strung across girders over a thousand feet in the air. Not much held them in. Looking at his dead screen, he knew the commodities exchange would halt and he wondered if the New York Stock Exchange had shut down. Not much left to keep him there, to keep the whole thing going.

He figured the building had been bombed, but Eldred Spell did not care.

Out his office window, the traffic up to midtown looked the same; but he saw down at the Trade Center Plaza that smoke billowed from the Vista Hotel. People fled across the white concrete, bits of black ash blown by a strong wind. Something meant for us, Spell thought. He could see that it would radiate from the towers, travel over the airwaves, fill the streets and subways and buildings with fear.

The first alarm rang somewhere, a faint voice in Spell's ears and he relaxed, tensions easing away, because he already knew what to do. He welcomed some reason to leave his office, and a bombing seemed appropriate—a perfect commemoration of the terse message he had read an hour before. It was an e-mail message, from Miss Brace, his mother's secretary. Spell had not heard from his mother in years, but the news she passed on to him was even more unpleasant than usual. He had looked away from the screen, but nothing he saw in his office comforted him. Carpet, chairs, walls, and ceiling were all white, as he had ordered them to be the year before, a color he had grown up in, and one he found blank and endless, one to be lost in when he wanted to be lost. But the message hovered in his head, words that rapped the front of his skull with a hammer's blow.

Out the window the sky was a ceiling of flat gray clouds, cold; below, Manhattan hugged the ground, the smaller buildings a tumble of dark square stones against the ridge of midtown skyscrapers. He put his hand to the glass and felt something alive and violent drawing into him, something he reeled in from the streets—it flowed up from traffic squirming among the buildings. Spell had made his fortune by being tied into the city, by feeling movements no one else felt, by turning what he knew into advice for big stockholders. He saw just ahead of everyone else, did not explain it, and the senior partners at Whitston Harris never cared how he did it, but gave him what he wanted as long as he saw a step ahead. He knew the science of the stock exchange very well, taking his MBA from Harvard, but he knew more that had nothing to do with science. Some called him the Voodoo Broker, but never to his face.

On Black Friday, as the numbers had hurtled hundreds of points, his clients were saved; he saw the crash coming and capitalized on it, advised to buy and sell perfectly just before the financial storm rained fire and brimstone on everyone else. He made a killing. Whitston Harris noticed, bid high, and raised him from the ashes of Black Friday to a perch on the 84th floor of the World Trade Center, in the midst of their commodities offices, just because he wanted to be there. And every year he made a killing, seeing just around the corner before anyone else, and they gave him whatever he wanted.

But in the hour before the explosion he had felt something coming that was bigger than a financial crash, something that would mean more to him than making a few million dollars a year. As he watched the cabs swim down Broadway like tiny dull goldfish, he could hardly breathe; the hair on his head stood rigid, as if he stood on a spot where lightning struck. He looked at his calendar: Friday, February 29. At his clock: 12:29 p.m. Spell stepped away from the window and leaned against his dark teak desk, saw its rich wine color become blood.

Now he opened his closet and threw coat, scarf, and gloves upon his desk. The coat shoved a file onto the floor, the papers like white leaves, dancing in the air slowly down to the white carpet. Just an hour ago they might have been important. No longer. Spell clenched his jaw.

On a shelf in the closet he found a large gift box of Godiva chocolates a client had sent as a get-acquainted gift several months before. He slipped off the plastic and filled his coat pockets with truffles. From the same shelf he pulled down a flashlight and extra batteries. Everything fit into his pockets neatly. Then from his bottom desk drawer, he fetched a loaded M1911A1 Colt pistol, an original from 1926, worth several hundred dollars. This he slid into a custom holster on the inside of his overcoat. For several years, Spell went in public with a concealed weapon—safety off.

He stopped, watched the empty blank screen. But he still saw the words from that e-mail, and Eldred Spell shoved the monitor off its stand, grimly enjoying the sound of shattering glass.

As the building rumbled, Kerry Womack slammed down the phone and scrambled out of his chair. When his computer went blank, he instinctively hit it several times. Ran out of his small, windowless office, and stopped. Before Kerry panicked, he wanted to make sure others were panicking, too. Blending in was always important. But most people had already gone for lunch. Things were too quiet, and he needed to talk to someone right away. Down the hall he heard Tereza Limon call out. She was Eldred Spell's secretary. Kerry checked the hall to see if any other big shots were in, but they had all gone to lunch some time ago. The light died, the hall went dark, Limon whimpered, and though Kerry felt a building pressure in his chest, wondering if it were fear, anxiety, or a heart attack, even as he wondered if the tower were going to topple over, above all he did not want to go to Spell's office.

Fumbling to keep his lighter on, he crept by.

"Kerry!" Limon whispered.

He stopped, peering into the darkness, where a match light illuminated Limon's oval, olive-colored face. Kerry thought she looked scary and beautiful. She kept him from running through the dark.

"What?" He stayed at the threshold of the office.

"What the hell is going on?" Limon lit another match.

"Maybe an earthquake."

"In New York?"

"Shit, I don't know."

"How are we going to get out?"

"Shit." Talking to Spell's secretary while the world was crumbling sent a shower of confusing sparks through his head. He couldn't move, could hardly speak.

"Where is Mr. Spell?"

"Still in his office." Limon lit another match. "He's breaking things in there."

"What?"

Limon just stared at him.

Why Spell? Kerry thought. He had no idea what to do; he could use a little direction. But all the other executives were gone. Kerry had never read the evacuation plan, nor had he ever been in an emergency (came close when one of his frat brothers in college almost choked to death while chugging a beer). Three ideas competed for attention in his mind. He had a picture of Tower 2 falling over, like some huge log slamming down on Broadway. Then he recalled the day Spell overheard that water cooler joke about the Voodoo Broker; Spell silently walked behind him, grabbed Kerry's left biceps, and squeezed hard. Spell had scary green eyes, bright and fiery, and he stared as Kerry stammered out apologies, and even after Kerry shut up for a long time, Spell kept holding on and staring. No one messed with Voodoo after that. And floating through Kerry's mind, like a nervous tic, were Limon's breasts, swelling at the top, softly lit, easy to grasp in the dark at the center of an emergency.

"What are we gonna do, Kerry?"

"Shit, we could fall over."

"What?"

"What if this tower just falls over, you know?"

"Let's get out of here," Limon walked close to him. "Let's get some place where it's light."

"Did he say you could leave?" Kerry liked how close she was, but he kept picturing Spell watching them. He stamped his foot on the floor; everything felt solid enough.

"No."

"Maybe you better stay."

"The hell I—"

Spell opened his office door, illuminating Kerry and Limon in dim light. He looked back once, beyond the debris of the computer on the floor, up to the thickening smoke outside his window. Very faintly, the far away chorus of a dozen screaming sirens called to him, telling him that his career was finished, that everything in New York and in himself had dried up long ago, waiting to be broken. Something else would happen now, a new direction, and it had nothing to do with his Harvard MBA, his white office, his clients, his bosses. He closed the door.

"We, uh, could use the light." Kerry said. "Can you open the door?"

Spell shined the flashlight in Kerry's face, blinding him, then turned to Limon.

"Let's go," Spell said.

"You see what's going on out there, Mr. Spell?" Limon asked.

"A fire, a bombing. Put your coat on—it will be cold once we get outside."

"How we getting outside?" Kerry asked.

"We'll see." Spell took Limon's arm and escorted her past Kerry, shining the flashlight down the hall.

Limon's boss had never touched her before, but feeling the pressure on her arm seemed scary, like Kerry told her it was. Mr. Spell was a big, strong man. And quiet, and weird, and probably the asshole some said he was. She hoped he knew the right direction, and was glad he had a flashlight. As soon as she had her own light, though, she would get away from him.

Limon was his third secretary in a year.

Spell pushed open the door to a large office, filled with desks facing the plate glass windows. In the dim grey light, he let her go.

Kerry saw the column of smoke outside—it seemed to come up from under the tower. Knowing a fire burned at the bottom of the building made him feel trapped, an animal clinging to a rope while the lower end burned. He didn't like the fact that just a few people were in the office, looking out the windows. The office here usually rang with phones and the voices of people, all adding to the muted clicks and twitter of twenty keyboards being worked over furiously. Now only a few workers were left, standing in dark silhouette by the windows, transfixed by the smoke outside.

"Let's go," Spell said to them. They followed.

He opened the door that led to the elevator and stairs. The hall was black. As he pushed open the door, he noticed a thin wisp of smoke slipping in, flattening out on the ceiling. The flashlight cut a beam through the thickening haze ahead.

"Can't go in there!" Kerry yelled. "The whole damn building is on fire."

"Let's go." Spell repeated, his voice flat like he chanted some incantation. He stepped forward and everyone followed except Kerry.

"I'll prop the door open, okay?" Kerry asked.

"You come with us." Spell said, walking away.

"I'll stay here and keep the door open." Kerry couldn't move.

"I will come back for you." Spell receded into the gathering smoke with the others. His words scared Kerry almost as much as the fire.

More people had come to the elevator, which was dead. They milled about, grey in the smoke and the faint beam of Spell's flashlight. Because he had a light, they looked at him, their faces like death masks appearing out of the black. They had the look of victims, Spell thought, and the strange thing was that they did not look any different to him now than they did every morning when they rode up the elevators, in a haze of cigarette smoke or with the pallor of too much pasty makeup, to get off and pull another nine or ten hours.

"We're trapped," Limon said.

"No way out," a man whose face was lost in the darkness said. "We're standing around in a chimney."

"I'll check the stairs," Spell said.

"Is that you, Mr. Spell?" The voice asked.

"Yes."

"We'll wait here."

Spell felt better to be away from them. He followed the corridor to the unlit exit sign. When he pushed open the door to the stairwell a plume of smoke engulfed him. He stood there, sniffing at the smell of burnt oil, wood, and plastic. The stairwell had enough air to be breathable, the smoke still too thin to kill. Just as he was going to turn back, he heard a sound, like whimpering, from somewhere above. Spell could not be sure if the sound was in his head, or up the stairs, but he had long since learned to heed such things and he started up.

They could not move, the two of them. Joanna and Travis knew each other well, their mothers were friends and lived in the same building in Brooklyn. Joanna and Travis shared the same kindergarten class, both had become introverted and thoughtful children after each observed a divorce. They had slipped away from the tour together, starting down the stairs, and it was all great fun until the lights went out and the smoke came. They whispered quietly to each other in the dark, and when they heard the quick footsteps of one person or another come down, Joanna and Travis shut up. They had learned not to talk to strangers, and these strangers, hurrying by in the dark, didn't stop to ask questions.

Now a man came up, shined a light at their feet, and knelt down before them.

"Come with me," Spell said.

Travis felt Joanna get up and he stood, too. The big man gently took them by the hand, bending slightly to stay closer to their level and out of the smoke, and they started down the stairs.

Spell had gone up two flights to find them. Such quiet victims, he thought, could not have made that much noise. What had he heard? He wanted to smile. As he took them down the stairs, the smoke thickened. He bent lower to them, and said that they would stop to meet some other people in a little while where they could rest for a moment. He let Travis hold the flashlight when they came from the stairwell, and soon the boy made circles and figure-eights in the air even though he was quiet and afraid.

Limon saw them coming, the boy and girl, and Mr. Spell, stooped so he could walk with them more easily. She wondered if he had children, and thought it funny that in four months with him she did not know. She bet no one in the building knew.

He stood them in front of Limon, and gave them each a big Godiva truffle.

"You've been good," he said. "Watch them, Miss Limon."

"Okay."

"How's the stairs?," the faceless voice asked.

"Filling with smoke," Spell answered. "But it will get worse if we stay here."

"What are we going to do?"

"Go down and out."

Some of the people began to ask questions, and Spell felt a discussion coming on. He did not abide discussion.

"I'm going to get Mr. Womack," he told Limon.

"We may not be here when you get back," the voice said.

"Yes you will."

Kerry Womack tried the phone again, got nothing but a busy signal, so he threw it off the desk. Where were the instructions? What about a safety plan? He wanted to make a great show of anger, a display of outrage, but no one was around. He was the animal clinging to the rope, pushing out against thin air. Wispy smoke filled the room and gave him inspiration, a decision to make, so he picked up a desk chair and slammed it against a plate glass window. He would make vents! The chair bounced back and hit him. No window would get the best of him. He ripped at his collar, threw off his tie, and picked up the chair again.

This time it smashed through, went sailing out with shards of glass following it down to the Trade Center Plaza. Kerry laughed, now he got the hang of it, and he threw another chair, shattered another window. The smoke outside had blown away from his side of the building; in fact, now the smoke along the ceiling started to drift out. He broke into a rhythm, had his eye on a desk—what a big crash that would make!

Someone pulled at his arm.

"What are you doing?" Spell asked, gripping Kerry hard.

"Making vents!" Kerry pulled his arm away, remembering old wounds. "Making vents, asshole!"

"We don't need them." Spell said. "We're leaving."

"The hell we are—I, I know damn well what I'm doing here." Spell had broken the rhythm, and now Kerry remembered where he was and who he was. He wanted to get back to the desk.

Spell considered leaving him. The mad underling hurling chairs from the tower, shattering glass and bringing in the rising wail of gathering sirens, made an interesting scene. When Spell left New York he thought it would be comforting to think of Mr. Womack up there, breaking glass while the flames rose. "Come with me."

"The hell I will."

"I won't discuss it."

"Get out of here, Voodoo!"

Kerry turned to work on his desk and something heavy slammed him in the back of the ear. He whirled around and received another blow.

"Come on," Spell said.

"You hit me!"

Spell shrugged. "I've got your attention."

"Who says you know what to do!" Kerry screamed. "I'm making vents!"

"No," Spell brought his fists up. "You're making a shower of glass for the people on the Plaza."

"What the hell." Kerry's ears rang, filling his head with a sharp headache.

"And your vents will draw more smoke up here."

"Oh." Kerry hated Mr. Spell.

"Let's go."

"What if I don't?"

"I'll shove you out that window."

"You would."

"Yes." Spell could see himself hurling Womack out the window; he wasn't sure if he was bluffing. "Follow me."

Kerry walked behind him, mumbling one last protest: "You're as crazy as they say."

Across the blackness of the hall they entered, Spell saw the words in front of him: "Your sister has died in an avalanche in the Park where the two of you used to play." He knew that the spare message was dictated by his mother; it had her tone.

"I was not crazy," Eldred Spell answered Kerry. "But this changes things."

III

The sun was setting, and the autopsy would wait for the morning, when Ellen Cheltingham would be transported to Fresno. Eli left the body in the Park morgue where she had helped lay it out. She washed her hands and face several times, pulled on her coat, and started out the door of headquarters. Nick Cairns blocked the way.

"You've had a rough day," he said in his over loud voice.

Eli waited, looking up to his broad smile, knowing that the Park superintendent had something unpleasant to ask of her. Looking at the way he had pushed his large body into his tight dress uniform, dark drab cloth draped over a hard, broad frame, she already knew what he wanted.

"You found her lover," she said.

"Yes," he raised eyebrows in exaggerated encouragement.

"You want me to go with you."

"We'll face Mr. Luttrill together." His smile grew even larger as he shifted about in his uncomfortable uniform.

"Where's Olivos?"

"Oh, he and I agree you're better at these things. Your chief always speaks very highly of your abilities."

Eli had learned that with Cairns, all sentences have subtexts. He rarely could say something straight, so complaints and orders always slithered about under a pretext of smiles and overdramatic exclamations.

"Olivos is very fond of me," Eli kept looking into Cairns's face, knowing that her direct gaze bothered him, as he was crossed between his desire to look away and his attempt to be commanding—meeting her gaze was tough.

"I suppose he is." The smile hardened.

She simply watched Cairns, until his eyes narrowed.

"Now," his voice lowered with his smile, pretexts dropping away. "Get into your dress uniform, and let's talk to the son of a bitch who is so anxious to check out of the Muir Hotel."

After she changed, they drove to the Muir, and now it was her turn to smile, as Cairns drove quietly, because she knew he hated for any of his real self to slip into the open. She wanted him to see her smile.

Mr. Luttrill had not bothered to ask anyone about Ellen. The hotel staff knocked on every door, asked every guest, to find out who knew anything about her. The assistant manager located Luttrill in the Hetch Hetchy Suite in the Muir. The man had been packing, and had heard what had happened to Ellen. Now he waited in his room for an interview with the rangers. Eli and Cairns crossed the large, softly lit lobby and took the elevator up.

Cairns knocked too loudly on the door, nearly pounded it, and stood back in the hall, feet apart, hands behind, at parade rest.

Luttrill opened the door, grey hair slicked back, shades covering his eyes, Ralph Lauren Polo teal shirt and tan slacks—a man of fifty bent on looking thirty.

They made introductions, and Eli thought both men were too noisy; she saw that Cairns was faltering under the protection of his loud voice and smile.

They all sat on a large white couch/love seat arrangement. Cairns removed his hat, studying the brim with his fingers, smile fading away. Eli wondered if he would get the words out, or if he wanted her to start. By now a long crease between Luttrill's grey eyes was gathering other lines; he was worried.

"Mr. Luttrill—" Cairns started out, loudly, officially.

Eli looked away, and then he surprised her.

"You know that we found Ellen Cheltingham this morning," he said very softly, in a tone of voice Eli had never heard before. "She happened to be at the wrong place—there was an avalanche at Illouette Pass. She was dead when we found her."

"How exactly did she die?" Luttrill tilted his head, leaned forward. Worry was running to curiosity.

"She struck a tree," Eli began. She searched for the right way to put it, looking for words among images of the body, of blood and broken bone. "I believe she was knocked unconscious immediately, and then smothered in the snow. We did all we could."

"Officer Ware was part of the rescue effort," Cairns's voice rose to official decibels again. "They saved two skiers."

"How far away is this place?" Luttrill asked quietly.

"Nearly five miles," Eli said.

"Definitely five," Cairns corrected.

"How in hell did she get out there?," Luttrill looked down, speaking to himself.

"She had snowshoes," Cairns explained. "Really, quite a hike."

"A hike." Luttrill took in the size of Cairns, then he looked at Eli: tall woman, wiry, lips tight. He wanted out of this room. He had done nothing wrong, but it felt like he needed a lawyer. Something about the way the woman ranger watched him.

"What can you tell us about her?" Eli asked. "What she was doing out there?"

"She was a temp in my office in San Francisco. I hardly knew her."

"But she came out here with you, spent how many nights?"

"Just last night." Luttrill turned to Cairns, wishing he would ask the questions. The woman bothered him. "I mean, we were talking and she told me how much she loved to come out to this Park when she was a girl. I took her. Got this room. Damn expensive room."

Cairns was about to say something, but he stopped. They waited. In the silence Luttrill felt that the woman ranger could read his thoughts. Could see what he saw when Ellen came a few weeks to work in his office while his receptionist recovered from a hysterectomy. Young Ellen, on the right side of thirty-five, a tight little thing, strong and quick. And hungry. No money but an appetite for good liquor and good times. She was a great roll without a past and a future that quit when his receptionist came back. A natural blonde, a fabulous little lay with an endless smile and an educated wit. Ellen Cheltingham was a much-needed vacation.

"Did you know she was drunk?" Eli asked.

"I know I was," Luttrill looked at the dark timbers in the ceiling.

"Did you even know she had left the room?" Eli doubted it.

"I was out. I didn't know she was gone until I woke up around 11 or so."

"Hung over?"

"Sure." Luttrill wondered why Cairns was letting the woman ranger run the show.

"Do you have any idea why she went straight to Illouette Pass?"

"None at all," he lied. All the way to the Park, Ellen had talked about summers in the Valley with her brother. She wanted to get up in the morning and find some little cave or something that they had found, where years before they made a secret shelter for themselves. That's where she was going. But Luttrill would be damned if he'd get into that with the ranger woman; he just wanted to get the hell in his BMW and head home.

He didn't say much more. As far as Luttrill was concerned, they could accept his brief answers or it was lawyer time. He gave them addresses and numbers where he could be reached, he gave them his lawyer's card.

"How will this play in the media?" he asked Cairns as the rangers stood up to go.

"It will be in the regional papers, probably make a few paragraphs in the nationals. News crews are on the way, there will be spots on TV."

Eli noticed how Luttrill clenched his hands. He had relaxed in the interview, but he tensed up again.

"Goodbye, Mr. Luttrill," Cairns said at the door. "We're sorry about all this."

"That's okay," Luttrill said. "What could we do?"

"Not much, unfortunately," Cairns said.

"Mr. Luttrill," Eli stood close to him at the door; a few inches taller, she looked down into his eyes. "Your wife might know before you get home. You should call her."

Those hands clenched again, made white little fists. And Luttrill shut the door.

They walked down the hall silently, and then Cairns asked, "you sure he's married?"

Eli pulled on the brim of her hat, giving Cairns a sidelong look. She wondered how he could be so dense. Cairns had been married for years, and though his marriage appeared to be his bane and certainly was the talk of the Valley, he still must have learned something about men and women.

"Hmm." He did not like the way Eli made him feel uncomfortable, like a fool. He had enough of that at home. "Tomorrow your day off?"

"Yes."

"Sorry." Cairns picked up his stride so she would fall back a little, but she kept up. "I thought all of you SAR people on this one would need a debriefing—a good, helpful counseling session to help you all through. Got it set up for tomorrow, noon."

"I told you—"

"Now, good lady," he said, in command now. "Do you know how hard it is to get the clinical psychologist to come out from Fresno on a Saturday? A lot of trouble. We couldn't miss you—you're important. Olivos says you're a crucial part of our team."

After a long pause, Cairns could not look at Eli, but did say in a very steady voice, "I'll see you at that debriefing."

She wanted to be home in time for the dinner Karol made. Some nights it was enough if she could get home before Sarah was read to by Karol and put to bed by Karol. For a time her husband had been letting Sarah wait up for Eli, but now there were too many late nights. And even though Eli would be home by six, she knew this was going to be a long night, knew that she would not get much more than half sleep. Somewhere tonight Ellen's and Sarah's faces would blend, and the headboard would feel like a rock face, and no heater could keep out the cold. She needed Karol, and figured he was even now pouring himself plenty of coffee, getting ready for the long night.

IV

Spell told them to go down and they did. One or two suggested going up to the roof, maybe wait for a helicopter to pull them off. But Spell said they would be too dependent on people with helicopters. And when they entered the black, smoke-filled stairwell they had to follow him—he was the only one with a flashlight.

He himself did not know why he wanted to go down, to descend nearly ninety floors to what might be a deadly inferno. Going up was easier. But he felt that he should go down, that there was nothing for them on the roof and they would probably have to go down anyway. Then someone with a Walkman heard that there had been an explosion in the parking garage, so Spell figured an explosion could be contained. Going down was safe enough.

But as he entered the stairwell, taking in the thickening smoke while he held Travis and Joanna's hands, he simply wanted to go down. It was right that these people should go and meet the remnants of the blast, descend to see what was really going on in their world—learn firsthand how weak the whole foundation had become, how ready everything was to fall, how easily people die. At first they were alone, but as they walked down the steps they picked up others. In the flashlight they all looked pale, a gathering of wide-eyed, coughing, crying faces floating down in the clouds. Lower, at each floor, more joined, the smoke and fire dislodging them from their offices, until they flooded the stairwell, a cascade of confused world traders, Port Authority workers, secretaries, underlings and runners, all flowing down to the inferno.

At times, stooping to avoid the smoke if he could, Spell hoped flames did await them, that the trip would end there. He held the children's hands tightly, encouraging them with melted chocolates, letting them handle the flashlight. Their innocence gave the trip meaning. Once Kerry tried to hurry down past them, and Spell planted the heel of his sharp Italian shoe in the fleeing man's back, sending him sprawling on the stair. People stepped over him while he hacked and screamed obscenities at Spell.

Two hours later they walked out of the building, through the Liberty Street exit, part of the outpouring of the living dead, their mouths and eyes ringed with black soot. Spell and Limon knelt down with Travis and Joanna, a small island in the moving crowd.

"You were good children," Spell said, trying to wipe some of the soot from Joanna's face. "You get out of here now, never come back." He tucked a hundred dollar bill into each child's pocket, as if he were giving them cab fare out of the city. "Here's the last of the chocolates."

They held out their hands.

"Good." Spell wanted to smile for them. He turned to Limon, "You take them to those officers there."

"Yes, Mr. Spell." Limon's eyes watered so it was difficult to see. Her lungs itched with toxin; she could hardly speak.

"Then you get out of here." He handed her a hundred dollar bill.

"I will." Limon wanted to say thank you, but she was too tired. She saw his chest, his thin white tie and white shirt streaked with soot, and then he turned from her, his black coat melding into the crowd and the red and blue flashing lights and the silver and black of the buildings, all distorted in the wash of her tears. He's maybe crazy, she thought, maybe not. For the first time, she wanted to know more about him. She even looked forward to seeing him again.

As Spell predicted, the fear traveled up Manhattan quickly. He turned the corner and started up Church Street. He walked in and out of police barricades—no one noticed him in the confusion of victims, gawkers, sirens, smoke, and broken glass. Passing the Plaza, he looked up at 2 World Trade Center, finding his floor and the three windows that Kerry had broken out. On other floors in both Towers 1 and 2 he could see several windows had been shattered. And below, smoke rose from the ground behind the Vista Hotel. By the great copper sphere in the center of the Plaza, firemen and police hurried, stepping over the pulsating canvas arteries of dozens of hoses.

They can put this back together, Spell thought, but the next bomb will be bigger. He stood, imagining Tower 2 reeling back into Tower 1, toppling toward Wall Street, making a tremendous avalanche of concrete and steel until it reached the dark canyon where the heart of finance beat and where it would be snuffed out. A police officer shoved him, and Spell turned his back on the World Trade Center and headed for home.

He turned the corner at the Hotel Millennium and took Fulton Street to Broadway. Then up the Great White Way, glutted with a stalled, frightened herd of vehicles, the screams of drivers and blaring horns roaring up the stone walls of buildings. Occasionally someone would glance at Spell, take in the soot on his shirt and face, but then the stranger would glance away. Though tired, Spell wanted to get away as quickly as he could, the smoke—a toxic mix of spent gas and oil—seemed to hover about him. Broadway filled with its own smoke, the idle of gas and diesel engines, and Spell felt the air was even thicker here than in the stairwell.

Once on Fifth Avenue, Spell thought it might be possible to get a cab. But at 34th, in front of the Empire State Building, he met a new tangle of panic and confusion. People poured out of the building and the traffic had frozen here, too, and in passing conversations of Empire State tenants he heard that a bomb scare was on there. He glanced back at the twin towers, dim in the grey light, slightly obscured by a gentle snow. Spell wondered when the Empire State was set to go off. Hurrying along Fifth, he gave up the idea of a cab.

His own personal cloud of smoke gathered about him, and no matter that by now he trotted up the street, the gritty, sooty air kept pace with him like a clinging ghost. Crossing 57th, Spell stumbled on a pothole, his slick shoes slipping on the dirty ice at the sunken curb. On the sidewalk he stopped, taking in the black pavement, thinking of all the layers of asphalt on the road. Everything in New York was covered, done and redone. Where the old buildings squatted, with heavy thighs of soiled brick and shoulders of black steel and pocked stone, Spell could see the phantoms of even older structures. Layers of varying architecture blocked out the sky and all of it weighed heavily on the trampled, sinking paved ground. Once, several years before, he had come from Harvard and looked up and saw history, progress, amazement. Here had been human activity in abundance, everyone did everything every day—protests by megaphone on the streets, artists painting in the plazas, vendors hawking bagels, knishes, vegetables, oranges, or watches right at the door of Wall Street, where everyone fed on the heart of commerce. Beautiful.

But now, at Fifth and 57th, the air felt heavy to Spell. New York was paved and repaved, new paths were impossible, and in this air, breathed and rebreathed, even a new breath was impossible. The array of buildings and their architecture stood as cold, heavy monuments to everything an artist could do. The protestors had nothing new to protest—sometime, somewhere, on every street corner someone had done it before them. Hawkers seemed tired by more than the exhaustion of competition and rejection, the vendors of a century before quietly leaned on them. A beggar with his sax did not have to look far down the street for the beggar with a clarinet, and just beyond were the sax and clarinet players of fifty years before.

Up in the buildings, behind the dull, yellow windows, Spell knew the people would have the same conversations people did when New York suffered the big terrorist bombing twenty years earlier. Even the bombers were working old territory.

By the time he reached 73rd, Spell was relieved to turn away from the park. It spread out to his left after he crossed Central Park South; the black, stark trees, huddled behind a moat of pavement and diesel fumes, offered him no comfort. Finally, in front of The Towers at 73rd and 3rd, Spell was home.

"You were at the Trade Center today, Mr. Spell?" The doorman looked him over.

"Yes," Spell slipped his pistol out of its holster before he threw his coat on the ground.

"Good to see you, sir." The doorman said nervously; he wanted to ask questions, but he knew better.

"Throw that away," Spell pointed to the crumpled coat and handed the doorman a hundred dollar bill.

"Thank you, sir." The weirdos are always the best, thought the doorman. So what if he's got a gun. "Sir?"

"What?" Spell did not turn as he walked away.

"Miss Newman is waiting for you." And she looks very hot for something, he thought.

"Yes."

The elevator up to the 39th floor went very slowly, and the sooty cloud around Spell filled it up, so he could hardly breathe when the doors opened at last.

Alanis Newman threw open his door before he could unlock it; she pulled him in, and slammed it shut behind them.

"My God!" she smiled, digging her nails into his shoulders. "You were in it!" Alanis buried her face in his chest and breathed deep. "You smell like fire and smoke." She breathed in again.

"I'm tired," he said.

"I know how to wake the dead." She took him by the hand and led him to the living room.

Once he had thought that he felt something for her. Once, for a short time after they met at the health club in the Hilton, the sight of her in his apartment, as he saw her now, smiling, breathing hard, fresh with sweat wrapped in her slick spandex outfit, strong bare calves and arms bulging from the flaming fabric, urging him on—once, it could have meant something. Hadn't it felt good and new, when they did the Tavern On The Green on warmer days, and she wore a sun dress? What was that he had felt when he looked into the creamy white apex of the cross her long neck, collar bones, and cleavage made? It wasn't here now, and he knew he could not share Ellen with Miss Newman. He could not say that his sister was dead, and the only thing the bombing meant in the face of that was he had learned how to clear out a building in record time.

Normally, Alanis would wait. She would like to chatter on about life as an acquisitions editor at Norton, fill up the long silence of his large apartment, and drive him with her words into the shower. Then out somewhere to eat, usually of her own choosing because he did not seem to have opinions about restaurants anymore, and then back again, where she could get one more time out of him. Spell was a good man, hard, and dependable. Although she had tried for a long time, she could find no one else to replace him.

But tonight she could not wait. The explosion sent waves up and down the city and electrified her nervous system and woke everyone up. Cabbies and doormen felt jumpy, asked questions, and everyone had energy that revved her up. Alanis was sensitive to energy, and she fed on it, came alive by it. She left work early and hit the gym hard but she could not slow down. Maybe he could bring her down—he was good—but if he didn't work tonight she knew others who might do the trick.

But Spell would do. Blown out of his building, he smelled of the fire and panic, and she pulled off his tie and slipped off his shirt, kissing his broad, slick chest, nibbling at the smokiness as if it were bacon. She took everything off and laid him out on his white couch. Alanis peeled off her slick outfit and tossed it to the floor. She watched his green eyes follow the spandex down and they looked wonderfully empty.

"What was it like?" She worked him over.

"An ending." Spell stared upward, beyond her to the ceiling fan, studying the still white blades. Sometimes her head, dark brows and short black hair, would dart in and out of view.

"But what was it like?" She moved up on his thighs now, and he was coming around like she knew he would.

"Confusion. Smoke. Fire." His body, despite the pain in his lungs, reacted to her licks and proddings. It hardened on its own, had nothing to do with him.

"Smoke," she said between breaths. "Yeah. But then what?"

"I led some people down." She had saddled on his hips now, settling down and up, and in the fluid movement arced down to kiss him on the lips. But he would not be able to breathe then, and he turned away. She rared up, as she always wanted to do, and did not try to kiss him again.

He looked away from her, and up from the white cross, and up from the underside of her chin and thin nose and black hair, bobbing and working way above him. His eyes went back to the still white blades.

"Then what?"

"I think I wanted to kill Kerry Womack."

"Then?"

"Then I almost fell in love with two lost children."

"Then?" Her voice was tense now, but not from what he said.

"I decided to give up my career and my life here. To get away forever. I'm finished." He could talk this way to her now, because he knew the times when Alanis just wanted sound and didn't hear what the words meant.

"Then, then?"

"Then—no, before." His body was moving with her now, as she wanted. It did what she wanted and he could hardly feel it. "I lost the only—"

"Then, then, then." She plunged her hands on his chest and shuddered. "Fire."

Alanis collapsed onto him, shoved her head under his chin, and turned to see his gun on the floor. Spell is good, she thought, good until I find another, if I find another, another. Can't find another.

He coughed hard, hacking, and shoved her off.

"I need a shower," he said.

For a half hour Alanis waited alone as he sat on the curb of the big white tub with the bathroom door locked. She called to him twice but then turned up the volume on his TV to listen to the special reports. Even after he heard the door bang as she walked out, Spell stayed in the bathroom and listened to the echoes of voices from the TV. Someone had planted the bomb that left a huge crater in the second floor parking garage beneath the Vista Hotel, shattering walls and floors and blowing into the PATH terminal. But what he thought of as he listened was what they would not say, what had happened to his sister. He did not sleep that night.

Early the next morning he threw on the same clothes, wrapped himself in stale smoke, and walked out to a news stand and brought home the *Times*. After pages of speculation–whether five or seven had died, what the financial impact would be–he found an article about his sister. A single column about the skiers and the woman the rangers had been tracking from the Park infirmary. How they pursued her across five miles, how they had been amazed at her progress. Nick Cairns, the Park superintendent, was quoted, saying he thought she was not lost but was looking for something beyond where she was found. He had no idea what she was seeking.

Eldred knew.

He lay back on the floor, the section of the paper still in his hand, and he watched the still white blades again until they blurred and expanded into clouds. Snow fluttered down slowly, twisting in a cold light that hit only the flakes and lit them up like silver. Now he stood, walked a long way toward a tiny square of green light, toward something he had seen many times before. Quickened his pace to get closer to it, watched the square grow slowly, so slowly, as he ran silently. Then he stood before the canvas, which had become huge and without borders. He wanted to step into the picture, walk through the oils and brush strokes. But could only watch. In the center of the great Valley he saw them, walking on a carpet of green between vast granite walls. He and his father. Too dark specks joined by a thin line—a brush stroke, or his father's hand holding the boy's. And they were frozen. He wished they would move. He wished he was in the picture, and not looking. He wanted it not to be a picture, not an image. His heart beat against the brush strokes, and he screamed to get in. Just to get in. The snow, waves of white blotting the view, crowded it out just as he thought he could see the two move, when it seemed he might be let in. The snow stopped everything, crushed out his chance. He screamed until ice filled up his mouth.

Spell shook himself awake. His mouth was dry from screaming. Breathing heavily, almost choking, he tore off his white shirt, threw off his pants, and stumbled toward the bathroom. Spell scrubbed in the shower, burnished himself with soap and water for a long time. Washing off the dream as he had so many times before, hoping the steam would clean out that picture of him and his father in the Valley in California.

Though always a part of his life, a recurring theme, the dream had come more often lately and had been building in intensity. Now, he believed, it had been leading up to Ellen. She had probably seen it too; it was a dream he had given her, told her about when she was a little girl struggling to live in the cold halls of the Cheltingham estate. A comforting dream, borrowed from a time Spell thought he had with a father he hardly knew, the man who fled the estate just before Ellen was born. Spell had his father's last name, but Ellen was christened with her mother's last name. Already, their mother was erasing any trace of their father.

Spell saw where the dream would take him, just as it had taken Ellen. Back to the Valley. For there, some summer day when he was three or four, his father had taken him. A trip that must have been just before he left. Despite everything his mother did to wash the memory of his father out, this one image remained. Spell learned not to ask much of his mother, but he asked again and again to be taken back to the Valley. He shared the image with Ellen, and when they were old enough they tried to live it by going to the Valley. But over the years that memory became framed in a picture, and by the time he came to New York he had been expelled from it. As a boy, he knew that he had to go back to save the image of his father. Back then it had been much clearer; now, Spell could hardly remember it. Sometimes he was not sure if the trip had been real or a part of the dream.

When he was ten, his mother finally let him go. She insisted he travel alone and, looking back, Spell realized she allowed it because the trip made a good way to kick him into adulthood, to test him, and beat back all fear. She had wanted to make him a tough boy, an invincible man. He traveled across country on Greyhound, for she said he should mix with the public and learn what was out there. The first few summers he came to the Valley, she set him up in a suite at the Muir Hotel and paid the staff well to watch him. When she considered him of age, at 13, she gave him a backpack, some money, and said if he wanted to go to the Valley he would be on his own. The trips became his reprieve—two weeks out of the year that she relented and let him run free of her. When he was fourteen, his mother let him take Ellen along.

In the beginning, as a child, he timidly went out into the Valley and searched for that place in his mind, searched for his father. When he grew older, and when Major McCrimmon at Jackson Military Academy stamped more reality into his frame, he abandoned the search. But not the Valley. Each year in June he returned, and then Ellen joined him, and they followed the river and creeks on the Valley floor, traveled on and off trail. Each year they put on packs and went up out of the Valley and learned the upper vales and jagged mountains well. Farther and farther out they went, escaping all clutter and noise of people, stretching out on the cold meadow grass at night by a fireless camp, studying the stars, or the dark clouds that blew across the moon. Now he remembered Ellen, as a soft blur of blonde in the dark, a line of little teeth, smiling.

By the time he arrived at Harvard, most of this foolishness of looking for his father's ghost in the Valley had been removed by his mother. He took his degree, looked for a life in New York, and had not visited the Valley in nearly a decade. Ellen took a degree in art history at Berkeley and then slipped away into a life on the west coast. Skipped from job to job, man to man, and Spell let her go as he plunged into a life on the exchange. Both had their ways of escaping home, and for a time he believed his had been more successful.

But sitting on the floor of his silent Manhattan apartment, he regretted every lost summer. The only true thing he had known was in the Valley. His mother, Major McCrimmon, and he himself had closed it off. And so the dream screamed at him. Ellen screamed at him. He saw her, little thin thing with crazy hair, bouncing along at his side as they explored the Valley.

Yes, he saw her in the firelight edging closer to him as he talked about black bears, or when she cried when a mountain bumble bee skimmed too close on a sunny day. Blue-eyed girl, jittery and scared, wrecked by his mother. As he was wrecked. Ellen had been going for the cave they discovered, their most secret place, a summer sanctuary. He should have been there with her. When she died, he had not even known she was in the Valley. While she was being tracked by Park rangers, running across an avalanche path, he was in the office and knew nothing. Even now, he did not know about the funeral. His mother would be there, so he would not.

Years ago on the exchange floor, in the kicking and screaming of brokers, he had felt some life there until one day something inside him broke out and he realized his world was stillborn. He had become successful, could not lose, and there was not a thing to push against. Just dead air. When he thought of his mother, and he had worked for years to train himself not to, he did remember how she believed a good life was one in conflict, a life with an edge to sharpen against. His old trainer, Major McCrimmon, had drilled that philosophy into Spell. Even when he learned that his life in New York was achieved, done, the World Trade Center still seemed majestic, two towers of Babel that worked and made money worth something. When Whitston Harris surrendered to his terms and gave him an office in the Tower, some fresh air was pumped into his career. Manhattan, Queens, and Brooklyn spread out for him every time he looked up from his desk. At the end of a day he strolled through the lobby—under the square, gold chandeliers that hung like ingots, row after row—and out into the plaza. On warm days people walked around the twenty-five foot high brass-colored sphere. Spell might see two lovers embrace on the concrete benches. And children playing. And occasionally a trader with his head in his hands, doubled up on a bench, given his walking papers and avoided by all the other sharp suits zipping by. Only the canned ones sat still, alone, while the red-jacketed security man hovered about nervously. Spell would watch these sacked men, as they ignored the inquiries of tourists, until finally they stood up and walked aimlessly around the plaza. For some time, Spell could look at them and think, not me, not me.

Now he began to see the way ahead.

He would call someone, sell off everything wholesale–original oil landscapes, rare books, crystal and bone china–have the place cleared out. But he would keep the guns from the shelves and gun rack in his closet. He would walk each one down, under his coat, to his Jaguar in the garage. His pistols were legal—they were the first when he began buying guns. At one time, he bought them as investments. But as he used them at the Manhattan Gun Club, shooting at targets in the basement there, he found out he liked remembering how he had learned to shoot, and how he had finally beaten Major McCrimmon. Firing the guns felt clean and hard, the kind of thing he liked, and his accuracy gave him pleasure.

Somehow, the illegal guns—perhaps because they were exotic—felt better in his hand. These came by courier, unseen deliverers who put the guns in the trunk of his car on prearranged streets at prearranged times, from the CB Gun Company of Ohio. When it was discovered by some patrons at the Manhattan Gun Club how much money Spell had, what class of man he really was, a satisfied CB customer quietly slipped him the company's name. So Spell wrote to a P.O. Box in Brulingham, and several months later—perhaps the time it took to check him out—he received a phone call. Spell told the voice on the other end—always a different one—what kind of gun interested him. The voice told him what would be sent and how, after he paid an exorbitant price for it.

He went to remote places in the Adirondacks to fire the guns, here and there, late on cold autumn nights. The dark, lonely treks along miles of winding, narrow trails felt best of all. Trying the guns gave him a reason to go, and in the last several months he had spent a lot of money on exotic automatic weapons and cases of contraband ammunition. The CB Gun Company favored East Bloc weapons.

Carefully, Spell would take his 9 mm Avtomaticheskiy Pistolet Stechkina down to the car (a clumsy automatic pistol that jumped wildly in his grip). Then the Hungarian 43M machine gun. With two steel boxes of ammunition, his trunk would be full. He would put his suitcases in the back seat.

Once the apartment was clean and everything sold, he would take his Jaguar out on the Jersey Turnpike. Some time that morning he had decided to go find the CB Gun Company in Brulingham, Ohio. After his dream he had awakened with the powerful urge to find the one type of gun he did not have: an accurate, long range rifle. The CB Gun Company was west, in the direction his dream told him to go. Spell did not ignore feelings, premonitions, and dream signs. These things had brought him more wealth than he ever wanted. Now, perhaps, with what he would take in the trunk—and what he might find in Ohio—they could bring him something else.

The voices from the CB Gun Company always reminded Spell that he must never visit Brulingham. Even his first contact in the basement of the Manhattan Gun Club whispered to him, urgently, that he must never try to visit the Company. But Spell saw himself, already driving toward the plants south of Jersey City, where the acrid smoke poured into the sky, and he imagined that final glimpse of the World Trade Towers in his rearview mirror—the world's largest markers over an island of monuments. He knew this was a time to go to places he should not go, and through to the picture in his and Ellen's dreams.

V

Karol Ensley Ware sat on a rocker facing the bed, watching the cabin's window above the headboard, and he waited for the night's sky to become pink. Karol rocked about once on the minute, and every five or so he sipped just a bit from his hot toddy, savoring the buttered sting of Johnny Walker Black on the tip of his tongue and the pictures of Eli in his head, images that came on a night like this. One of the best was the first, and he saw it over and over again, from ten years before, her first season as a full-time ranger, on a morning under a June sun, when she had fumbled in front of a dozen visitors while giving a talk on the Modern Ranger. Her long blonde hair had been a little lighter then, unfaded by worry and childbirth. Her brown eyes, always the same, clear and deep, had wandered over the group and, so he thought, kept coming back to him. And the moment someone asked a dumb question, and her long angular face had upturned in a white, relieved smile, he knew that he was going to stay in the Park longer than he had planned.

She shifted uneasily under the blankets, and in the early grey light he could just make out the curves in the big blue comforter. She had always been very strong; her father saw to it that as a little girl and young woman she marched all over the mountains, knowing his Park as he did, inch by inch. Every year she grew harder than the season before, long limbs wound up, finally tuned, delicately balanced. To see her run across a meadow, to stretch her neck, lift her long chin toward the sky—there was a grace and power he could never hope to capture in his poetry.

Karol finished his toddy in one long last draw.

The light was almost that shade of pink he waited on, and it slowly spread over the room. The pine and timbers of the cabin walls and ceiling were very old and dark, leaden, it seemed to Karol then. What it comes down to, he thought, is this cabin, and her father, grandfather, and great-grandfather, who together make this place her joy and her weight, make her strong and burden her. It's become a price to keep it.

The light became that pink, and Karol stood up, gathering the Golden Grizzly Bear rug around him. The fur hung heavily on his back, the huge bear picked off by her great grandfather in 1910. He breathed deep, the dust from the trunk where he had found it tickling his nostrils. And under it, he believed, he could smell the wood smoke of a fire some eighty years gone, and the honey pollen of flowers extinct for decades. The bear's great head hung over his shoulder as he walked to the bed.

He tapped her forehead gently with the bear's left paw.

Eli opened her eyes.

"Me and the bear are here," he announced softly.

"Oh no." She rolled over.

He brushed back her hair with the paw. "Your great granddaddy's bear says we must go."

"No."

"It's an appointment."

"If my dad knew you had that—"

"Your father won't be where we are to go." He leaned down to kiss her on the cheek and the bear nuzzled the back of her head. "He will not be born yet."

"What?"

"You know me."

"Yeah," she looked up at him with a wry smile.

"Then come." He pulled the comforter back.

"I can't sleep?"

"No."

"That's my life," she stood up. "Pushed around by my men."

"It is this bear that is moving us now." Karol enfolded her in the fur. "And I believe the bear is female."

They went down the hall, paused to hear Sarah breathing heavily, and came to the back door.

"We're going out?"

"Yes," he opened the door.

"I'm just wearing a nightshirt."

"And I'm just wearing a bearskin," he said. "But it's enough."

They stepped onto the meadow behind the house, the snow biting their feet, and the frigid wind huddling them closer in the bear rug.

"Cold," she said.

"Damn, so it is."

"The feet and hind of this priceless heirloom are dragging in the snow."

"That was the bear's problem," he looked at the stand of dark pines across the field. "That's why your great granddaddy was able to get off the shot that killed her. But our four legs will carry her now."

"Where are we going?"

"You know—now!"

They ran across to the pines, following a trail to a small clearing, deep in shadow, but lit up from above by a ceiling of pink and grey clouds.

"Here!" Eli tripped him in the center of the clearing and he fell forward; she pulled him close and fell on top of him, his head cradled on the base of the bear's head. Eli felt him pull her briefs down and she settled on his hips very hard. He moved up into her like a root from the ground, and she looked down into his eyes, wide and blue, his tan, lean face tinged with the pink of the opening morning. Then his face disappeared under her hiked up nightshirt, and he kissed her hanging breasts, cold and white in the winter air. Eli and Karol made their heat for as long as they could, racing against the gathering cold, and she looked up at the trees, breathing in the smelly old fur and the citrus of pine needles.

At last she gathering into him and he folded the rug over them.

"There is no time," he breathed heavily.

"No." She knew by the deep tone of his voice that Karol was going into his little incantation, a ritual he had made up for her. She wanted to hear it.

"And if we chose to we could get up and none of it would be there. We could walk out into these trees and it would be like it always has been, through the centuries, and you would find no cabin back there, no paved road, no smell of exhaust. But we will not so choose."

"No." She put her cheek against his soft skin, and slid her arms under his back and squeezed hard. Eli cried silently, privately. She recalled the night before, coming home to a sleeping daughter, to a silent husband as she spat out bitter words about Cairns, Olivos, stupid skiers, adulterers, waiting slabs of wet snow. How the Park had become no place for an interpreter, how if he wanted to remain a poet he should flee the Valley, find better ground. The Park was a place for SAR teams, trained dogs, accidents, drug busts, autopsies. Then she would not cry, but wait for him to speak one word awry, say one thing wrong, and she would fly at him in a rage, try to beat him senseless. He would receive her rage with grace, for he knew it had nothing to do with him.

But he had little to say on those nights, as he listened. When she had first met him, somewhere, now she did not remember where, she found he was unlike the others. A poet from North Carolina who wandered into the Valley, a patient man long rested in the old, old mountains of southern Appalachia. Never any hurry about him, no need to break down or control. She had known nothing like him. And she felt him now, dark, thin, willowy, like a jigger of Wild Turkey. While she embraced Karol she almost felt a panic, like there was not enough of him to hold. But he was there, and soon she relaxed, eased down into his smoother rhythm.

"The sun is about to crest White House," he said after a time. "And if we don't get up soon I believe you'll have to make a fire to unstick my behind."

They stood up, sorting out the aches in the cold air. They took a few steps and something fluttered down out of the bear rug.

Karol bent down to retrieve it, and he handed it to her.

They came out of the trees, and stood before the cabin across the meadow.

"You tell your boss you don't need to go to that meeting today."

"How's that?"

"You tell him you've already been properly debriefed."

Eli laughed and then yelled, "Go!" They ran across the snow on blue feet, stumbled into the cabin and stamped on the wooden floor, giggling, waking Sarah. She came into the hall, blinking at her parents in the bear rug. The girl was invited to join them, and she curled into the rug. Sarah had seen them come in this way before.

Sometimes Karol Ensley Ware knew what to do with his wife.

VI

Nothing about Brulingham seemed right; from the time Spell drove within twenty miles of it, when he crossed the Ohio River from West Virginia, he felt apprehensive. On the Ohio side a huge coal-fired power plant sprawled along the river, clouds of steam rising from two gigantic, squat stacks. Beyond these, reaching hundreds of feet in the air, a single thin stack released a sulphurous plume into the late afternoon sky. The two-lane road that broke west away from the river, toward Brulingham, went into tired, dormant fields and tangled woods of young trees—sooty upstarts from the last clear cutting of a decade before, now waiting for the next round of chain saws.

Something about the hazy angle of light through the trees and on the clearings opened memories in Spell and, alone in the car with few distractions, he allowed himself to briefly walk in his past. Something about the feel and look of the landscape returned him to Jackson Military Academy as a boy, just thirteen years old. In 1967, Jackson had come close to its end, with its empty dormitories, broken equipment, dirty walls, and dusty playing field. At the time, Spell could not imagine why his mother had sent him there, when she could afford the very best. Later, he learned why.

He had been there nearly a month before his real education commenced, a day when all the boys were worked hard on the parade ground and the running track just below the old red brick buildings on the hill. They had sweated, groaned under the new physical regimen and the flaming orange heat of a late Georgia summer. That day, when the other boys were walking off the field to eat dinner, Major McCrimmon grabbed Spell by the arm and walked him away from the others.

"Where are we going?" Spell had asked, looking up at the major. The man was not old, in his early forties, but his hair had already become white, clipped short and perfectly flat on the top. His pale, dull blue eyes hid any of the life within—more important to Spell at the time was the clenched jaw, silently signaling some kind of rage, and the square strength of the man, coming down into the sharp grip that bruised Spell's arm and sent him stumbling forward.

"Into the woods." The major wore a camouflage outfit that was army issue and had nothing to do with the uniforms of the academy. The major would never wear his grey academy dress when he took Spell to the woods.

"Why are we going?"

"Shut up."

"Why are you taking me?"

Spell had seen the major look back, and the boy followed the man's gaze to the empty field behind—the other boys were gone. He tried to stop but the major pulled him into the forest, dragged him along a narrow trail cut through a deep cedar grove and the undergrowth of poison ivy. Spell staggered along as best he could until the major shoved him into a tiny clearing. The boy fell to the ground, panting.

"Who the fuck are you to ask me a question?" McCrimmon stood over Spell.

"I don't understand." He met the man's eye and knew he should not cry. Under any circumstances, according to his mother, he should not cry. Look it in the eyes, was her motto, face it down or learn the advantages and win. But never cry.

"I've watched you at play with the other boys," McCrimmon said. "You don't fit in with them, do you?"

"I don't know." But he did know that, unlike the others, he had not yet paired up with a friend nor fallen into a group. His had been a solitary childhood, and it showed at the academy.

"I think you do." McCrimmon kept looking down, but Spell did not look away. "I see you play soccer—you anticipate the opposition's moves well, play hard, but you're not really a team player."

"I could be," Spell said. "I try. I score for my side."

"Part of you wants to be on the team, but the bigger part of you plays for yourself—you take the ball, run down the field, and score for yourself." McCrimmon leaned down, close to the boy's face, locking their eyes with the intensity of a death grip. "That's the part that interests me: the animal, Mr. Spell, the insane fucking animal in you. We'll coax it along."

Spell looked away, breathing hard with fear and, despite himself, excitement. He looked for a break in the woods, a place to run. He stood up quickly and turned away.

The pain to the back of his head was white and sharp, and as he staggered forward Spell felt his feet kicked out from under him; he grabbed for a tree, missed, and fell face down in the dry red earth. He rolled over, his eyes meeting McCrimmon's again. The major knelt down, bending his large face very near.

"I must learn to hate you." He made a small smile, rigid, muscles tensed with some effort. "That is the way to do it." The major looked up and spoke softly, as if to himself. His smile faded away. "That is the way we have to do it."

"Do what?" Spell worked hard to control his breathing and beat down the urge to cry.

The major stood, still looking away. "Now, I'm going to disappear, and you try to get back to the field. But don't let me catch you."

Spell looked at the red earth and took a deep breath. When he glanced up, McCrimmon had gone, had moved off into the woods without a sound. Spell stepped quietly onto the narrow trail back; the heavy limbs of the cedars darkened as the sun set. He already knew that the name of the game was to move silently; he struggled with his heavy breathing and it seemed with every step he broke a twig or kicked a leaf. His new canvas shoes whispered on the dust.

McCrimmon appeared directly in front of him, and slapped the boy's head about with quick, open palms.

"You're not crying," McCrimmon's face was without expression as he slapped Spell again. The boy would become used to the slaps that first year, just enough to sting but not enough to leave a mark.

He tried to kick the major, but was thrown on his back.

"And you fight already," McCrimmon said in a less harsh tone, with a hint of pleasure. Then, with the side of his boot, he kicked Spell's ribs.

The boy blinked his eyes and the major was gone again. He sat, listened to the evening breeze in the trees, and he cautiously stood up. His side ached, but when he lifted his shirt and checked, he could see no mark. Slowly he walked.

When Spell came to the edge of the field, he heard the major's voice. Stopping, he looked around, took in the entire sweep of the dense woods, and could see no trace of McCrimmon.

"First lesson," the voice seemed to be in his ear. "And the one rule you must remember: don't tell anyone. Not an instructor. Not the colonel. Not your mother. No other boys. Discuss this with no one."

"Now," the voice somehow had shifted to his other ear, but still Spell could not see McCrimmon. "You ask why. I will tell you this once. If I don't kill you in your years here, if I don't have to kill you, I will make you into something wonderful. Set apart. A Pathfinder."

"Move out. Keep your mouth shut."

Spell trotted out to the field, and when he was in its center, he slowed. The red brick buildings, turning grey in the fading light, blurred ahead. He stood, the tears pouring from his eyes, but he controlled his breathing and would not allow the sound of crying. When he had finished, and walked by the dining hall to see that dinner was over and he would have to go to his dorm without anything to eat, McCrimmon walked by. Somehow, the man had gotten ahead of him, had even put on his grey Jackson casuals.

That first year, as Spell was pulled day after day into the woods, and sometimes not allowed to escape until late into the night, fear created a wall between him and the other boys. Their fear. His strange absences, which he would not explain, set him apart. Although they were all going to the same school, his experience there became so different from theirs that he had little in common with them.

By the end of the year, taller but ten pounds less than he weighed when he started, Spell had summoned the courage to talk. He had planned to tell his English instructor, or maybe the colonel. But he argued with himself; as much as part of him hated the major and the game in the woods, another part recognized the value of what he was learning. He knew he was receiving a superior education. If he told, which was the coward's way out anyway, he would stop learning, would never reach his potential, and, what was becoming most important, he would never have the chance to beat the major. When Spell returned home, seeing his mother for the first time in nine months, he did tell her. To his surprise, he wept as he spoke, crying before her like he had not done in years. She had looked away, and when he finished she walked from him, glided across the great white salon and looked out the window. "He is trying to make something of you," she had said. "You know that. The way he does it—that's something I will not discuss."

Sometimes, on his trips to the Valley with Ellen, he would wait until they were in the dark of the night and he would tell his sister everything. She listened, but said nothing. Quiet was the rule in the Cheltingham house, and Ellen's silence told that she understood perfectly.

Spell had expected Brulingham to be a bucolic farming community amid cows and cornfields, but several of the farms on the way seemed dead with gray, crumbling houses and listing barns faintly advertising the merits of Mail Pouch Tobacco. Although he couldn't see it in the low-hanging grey clouds, Spell believed the filth from the plants on the river traveled with him to Brulingham. On a hill at the outskirt of the town, an old academy of Victorian-style buildings stood. Upon a black wrought-iron gate someone had strung a banner, hand-painted and tattered with age, proclaiming: "Save Agassiz College." The gate was padlocked, the lane up to the buildings strewn with mud and leaves.

He crossed a bridge, spanning a shallow river, and entered the town. The main street was paved with bricks, some broken or missing, so his Jaguar bounced about in the holes like it might on Broadway. He searched the vacant street for the gun company, but instead saw several closed shops on one side, an entire block burned out on the other. The nineteenth-century brick facades, though black with rain and ash, still stood—behind them a jigsaw of broken beams and debris. He stopped at a BP station and checked the phone book; no CB

Gun Company was listed. He asked the station attendant, who said he had never heard of the place. So, Spell thought, try the bars. He had seen several.

At each place he went no one could help him. By nightfall he decided to find a motel, and checked into the College Inn. One building with rooms had closed, and the remaining building held no guests. He stood at the desk, watching the man there, who glanced at an episode of *LA Law* on a TV hanging from the wall. The clerk was a heavy man, with pectoral fat that hung like breasts under his T-shirt. He had a habit of rubbing them. When he filled out the card, he focused his small blue eyes on Spell.

"How long you stayin'?" he asked.

"Just tonight."

"What you drivin'?"

"A green Jaguar, '93 model."

"Jaguar?" The man rubbed the grey stubble on his heavy, yellow cheek, glanced at *LA Law* once more, and did not bother to fill in the space on his form for the car's license number. He stuffed the cash Spell gave him into the register and handed over a key.

"Room 1, next to the office."

Spell looked at the key for a moment; the man at the desk had already turned to the TV.

"Do you know where I could find the CB Gun Company?"

"Eh?" He turned down the sound and looked into Spell's eyes. "The CB Gun Company?"

"Yes."

"Don't know it."

But Spell could see the clerk knew something, because he stared now; he seemed quietly excited.

"I've come a long way to find it."

"How far?"

"New York."

"Don't have gun shops in New York?" The man smiled.

"I didn't know it was a shop," Spell leaned forward. "I thought it was a company."

The desk man looked away, puffing up his cheeks and then exhaling loudly, his lips rattling. "Well, sir . . ."

"Where is it?"

"Can't say." He looked at his TV program again, turning up the volume. "But people know a lot more about such things at Herb's Ore Car."

"What's that?"

"A bar."

"I've been to the bars."

The man kept his back to Spell, looking at his program but not paying attention to it. "This one's in that burned block uptown. At the corner; the only thing that didn't catch fire. Except the sign. They lost that."

"I'll go there."

"You do," the desk man stared intently at a commercial. "If you want to go through with it."

Herb's Ore Car kept the west side of the block upright. The facade in front had been draped with soot carried down by the water from fire hoses; the one window had not been cleaned, so the light from inside dimly shown through the black film. Before Spell opened the door he stopped, looking around. The street was empty, and the sleety rain fell like dirty nickels by the few streetlights. He clenched and unclenched his fists; nothing in Brulingham seemed right.

Inside, the room was long and narrow, with a low ceiling that sagged in the middle from the weight of water and snow. One large beam had been jammed at the center to hold things up. A lamp lit the bar, but the rest of the room was dark, with one couple huddled at a small table. A few men sat at the bar, two without drinks, and they all turned to stare at him. Spell felt like he had just walked into someone's living room.

"Something for you?" A heavy woman smiled at him from behind the bar; Spell was beginning to think that everyone in Ohio carried too much weight, they were all ballooned out with bratwurst, salts, and nitrates. Her face seemed slick with grease; the smell of fried pork thickened the warm air.

"I'm looking for the CB Gun Company." Spell wanted to get to the point and leave. "Someone told me you'd know where it is."

"Who?" Her smile faded away.

"The clerk at the College Inn."

One of the men slid off a stool, poured change into a juke box, and the room split open with a Billy Idol tune.

She said something, but Spell could not hear her.

"What?"

"I said I don't know that place." Her smile returned. "It's not here."

"I've come from New York." Spell hated yelling over the noise. "I want to make a special purchase."

"It's not here."

"Listen," he leaned close, and she bent close to hear him. "I'm a regular customer. I'd like to make some extensive purchases."

"So what's your name?"

"Eldred Spell." He thought he was getting somewhere.

"Don't know of any gun company," she said.

Spell bought a Bud—they had no Guinness—and he sat in a corner table. The two men at the bar left, looking away from him as they walked out. One young couple stayed at a table, slowly working on beers and a plate of brauts and kraut. The man was hungry looking, like a big rangy dog. He stroked his beard and smiled when the woman talked. She seemed tight in her jeans and flannel shirt, tight in her skin like most young people who gain weight fast. She smiled when he talked.

Watching them, Spell felt a sharp thump inside, down in the dry, hollowed marrows. He could go back, to the relief of Whitston Harris. He could be back to his place, redecorate it anew, please Alanis. Maybe see a therapist, though the idea made him frown, but maybe he could use some psychiatrist long enough to get a prescription. A good, synthetic drug might deaden his feelings just enough so he could see around the corner to serve his clients but nothing more. No one said his life in New York was over, including himself. Something bigger than him said it was over, injected this feeling into him. Well, a drug could kill the sting of that needle. Ellen was dead, tracked down by rangers right into an avalanche, and perhaps going there would do no more for him than it did for her.

What's the matter with me? He drained the Bud. There's nothing here.

As he put on his coat, he noticed the woman at the bar was gone. In the empty room the light grew darker, the walls and ceiling narrower. Something was wrong.

Spell went out on the vacant street. He was a man who never allowed himself to trot in fear along the streets of New York, no matter if he was alone and the hour was late. But he trotted now, while his Jaguar down the street seemed to get no closer, as if he were in a dark dream. As if this were a moment he had seen somewhere before.

The muffled footsteps came up fast behind him, and before he could turn someone kicked the back of his knee, like they used to in elementary school, and Spell lost his balance. Arms gently caught him, then closed their grip, dragging him back into a gaping hole in the facade, into a black jungle of broken glass, twisted steel, and shattered timbers. The first blow to his head came from behind, slow and heavy, knocking him forward into a sharp white fist between his eyes. A body slammed him and he fell, sprawling across an uneven floor of cement and glass. He moved his hand back to try to get up, but someone stepped onto it, grinding it into a shard of glass that sliced the delicate web between thumb and index finger. Boots closed on his ribs from both sides, and now it seemed slowly done, even painless to Spell, as if he were insulated, like things happen in a dream. He looked up, squinting in a warm stream of blood that ran down his forehead. Hard to believe he had been taken so easily—Major McCrimmon would have laughed, would have loved to see this. Ahead he saw a streetlight through a hole, and the sleet had become snow, yellow and sulphurous. Spell could hardly breathe. Then nothing.

"How is he?" A man stepped away from the body. "Doc?"

Another came in from the street and knelt down, checking over Spell with a penlight. "You all did fine. Well done."

"Yeah," said one man. "A bad night for this city boy."

"At least he found his gun company."

VII

Some years ago, they had reached an unspoken truce, and shared dinner together only three times a year: Thanksgiving, Christmas Eve, and the first day of Spring. Other times, Karol would leave shortly after Eli's father arrived at the house. When Eli and Sarah visited the old man's one-room cabin across the meadow, Karol might make a polite appearance and disappear. His absences caused no squabble anymore; this was the comfortable rhythm of things, a way out of inevitable storms. But three times a year they tried a meal together, each, with the exception of Sarah, wondering just how badly it would go.

Eli looked out the kitchen window; her father cut a square, dark patch in the early spring stubble. Sarah trotted behind him, trying to keep up, straining to hear something he was telling her while he looked ahead. The sun had set, the pine trees black and the mountains grey, capped in pink snow. Eli watched them come while she listened to "Marble Halls" on her *Shepherd Moons* album. She admired the meadow and her daughter's persistent trot against her father's march; Eli thought how this is what her own mother would have seen, had she not left the Park for good when Eli was two. Well, Eli thought, tonight I'm mother to all three of them.

"Karol, they're almost here."

"Very well," he said in a flat tone from the small living room, where he sat before the wood burner.

"What are you reading?" Eli asked, already sure of the answer.

"I'm preparing."

"You're reading some of that damned *Portrait of a Lady* again, aren't you?"

"I'm steeling myself, and I've read twenty-five pages this afternoon. A record."

"Put it away."

"Yes," he said. "Here's the real thing come to the porch."

He hated *The Portrait of a Lady*, and had been picking at Henry James for years, reading passages when he had the perverse desire to become irritated. He pulled it off the shelf only three days a year.

Eli's father, Jack Hattan, did not knock, but threw open the door.

"Happy spring," he announced, with Sarah coming in breathlessly behind him.

"So it is," Karol held out his hand, and they shook very formally, fumbling with smiles. "Good to see you, Jack." Karol shut the door.

"Likewise," Jack Hattan never spoke Karol's name.

Jack laid his leather day pack on the round coffee table, setting it on the spine of *The Portrait of a Lady*. He pulled out a bottle of whiskey.

"Old Jack Daniel's," he handed it to Karol. "For the southern boy."

"You can't find a smoother cliche." Karol opened the bottle. "Let's you and I try it out."

"There's a thought," Jack said.

"How about me?" Sarah asked.

"We'll wait a year or two," Jack said, throwing his old brown leather jacket over the day pack. He rolled back the sleeves of his rough flannel shirt. "But you can serve."

Everyone was quiet as he did this, and Eli watched them. As bad as it might be, she savored the moment, having the family in one room. Sarah reading the J.D. label, Jack settling in the leather easy chair, Karol sitting in the one on the other side of the picture window. For a moment the men looked at her, as if waiting for some instruction, and she wished it were not like some fragile experiment in mixology, like when her father spent a year playing with the Tequila Sunrise, when the beautiful color in the glass happens just at the right balance, and the slightest shift in temperature or measure makes everything darken and sour.

Eli took the bottle from Sarah's hands and led her into the kitchen.

"There's a trick to serving your grandfather his whiskey," Eli whispered to her daughter in mock conspiracy.

"You get the biggest glass in the kitchen, fill it with ice and a little water, and put in as little whiskey as you can get away with."

"Does daddy like it that way?"

"Right now, he doesn't care how you do it."

Sarah stuffed the tall glasses full of ice, added some water, and heaved the bottle over the lip of each unsteadily, her mother pleased to see dollops spilled on the floor.

More spilled when Sarah put the drinks on a serving tray, then she put the bottle on the tray. Eli took it off. "Never bring your grandfather the bottle."

"Isn't that a polite thing to do?" Sarah asked.

"In polite company." Eli bent down to Sarah. "But you really don't want to do this any way Grandpa likes it."

"Why not?"

"So he won't ask you to serve him again."

"Mom," Sarah pursed her lips. "Now I don't know how I'm supposed to—."

"You're fine. Go ahead."

"Mom."

"Go. It's okay."

Sarah left with the tray, and from the living room, Eli heard her father: "Damn—" then he stopped. "Thank you, Sarah."

"Why, Sarah," Karol smacked his lips. "That's the best iced tea I've had since I left North Carolina."

In a moment, Jack came into the kitchen, muttering, "where the hell did you put that bottle?"

"Here," Eli handed it to him.

"What'd you do?" He squinted at the J.D. "Pour some down the drain?"

"Sarah did her best."

"Yeah," he lowered his voice, frowning. "Seems she's learning from you—never knew anyone who could water down a good drink like you."

He stamped out of the kitchen.

The men drank hard, as they usually did when trapped together, and the room filled with Sarah's voice.

A half hour later Eli called them to sit down, and she saw the bottle her father brought with him was nearly empty. His face was flushed, and a grey film had formed over his eyes. But he came on straight, took his chair as if he were sober.

Karol came in less steadily, taking a moment to navigate the room and settle into his chair. His face set dark against his broad white cotton shirt; eyes, long nose, small mouth shrunk into a point. Karol's mind jangled with the grate of Henry James' syntax and the close, hot presence of Jack.

A cloud settled over the table, a silence draped upon them all after Sarah stuttered through her great grandfather's grace. Eli watched the steam rise off the serving plates: leg of lamb, mashed potatoes, pickled beets, hot herb bread. A starchy menu with which to celebrate spring, but her father insisted this was how Hattans always did it, from the time they helped beat the Miwok tribe out of the Valley in 1851. Eli could never convince him to deviate from the menu, nor the date. The first day of spring seemed too cold to celebrate the season, she thought.

Dinner came to a close, no one wanted seconds, and Eli thought that they just might make it through. She could not eat, the little bit of mutton she tried sunk in her stomach as she watched her silent men. But now it was almost done, and her father would saunter off safely, ready to hibernate in his cabin.

But he woke up suddenly from the stupor of his bottle.

"Sarah, my dear," he turned to her, dropping his fork on his plate. "Why do you think we're here?"

"To celebrate the spring," she said cheerfully, relieved that someone was finally talking, and to her.

Karol stopped eating, pushing his plate away, looking down in his lap, his lips pursed more than ever.

"What else?"

"I don't know," Sarah said.

"Of course you don't—who would teach you?" Jack looked around the table, challenging anyone to speak, lost in the preparation to fight until he refocused on his granddaughter.

"She knows about her great great-grandfather," Eli said, picking up her unfinished plate. She knew the celebration was over.

"Yes, I do." Sarah offered, "He—"

"You don't know. Who would teach you? Not your mother, or the romantic poet here."

Karol picked at the edge of his eye with his long thumb and forefinger.

Eli removed the good china and crystal from the table as quickly as she could.

"Eli was his name—"

"I know—" Sarah started.

"No," Jack snapped. "Eli was his name, your mother's namesake, even though she hates the name."

"Dad—"

"Your mother hated it," he looked at Eli's eyes. "Hated it, like everything. Wanted to call you by some pussy handle, can't recall." Jack found Sarah again. "Your great great-grandaddy came into the Valley with riders, and he helped clear the fucking Indians out, cleared out the whole damn place to make it his own. Wiped it clean. And it wasn't the cesspool your mother runs around in, with all the lowlifes and pushers and—" He looked hard at Karol. "And assholes, kooks, would-be poets, and other fairies."

Karol slammed his hand flat on the table, just as Eli had cleared the last of the dishes away.

Jack looked for Sarah again, smiling. "He built that cabin I live in, my father built this one." He pointed to the rough pine beams in the ceiling. "And in this whole damn Park, these are the only two private homes left. First and last. The feds want to take it away, but me and your mother have stuck it out, joined up with their damn army of rangers, so they won't kick us out. Know why?"

Sarah shook her head, looking at her father until Jack Hattan caught her attention again.

"They won't kick us out because these logs pump with the hard-won blood of my family, blood mingled in pine tar, still pumping. These walls would reject anyone else. That's what we celebrate, my dear. And that blood, though diluted by a stranger or two—" He paused, to take in the effect on Karol, then went on: "that blood is in you, makes you a part of this Valley, set apart from all the shit heads—"

"Darlin'," Karol craned forward toward Sarah, elbow on the table, chin cradled in his hand. "This magical load of western bullshit that your granddaddy has brought before us can be blown away by one little fact." He pulled himself up, looking at Jack. "Sarah has my blood type, not yours. O negative, I believe."

"Sarah," Eli called to her from the living room.

Jack stared at his son-in-law with his mouth open; Karol smiled broadly, satisfied at the result.

Sarah slid out of her chair and hurried away.

"Let's take a walk." Eli, already in her jacket, threw on the girl's coat and pulled a wool cap on her head.

"Are we going far?" Sarah whispered.

"Just far enough."

They went out the front door, down the steps, and onto the road in front of the house.

The men did not notice.

Eli and Sarah walked slowly, breathing steam into the night air, listening to the voices from the cabin rise. Jack began yelling first, his voice rumbling. They did not hear anything but his voice until he said something about faggoty poetry, which brought a sharp jab from Karol about an old man's castrated vision. Soon the voices became muffled over the meadow, they faded away when the road plunged into the pines.

"I wonder about something Grandpa said," Sarah broke the quiet. "Does he believe there are fairies here?"

"He used to tell me they lived in the hollows of dead trees, and skip about in the woods at night."

"What do they look like?"

"Small, I think." Eli thought she heard the faint sound of breaking glass, a hiss or tinkle far off, and decided that she would make them both pay if any of the china was broken. But she didn't think Karol, drunk as he was, would get that ridiculous. She could trust him. "Small, Sarah, and they make a little noise here and there, but it doesn't amount to much."

"Do you believe in them?"

"I believe anything could be in these woods, Sarah. You just need to look and listen—see what the woods have to offer."

"That's what Grandpa says."

They walked on, until the pines gave way to a much larger meadow, and the lights of the Muir Hotel, like a chandelier, lit up the glade and the trees.

"Are we going to the hotel?" Sarah asked.

"We'll have some dessert, if that suits you."

"Sure."

"We're not dressed for the dining room, but Stan will let us in the kitchen."

"You know what, Mom?," Sarah grabbed her mother's hand. "I kind of like it when Dad and Grandpa fight."

"Why?"

"Because we always walk to the hotel for dessert."

Eli felt the little warmth in her palm as they walked, and the knot in her stomach finally loosened. Her father's rages would mean little to Sarah, because there would always be someone to take her away before things became ugly. And Sarah would never be the object of his frustrations, would never be the only one in the room with him, never be the one to take a sudden blow to the face. Eli wondered how it would have been when she was a child, if her mother had been there, to take her by the hand to the Muir Hotel while her father went on.

"Take it easy," Sarah complained. "You're squeezing my hand too hard. You always do that, Mom."

They both chose raspberry mousse in chocolate cups, and they ate them in the middle of the stainless steel clatter of the hotel kitchen, free of charge. Stan, the executive chef, asked Eli how the family dinner was going and winked. The last quarter mile home, Sarah quit walking, and Eli threw her over her shoulder and took her the rest of the way. She stopped near the front door, listening, and did not hear any yelling.

Eli kicked open the front door and dumped her giggling pile of daughter on Karol's lap in the easy chair.

"Where the hell you been?" Her father stumbled out of the kitchen. "And where the hell is my jacket?"

"It's still here," Karol smiled crookedly, lifting it up from the floor with his free arm.

"Did you tear up my kitchen?" Eli asked.

"We cleaned your whole damned mess." Jack took the jacket from Karol, looked at it absently, and dropped it again.

"We did," Karol looked up at her, blinking, as he stroked Sarah's hair.

Eli could imagine the wreck that he would have to clean up tomorrow, under the shroud of a hangover. She did not plan to eat in the kitchen until he finished it in the morning.

"Grandpa, we had free dessert at the hotel," Sarah said.

"You're a special girl, living in a treasure of the world." Jack bent down to kiss her good night but missed heads and almost kissed Karol instead. He recoiled, stumbled, and hit the floor.

"Very fine display, Jack," Karol peered over the chair with Sarah.

Eli helped him up. "Don't you want your jacket?"

"Hell no. It's spring."

She took him through the kitchen to the back door, and he lurched out of it.

"Good night," she called.

"Thank you, daughter." He wandered across the meadow, headed home. Faintly, half way there, he called out, "your husband's an asshole."

"He was in good company tonight," Eli said.

He stopped, and then he resumed walking. She waited a long time before she saw the light go on in his cabin.

She ignored the kitchen, sliding the unbroken J.D. bottle out of her path with her foot, and went back to the living room. Sarah stared at nothing, just this side of sleep, her head nestled in Karol's white shirt. He looked up, eyes bleary, at Eli.

"We were too tired for a fight tonight," Karol offered Sarah to Eli.

She took her daughter up, grunting. "She's really too big to carry."

"Not for you," Karol smiled.

"My father informed me that you are an asshole."

"So what do you think?"

"You have a lot of housework tomorrow."

"Spring dinner," he stood up, walked a few paces, and carefully picked up *The Portrait of a Lady*. "How many months until Thanksgiving?"

"I think you enjoy his visits." Eli shifted Sarah's weight in her arms.

"Sometimes you can have screwed up characters." He tried to put the book in its place on the shelf, missed, and tried again. "And the ending can come out all right."

He dropped the book. "But more often it doesn't."

VIII

When he had awakened that night, he found they had put him back in his motel room, undressed him, and draped him on a bed. At the time, he did not care where he was or how he had arrived there; all Spell wanted was to curl into a ball, pulling a cover over himself slowly, with what seemed to be his good arm—the one that pained him least when he moved it. An ache in the back of his head pushed his face forward, closed his eyes for him tightly, and sent him down into half sleep not deep enough to relieve him from the pain.

In the morning, a woman knocked on the door and let herself in. He could see her clearly—they had not blackened his eyes. A young woman, maybe twenty, slim, with a thin, sharp face half covered by slick black hair. In jeans and an old Agassiz College sweatshirt; later he would notice that her dress rarely changed. She wore her sweatshirt like a wish.

His view filled with her, a face pale from thick, white makeup, and hers were black eyes, encircled by black mascara. She wore teak-colored lipstick. The whole effect made the young girl look as if she were dying.

Spell tried to look away, but his neck was stiff.

"What the hell happened to you?" Her voice sounded deep, intelligent, and did not belong to the young, over-made face and the ragged sweatshirt.

"How did I get here?"

"I have no idea." She slowly pulled back his cover. "Do you want me to call a doctor?"

"Who are you?" Spell closed his eyes.

"Thelma."

"Are you here to clean?"

"I'm supposed to make sure you don't die or something."

"Who sent you?"

"Do you need ibuprofen? I have 600 milligram tabs here; might help bring down some swelling, too."

He rolled over carefully, to get to the edge of the bed, and put his feet on the floor. He walked slowly, forgetting he was nude as he tested the severity of bruises and scrapes. The worst was the slice in his hand, and he held it to his chest. Thelma quietly watched as he walked into the bathroom, leaving the door ajar.

He felt the first stir of emotion, anger, as he looked at himself in the mirror, at the deep scrape down his forehead, at the green bruise along his jaw, the cuts and welts and seeping bruises down the length of his body.

"Who do you work for?" he said in an even, between-the-teeth voice that he saved for those times he wanted executives to pale and secretaries to get out of the way.

"Let's say Cleveland, the desk man."

He did not like the relaxed tone in her voice, nor the irony.

"Who does he work for?"

The motel door clicked, and Thelma was gone.

They had been careful. No bones broken, no cuts deep enough for infection to set in, and soon the headache in the back of his mind withered away. They took no money—his billfold remained full. Out the window, he could see his Jaguar parked in the lot, and he found his keys in his pants pocket.

And they gave him Thelma, who brought food, bandages, over-the-counter drugs as needed. She kept accounts straight with Cleveland, had Spell's clothes cleaned, and let him ask questions that she did not answer.

For a week Spell stayed in his room. He did not want to bring the police into anything, as he had come for illegal guns and he still wanted them. Spell believed this was a test—if he waited, the gun company would come to him. The major had taught him about tests. And responsibility—everything that had happened to him was his own fault; he had not been alert, he had let a bunch of hicks get the best of him. On the other side of responsibility was revenge, to take the punishment these people deserved into his own hands. Spell knew he could not leave until they paid their debt, and he must have the long-range sniping rifle that grew more important in his thoughts every day. He wanted no connection with the police. He would return to the road clean.

For the same reasons, Spell did not want to create any records at a local hospital. So he waited to heal; he did not want to hop in his Jaguar and drive as a conspicuous mess—the guy who lost a barroom brawl somewhere. When the time was right, when the scabs fell away, he would go west, to the Valley, where he could be right again. Above all, he wanted that gun and to go west. There was no rational explanation for his desire beyond the fact that he was running after that image of his father in the Valley, returning to it. Maybe, he thought, it was a pattern in the air, an imprint from long ago: you go west, you bring a long rifle. More and more, he knew, he wanted to make the Park rangers suffer; always in his mind was a picture of his sister running with the rangers and their dogs behind.

As the pain subsided, and he brushed off the dead, damaged skin, dropping it in the toilet, his anger grew. The big round bruises went from black, to green, to yellow, like opening cat's eyes, and his anger grew. The heater pumped dirty air into the room, hot with the smell of electrical coils and tainted with the diesel from trucks rumbling by outside, and his anger grew. The quieter Spell became, the more he looked at Thelma.

"You've been reticent," she said after she set down his dinner, a sack from Burger King.

He noticed the flecks of snow, like dandruff, in her hair.

"Reticent is a word I learned in English class, in the last semester at Agassiz."

She had caught him while he was taking a shower, and he stood watching her, dripping, with a towel wrapped around his waist. In the last few days she had taken the habit of entering while he took a shower, as if she were listening outside and timing her visits on purpose. The food she brought was always stone cold; maybe she did wait outside, listening.

"Who did this to me?" Spell walked up to her quickly, and the closer he got the more something hot wanted to crawl out of him.

"Like I told you—"

He grabbed her arm and squeezed it; her biceps felt small and hard in his grip.

Thelma looked down at his other hand, clutching the towel at his hip, and she smiled.

"Tell me." He knew the look he showed her, dead and angry, the one his mother had suggested would freeze on his face if he used it too much as a little boy. He used it to freeze other people.

"Can't say." She laughed. "You're a bit randy tonight, eh? Randy's another word from that English class. I think it's cute."

He shook her, with both hands, and he hated the slick mask of makeup, the lifeless eyes, the smell of a burger on her breath.

Thelma giggled. "I could pull off these clothes, you know, and we could settle you down."

He let her go, breathing hard, glancing at the towel around his feet.

She made a move to pull up her sweatshirt. "So, what do you think?"

"Get out."

She leapt forward and pushed him, so he fell back on the bed, then she jumped on him, grabbing him between the legs and rubbing him against the cold, sharp zipper of her jeans.

"So, how about it?"

They were both very still for a moment, then her smile softened, and she let him go. Standing up, Thelma went to the door, watching him all the way.

"You'd fill a big codpiece, Spell." She opened the door wide, and Spell pulled a cover over his lap. "Now if you don't know what that means, you look it up. That's what they always told me to do." She left, closing the door behind her.

Spell stared at the Burger King sack, his mind blank with rage and frustration. He sat on the edge of the bed for a long time and the room felt cold. As his mind cleared it brought him back to Jackson Military, where he had been beaten so many times.

When Spell had returned to the academy in his fourteenth year, part of him still had hoped the major would be gone. But McCrimmon was there, and Spell went deeper into the woods, where he was attacked in rain or snow, where he listened to the faceless voice in his ear: "you must disappear to get by me, go quick, run silent, predict my moves."

By his sixteenth year Spell had looked forward to the woods. Jackson lost more enrollment, spiraling into small classes with part-time instructors as the good faculty left. It became a place of flaked paint, rusted screens, weeds through the paved drives, and meals served that were hardly edible: lukewarm concoctions of ground hamburger and tomato sauce. The war in the woods carried on. Sometimes Spell almost won, trekked several miles, off trail, until he came close to the field. But he never made it. The better he became, the more brutal the major's attacks. Spell fought back, now that he had grown as tall as the major, though he was not as strong. Spell did not go out for the other sports. Child's play. No coach ever asked him to try out, the colonel never asked why he wandered in late to his dorm room. Spell knew that they were all in on it; the major had free reign at Jackson Military. And the boys, with their complaints of the easy regimen, their training without beatings, bored him. They did not live his life. They remained children. But he knew he was becoming something more, would have to if he was going to beat the major.

At home in the summer before his senior year, he ordered his own gymnasium built in one of the old greenhouses and his mother paid for it without question. She hired a trainer for him, an old Olympics coach who worked Spell without mercy. She hired college boys, wrestlers and boxers, and paid them a year's tuition to beat up her son. She paid their medical bills when he won. He took his annual trip to the Valley, where he practiced becoming invisible and trained hard in the high, thin air. For Ellen he played hide and seek, jumped out of the woods at her and made her laugh. For two weeks out of the year he allowed himself to act as a child, as a young man, and Ellen was the only one who saw this side of him. The only witness.

As he packed to leave for his last year at Jackson, his mother was almost kind to him. She touched his arm, and told him, "beat the shit out of that man, Eldred." The fact that she used profanity and called him by his first name showed him as much feeling as she could; it was as close to a mother's caress as he would ever feel.

That term the colonel retired in October and Jackson Military staggered to complete its last year of existence. The school had already become a phantom to Spell; he looked right through it and into the woods. Miles in, deep among the cedar trees in a blinding November rain, Spell had run fast, calculated where the major would go, and he froze against a tree, became a part of it, as the major had taught him. Spell never felt as much joy as the moment when he saw McCrimmon's hard back materialize out of the rain just ahead. The man had crouched low, silently searching. Just as he turned, Spell leapt high and hit the major across the face with the heel of his boot. The major staggered back and Spell moved in for the kill.

Then he saw McCrimmon smile as the rain washed blood from his nose. Spell turned, but too late. Powerful hands grabbed his arms, and he saw men in the same camouflage gear the major wore. He had never seen the men before, and they held him fast.

"You thought I wouldn't be ready for you?"

McCrimmon tightened his fist until it flattened like the head of a cobra, then he struck quick and sharp in his student's groin. Spell had doubled over as the men released him, retching as a swift boot sent him sprawling into the mud. He sucked for air.

IX

The early spring grass of Paw's Meadow rippled delicately away from the wind of the chopper blades. Every member of the SAR team smiled heartily; strong arms almost threw the two children into the Huey. Even the children smiled, despite a long cold night alone in the forest. Cairns, towering over them on the deck of the chopper, patted a boy roughly on the head. "Very tough kids," he boomed, and then turned to Eli, who began to climb into the helicopter.

"Hold on," Cairns said, putting a hand up.

She jumped down.

"I've got a job for you: I want you to go with Olivos and take the trail back to the point where these two kids got lost. Parents said the rock wall tumbled down—we need it fixed right away."

"Can't I call it a day?" Eli yelled over the beating blades.

"At 2 p.m.? Olivos has got the tools. Have a nice walk."

"What about the conservation corps?"

"Can't trust those misfits to fix it." He gave the pilot the thumbs up. "I'll put in a good word for you with the press. You done good!"

He ducked back to strap himself in. The Huey pulled up into the cool blue sky, banked over some redwoods, and disappeared.

"Some day his regime is going to end," Eli said to herself as the noise of the rotor faded. "I'll outlive it."

Olivos, already on the trail at the edge of the clearing, waited with two shovels over his broad shoulders. He watched how her long hair unraveled and flashed out when the helicopter rose, and how she stood for a time before she bent down to pick up her hat. Some women could remind him of animals, something in the movement that might be stocky and pig-like, or timid and rabbit-like. Some women were snakes, which on the right night could be good. But the best ones, he thought, were like her: long limbed, sleek, graceful, with a long mane of hair. He admired her stiff spine, the strong curve of her flanks.

"Quit staring, Olivos." Eli tramped by.

"Hey," he started after her. "Why don't you carry one of the shovels?"

"Who figured out where the Hazeltine children would be?"

"You did."

"Right." She picked up her pace. "Who goes to talk it up with the press?"

"The boss."

"Right." On the incline she went faster, with the faint hope of losing him, but she knew his strength—knew that if not for his weird habit of always following her, he would be way ahead. "Who always sucks me into some shitty job?"

"Me."

"So you carry the shovels."

"Okay—"

"And you shut up."

"Aw, hell." His eyes traveled up the V from her waist, where her uniform went a little tighter just under her shoulders; he could see the curve of her right breast if he looked hard enough. Her shoulders were wide. She stood just under six foot. Nice line. Good stock. "You let Cairns rattle you."

"Put it together, Olivos." She trotted now, where the incline became even steeper, and she could hear the shovels jangling on his back as he stayed with her. He would never ask Eli to ease up, so she could go as fast as she wanted and let his pride push him along.

"What?"

"Cairns puts me on the SAR team for this one—yanks me out of a tree walk I put together for a group. Puts Sandra on that—"

"She's good." That would get her, he thought. He loved to get her a little riled—but not too much.

"Of course she is." She could hear Olivos falling back; then he kicked into low gear, moving very close behind her. Rumbling up the trail like a four-wheel drive. "But it was my job today. Not to get up at 3 a.m. and join a SAR team."

"You figured it out." He huffed now, feeling the dust of the pumice floor in his nose, breathing out in hot exhausts—not too loud, so she wouldn't hear. He kept his voice even. "You estimated the kids' route, the terrain they'd cover, how far they'd go. It's the kind of thing you're good at."

"I'm good at too many things."

"I can imagine," he licked the cold sweat from the bottom of his mustache.

She broke into a run and he chased her, working hard to keep just behind. After nearly a mile, Eli stopped abruptly, and Olivos, hypnotized from leering, nearly ran into her. They both breathed heavily, staring at each other, with nothing but the hiss of the wind in the pines. Olivos enjoyed it until he saw her eyes narrowing in that way that made the whole upper half of her face seem to grow pale; something of her father in this gaze, which became focused and icy.

"I'm going ahead," she said. "You stay back."

"Okay."

She ran ahead, quickly out of view.

Olivos felt the dull ache across his shoulders where the shafts of the shovels had bruised him. He let them down, dragging them behind him to stretch out his muscles. Listening to the steel drag on the ground, he felt the vibrations run up his arms as if the backs of his own hands were sliding along the trail.

Some men are slow to learn women, he thought. For the first ten years in his relations with them, they were meant to coax into bed, to play slap and love hard and quick. On his twenty-fourth birthday he had meant to prove something to himself, saved himself up for it, and took two prostitutes in a Fresno motel, working them over with images of his physical power tall in his head. When he was spent, and one of the women left for another appointment, he stopped the other, handed her an extra twenty, and asked her how it really had been. "Rough," she had smiled sadly, and left.

He gave up on prostitutes and invested in relationships that were a step up. Women his own age had seemed too difficult, and he took to the teenage girls in the conservation corps. They usually liked to play his way, a little gentler than he used to be, but still these affairs came flesh toned, adventures of breast and thigh practiced hotly in his small house outside the Park. By the time Cairns put a stop to these affairs, Olivos felt relieved. Teenagers bored him.

At thirty, in his prime, he wanted women about five years younger. Olivos wanted them pretty, and he could attract them as he pleased. Some he kept long enough to lure into his house. But he grew tired of sitting at home or at a restaurant, sipping a beer, telling the same stories over and over. He had rerun his adventures, his rescues and busts, so many times he could hardly tell them. Every time he heard his voice filling up the room, saw her eyes glazing over, he knew another relationship was spent. Lately they had been burning out quickly. There were too many women. He was afraid he was getting the reputation that he had always wanted when he was younger.

Eli was his one friend among women, and she could teach him some things that might make him step up once more like the time after the prostitutes. He knew he needed that step but he could not seem to do it himself. Olivos wanted her to like him, but what it was in him that wanted her to love him always lurched forward and—well, here he was again, on the trail alone. "She's pretty damned complicated," her father had told him once over drinks at the Muir Tavern. "It would take something to win her from that poet she's married to."

Olivos picked up the shovels, holding them up by the necks, when he reached the bend in the trail where she waited. There was a small overlook, and the low end of the Valley spread out before them, gold and green in the afternoon sun. April Fool's Day, and the snow down in the Valley had begun to recede. A rock wall two feet high lined the outer edge of the trail, and a large middle section had been pushed over the edge by expanding ice in the winter. The Hazeltine children, too far ahead of their parents on the trail, had crept out through the break, ran down a slope a hundred yards, and began their wandering trek in the woods below.

In the quiet, Eli had listened to the far-off cry of a red-tailed hawk, and her anger had eased away. She sat on a crumbled edge of the rock wall, legs tucked up with her arms across her knees. Watching Olivos. As he walked up, he would not look her in the eye. She could depend on him to keep his mouth shut for awhile.

"Let's go," she said.

He gathered the cut stones, which had not tumbled far down the slope, and she fitted them into the wall. Straddling it, she lifted a rock into place, fitting it into the puzzle neatly. She did not wear gloves, and her fingers chaffed against the granite pieces and stung in the cold breeze. When a stone weighed as much as seventy-five pounds, she bent her knees and pulled with her arms, protecting her back as much as possible. The job was nearly done when Olivos started talking again.

"You think Nick Cairns is hard on you, right?" Olivos set a heavy boulder down by her.

"You're saying this is my reward for a job well done?"

"No."

He paused, and Eli could tell he chose his words carefully.

"He's trying to get something better for you."

"I like where I am."

"An interpreter on G-7 pay?" Olivos stopped his work, looking at her as he rubbed dust from his cheek with the back of his hand. "You're better than that."

"So if I'm better, I have to join you people in protection?" She heaved a very heavy boulder up on the wall.

"That's what Cairns wants."

"Oh." She let the boulder slip, giving it a small shove, and it rolled down the hill, bouncing until it hit a tree far below.

"Shit." Olivos went down after it.

Eli kept working on the wall, listening for her red-tailed hawk, and had most of the boulders in place. Occasionally she glanced down to see Olivos' progress; with the heavy rock tucked under one arm, he walked up quickly. Breathing heavily, he came back up and set the boulder by her.

"Now," he said, wiping his brow. "You got to get things straight. You have all this training, and more and more the Park needs someone in protection like you."

She set the boulder on the edge of the wall.

"The government wants more women in protection anyway—"

"Not again!" Eli let the boulder tumble down the hill. After it dove into the woods below, she turned to him, "if you're too tired, I'll go after it."

"I can go down and get the damn rock."

"You're not tired?"

"Of course not."

While he walked down, she hurried and finished the job, so that just the large boulder was out of place. Eli sat on the wall, looking over the edge. He came out of the dark tree line with his rock, coming up faster than before. She admired the thickness of his frame, the way his heavy quads pumped up the hill, and she wished he would stay that way: a fine, quiet picture walking at a distance.

"I'll do it," she said when he came up.

He handed her the rock reluctantly.

She balanced it on the edge of the wall.

"How about if we don't talk about your career?" He sat down on the wall, watching the boulder.

"Done." She fit it into place.

X

The morning after he attacked Thelma, Spell decided to leave Brulingham. His loathing of the place at last overcame his desire for the gun. He would wait no longer to go the Valley. Spell desperately needed to be there. He had spent a sleepless night in the suffocating room, and at first light he carefully put his clothes away in his suit bag, set the room key and five hundred dollars on the night stand, and put everything in his Jaguar, settling in at last to hit the automatic locks.

Just before he turned over the engine, Cleveland tapped on the window.

"Checking out?"

Spell shifted to reverse.

"You go out to Agassiz College, say, in about an hour." Cleveland licked his lips; steam puffed out of his mouth at every word. "Take the main road up to the front of the old administration building—big building, looks like an old-fashioned hotel. You wait there."

"Why?"

"What you came for, Mr. Spell." Cleveland smiled.

"The gun company?"

Cleveland walked away.

Spell drove slowly through Brulingham, past the burned block where a crew lethargically pulled out debris, stirring the stale dust of wood smoke in the air. The entrance to Agassiz was open, the gate unlocked so the "Save Agassiz" banner lay on the frozen mud. The Jaguar could not get up the hill, its wheels spinning on ice and caked leaves, so Spell parked under a canopy of white sycamore limbs. After getting out, he put on his overcoat, leaving it open so he could quickly reach the pistol in the holster. Opening the trunk, he pulled out his Karabin wz63 submachine gun, unfolding the stock and pistol grip, and sliding in a clip. He had another clip in his pocket.

Walking toward the central administration building at the top of the hill, he went between two other brick structures, openly brandishing his weapon. The feel of the guns renewed him, reminding him of what the major and his mother had made of him. He did not care now if the police caught him; in fact, as he walked among the abandoned college buildings, still favoring the bruised muscle in his left leg, he hoped someone tried something. He wanted to open the Karabin on someone, and he did not care what happened after that.

Thelma had told him Agassiz died the year before, but the buildings and weedy grounds looked like they had been in decline for longer than that. A kiosk in the center of the quad opened at the top like a flower, the grey, peeling boards leaning away from each other like petals. In the cold breeze, the tattered remains of a poster waved from its tacks. He went into the central quad slowly, staying in the middle, looking up at the dark walls.

Through a dirty window pane in the old president's office, Clyde Bumber peered down upon Spell. Clyde was the only employee left at the college; the chief of maintenance, he stayed on as caretaker while the board of trustees negotiated endlessly with a reluctant Japanese buyer. Clyde made himself comfortable in the president's office—he had been the head of his own company for some time now—and he did as much cleaning and maintenance as the previous president of Agassiz. The trustees didn't know it, but Agassiz had become the headquarters for the CB Gun Company, and most of Clyde's old maintenance subordinates were now his underlings in the gun trade.

Lean and well-groomed in his Eddie Bauer hunter's outfit and Rockport shoes, Clyde had evolved into the upscale look very naturally, while those below him remained the backward mountain types he preferred. One-dimensional men, Clyde called them, and precisely the kind a three-dimensional man like himself could lead by the nose. Briggs Sutton and Rex Lerned, joining him at the window, were one-dimensionals. Briggs still wore his old Agassiz maintenance overalls.

"Right on time," Briggs grinned through his chaw. "Cleve's been watching this guy close."

"Practically livin' in that guy's pants," Rex added.

"What do we have here?" Clyde studied Spell's submachine gun. "He's packing that 63 we sent him six months back."

"Right out in the open." Briggs spat, missing the president's waste can.

"Damn it, Briggs, be more careful with the snoose grits."

"Sorry."

"No problem," the expert carpet cleaner in Rex emerged, "you just hit that with some—"

"Never mind." Clyde set down his coffee cup. "We have a lunatic down there."

"But a rich one," Rex said.

"You think he knows we beat the shit out of him?" Briggs grinned.

"He hasn't met us yet." Clyde holstered a 9 mm automatic and put on his coat. "But when he does, he'll figure it out."

When they came through the doors, Spell was already waiting for them on the portico of the administration building. The middle man, smartly dressed, did not appear to be armed. The two with him, who came out first, brandished shotguns and menacing looks which Spell thought they learned from too many movies on HBO. He pointed his Karabin down, moving his hand from the trigger, thinking that he looked like he belonged in one of those movies, too.

"Ah, Mr. Spell," Bumber put out his hand while he looked at the submachine gun, the open coat, and the green bruise running down the stockbroker's cheek. "It's a violent country."

"Yes." Spell took his hand.

The men of the CB Gun Company waited for anything more, listening carefully to the silence.

"So, what brings you here?" Bumber asked, watching the distance between Spell's hand and the Karabin's trigger.

"You're the gun company?"

Bumber wanted to say they were merely representatives, but Briggs said, "yeah, we are."

"Strike two this morning, Briggs," Bumber said, without turning from Spell.

"I'm going west," Spell said.

Silence followed. While Bumber waited, he could read nothing in Spell's face and had no idea what the man was planning. Clyde rubbed his stomach in a casual way, but kept his hand as close to the automatic as possible.

"So?"

"I want a long rifle."

"What the hell is that?" Briggs asked. "You lookin' for a musket?"

"I want something very accurate, long range."

"You mean a target shooter—a sniping rifle?" Bumber asked.

"Yes."

"Why didn't you go to your local Wal Mart?" Bumber laughed; soon Briggs and Rex joined in. God, thought Bumber, this guy is nuts. Everything in him relaxed, suddenly, except the hand he kept on his stomach.

"Is this amusing?" Spell asked in a flat voice.

"Yessir." Bumber settled down. "What you're looking for, Mr. Spell, is perfectly legal." He wanted to say all of it—his trip, the beating, what Thelma did—all of it was unnecessary. But he didn't.

Spell looked away.

"But as long as you're here, Mr. Spell, I can show you the best sniping rifle in the world."

"Fine."

"It will cost you a lot of money."

"Fine."

"We'll pick you up at the College Inn tomorrow—take you out with it, let you shoot it."

"Tell me about the gun."

"You'll like this one—it's not quite legal. A prototype weapon smuggled out of Russia after the Soviet Union blew up." Bumber grinned wide, still amused, thinking how much he would charge Spell. The sky was the limit with this guy, no doubt. "It's a refined Snayperskaya Vintovka Dragunova, cutting edge, a real beauty from the old evil empire. Actually, you'll love it, Mr. Spell; no one else on the block will have one—that, I guarantee."

"Tomorrow morning?" Spell asked without expression.

"10 a.m. This morning's a little early for me, Mr. Spell. I keep the banker's hours."

"Yes."

They followed him through the quad, then stopped, and watched Spell go down to his car, put his guns in the Jaguar, and spin his wheels in the slick black ice. While the Jag's engine screamed, sending clouds of blue exhaust into the freezing air, Bumber studied the man at the wheel. This is Mr. Spell, he thought. Doesn't say much. Going west. Rich stockbroker who made nearly a few million dollars last year. Keeps an arsenal in the trunk of his luxury sedan. Content to take a beating to find his long rifle. Dapper fellow who tried to rape my daughter. Well.

"You boys help out Mr. Spell. Give him a push."

Briggs and Rex shouldered their shotguns and headed down the road.

XI

Spring runoff shot over the rocks, roiled like dark glass fingers into the pools, flashed white into Eli's scuba mask. She stood, pulled her torso from the icy foam, and looked up at the grand apron of Cascade Falls, felt but could not hear its thunder as it reached down 500 feet and split the silver morning sun into a thousand shards. She heard nothing but the water in the pool, crashing against her. The harness seemed secure and tight against her wetsuit—she checked it minute by minute—felt its hold on her every time the water pushed a picture into her head, images of being cut loose, tumbling with the current, spilling over the lower falls down stream, water hammering 800 feet into the blunt granite rocks below.

She held up her hand, and they reeled her in to the bank at the right. On the left two men let the harness lines out, on the right two pulled her in. She stepped carefully, muscle and bone frigidly set against the heavy water at play against her.

Something long and pink—at first she thought it some kind of fish but then she knew. She bent over, peering into the water, and saw the cleaned flesh whipping back and forth. Stepping forward, Eli reached for it, slick in her hands, it came from the rock easily. Nearly three feet long, pink and veined. Carrying it to the rocky shore, she dropped it into a plastic bag Olivos held for her.

"A good chunk of his colon, I'd say." He handed the bag to Saunders and looked to the head of the pool. "This man's close."

"At last." Eli crouched down, shivering. The scuba tank felt like a small refrigerator on her back. "So that's, what, part of his shirt, car keys, pieces of flesh, and now this intestine?" Her mind was numb.

"That's it." Olivos handed her a cup of black coffee, strong.

"I'll go back in a minute," she sipped from the hot tin rim. "One more time, that's it."

"Cairns says with the mild weather today, sunshine and all, we better find him." Olivos looked down on her, smiling, waiting for the effect.

"Hell with that bastard," she handed the cup up to him. "Get his fat ass out—"

She saw how the men grinned.

"Maybe you should go in, Olivos." She smiled. "Or maybe you, Saunders, because you look pretty nimble and willowy."

"Oh, now I ain't as strong as you, Mrs. Ware." Saunders set the plastic bag in a large cooler with other bags.

We need someone nimble, willowy, light, Cairns had said. Then looked at her. And strong, he added. All the way up the trail that morning the SAR team had a laugh about that, but now they were closing in on the body and the jokes seemed strained.

Three days before, just at sunset, a couple had left the dining salon at the Muir Hotel. Walked out into the meadow just as the man had planned it for months, and then it was really happening: he had her out there, in sight of the distant falls, water glinting in the sun just as he had pictured it. Her eyes glistened, her breaths came in little puffs, while his black shoes settled in the damp snow and he almost asked her to marry him when she said she saw something go down the falls. A black speck, she had said. And before he could get out the big question she became convinced, as she reeled the image through her memory, that the black speck she saw fall through the water was a person.

That night two rangers, one of them Olivos, had checked the base. Flashlights probed the lower cascade, beams bounced off thick columns of ice looming over the rock. They found nothing. But Cairns was thorough, so the next morning he sent a ranger up the safe, long trail to the top of the falls. And then the day pack was found, with $500 in travelers cheques and a Swiss passport: Janslow Grueben. In the doctoral program at Berkeley: physics. Fog and cold wrapped around the falls for two days, but on the third day the weather broke, became unseasonably warm and open with sunshine, so Cairns sent a team up to find Grueben.

Eli had planned to take a group of tourists for a meadow meander that would wind up at the base of these falls. But had to find Grueben instead. Cairns needed someone light, someone easy for the men to hold in harness against the current. Someone nimble and willowy.

She stood, grateful the air was still, without a biting wind, and she looked once more at the falls above, squinting at the place where a cut of blue touched the brim of the upper fall. Then Eli waded back into the water.

They walked ahead of her, keeping the lines taut. She moved in slowly, fast white water cutting her in half so she could not see below her waist, and had to feel the bottom, searching for a stone to secure her footing by. At the head of the pool thick coils of water spilled over a gap in the rocks; she could not meet that head on, so she eased to the left under the shadow of a granite wall a dozen feet high. The current went back on itself here, swirling, and she thought this could be where the river left Grueben when it was done with him. She plunged her head in, deep under the foam, and saw nothing at first in the dancing shadows and beams of sunlight.

Then something.

A hand, white as eggshell, dipped down below the bubbles just where the water fell into the pool. Then the hand shot back up. She watched it do this several times, all she could see, and after awhile the roar of water faded in her ears and it seemed the rapid breathing amplified by the scuba gear was all she could hear. She bent down deeper in the water, took a step forward like an old woman with back trouble. The steps came easily, the swirl of the current pushing her forward slightly, gently, toward the rushing water and the beckoning hand.

Someone tugged on her rope. She stood up, almost chest deep in the water now, and she could see Olivos waving frantically at her. She saw the problem: the men on her left could not secure her from the granite wall. They could not keep ahead of her, so that she was now ahead of the line. If she slipped, there would be too much lead and when they pulled they would have to jerk hard; she could be lost.

She almost nodded to Olivos, almost let them reel her in, but something in her liked to see him frantic. No joking from him this time. A voice like her father's wanted her to grin, told her to let him sweat. And Eli just wanted to get the job done.

Back down in the water, crouched deep under, inching forward she could see more of Grueben now. Hand, arm, shoulder. Raked by long strands of foam, his long blonde hair fluttered in the current. His face turned toward her—half a face; the rest, with the head, sheered away. But one glazed blue eye, set in white plastic flesh, looked at her. Torn lips peeled back away from broken teeth in a crooked grin.

She felt another tug; gentle, they could not risk pulling her too hard.

The current eased her forward and Eli reached for Gruben's hand. Within inches of it she hit an invisible wall: the current from water pouring into the pool. She found a solid boulder and braced her foot hard against it. She reached for the hand again, pushed her black glove closer and closer, shoving it into a current thick as membrane. His hand shot down again and she gripped it hard. He would not come from his perch in the rock. Body jammed in.

The rope tugged harder this time.

She yanked and half of Grueben, chest and broken, exposed hip bones like flippers, shot out of the rock. He pulled Eli into the hard current before she remembered to let go. The water hit her like a boot, kicking off her mask and shoving her backward.

She felt a stiff jerk from the left and she flopped over like a heavy trout on line. The left let go, and she swung away, hitting rocks on the bottom, going downstream fast. Then another hard jerk and she stopped.

The right held.

She scrambled for footing, fighting the urge to gulp water, her respirator trailing somewhere behind. She found a boulder and wedged her foot against it, managing to stand. The water was only three feet deep. Olivos and Saunders had been pulling hard, and when the men on the left lost her she had swung across the pool. She walked out of the water, Olivos and Saunders pulling her forward.

"Eli, what the hell were you doing?" Olivos dropped the line and ran to her.

"I had him," she gasped.

"Grueben?"

"Big part of him." She sat down, and it seemed the cold broke through and seized her.

"I didn't see anything."

"Me neither," Saunders threw a blanket to Olivos.

"He almost got me." Eli looked downstream as Olivos wrapped the blanket around her. Then she saw the men on the other side, standing, the line limp at their feet. "I guess he's swimming from pool to pool all the way down."

She smiled, knowing that kind of talk would frighten Olivos, and could tell it did by his silence. She also knew that later, when she warmed up, when she saw Sarah—sometime in the night what she had done would grab hold of her.

XII

Spell and Bumber took the Jag, with Briggs and Rex riding behind in a green Ford pickup. They stopped at the end of a gravel road which ended in a dense thicket of young buckeyes.

"We take the trail, Mr. Spell," Bumber said. "And you leave your guns in the trunk."

"So do you." Spell pulled a pistol from his overcoat and laid it down.

Bumber did the same. "You can disarm me, Mr. Spell, but these boys here don't go anywhere without their shotguns. It's just a part of their natures, you understand." And a part of my nature to have them ready with their guns as we walk, he thought.

"Fine." Spell shrugged.

"You fellows forgetting something?" Bumber looked at them, and they stood for a moment, shotguns drooped, thinking. "We have a sale to make."

"Well, shit." Briggs grinned. From the long toolbox in the back of the truck, he pulled out a flat, three by two aluminum case.

Rex set his gun in the wet snow and grunted as he pulled out a larger grey steel box.

"Think we should bring that, Rex?" Bumber walked to the truck, waving Spell to come with him. "How about we save your back and bring along ten rounds for the test, eh?"

Rex put the box back in, and then opened the lid.

"Get your gun out of that snow."

"Okay."

Ah, thought Bumber, good, dependable, one-dimensional men.

"Look at these shells, Mr. Spell." Bumber smiled, picking one out of the case, where hundreds of them were set points up, like so many tiny ballistic missiles. "Hold one."

Spell looked at the long, heavy shell.

"It's a .30 caliber, or 7.62 millimeter if you prefer to think metric, which I do. Weighs 2,000 grams." He could see something flicker in Spell's green eyes, lit up by the sun's reflection in the snow. Bumber jacked the asking price up higher and higher in his mind. "These are special shells—prototype for the gun, for maximum range."

"Aside from this," Spell looked at the case, "can you get any more?"

"No, but NATO has a 7.62 that will work. You save these for special occasions. Of course, you have enough here for about five hundred special occasions." For a second or two, Bumber wondered what the stockbroker was going to do with the Dragunov, but he had long ago trained himself not to care.

Now for the kill, Bumber thought. He opened the case and pulled out the two pieces of the sniping rifle.

Briggs and Rex leaned close; they had not seen it before.

Bumber fit the barrel into the stock with a precise click, and then attached the scope. He worked with the shiny, black parts carefully, feeling his customer's gathering hunger, as the cold, metal rifle came together. He quietly set the Dragunov down in the trunk of the Jaguar, and filled the ten-round clip—this he put in his coat pocket. Then he handed the rifle to Spell.

"Here is your long rifle." Bumber watched the man silently admire it. The asking price kept climbing in Clyde's mind.

Spell gripped the sleek underbelly of the rifle just ahead of the trigger. He ran his other hand along the two-foot length of barrel, feeling the thin grease of a new gun. It felt light and balanced in his hand, and made every other weapon he owned seem hopelessly clumsy. This was what he had wanted all along, even before the day he bought his first gun: a long, accurate weapon, deadly, functional, traveling—far better than any investment in art or books. This was the thing he would have with him in the Valley, as he trekked in the dark, flying nimbly over rock and under redwood. If it worked out that he had to pay for the rifle, he knew he would pay anything for it. This was an important part of going west, the stuff of dreams.

"And that's not all, folks." Bumber took out a six-inch long black cylinder, slightly thicker than the muzzle. He looked into Spell's eyes as he gently brought the barrel around, just short of pointing it at himself, and carefully screwed the cylinder onto the end.

"Other countries make sniping rifles, maybe as good as this one, but here's where the evil empire outdid them all." Bumber saw that Spell almost smiled. Oh, he thought, the sky's the limit with this man. "This is a suppressor which almost completely dampens the sound of the weapon while, as far as I can tell, not affecting accuracy at all. That's what makes this a one-of-a-kind rifle, sir."

"No shit," Briggs muttered. He wanted the gun.

Even Bumber forgot himself for a moment, and while Spell admired the weapon, the gunrunner's legs moved apart, and he took a military stance, going over the gun's points less like a salesman and more like the drill instructor he once had been.

"Your weapon weighs 4.5 kilos loaded. Overall length: 1,225 millimeters. Barrel is 610 millimeters long, with four groves, right-hand twist. Magazine is ten rounds, detachable box. Equipped with a PSO1 site. Maximum range: five thousand yards."

"I want it," Spell said, not looking up.

"Of course you do," Bumber, the salesman, returned. "This is a precision instrument, light, quiet, accurate. The best. And you'll be the only one in the western hemisphere who owns one."

"How much?"

"I'll let you try it out before we discuss price."

Spell shrugged. If he had his chance, the price wouldn't matter anyway.

Bumber held out his hand and, with some hesitation, Spell gave up the gun. Then he heard Bumber rapidly insert the magazine, and his heart skipped. The company president led the way, followed by Spell, and they all went into the woods. As they wound along the narrow trail, Bumber was overcome with the money. He knew that once he showed Spell what the gun could do, the man would go wild. A man worth a lot of money—and no Fed, either. He had passed that test. This guy is on his own, and loaded. The gun could go for twenty grand, easy. Hell, no, more than that. Could up it to thirty.

They came to the edge of the wood.

Could up it more—one of a kind gun. Crazy buyer. How about forty—.

Bumber saw several grey dots on the patchy snow across the lumpy, dormant cornfield. He waved the men back. Bumber crouched, put the head of the lead deer, a few hundred yards away, in his sight. The big doe put her head up, tensing, ready to run. He pulled the trigger, the action was smooth, and the deer's head blew up. The others ran, but Bumber caught a young buck in the rump and it crumpled headlong into a tree at the forest's edge.

"Two down."

"Shit," Briggs muttered with awe.

Maybe fifty thousand dollars, thought Bumber. Cash. The gun was fantastic. The best merchandise he ever moved. He'd send an extra grand to his wife's brother, a Marine guard stationed at the embassy in Budapest—Bumber's European connection. But no. Hell, he paid him too much already. He breathed in the cold air, feeling alive, and he figured that night he'd play rough with Melanie when he picked her up from the night shift at Pizza Hut. Damn, maybe he'd even get after his own wife, too.

"You boys dress out those deer and take them back to the truck."

Rex started to go, but Briggs's mouth dropped. "I'll go with you, Clyde-o."

"Yeah, Briggs. Just follow behind our customer here. But keep quiet while I conduct the business."

"All right." Briggs sighed and shouldered his shotgun.

Bumber turned to Spell. "Now, let's go to the next field, beyond the trees—this place is thick with deer."

He led the way across the field and into another dark wood. Spell tramped behind him. Heavily laden with money, Bumber thought. Maybe fifty-five. No less.

Along the overgrown trail, stepping carefully around the spiked arms of dry briars, looking up at the sun glinting through the icy branches, Bumber continued a conversation with himself in his head. He listened and the voice spoke. No one has done it like you. You're an original. Friends, people here and there, across the world, sending in arms while you sit in the president's office, maintenance man, sending out arms to jokers like Spell. The one dimensionals with suits. You check them out like no one else. You beat a man and watch. If he's a Fed, someone will pick him up, rush in when you dump him at Cleve's. If not, you send in Thelma, see if he goes for her. If he does, he ain't no Fed.

Then it occurred to Bumber, as they came to the edge of the wood, with the sunlit field opening before him, that the money wasn't everything. That the game was fun the way he played it. No one in the business did things like him. No one sought adventure. Few ventured out to the frontier.

Up ahead, the deer silently crossed the clearing, skittish, broken off from the same group that had just lost two members. Bumber stopped and without looking back, gave the military hand signal for Spell to come up.

He came, waiting.

"You see them?"

The deer stopped, tense, right in the line of fire. "You ready, Mr. Spell?"

"Yes."

Bumber handed him the Dragunov. Once Spell brought one down, Bumber thought, looking ahead, he would pay anything to keep the rifle.

The deer sniffed the air and bolted, their hindquarters and white tails waving goodbye to Bumber.

"Fire."

"Not yet."

Behind Bumber, something fell heavily in the snow.

The deer disappeared into the gray woods far ahead.

Bumber did not move. He heard a crack far off, a branch laden with last night's wet snow collapsed somewhere and hit the ground with a thud. He recalled a student at Agassiz who died instantly when a limb fell on her in the quad during an ice storm. It was always that way, when he became happy, swelling with life—that's when death crossed his mind, reminded him he could lose it all, snapped his synapses with the shock of reality. I'm an asshole, he thought, his heart beating hard. I deserve to fucking die now, and I probably will.

"Shall I turn around, Mr. Spell?" Bumber tried to sound calm.

"Yes."

Above the barrel pointed at his chest, Bumber looked at Spell's eyes. Briggs was sprawled upon the snow; on one side his face grew an ugly welt that had the shape of a rifle's stock.

"Undress," Spell said.

"About thirty-five degrees out here."

"You mean about five centigrade."

"Yeah."

"Take everything off." Spell took that tone again, the icy one he used for disagreeable people at the Trade Center, but it seemed more fitting to him here. Already the Dragunov gave things more meaning, made them sharper.

"I was going to ask fifty-five thousand for it." Bumber pulled off his coat and sweater, feeling the bite of the air.

"I would have paid it."

He took off his clothes as slowly as he could, straining to hear or see any trace of Rex. At last, Bumber stood white against the snow, his body hair pricked up in the cold—a black, skinny pattern along arms, torso, and legs that was a shadow of his primitive forebears.

"Walk away from the clothes." Spell waited. "A few more steps into the field. Stop. Turn away from me."

Bumber looked at the woods, two hundred yards away—too, far to run. He forced the picture of blood on the snow out of his mind. He hated the silence behind him.

"You won't get past Rex." Bumber shivered, shifting the balance of his weight from one blue foot to the other.

"He won't see me coming any better than you did."

Hell, Bumber thought, and for the first time in his life the word had some weight to it. Fucking *fourth* dimensional man.

"You were right about one thing, Mr. Bumber."

"What?" He closed his eyes.

"It is a violent country."

XIII

Karol did all he could: had John Williams playing the Canarios of Gaspar Sanz on the stereo, down low, kept Sarah out of the way by reading some Robert Frost to her. She liked the lyric poems, made Karol read "Design" over and over, but didn't care for "Home Burial." They stayed in the living room.

From the kitchen, a dish shattered. Eli had insisted on cleaning up after a very quiet dinner. Another dish crashed, its pieces scattering across the floor, banking into a wall near the entrance of the living room.

"I know what's the matter with Mommy," Sarah curled up next to Karol in the big chair, pushing aside the book of Frost poems.

"I'm sure you do." Karol hoped she wouldn't talk about it; he could just see what would happen if Eli came in and found them talking about her. That kind of thing did not go over on a night like this.

"She's like a storm," Sarah whispered.

"Yes, that's good—but let's not talk."

"No, listen—"

"You going to insist on talking about this?"

"Yeah, listen—"

That was the excuse Karol needed. "Okay, but first let's go outside. Quietly."

They slipped out the front door without a sound, accomplished with a lot of practice. Karol regularly oiled the hinges. Sarah had a sweat shirt on, not really enough for the cold, and if Eli saw them come back in he would catch hell. But sometimes, on a night like this, sneaking out was the best thing to do.

They walked from the soft amber glow of their cabin into the moonlit night. The air hung still but cold, and walking into the meadow felt to Karol as if he and Sarah stepped into water; breathing in the deep air, he reached for and found his daughter's hand for guidance. His foot hit a slushy patch of snow.

"Which way are we going?" Karol asked her.

"Northwest. Almost exactly. See that glowing through the trees?"

The Muir Hotel made a dome of faint gold light beyond a thick stand of pines.

"The hotel's northwest."

"Very good—hold up." Karol pulled his pipe from his pocket, felt for the pouch of Captain Black, put a pinch in the bowl, and brought up the lighter. He stoked his pipe, looking down to see the line of Sarah's face, eye, nose, chin, in his weak fire. She would grow up with the sharp features of her mother's face, he thought, as the baby fat melted away there would be a woman very much like Eli—tall, sharp, but with his darker coloring. And probably his temperament. And none of the grandfather, no, none of the thicker peasant features, thank God.

Sarah pulled him and they walked deeper into the meadow; his eyes had adjusted enough so he could make out the melting humps of snow scattered about—in the dim silver light they reminded him of cloud tops.

"Now, about Mommy," Sarah stopped. "I've made an observation."

"All right."

"She's like a storm. All this heat rises up inside her."

"From her job."

"Yeah. And then there's the good part of her, like cool air, and the hot and cold hit—"

"Gathers up in the mountains."

"That's right. Backs up into the mountains and then she's like a June storm. Bang."

"Very impressive, Sarah." He pulled her into his side with one arm. They headed toward the White House cliffs; he saw the rock cut like a moon face against a faint scattering of stars in black sky.

"She's like a storm because they just happen and you can't blame storms for happening."

"There's a poet in you, Sarah."

"Thanks," she walked ahead. "Dad, do poets make any money?"

So much for the sublime, Karol thought.

In the kitchen, Eli swept up the broken glass. When the last dish shattered she felt foolish, and then her anger faded down deep inside her somewhere when she heard the front door gently shut. She had chased them out again. When she put the dishes away and swept up the last of the glass, she went out the back door.

Blinded by the kitchen light, she walked across the dark meadow to her father's cabin. At the porch, she could see Jack through a window; he sat inside by the light of an old railroad lantern, carving a piece of cheddar with his buck knife.

Eli came in without knocking and pulled up a chair at his table. Next to a big wad of pemmican she saw a blackened, overturned TV dinner tray, dark gravy oozing around the base of his bottle of Jack Daniels.

"Dinner?" she asked.

"That TV crap come out black as cinder." He popped the cheese into his mouth and talked around it. "So I declared war on electricity. Kicked that piece of shit for a stove and pulled the breaker on this place. Got this old lantern here. Cheese and a plug of pemmican—that's all you need."

"And the JD."

"Yeah, the JD." He got up and felt around, until he found a shot glass. He shoved it across the table at her. "Now, daughter, you need a drink."

"How's that?"

"Olivos told me about your playing with a dead man up there in the inner gorge of the falls." He poured the glass full until it overflowed, the whisky going with the slant of the table into the coagulating gravy. "Drink up."

"All my life you wanted me to be an alcoholic." She picked up the glass and sniffed the whiskey. "Something like you."

He ignored that one, but smiled at her mood. This was how he liked her. "Something like me in you wants a drink right now." He picked up the bottle, swung its base toward her and waited until she clinked the glass against it. "Gotta roll with the punches," he upended the bottle, brought it down hard, and sighed long.

While he had his eyes closed, she gulped the whiskey. Eli felt the heat and pain down her throat, fought the push to cough, and put down the glass for another. He filled it.

"Is that Johnson's pemmican?"

"The one and only." He carved a hunk off and tossed it to her; she gnawed on the stiff, salty beef. And she reclined in the rough pine chair, took in the cabin, letting the JD move her mind downstream. With the second shot, as he munched away without talking, Eli felt numb, felt time folding in around her. In the flickering light she could just make out the rough cupboard, rusty enameled sink, same greasy white curtains hanging on the window. His backpack hung by a nail on the wall, his gun racks: shotguns on the top down to the .22 rifle that he used to teach her to shoot. She felt the leeward drift of the entire cabin, its foundations sinking, timbers rotting and fragile. Everything all tough to look at but worn and delicate—ready to cave in any moment. Like him.

"So, Eli," he spoke up suddenly. "You're swingin' by one line, just dangling over 800 feet of falls, chasing after some dead farmer. Got you up there near the peak of the spring runoff, current runnin' its hardest, falls just itchin' to get another fool. What in hell were you doin'?"

"My job."

"Job hell. I thought you were a park interpreter, going to take the assholes out to appreciate nature, pick flowers, shit like that." In the gray haze of his whiskey, he saw her tense up, jaw clench, just as he wanted.

"They don't pick flowers."

"Oh yeah, they do. You show them a colony of wildflowers and what do you think? Soon as your back's turned off they go, back to what you showed 'em, and I see them with bunches of wilted shit, and they're happy skippin' down the trail, kids and all. Every time I go out I see less and less flowers each season. Thanks to you interpreters."

"Right." Eli looked down.

Well, damn, he thought. This ain't working. He tried another tack. "Course, today, you were too busy swimmin' around the inner gorge with some dead Viking."

"He was from Switzerland."

Now he saw how she stared at him, eyes lit up, and he noticed how her long hair was pulled back tight, forehead hard and white. This was better. "Don't you have any sense? Didn't you learn anything I taught you? You should have told that bastard Cairns no, you weren't going to risk your life for a corpse today. Thankee, asshole, but no sir."

Eli sat rigid in her chair. "When you were a ranger, since when did you tell your chief no?"

"Oh, I had the balls to when the orders were foolish. 'Course, it's your lot not to be so equipped." He saw that she stood up, and was let down a bit because he had played her too hard and she was just going to cut loose and go. "Now, don't get worked up."

"That's what you like to see," she said to him as evenly as she could. "All my life. This game gets a little old, don't you think?"

"Game?" He looked down. "Oh, the hell with you."

She went to the door, shaking. "This how you drove my mother out?"

"Here we go again." He rolled his eyes. "Don't be stupid. Now, sit down here and have another drink."

"Always testing me. Test everyone, don't you?"

"Aw, c'mon, sit down."

"Lonely, broken down, old drunk. Why do I bother to see you, talk to you at all." She wanted to scream, tell him she came to him for comfort, some kind of instinct of a daughter, to go to her father, to say she almost died today and expect something from him. She knew better, but she kept coming anyway. To tell him now what happened, how she still shook thinking about it, that would be weakness. Jack Hattan would just make her feel worse.

"No one loves you," Eli said.

"Who needs that." He growled, standing up. "Who ever gets that?"

"Got you," she smiled hard and slammed the door on him.

Late that night Eli sat alone in her living room with the curses he had hurled at her as she had walked back across the meadow. She stoked up the woodburner, shoving as much wood as it would take, and when she worked up a sweat she threw off her clothes, standing before the hot black iron until she could hardly stand the heat. And then she went into her room and pulled Karol out of bed, pushed him mumbling down the hall, kicked his boxer shorts in the rear and spilled him out the front door. She shoved him down deep into the cold prairie grass, jammed her breasts into his face until he could no longer resist nor reason. Eli pushed his head down into the earth, pried open his lips with her tongue. Then he threw her over. She hit him hard in the chest with her fists, but he kept on until she pushed him over. And back and forth they went, rolling in the stiff cold grass, all musk and diminishing heat under still, stars.

Finally she stood up, ready to run away.

Karol puffed, spent, making out her long hair and the curve of her rump. She stepped away lightly, like some animal, and he called out after her, "sometime let's try this in the comfort of our warm bed, darlin', like the normal folks do."

She stopped and laughed, and then stood over him again. He felt her hand close on his, cold and strong. Eli pulled him up.

XIV

Spell fell across the continent. Dropping down to Tennessee, slipping below the scattered northern snows of early April, he pointed the Jag west on I-40 and drove tirelessly. In Memphis, news of the flood poured off his radio—disaster a few states up in Iowa, working on down the Mississippi. He passed the big glass pyramid almost completed on the banks of the river and drove on, tuning into NPR and a feature about global warming and the recent blizzard and impending flood. He went to high ground, left the basin of smothered houses and hog futures, climbing to the high plains. He slipped between storms, entering Amarillo through a pocket of blue sky, which expanded in front of his hood while the flat land lowered out of view. Huge diesels shoving past him blew away the effect of the open skies; in the cockpit of the Jaguar, sealed tight against the cold air, exhaust shot through the vents. The Jersey Turnpike always hovered in his backseat.

Early one morning at Williams, Arizona, he turned north. A stunted forest of ponderosa pines lined the highway, dying, he had heard, from acid rain dripping off the sulphurous effluvia of coal-fired plants. On one of his few vacations, two years before, he visited the top of the Great Smokies, riding along the Blue Ridge Parkway, where the Frasier Firs had died, grey skeletons reaching into the sky, knocked out by an imported adelgid and acidic mist from the northeast. He had returned to New York a week early.

When he reached the south rim of the Grand Canyon, the weakened trees gave way to the bare red rock, and he found himself in the crowded parking lot of a tourist center—the back of the El Tovar Hotel—and he spent more time looking at the brown dumpsters there than he did the canyon. Spell never got out of the car, but raced back to Williams, turned right, and fled west on I-40.

At the California border, late in the afternoon, he slowed when he saw an agricultural inspection station. Officers in brown shirts bent to the windows of the cars ahead, stopped in the gates. Spell had forgotten about the station; he had not driven to California in over a decade. The cars were backed up. Some were ordered to park in a lot on the right for more careful inspections. He had a few minutes. Highway patrol cars were parked to his left, ready, like they are at toll booths. No way to turn around. Illegal guns in the trunk. Each second brought him a little closer to the gate.

He nosed the Jaguar toward a female officer. She was a blonde, about thirty. Spell was furious with himself, furious with these officers out in the desert. How could he have forgotten? Why didn't he see this coming? It was like Brulingham again. He had screwed up. He could picture Major McCrimmon: *well, Mr. Spell, you're not so special, eh?* Eldred felt sick.

If something went wrong, he imagined he would reach for his .38 under the passenger's seat. He would hit her right in the bridge of her sunglasses. Then he would pop the trunk lid, pull out one of the submachine guns, already loaded, and take out the others. They wouldn't be ready.

She was two cars away.

He undid his seatbelt.

Now one.

None of them would be ready. But what chance would he have after he sped away, down the highway, surrounded by nothing but empty desert? He argued with himself. What could he do? Just let them pull him over? Give up at an agricultural inspection station? No.

"Good afternoon, sir." She wore Ray-bans. "Where are you coming from?"

"New York." He wanted to say from somewhere else, but that wouldn't square with his plates.

"Long way." She smiled. Younger than he thought, maybe twenty-five. "Do you have any fruits or vegetables with you?"

"I haven't any food with me."

She nodded, but looked about in the car. Then she paused, looking at him. Her smile fell a bit, as if something mildly troubling crossed her mind.

He slid his hand toward the passenger's seat.

"California has a seatbelt law, sir."

"Oh, yes." He fastened his belt.

"Have a nice day."

"Thank you."

That night he stayed in Needles. The next morning he drove out into the desert, past the borax mines. Spell had felt no sense of relief when he left the inspection station. Out in the emptiness, driving along a pencil line of grey road, with patches of tan, burnt earth on each side, he asked himself, over and over, if he was disappointed because he hadn't killed them all. When he settled on an answer, Spell decided to drive north, along a string of small towns in blank land, and avoid Los Angeles altogether.

West was a direction that failed him at the southern end of the San Joaquin Valley. Whatever Spell thought he would find at the end of West was not over the Tehachapi mountains; he knew about the coast, walled off by highways, cities, and oil rigs in the ocean—the West's big wall, erected by westerners over a century before, the dreamers from the east, come to escape the east, only to bring it all with them.

Spell drove up the highway that divided corporate farms, vast acreage trimmed, fertilized, poisoned, and weeded like any lawn in Connecticut. He wondered what had been in the land before it had been laid out in flat grids, portioned out for Del Monte and Dole, coaxed and beaten to fill supermarkets with frozen packets and cans. He couldn't guess. In his eyes the San Joaquin narrowed into the back of a diesel on the road, or the rotor on a helicopter sprayer. Exhaust, fertilizer, and pesticide pumped into the Jaguar from the vents, and when he rolled down the windows the air smelled the same.

He saw the sign for the High Sierra, and took the offramp toward the Valley. His Valley. The road cut through a city that seemed to have sprawled out like so much crabgrass, and he passed every fast food chain on the stock exchange, new car lots, used car lots, until the city gave up and he drove on rolling country. The suburbs disappeared, developments dwindled, and then there was tall dry grass, a few horses, and hills.

The air grew cooler as he climbed, fresh for the first time in three thousand miles, and Spell let down all the windows. As he shivered, something in the late afternoon shadow of the hills, in the delicate scent of dormant sage and earth, brought that picture to his mind, even magnified it. His small hand covered by a larger one, looking up to his father who told a story of where the Spells came from, something about a ragged Indian out from the west who didn't act like other ragged Indians, who went to New York and, somehow on the edge of the Gilded Age, made a fortune, turned the Spell name into a monument of money. The story came and went in Spell's head, prompted by a feeling or a scent in the air, and he never knew if it was true or something he had dreamed.

His mother had not explained why his father left. She denied that the Spells were Indians, said she'd never let her son take the name if it were so, and took him by the arm to his father's portrait on the wall, to point out the green eyes, with the darkened skin having all to do with a bad artist and not race—she showed the boy how silly he was to persist with his story. You were too little to remember your father, she would say, and he would never have talked such rot. If Spell persisted with the memory, she warned him that she would change his name to her maiden Cheltingham, which was a more proper one anyhow. He would shut up then.

Spell welcomed the habit of thinking his mother had died, and to maintain the illusion he had stopped visiting her years before. Ellen dutifully visited her on holidays, but she would call and remind Spell how unpleasant the old woman could be. He was wise to stay away.

As he wound along the two-lane road, darkened now under tall pines, he listened to the air whistle by. Spell felt he was coming close to home. Patches of blue snow lit up the deep woods as he peered in; he found it hard to keep his eyes on the road. By looking into the forest he could ignore the oncoming headlights and the blinking road signs enticing tourists to buy trinkets or ride the old logging train.

When he came to the Park gate, the fact that he had to pay a fee annoyed him, and he threw a five at the attendant and did not wait to be handed the brochures. He left the lighted gate behind; nothing was before him now but mountains and trees, and as the sun set behind a high ridge the air in the car grew bitterly cold. Spell blew warmth into his hands but enjoyed the chill; it felt better than those nights he scrambled over trails in the Adirondacks. Those were polluted hills, manicured by sad rangers for the pleasure of the city dwellers—a heaping litter box with dying trees and weakened vegetation.

Nothing about it had been home, those nights in the moonlight were only a premonition of home. The winter place in Concord, his mother's ice mansion a stone's throw from Hawthorne's Old Manse, never had the feel of home either. The summer place on Nantucket, rivaling the Johnson and Johnson mansion, had been a big blue and grey chimera, flapping with billowy curtains, perched on the wide empty beaches. Days at Jackson Military were, as his mother said, a place for toughening, and nothing more. She and McCrimmon had seen to that. Spell had tried to make a life for himself in New York City, make it work with a lot of money he thought he wanted until he learned when he was rich that the money did not interest him. Life in New York—that life never worked because he knew, deep inside, it would never work. The painting in his mind, of him and his father on a visit to the Valley, was the one thing that seemed pure, down to the root of what he was: a Spell.

He emerged from a black tunnel and pulled off onto a stone overlook. Spell turned the car off, killed the headlights, and slowly stepped out into the cold blue twilight. The Valley spread out before him, the flat floor hundreds of feet below nearly obscured in the dark shadow, but the cliff faces rising from the floor were brightened by the last pink from the sun, and above these the mountains stood with heavy brows of snow. Thin clouds slithered in and out of the mountains like grey phantoms.

Something, like an animal, screamed out one long, fulsome cry, closing off shortly with a sound almost like a word.

Spell smiled.

Night came as he stood on the edge of the overlook, wishing he had wings, and could take the long rifle and leap off the cliff, swoop over the trees, and fly up to the rock faces, touch them with his hand. Light remained, for the moon was up, growing stronger as the twilight ebbed away. In the silver air, he caught sight of a falls on the other end of the valley, as crystalline and thin as the stem of a wine glass.

This has always been home, he thought, this is what my father said to me.

A large, missile-shaped RV chugged into position alongside the Jaguar, blinding Spell in its headlights. The driver kept them on, and left the diesel idling.

"I'll be damned," the man leapt from the cab. "We're finally here."

"You going to help me with the kids?" his wife called from inside.

"C'mon out, kids!" He walked to the edge.

"Thanks, Tim," she said sarcastically from inside.

"C'mon out," Tim called again. "Shit, woman, no need to get jackets on. We're just out for a minute to see the view."

A young boy scrambled out to join his father; the wife came after, a little girl in hand. At the edge, the family murmured approval of the moonlit scene while the little girl quietly pulled loose from her mother's grip.

Spell walked away, out of the headlight's beam. He tried to focus on the Valley again, but the RV's idling engine broke the moment. He started back to his car, nearly bumping into the little girl.

"Hello," he said, bending down to her level.

Her pale face half buried in thick black hair, she turned away and looked out over the Valley.

"What do you think?" Spell asked her.

"I don't know," she whispered.

"Watch it carefully," he said in her ear. "It's rare down there, and beautiful."

The mother only heard him say beautiful, and she did not like the intensity of the stranger's voice, so she pulled her daughter away abruptly. The girl looked back, her black eyes reminding Spell of Joanna in the stairwell of the burning Trade Center.

He watched them gather together, the woman muttered something sharp. The husband looked at Spell and said, "yeah," and the family packed into the RV. It roared away. Spell waited for the noise to fade and the exhaust to clear out; he studied the Valley, waiting a long time for the animal to cry out again, but it never did.

He drove down into the Valley.

The Muir Hotel rose out of the center of a meadow like it had grown there, stone and timber with tall clerestory windows, a high church of twenties architecture deep in the Valley. The only room available was a grande suite, at $700 a night, and Spell took it. He gave the porter $50 to make a fire in the stone hearth of his expansive room, and paid more to have beef tartar and a bottle of fine cabernet brought up. After Spell had eaten, he took the bottle out on the balcony, looking over the moonlit meadow as he shivered. The dark pines beckoned, he thought, but he kept pouring the wine into a goblet, finishing one after another, until the bottle was gone. The air told him to lose control.

By the time the moon set, he put on his hiking clothes, pulled on his heavy black jacket, and walked through the great empty halls of the Muir, his new boots clicking on the stone floor of the silent lobby. At his car he removed the Dragunov from the trunk, loaded the clip in the moonlight, and went into the trees. Despite the heaviness of the wine, he felt light, skipping over snow patches, following the dim light here and there, just missing icy brooks as he hopped over them. The more he ran, the clearer he felt, the lighter the gun felt. He believed the effect of the wine wore off as he shook off the New York man and became the kind of commando Major McCrimmon had made of him at Jackson. The major had spared no cruelty to see that Spell was hard, ruthless, and above all, invisible.

He came to the Merced River in the middle of the Valley and followed its banks for a time. Music echoed off the water as he skirted a camp, across the river from him, with a fire blazing and people huddled about it, a pillar of smoke rising above them. The sight of young women laughing, men with their beers, and the sound of grunge rock reverberating off the trees weighed him down and he went back into the trees.

Coming into a meadow he saw the silhouette of a deer, or a bear, standing on the other side. Bear, he decided. Could only see so much in the moon's afterlight. He narrowed his sight on the creature, had its head in the cross hairs, and saw the bear zip up his pants and head back to camp. He tracked it, and came to a huge tent city, an encampment that, if not for the parking lot before it, might have been a Civil War-era camp with its square grey tents, row after row. Quietly he stepped among the tents, each one spewing smoke from stove pipes. He gripped the Dragunov, ready for someone to spring out—ready, if necessary, to use it and disappear into the woods. Something about the gun urged him to use it. His step was light and without sound; perhaps McCrimmon would have been pleased.

One whole section, a city block of tents, was filled with the laughter of a loud group of Japanese tourists. Beyond that, a section of snorers. He sprinted through the center of the tent city, by the glass windows of the cavernous cafeteria, over the decks of the gift shop plaza, and back among the tents, following the shadows perfectly. At the edge of the encampment he stopped, listening to the loud moans and high-pitched cries coming from one tent by the trees. The lovers went on and on, and thoughts of his recent loves fluttered by—a feeble twitch of the New York man within him.

"Whoa!" He heard a hoarse teenage voice exclaim from another tent.

"You hear that, too?"

"Shut up, boys."

Spell sprinted away. He kept running until he could hardly hold the gun, panting, dizzy as the wine worked on him. Now he saw a lake emerge from the trees, with the pale white face of a great cliff upside down in dark waters. He leaned against a redwood trunk, breathing hard, putting the gun across his knees and closing his eyes.

"Is this home?" A voice inside him said very clearly. In the gathering haze of exhaustion and a bottle of wine, Spell had to concentrate on the thought that the voice was part of him. Yet it sounded like it came from somewhere in the wood, from somewhere outside his head.

"I don't know," Spell said aloud. He opened his eyes, looked slowly about, seeing something in the air ahead of him; the thin arc of a shooting star. Could have been in the lake, in the reflection with the other stars.

"It doesn't feel right." Spell sat down, set his back against the tree as he drew up his knees and cradled his head in his hands. He thought of the crap he had come through, the long run from the Trade Center, Brulingham, the noisy camps in the Valley. The whole mess. And though it was clearer in the Valley, a bit more pure, that dead air from the Trade Center had come with him. Smoke hanging in the air—there in the streets of New York, and Ohio, and even here, even now, drifting from the camps. The pristine picture, he and his father and the solitude, the purity of it— would be gone tomorrow, impossible to find as it always had been. He could hardly breathe when he thought of Ellen, and what happened to her when she came searching.

"All these people." That strong voice again—stronger, it sounded more like something from somewhere in the trees.

"All these people," Spell repeated. "If we could be rid of them."

"Clear the Valley."

The words, as he heard them, did not seem like his own; this was not his idea, but was his idea. Something big moved here, had been moving since Ellen died and the explosion in New York, and it thumped him in the brain. Everything came together now to a point in the front of his mind, like a highly magnified object in a telescope that swims in haze just before the eyes and then suddenly sharpens. What he was in New York had been an obscurity, a cloud over his vision, and it took an explosion in his building and a beating in Ohio to blow it away, to see how far from himself he had been. How out of focus. The image that had led him so long, and so far across the country, could become clear at last. And Ellen had led the way.

"Clear the Valley."

Spell staggered up, felt the stiffened skin of the redwood with one hand. He listened. No one was near. He wanted to be sure of that.

XV

They had gathered at the end of May, a group of twenty, in Tokyo station, navigated the underground city, picked up some last-minute $150 bottles of scotch in a shop, then taken the train to Narita, boarded the JAL 747, sat down with their obento and sake in first class and studied the scenes on the plane's big screen: cowboys on the range, cattle drives under tall snow-peaked mountains, country music. Got in the mood and fell asleep over Alaska. Arrived in San Francisco on time, boarded the deluxe coach for the Park, had cocktails, and by nightfall were checked into the Muir Hotel. Met up with four other parties, one hundred travelers in all, took over the lounge, and partied bleary-eyed into the night.

At 7 a.m. they were up, had a big breakfast in the grand salon, most of them rejected the omelettes—too much cheese—but they embraced the fried potatoes and the fresh fruit. By 9 a.m. they were in the hotel shops, picking up film, tour books, and then to the Ralph Lauren clothiers, where they pressed the retailers there with a frenzy of outfitting, dealing, and laughter. At noon they returned to the salon for a deluxe lunch—most took the fried chicken. Had cases of Asahi beer on ice brought out to their tables. At 2 p.m. sharp the twenty from Tokyo stood out under the east awning and waited for the tour to begin.

They were junior executives from NTI, all in their twenties, except for one middle manager, Kiyoshi Sugiyama. Some of the men walked nervously about, looking up into the blue sky that had been broken by a wall of dark thunder heads; others peered at a filthy group of ragged backpackers squatting out in the hotel's meadow. The nervous men had read the travel books, knew America from the staggering crime statistics in the cities down to the frequency of lightning strikes in the Valley. Most others crowded around Sugiyama, took pictures, laughed loud at his jokes. Several checking their watches: 2:10 now. They were attached to the division of NTI that owned, among other properties, the Park concessioner: The Heston Company. The division had done well, serving over a million customers in the Park in the last fiscal year; the CEO was magnanimous, and these juniors were sent to enjoy a whiff of the west. 2:15.

They waited. A distant boom of gray thunder pushed in a breeze that shook the white and green striped canvas awning.

"Ah, there," Sugiyama pointed across the meadow.

They saw her come from the trees, olive hiking pants and tan shirt, WWI-era hat and thick blonde hair tucked under. Bronze belt buckle and badge polished. She walked steadily toward them, fast, hat slanted against the gusts.

"That is the ranger," Sugiyama said in Japanese. "She is quite long-legged." Several men laughed.

"Hello," Eli called to them. "You are the NTI tour?"

The men smiled, nodded, and waited for Sugiyama to speak. He went forward and shook her hand.

"I hope you had a good trip," Eli said.

"Like clockwork," Sugiyama grinned. "But you are a little late, I think. I'm Kiyoshi Sugiyama."

"I'm Eli Ware, your Park guide." She looked at the group, felt some eyes on her legs. Should have worn the trousers, she thought. "I'm sorry I was late, but I checked the weather reports just now. As you can see, a storm is coming in from the west."

"Electric?" One of the nervous men looked at the sky again.

"It might be severe," Eli spoke up. "Possibly dangerous."

"Should we cancel the tour?" Sugiyama asked.

"No. I'd say we have an hour. We can't take the falls trail, but I'd like to go to the lower end of the Valley, along the river–if we can keep the light, you should get some great pictures."

Sugiyama explained the change to the group and assured one man who asked about the lightning. He turned to Eli, "Let's go now."

They walked a half mile down through the lower grove of ponderosa pine, on a paved trail between the river bank and meadow grass. The wind shook the trees fifty feet above but the air below was still; patches of light passed quickly along the forest floor, old stiff pine needles left from winter came down like rain. The men snapped a lot pictures.

The river opened into a field and the wind swept down. Invisible columns of dry, electric air spilled over the granite cliffs of the valley, piling into the field. Sunlight still shot through. The men from Tokyo woke up, forgot the statistics, and took video tape, took 35 mm photos, wouldn't listen to Eli's lecture about the sedge and moss but instead had her pose with each man in the group. Big grins all around.

Then the storm sped up, broke open in thunder and lightning, and a curtain of rain swept the meadow. The men scurried to get their equipment into leather cases and day packs.

"You misjudged the storm," Sugiyama said to Eli over the wind. He smiled, enjoying his observation and the sight of the junior executives scrambling about in this moment from the West.

"Yes—sorry," Eli said.

"No," he patted her shoulder. "This is very fine. But can we get out of the rain?"

"Take the trail to the right, not the way we came." Eli thought for a moment. Karol and Sarah would be home; he would not like it. But, oh well. "We can get shelter in my cabin."

"Your cabin?" Sugiyama looked puzzled.

"Yes, let's go to my house."

"Oh, no."

A lightning bolt came on as bright as a flash bulb, and everyone blinked. The nervous men ducked, and the clouds rumbled.

"We must go now," Eli said and led the way.

They ran, Sugiyama speaking sharply in Japanese to the scampering men; when the thunder cracked he laughed hysterically. "Oh, this is fun, eh?"

"Fun," several men repeated, running for their lives.

"You are a fast runner," Sugiyama yelled to Eli, panting behind her.

"I can slow down."

"No, move on." Her hat had blown off and he liked the way her long pony tail swung against her back. And the water ran down the curve of her spine, the cloth of her pants stuck to her backside, quite muscular. Ah, he thought in Japanese, this is a good adventure. Wild west, indeed.

By the time they reached the cabin, the lightning had become wicked. An electrical storm with an intensity that the national weather service had not predicted. The tin roof of her cabin lit up in flashes, each time looking as if it had been hit by a bolt, and each time sounding like it in the black thunder. The lowered branches of the big oak by the cabin lifted up, the pines nearby sang in the wind, bent, chords strummed by a giant hand.

Eli sprinted ahead, went for the door, opened it and let the wind and scattered raindrops into the living room. Sarah worked on a watercolor at the table; the paper blew out of her hands.

"Can you close the door?" Karol put down his book.

"Can't," Eli grinned at him. "I'm holding it open for twenty Japanese tourists. Clear the decks."

"What?"

"Hurry. Move the table to the wall." The men had run up to the porch and stopped. "Move the chairs. Karol, I'm not kidding."

He looked out the window. "Well, what do we have here?"

Sarah took one look and fled to her room.

Karol shoved the table back and put the chairs to the wall. "I'll bring in every chair we have."

They had packed onto the porch, pelted by slanted rain, still jumping with each blinding flash.

"Come in!" Eli yelled.

Sugiyama started to take off his shoes.

"Leave them on. The rain's getting in!"

They followed Sugiyama, the nervous men first. Eli could finally shut the door, and they stood about in the kitchen and living room. Dripping wet. Very quiet suddenly.

"I'd like to introduce my husband, Karol Ware."

"Pleased to meet you." Sugiyama shook Karol's hand and the others followed and suddenly there was a kind of receiving line in the small living room.

"You look cold," Karol looked around, edging back toward a wall. "You boys need a shot?"

Sugiyama smiled. More silence.

"You boys drink Jack Daniels?"

"Yes, Jack Daniels." Sugiyama turned to the group and announced, "J.D." They came to life.

Karol finally had to settle for paper cups, a splash of his last bottle in each, and ice. Sarah crept out of her room and was greeted with such enthusiasm that she brightened up and did not mind being enlisted as a waitress by her mother. Eli called in to explain where she was with her group. Sugiyama looked at the rain splashing against the windows, took in the fire that Karol had stoked, and called the hotel to order a van load of drinks.

"What kind of beer shall I order, Mr. Ware?" he called over the chattering junior executives. Even the nervous ones reclined happily on what chairs they could find. They submerged the sofa.

Karol did not drink beer, so he thought hard. "Bass?"

"Bass," Sugiyama said into the phone. "Two cases on ice."

The hotel van came rushing to the door, braking on one of Eli's tea roses. The men formed a line, juniors outside in the rain, unloading the goods. Then Sarah, coming into the party spirit, unveiled the stereo.

"Should I put on Donald Fagen?," she asked Karol.

"Sure."

"What is Donald Fagen?" Sugiyama asked.

"Something like jazz," Eli said.

By 5 p.m., with the music up and thumping in the boards, Sarah began to dance. Then they called for Eli. She joined in, did the bump and grind with each executive until the men staggered away. The house roared with the music and filled with the sweaty heat of people. Sarah opened all the windows and the cold mountain wind blew through the house like a cool stream, scattering napkins and empty beer bottles.

"You're a southern boy, Karol?" Sugiyama was back on the phone.

"North Carolina," he answered from the haze of his sixth beer.

"You like barbecued ribs?"

"Naturally."

The van from the hotel came and plowed down a second tea rose. They formed a line again, bringing in racks of ribs, with boxes of spicy fries, tubs of beans and slaw, several loaves of hot garlic bread. The rain had stopped and the clouds parted. No one noticed.

"Very southern, eh?" Sugiyama inspected the piles of food in the kitchen, a cigarette dangling from his lips.

As they finished eating, Sarah announced her father was a poet. They turned to him, and then to the Park guide. Eli nodded. They had to have his books. Karol brought in a box of his last edition and they bought up the copies. He had an impromptu signing party and sold all fifty books. He inscribed for an hour, hands shaky, doing his best to spell out names phonetically. Sarah collected the money.

Jack Hattan came stamping up the porch, threw open the door, and yelled at Eli, "what the hell is all this racket?"

Eli noticed that he was in easy earshot of Sugiyama, and she tried to push him out the door.

But he lurched forward, ever closer to Sugiyama.

"What the hell. You got a house full of Koreans here."

The tone of his voice hushed the crowd, brought the volume down, which, to Eli and Karol, meant that things were going to take a turn for the worse.

"We're having a party," Sugiyama came forward, taking Jack's hand.

"Korean bastards!" He pulled his hand away.

Sugiyama stood back, took a long draw from his cigarette and winced. "We're not Koreans. We're Japanese."

"Oh," Jack scratched his beard. "Yeah, I can see that. Glad you ain't Koreans; I fought those bastards in the war, you know. They're animals."

"Indeed," Sugiyama grinned. He turned to the executives, and told them in their language that the old man had thought they were Koreans but was pleased they were Japanese. The men cheered, raised beers, cigarettes, and rib bones to the sky.

"Damn straight," Jack now shook Sugiyama's hand vigorously. "I'm Eli's father."

"Oh, then what will you drink?"

Karol slithered to Eli's ear and said, "He knows how to play your father's game."

No one saw the sun go down. Sugiyama, who had read American and English poetry avidly in his youth, had Karol's book and was spontaneously translating the verse aloud for the junior executives. When he was done with a poem, they would applaud him. Karol sat back at the door, his arm around Eli, listening to Sugiyama's deep voice, not following the words but enjoying the sentence sounds and cadences.

"Beautiful!" Karol yelled when Sugiyama finished another one.

When the book, or Sugiyama, was spent, Eli called for their attention. After some time, she had it. "As your Park guide, I'd like to invite you outside."

They went into the meadow, the cool grass soaking their shoes, and she directed them to look up to the sky.

"This is what you came for."

The storm had cleaned out the high mountain air, polished the stars. The wide, ghostly band of the galaxy hung over the middle of the valley, rogue stars further out in the intense black. These, and the cold wind, the rustle of the oak and pine, silenced the junior executives. They leaned back far, a few fell over, into a night without chirping signals, buzzing cars, city lights, shimmering Pachenco parlors, nor jagged neon signs.

Sugiyama found Karol, spoke into his ear intensely.

By 11 p.m. two hotel vans picked up the executives. They cheered Eli, praised the brilliance of Karol's poetry and his Japanese translator. They struck up a song in Japanese and it and the hum of motors echoed over the meadow. In the quiet, Sarah crawled to the sofa and fell fast asleep. Jack had already stumbled home.

Karol hugged Eli, and pulled her down with him so they nearly fell but somehow managed to sit on the steps of the porch. The planks of the floor were faintly illuminated by the warm light from inside, and cut an edge against the black meadow. Karol felt dizzy, a bit of vertigo, as if they could slide off the edge of the porch and find themselves falling in among the stars.

He closed his eyes and settled on a favorite image, Frank Benson's impressionist painting ,"Sunlight." The woman stands on a hill of daisies, he remembered, erect in a long white dress, one hand on a hip, the other on her brow, shielding her eye from the sun. It is a profile, and the woman peers intensely toward the sea. Clean and sharp, brushed white by sun. To Karol, the woman was Eli. He had admired the painting since his childhood, and when he met her that was why she already had the look of an old friend.

"Thanks for bringing your interpretation to our house," he opened his eyes and kissed her cheek. Studied the dim illumination of her profile as she peered into the meadow. "Sunlight," he thought.

"Oh, the Japanese," she said.

"Good people."

"Yes, they are," she laughed.

"Sugiyama is a wise man."

"Think so?"

"While ago he whispered into my ear, said, 'your wife is the most beautiful woman.' Said it over and over."

"Hmm." She focused on the meadow.

"You know what I said?"

"What?"

"I said, 'she's your American beauty.'"

"Oh God."

"I said, 'Kiyoshi, this is how it is in America, with the big country, big women.'" He pulled her close. "I told him, 'We have parties like this every day in America, with these kind of women.' You know what he said?"

"How about another beer, yankee dog?" She turned toward him, caught the flash of his teeth in the light. Eli felt a little embarrassed for him, a little dizzy too.

"No. He says, 'It's the same in Japan.' You got to love that man."

"You got to love everyone." Her face flushed; she could not look at him anymore, nor talk any more foolishness, and so she turned his head with her two hands, closed her eyes, and kissed his mouth for as long as he could take it.

XVI

After that first night in the Park, Eldred Spell searched for a proper supplier, starting in San Francisco and working down the coast. He had no address, was too nomadic for catalog companies. In April, driving a rental car, he checked every outfitter in wilderness clothing, packs, food, and survival supplies—from tiny shops to huge chain dealers. Nothing felt right. Then, one afternoon in Carmel, he knew almost immediately that he found the supplier he needed to do his work.

The Vantage Point was a small shop at the end of a side road off the main street. Spell stood outside the shop, noting the old Victorian house that had been refurbished, that it stood in one of the larger yards he had seen in Carmel. He watched the cypress trees that shadowed the house, saw a bluejay chattering in a limb, the afternoon sunlight dropping through to the grass and begonias in golden pools. Heard the ocean breeze in the trees, wind chimes in the garden, and a little girl sing out from the floor above the shop. Owners live there, he thought, a family on its own, disconnected from chains and corporate computer networks. A small outfit he hoped he could control.

Inside, looking over the walls and shelves laden with expensive merchandise, he felt even better. In his week's search he had come to know the best brands, and here they were, in backpacks, tents, sleeping bags, coats, hiking boots, made from old-fashioned to space-age materials—things for all seasons, made for endurance. And most important, the tags on products pushed for the environment: aluminum frames on backpacks 100% recycled, camp stoves approved by the Sierra Club. On the walls, pictures hung of Zodiac rafts battling whalers, posters of the spotted owl, of ugly clear cutting in Washington, a satellite image of the ozone hole. To Spell, everything here added up and felt right.

Now to the owner: a lean man, early thirties, yellow hair and gold-rimmed glasses, bald spot shining as he bent over a catalog with one hand working a calculator. Nervous, Spell thought, playing the same series of numbers over and over. Can't believe the overhead. Income isn't making it. Spell thought how he would work this fellow over with a fat pocketbook, and saw a glimpse of himself from the early New York days, in the pit of the stock exchange.

Doug Evers had been lost in figuring the break point for a new line of mountain bikes that he could not purchase. His three-year-old, Chelsea, kept singing the same tune, distracting him, and he wished Maggie would make her stop. The girl kept singing a jingle from a McDonald's ad, and he figured this was another reason to get that TV disconnected. Doug looked up to call out to Maggie and he saw Spell. Usually he heard customers come in, but somehow this man had walked up to the counter without his noticing. And this customer stared at him.

Doug's mouth opened but nothing came out. He had never seen such green eyes, glittering from a sharp, long face. Depthless black hair. Everything about this man was long and graceful and the sudden impression of beauty startled Doug. He could not read the unbroken stare, but it had none of the inquiry of a customer with a question. What was it? Doug felt his heart thump and his hand at the calculator shiver. Perhaps he had drunk too much coffee. Would go decaf tomorrow.

He shook himself. "Can I help you?"

"Yes." Spell took him in, and did something he rarely did on first contact: he leaned over the counter and shook Doug's hand. He felt its weakness, and he held it for a moment too long. Stared at Doug intensely and measured the effect. "Are you the owner of this store?"

"I am." For some reason, Doug did not mention his partner, Maggie, and he was grateful she and Chelsea were now quiet upstairs.

"Good." Spell released Doug's hand. "This part of a chain of stores?"

"No." Doug smiled. "I'm on my own."

"I'm glad." Spell looked around. "I want to make some big purchases, in cash, and I hate to see my money go to a faceless conglomerate."

"I can understand that." Doug came from around the counter.

"I want equipment designed for low impact on the environment; I don't want to leave a trace where I'm going." Spell stepped close to Doug, saw the smaller man's hands shake slightly. "Big companies can't understand that."

"Absolutely." Doug stepped back. His mind went blank.

"You've been a member of Greenpeace and the Sierra Club for a long time, haven't you?"

"Well, yes." Customers rarely asked. "Been a member of both since college."

"Member of the Nature Conservancy?"

"Sure." Heart beating fast, and busy trying to figure out why. "And several other groups. How did you know?"

"By the posters on the wall." Spell caught the man's pale blue eyes. "By your selection of stock. You're not here just to make a profit—you believe in the environment."

"Of course I do. Not everyone in this business feels that way. You'd be surprised." The salesman was coming back to life in Doug; he recalled this customer had said cash sales.

"You're really committed," Spell lowered his voice. He moved into Doug's personal space once more. "I'll bet you give to these organizations, tithe your profits to them."

"You're right." He grinned, complemented, but he knew ten percent of his profits would be over Maggie's dead body. He gave two percent at best. The thought brought back some bitter arguments from last year.

Spell put his hand on Doug's shoulder, looking at him intensely, focusing on the man's eyes all the time. "Have you been active in these organizations? Really put yourself on the line for the cause?"

"Of course." Doug felt a little fear now, somewhat thrilled with the pressure of this man's hand on his shoulder. Saw in his mind a dark night with the group, spiking trees marked for logging; wondered if his or someone else's spike caused the kickback in the chain saw that lopped off the lumberjack's forearm a month later. Read about it in the paper, spent a lot of long nights sweating that one out. They never caught him. He never told Maggie. And the spiking did not stop them from logging the old redwoods.

"I've made a few speeches," Doug said. "Been to a few rallies."

Spell had seen the man struggle with the question and suspected that Doug had at least thought of doing more than giving speeches.

"Well," Spell released his grip on Doug's shoulder. "You're my man."

"How can I help you?" Doug felt a bit relieved and let down that things were back to the level of just plain business.

"I'm going on an expedition."

"Where to?"

"Can't say." He looked over the shop again. "But I'm going to need gear for every contingency, for all seasons. I'll no doubt make some special orders—I need more than what you have here."

"We can consult my catalogs and find whatever you need." He licked his lips. "I have relationships with suppliers all over the world."

"I'll need to order several complete outfits, clothes and all sorts of gear. There will be a lot of redundancy."

"For caches? This the kind of expedition you'll need to set up caches along the way?"

"I didn't say that." Spell went down the aisle, and Doug followed him. "But I tend to order several copies of whatever I buy. Force of habit."

"That's fine with me."

"Yes. Now, let's see what I can pick up today."

Spell left with a lot of spring and summer gear. He paid over three thousand in cash for the supplies Doug loaded into the rental car. He ordered nearly three thousand more in winter wear and equipment, and assured Doug that this was a beginning. Just after closing time Spell held Doug's hand again, and tipped him an extra five hundred for the help. He saw how the salesman took that money; Spell had control now. Doug Evers was just the kind of supplier he had been searching for—vulnerable, and very dependent.

"I want to keep these transactions between us," Spell said at the door just before he left.

"Why?"

"It will be in your interest, and mine, to keep this between us." Spell gestured to the posters on the walls. "And in the interest of the environment."

"All right," Doug gulped. He wondered if the customer had been buying for several people, and he realized he was getting himself into something.

"I won't say anything." And I will figure out a way to lose all records of this, he thought. He gave up the idea of asking for the man's name.

"Then I'll be back."

Spell started on his way to the airport in Portland, where he had left the Jaguar.

Doug went back to his counter, looking at the cash that was so much the tray in the register could not handle it. He made a big stack of one hundred dollar bills. The calculator had been buried in a pile of cash, to which he added the five bills in his hand. He felt weird, perhaps a little guilty. He had sold the most expensive clothes, the best jackets, even the self-heating ready-to-eat meals he thought he'd have to discount. Everything went at original markup. He'd lost track, couldn't even make out a receipt for it all and the customer had insisted he did not want one anyway.

He started to recount the money and stopped. Thought of the shining green of the man's eyes. And Doug felt some kind of excitement, something beyond the money, run through him. He shook, thinking how he'd take Maggie that night. Get Chelsea to bed and then Maggie. . . . But he knew that wouldn't be enough, wouldn't quite satisfy. The feeling was strange. He couldn't wait for the man to come back.

Chelsea started singing again upstairs, must have awakened from her nap, and he could hear her solid little steps as she came down to see him. He shook the odd feeling, tried to focus on Maggie and how much he would tell her about the sales. He'd also ask her to buy decaf from now on.

XVII

"Coffee?" Cairns asked.

"No," Eli said.

"You don't drink coffee?"

"Yes, I do."

"But you won't drink it now?"

"No." Her stomach recoiled at the thought of coffee, curling in a state of nerves. She looked past Cairns' plaques and awards on the wall to the clock. The slight hangover from her interpretation with the Japanese did not help. 8:45. This would be a long morning.

"So." Cairns returned from the coffee maker in his office and sat down with a huge mug in his hand. He glanced at the open file spread out on his desk. "Well, here we're getting through May already. The annual performance evaluation."

"Yes."

"Are you ready?"

"I've been ready for ten minutes." Eli regretted her tone. She had promised herself and Karol that she would be careful, control her temper no matter what. Her father had blown up at sessions like these and missed promotions the last fifteen years of service. She could play the system better than that.

"Of course." Cairns sat back. He knew exactly what she wanted more than anything else: to stay in the Valley. That gave him an edge. She seemed pale this morning, probably her time of the month, but her brown eyes cut into his. Saw her clench her fist until the fingers were white. He didn't want her to get mad, really, so he would work her carefully.

"I see some very good work here," he said, feeling better staring at the paper and not catching those eyes. "You completed your coroner's certification, dressed out some bodies for us. Filled in nicely there since Parker went to the Smokies."

"Yes."

"Did you enjoy that work?"

"I thought I was useful." But who in the hell enjoys laying out dead people, women and children? Keep calm, she thought.

"And you participated on more than a dozen SAR teams this year. Olivos writes you were always the best on the team."

Damn Olivos. She crossed her legs.

"Very courageous stunt you pulled up there on the falls awhile back. Glad we didn't lose you."

"For a dead body."

"Right," he chuckled. But that was under his orders, a mistake he admitted to himself, and he felt his face redden. She often had this effect on him, making him feel uncomfortable, and if she weren't a woman he would have transferred her ass out in his first year as superintendent. Then there was her father; Cairns knew that if he transferred her, Jack Hattan would probably come down on a wild drunk and attack him.

"And you even participated in our big drug sweep last October." He kept building his case. "You made how many arrests?"

"Two—it should be in there."

"So it is." Right under his finger in the file. Pause.

Eli saw herself with the other rangers, sweeping through the housekeeping cabins, rounding up two dozen Heston part-timers on possession charges just a week before they were to leave for the season. She chased after one woman, running across the meadow in the cold morning, the suspect running ahead wearing only panties, nightshirt, no bra. Eli remembered shoving the running woman down, cuffing her, hauling her back. Even her father figured that was the low of Eli's career, and he was right. All Cairns' idea. Very bad P.R for the Park.

"That operation was problematic," Eli said. Told herself to shut up.

"How so?" Cairns's eyes became small. Shirley Weaver, the manager for the Heston Company, had complained about the sweep, screamed to Washington that the arrests just meant media trouble, would make it harder to find cheap summer labor, and that they reaped few convictions. Cairns had a call from the assistant secretary of the interior on that one.

"Just bad press."

"And look how you helped us there." Cairns smiled now, because she walked right into it. "Heston was all set to haul us up on brutality charges with that woman you tackled. But turns out she was even bigger than you. Now, if a man had made that collar, we would have been up the creek. Sexual harassment, the whole nine yards."

She did not say a word. Because he was smiling so broadly, leaning forward so eagerly, she knew she had blown her case somehow.

"Do you know what your file tells me?"

She waited.

"I see a female protection ranger." Cairns stood up, went for more coffee, kept watching her. Hitting home now. "I see one hell of a SAR person, one hell of a ranger on busts, a criminologist, and to top it all off, a woman. And we need women in this end of the business."

She started to speak up, but he cut her off. "It's more than that. Olivos, my right hand man, says you have the potential to be the best in the Valley. Hell, give it time, and you could be sitting in my seat." After my retirement, he added to himself.

"His judgment's clouded." Eli's muscles tensed, tendons pulled from some point at the top of her skull where her headache was opening. "He's in love."

"Don't belittle yourself that way." He sat down, brows furled, looking into her eyes. Being earnest. "Everyone can see how good you are at being a protection ranger. It's in your blood. From your father, you know this Valley and the mountains around it like no one else. It's a part of you. And so is protection, part of you, being tough—I know enough about how he raised you—"

"Stop right there." She put her hand on his desk and looked at him with the intensity of her father's eyes.

"Yeah, I know I'm being too personal. But you're no interpreter."

"I'm good at it." She sat back, on the defense. "Like you said, I know the Valley."

"You're just not made to talk to tourists about chipmunks and geology." Had her on the run now. "Sandra completed animal ecology at San Francisco State, bust her butt to do it. Same time you were working on a coroner's certificate. Now, what does that tell you?"

"That I submitted to your request at an evaluation two years ago." She looked down, away from him, could hardly hold her temper. But she couldn't blow it now. Cairns could transfer her away with a signature.

"You like working at G-7 pay?" He tried another tack. "Interpreters are a dime a dozen now. We need excellent protection rangers. You change job descriptions and I could put you up to G-9 right away. You'd be G-11 in no time."

She studied her boot. If she spoke, she would tell him what she thought of him and his underhanded manipulations and that would be the end of her career in the Valley.

"You want to stay here?" He decided to go all the way, get this over with once and for all. "I need you as a protection ranger. If I can't have you that way, then I'll find some other woman to fill the bill." Cairns almost added that he could pull strings to bring imminent domain into play, kick her and her father out of the Valley, make their cabins into historical landmarks for Park visitors to check out. But he was afraid to go that far.

Eli shook, all nausea gone from her stomach. He had been shaping her career for the last five years, sliding gates open and shutting others in the maze, until now here she was, a qualified protection ranger despite her best intentions. What she didn't say was why she did it—to stay in the Valley. But she knew what was going on in his mind, his trump card.

She decided to let the anger take her, nothing could be worth looking into his huge square, grinning face and taking it. The hell with this whole thing. Let her father save the ranch; she was tired of the job. She took a deep breath to tell Cairns what she had wanted to say for years.

The phone rang.

Cairns picked it up quickly. "I'm in the middle of an evaluation here." He swung his chair around and looked out the window.

Eli listened, taking deep breaths, calming down, pulling back from the edge.

"You think a sniping rifle?" Cairns swivelled back around. "See if you can find a slug. I'm on my way." He put the receiver down, stood up, and put on his hat.

"We'll have to cut this off, Eli," he said, pulling on his jacket. "Olivos thinks a sniper just blew the head off a dog in the tent camp."

XVIII

Spell missed his deadline; he was not ready to begin his takeover of the Valley until two days after Memorial Day.

After that first night at the Muir, he wanted to recall the Valley and surrounding Park, know it even better than he had in his youth. Spell could reclaim it in his mind, knowing it as he had learned the stock market: through numbers. In the Georgia hills outside Jackson Military, Major McCrimmon showed him many ways to learn a country so well you could travel it fast, at night, with little light. Spell had a natural inclination to numbers and probabilities, so he mapped the hills around Jackson, and later parts of the Adirondacks, by his own grid system. He worked one out for the Park in a few days and nights at a rundown motel on the coast at Bodega Bay. Gave the clerk a false name and the wrong license number to his rental car. Paid everything in cash. He bought U.S. geological survey maps, studied these, and on one carefully penned in a series of small grids, each representing an eighth of a square mile. Staked out a grid of twenty square miles, broken into 160 squares. In and out of the grid area were eighteen known trails, escape routes, and he planned to make some new paths of his own.

He had moved from motel to motel, town to town, using different names and different cars. He hiked a new trail into the Valley each time, came from as far out as Wawona or the Devil's Postpile. Some had not been well traveled, buried in pine needles, overgrown, blocked by trees fallen years before. He hiked in all weather, pushed himself in freezing rain or light snows in the higher elevations. After he met Doug Evers, he ordered night-vision headsets. Scrambled over trails day and night. Slept little, never had anyway, but became used to the ready-to-eat meals. Made sure he didn't lose too much weight and kept supplied in high-energy supplements.

He listened carefully on the trails, listened for other travelers, and most of the time he hid from the occasional hiker before he could be seen. Spell soon learned that his gift had not left him—he could still see around the corner, see a step ahead. His prescience meant much more to him now than it ever had on the stock market. Even if he could not hear someone coming, he felt someone there. Very few caught him by surprise, even as the season came and the trails had more travelers. No ranger had seen him; he planned that none would.

By the end of April he knew the escape routes, in high country and low, and he had found a few short passes out of the Valley that were not on any maps he had read. He marked his grid. Moved across the Valley, square by square. Some could not be navigated, containing a sheer cliff or covered by a lake. Spell would come to a square, measure by compass, survey it, reacquaint himself with it; he would study its slope, learn how many places it could be passed through, seeking out its hiding places and vantage points. Sometimes he would squat down in the dark of a tree, rain pouring down, and imagine ambush points, lines of retreat. Tried to picture how that square would prove useful; imagined ahead to see what his stock would be there if they found him, if he had to live or die. At night, returning to a square, he would study it through his night vision goggles. He practiced moving from one square to another, day or night, without ever being on a trail.

Up at 8,000 feet, following along the base of a crumbled granite wall, bare of all but some lichen, he searched. Felt something—a puff of cold air at his side, maybe nothing. He crept up to the wall's blue face, looked up into the golden sky of a cloudless, still sunset. Held his hand out and felt the cold air faintly on his fingertips. Ran his hand along a vertical black vein in the rock, a deep crevice an inch across but widening as he moved his hand down, widening to a foot across until it hit a jumble of broken rocks at his feet. He moved these aside. A deep crevasse two feet wide. Night came, but he kept moving the rocks until he had an entrance he could slip through. Spell peered into the black night and sensed no one was near him. He shined a dim light into the crack, could see that he still would be able to squeeze into it. It went down and opened wider. Here was the passage into the belly of the mountain, and not on any guided tours or maps. Eldred would not go in; he perched at the entrance, looking into nothing, until he saw her face. He tried to picture her as the little girl who discovered the cave, their little place of refuge. But instead he saw Ellen as an older woman, insanely seeking this place when it was under several feet of snow. Tracked by a posse of rangers with dogs. He sighed, got out, and carefully closed up the little entrance with the rocks.

On May 15 Spell began to place his caches. He made small bundles of clothes, cash, food, water, a gun—loaded, oiled, ready—and ammunition. They were packed very tightly, all sealed in plastic—colored to match the terrain in which they were hidden. Some went up into trees, some buried, one in the small unmarked cave. Eight in all, evenly spaced over the Valley. All off-trail. All along intended paths of escape, conforming to strategies he had made against the future. Spell packed them in and placed them at night; no one saw him go in nor out.

On the Tuesday after Memorial Day Weekend there was one last step. Seven squares left to explore: The center of the Valley, from the north with the huge tent camp, down through the shops, the little city and Park headquarters, to the Muir Hotel, and finally the South Meadow with two old cabins.

Spell came in from Fresno, bought a ticket on a tour bus, called himself Rick Hanes on this trip. Dressed in pants and T-shirt, with a large day pack, all from Wal Mart. The bus left at dawn, and to avoid conversation he pretended to sleep all the way. But he peered out the window through his sunglasses, from under the bill of his Dodgers cap.

They descended into the Valley, part of a slow-moving caravan of smoking buses and grunting RVs. Things had changed since he had arrived in April: more and more people, crowding into every part of the Valley floor. Passing a family on the road, he heard the mother scream at her small boy. Passed a large clot of Japanese tourists shooting pictures of each other and the Valley walls. Passed a ranger writing a ticket to a teenager idling in a red Miata coupe. Came into the Village: a blur of shorts and bright t-shirts, people trudging along, already haggard in the morning. Stopped at last by a knot of struggling old apple trees in the center of a huge parking lot, flanked by wandering cars searching for spaces, by other buses spewing passengers and smoke.

What a mess, Spell thought as he stepped off the bus.

Earlier he had bought a handsome picture book, *The Valley: A Cycle of Seasons*, and in all of the beautiful shots he could not find a single person. Such books were an illusion, a Valley with the people framed out. But here he found the reality, small chunks of Los Angeles and San Francisco, and other cities from all over the world, dropped into the Valley. Thousands scurrying about in gift shops, lined up with trays for the cafeteria, camped out at dawn for backpacking permits, waiting at restrooms, gift shops, ranger shows. He had seen from the rim of the canyon, with his binoculars, that people crowded to the outdoor amphitheater at night to see the park via a video presentation projected on a screen big enough for Times Square. Pictures of the Valley on TV, for many people the only way to make the Park real.

With the diesel fumes layering the air, the heat of asphalt, the crushed and dying meadows (roped off now), the paved walkways, the open tour trams, with all of this they had made the Valley a kind of Disneyland. Wildflowers picked, butterflies trampled, squirrels running from yelping dogs, blue jays flitting through clouds of smog, a grey haze muddling the pines and granite walls. The Merced River itself a cesspool of dirty disposable diapers, glistening beer cans, foam from hand soap—this is how Spell saw the Valley.

He would change all of it.

Give them time, he thought. The pressure of money he knew too well would increase the Village, build a new one. Add another gas station. Scrap a meadow for a parking garage. He had hiked Mammoth Mountain outside of the Park, had seen how they ripped trees off it and planed the slopes for easier skiing in Winter. Built another chalet. What they forgot was how the mountain looked without snow: a stripped desert, something like an artillery testing range. Money eroded the earth faster than any river or glacier. Supply was limited, but demand for what was left of the mountain was high.

No one could save Mammoth—it was too late. But the Valley still had a chance.

He found it quieter at the Muir Hotel, an escape from the middle class. From the wide veranda, hooded by a canvas awning, the wealthy sipped drinks, chatted, looked out on the Muir meadow as if it were a golf course at the club. With a crack of thunder, people hurried in and Spell followed them. When the rain blew itself out, he walked through the cool, wooden cathedral lobby, walked out the long stone entry. Noted the people checking in and the red-coated attendants carrying bags. The rich were insulated here, could buy a bit more peace. Spell felt comfortable, admired the order of the place, what these people had achieved, and then he looked out over the drive up a wooded slope behind the Hotel. He could hit the backside of the Muir from up there, windows of the rooms completely exposed, in range.

Farther south he found the Park Headquarters. As the Valley closed in here, he saw the offices could be hit from several vantage points. His Dragunov had a range that would surprise them here. He passed by the small medical clinic, the fire station, the maintenance garage, the headquarters building itself, and, down wind, a garbage collection station. Something occurred to him. He walked back to the headquarters, stopped, took a deep breath, and walked in. Found the Park superintendent's office and, when the hall was vacant, he peered in quickly. Looked through the superintendent's window. Then he went outside, found the window, saw where it faced. He knew a secure spot from the slope above; he could just about make the shot if the need arose. He walked by a woman ranger coming and looked away, as if he were intently reading a first-aid poster on the wall.

At dusk Spell finished surveying the populated areas, and circled in on the two cabins. Standing on the edge of the South Meadow, he heard the stereo from the larger cabin, watched the people dancing to some Dave Brubeck. Their laughter came across the field like musical notes, mixed with the jazz, and through the windows into the amber lit cabin he saw a tall woman being swung by one Japanese man to another. Apparently, she was teaching them a few moves. Saw her dance for a long time, as the night came on, and admired the way she threw off her shoes and shook her long hair out of its pony tail. It fell in the soft light when she stopped twirling.

Closing his eyes, Spell went back a few years. To the nights in the clubs in Greenwich Village, taking in the jazz—even Brubeck live—when for awhile he thought life in Manhattan would work. Hadn't there been a blonde woman, tall and graceful, in his life? A momentary flicker of someone he had thought he might introduce to his mother. Someone before Alanis, who he met at the clubs, who helped him shut out the noise of the city. No, he thought, there hadn't been anyone quite like that. Some women seemed that way at first, but eventually they all burned out with him, like Alanis. Beauty always ran skin deep in New York City. Or perhaps it was him.

He walked the perimeter of the meadow, far out of the circle of light, and went to the darker cabin. Stopped suddenly. Ten yards in front of him a man, old by the sound of his voice, mumbled as he relieved himself near the doorstep.

"They're not like those other slopehead bastards," the man said to himself. "No wonder the Japs are kicking our ass."

The man zipped up, went into this cabin. He did not turn the lights on.

After awhile Spell walked close by, and heard loud snoring. As he headed north he listened hard for the jazz and laughter, heard these through the trees until they were blotted out by the rumble of an open-air tram. He came to the road and the tram—a train of three tourist-filled trailers—lurched by. "If you'll look up northwest about 11 o'clock you'll see . . ." A guide's voice mapped out the constellations over a crackling P.A. system. In a cloud of exhaust, Spell crossed the road.

Feeling lazy and tired he headed west. He found a large redwood, an anomaly among the other pines, that he took as a landmark. Flashing a small light every now and then to keep his bearings, he went off-trail for a few hundred yards until he found a thick stand of manzanita. Burrowing in he came to a small clearing he had made in the middle, a little coffin-shaped space deep in the knotted scrub. He ate some crackers and cheese pulled from his day pack, drank a V-8 and a Perrier, then sealed the trash in a ziplock bag. Next he unpacked a thin black plastic thermal blanket, wrapped himself in it, and set his day pack beside him. He felt the hard bulge of his disassembled Dragunov at his side.

Looking up through the manzanita and the high pines above, he recognized the brightest star in Cassiopeia. He took off his new cap. Pine needles and sticks stabbed the back of his head; the wet, cold ground dampened his hair. But in the last two months he had slept out often, and the night seemed warm and inviting to him.

None of them know the Valley, he thought. Wrapped in walls, electricity, appliances, and TV static they can't know it. Through the ranger's video show they can't know it. Then his mind skipped to visions of any of a number of attractive couples he had seen—now, probably, making love in the tents, or in the rooms of the Muir Hotel, perhaps to the gentle riff of a Gershwin piece on piano. He pushed these thoughts out of his head, watched his star.

Part of him had always longed for that world, a part that tried to like life in New York as a wealthy stockbroker. But the other part of him always broke through, pushed him on some detour. That darker part of him, he knew, had grown up considerably at Jackson Military. Major McCrimmon had nurtured it.

By the end of his last year at Jackson, Spell had been escaping the woods regularly. He could not get at McCrimmon, but he could get away. The fact that Spell was winning pushed the fury between them higher and higher; when Spell was caught, the major didn't care how he marked his student. Spell's bruised face and swollen eye made some of the other boys stare, but they knew not to ask questions. With the colonel gone, Major McCrimmon took charge of Jackson Military Academy's last semester. Most of the group of fifty who made up Jackson's last class were afraid of Eldred Spell, and the strange world that seemed to follow him from classroom to classroom. He was the only student at the academy who had somehow won the right to a private room.

Two weeks before graduation, Spell stood behind a tree in the woods just at the edge of the faculty parking lot. He watched McCrimmon's new cherry red Mustang. This was his one chance, the time he had been waiting for: a thundering night with the warm spring rain coming down in torrents. A rare time when the major parked at the far edge of the lot, in dim light away from the two lamps that illuminated the area. Even rarer because he was leaving late after a planning meeting for the final graduation ceremony.

Spell saw McCrimmon run to the car door, and felt a surge of joy as the man fumbled with his keys. Barefoot, and buoyed with the speed and fury of years, Spell sprinted across the short space of parking lot as silently as an owl on the wing. He crashed into McCrimmon, driving the major's face into the door window, and before the major could turn Spell put the blade of a military knife to his instructor's throat.

"You kill me, and maybe you'll make it to prison." The major's voice sounded the same—not a trace of fear. "But I have friends who will find you wherever you go. You've met them in the woods."

"And do you think I care?"

"No. I suppose you're a Pathfinder now."

"You answer one question, and I won't kill you." Spell could feel the major's body tensing, so he kept himself hardened and ready; if the major moved at all, he would pull the knife across the man's throat. Otherwise, Spell knew, he might be dead himself.

"I want you to tell me why."

"I was to make you a Pathfinder. You are one—the Army brass would shit bricks to have you on their team, if you're so inclined."

"I'm not. But that's not why you did this. You don't give a damn about me—I know that."

"I'm getting tired of standing here, you little shit."

"Tell me why." Spell pushed the knife in, just slightly into the major's flesh, and he worked hard not to go all the way.

"Money."

Spell felt the major swallow against the blade.

"Your mother paid me."

Spell could tell by the easy tone of the major's voice that he was smiling.

"For kicking your ass all these years, I get a four-bedroom rancher, twenty acres, and that brand new Mustang."

The boy lost some strength then, and he stepped away, still holding his knife in the ready position. The major took his time turning around, ran his fingers along the front of his throat, and looked at the blood. He turned up his palm to Spell, as the rain beat the crimson off his white skin.

"My blood, Mr. Spell." His expression was flat, lifeless, as he looked directly into Spell's eyes. No smile. "I'll forget this. My graduation gift to you."

Spell had stood in the lot for a long time, watching Major McCrimmon drive off in the shiny red car. He had studied the red tail lights, looking in that direction long after the car was gone.

At dawn, after a dry, cold breakfast, he packed everything neatly, brushed pine needles over his tracks outside the manzanita, and headed for a site he had picked in advance on a cliff. By 8:45 a.m. he had hiked to the spot. With no trail, he edged out to a bent Jeffrey pine that was draped over a jagged outcropping of rock. He assembled the Dragunov in a minute, locked stock and barrel in place, affixed the suppressor and the long-range scope.

Then he slid out on the rock, the pine needles from the scrubby tree digging into his back while the rugged granite scratched his chest. Concealed, in position, he peered over the edge. A straight drop 500 feet down to rocks and the Valley floor. Across the river, at the edge of the tent camp, he picked out a couple setting up breakfast. The camper's grey hair, his spatula, his Coleman stove all jiggled in and out of view. Through the scope the man was hard to keep in target, as hard to track as a distant planet through a powerful telescope. Then his wife, black hair tied back, older, heavy. The dog walked into view, a lap dog like a hairy footstool, begging, its two white paws in the air.

Spell closed his eye. How to begin, he thought—heart beating, palms beginning to sweat despite the cold morning breeze. How to begin.

He opened his eye. Fired at last. The first shot missed and he saw a puff on the ground. They did not notice. It was as soundless among them as they were to him, talking without sound in the scope, the dog barking without noise, balancing for his treat.

Spell fired again. Direct hit, dead center. The silent explosion in the scope, the blur of pink, startled him. He would become used to it.

TWO

XIX

Eldred Spell watched the sun reflect off Silver Veil falls and he wondered at himself. Looking for the second dog, his Dragunov tucked in the shrubs behind him. His feet dangling over the rock ledge as he munched on a late afternoon snack: string cheese, an apple, Austrian chocolates. Beyond some wind-twisted pines, the rim of the wall turned until it came to a notch nearly facing Spell; from there water poured down six hundred feet, shattering in the rocks below. The sky behind the falls was dark blue, a fresh bruise, as the wall facing the sun melted from flesh tones to red. He would catch a splash of water in his eye and follow it down to the bottom, always skipping ahead to look at the rocks as the water hit. Then catch another splash at the top and see it go.

He realized shooting dogs would not drive people out of the Valley. They would just stop bringing their pets. Less dog excrement on the trails, that's all. A little fear. He had not planned on shooting dogs, but he'd just started, a warm-up for bigger things to come. With the cool breeze blowing up the wall, he put on his Dodgers cap. Ate another chocolate.

Something interesting about shooting dogs, he thought. He had wanted a dog once. His mother had eased up, bought her nine-year-old son a full grown bulldog that Spell was allowed to name Buddy. The dog didn't take to him; looking back Spell could understand that it had a master somewhere, that it looked for the owner who had sold him. Buddy didn't come to his new name, didn't play, looked depressed. A prize bulldog, fit for shows, came with a lot of responsibilities.

Spell saw himself as a child, watched the memory play out as if it were shot for a documentary. There he was, rubbing down Buddy, the dog looking away. Trying hard to please the dog. He recalled the day he had overturned Buddy's water dish on the veranda. An order came down. The gardener, an old Scotsman with a mat of white hair, watering grey eyes, and cracked grey hands like shark's skin to the touch, took the boy out by the hand, led him into the work shed among the sacks of warm peat moss. Gave Spell a few light whacks with a bamboo switch from the greenhouse, cutting cobwebs and dust in the upswing. The gardener stopped, looked at Spell, waiting for him to cry. Smiled. Something good to report to your mother, he said: you did not cry.

Not much later, Buddy's jaw had begun to swell, teeth pushed aside, lower lip shoved down, as a growth advanced rapidly. When the black tumor swelled to the size of a baseball, the dog wheezed through its pinched throat, stumbling, and another order came down. The gardener had Eldred put Buddy on the leash. The old man did not have to explain why he held the heavy revolver—Great Grandfather Cheltingham's Dragoon pistol from the Civil War—long, heavy, polished blue barrel. And Spell could see himself standing in the field behind the big white house, planted in one spot by the gardener. Eldred let the leash go and the old man picked it up, taking the dog ten steps ahead. The boy called to Buddy, but the bulldog looked away, toward the hills. The gardener pointed the gun at the back of the dog's head, also looked away, and fired.

Then the gardener dropped the pistol, walked to Spell, and hugged him. Eldred did not return the embrace. Buddy hadn't cared, so neither did the boy. The gardener didn't understand that—Spell knew now—couldn't understand a lot of things going on at the house. He would soon be fired.

That night, his mother had told him, "See what good Buddy did you."

Spell replayed Buddy again and again in his mind. Then he decided that the time had come; far below him a small platform—the falls lookout—was crowded with people and, often, their dogs. He knew, despite the shootings, people would still bring dogs, would always be careless.

Even though he was a quarter mile from the nearest trail, he listened for people. Nothing. Spell plunged deep into the manzanita, the hard limbs grabbing at his head, and he pulled out the Dragunov. Took it from a pack, unwrapped it, assembled it. He slid up to the edge, focused on the crowd below. Saw a dog in a special harness, apparently leading a blind woman. No. Saw a girl chasing a small cocker onto the platform. Difficult, jumping target. No. Saw a German Shepherd staring at the waterfall. Spell put the back of its head, the apex of two pointing ears, within the fine cross hairs, pulled the trigger, and watched the dog disappear.

Over the gentle roar of the falls he could not hear the people scream and yell, but within seconds they recognized what had happened and they ran. They looked like the people he had seen fleeing the Trade Tower, scattering like dry ashes in the wind. As he quickly broke down the rifle and packed it away, Spell realized that his plan would eventually work. The people would be driven out, the Valley at peace for the first time in centuries. No one would catch him, because they did not know the Valley as he did. Wherever he found himself, he was always one step ahead.

Shoving his way through the manzanita he came to an open wood and he ran light-footed among the trees. Crossed an empty space of trail and worked up to his third cache in the cleft of a rock. He put the gun away. Looked back where the cache was hidden: nothing but a dark crack among thousands in the base of a huge wall, all hidden away in the black shade of shrubs and old trees. Just off the trail he waited for a large group of backpackers to pass, and he slipped in behind them, listened to their chatter. Headed for the high country. He reached up to adjust his Dodgers cap but it was gone.

XX

Lars knew the business with the cap would be trouble. Everything would fall to him, and even more to Blackie and Buck. He was the Park dog handler, had been living with professional dogs in a cabin outside the Valley for fifteen years. His friends in the Park came and went, bosses were transferred out, his one marriage lasted just four years. But the dogs were solid, hung with him until they died, their good qualities living on in puppies and generations. His dogs were the best:

participated in most SAR operations, in rain and snow, and in summer they helped in the drug raids, even tracked a runner or two. In the down times they lived in the cabin on Dills Creek, trotted alongside the stream while he fished trout. The dogs ate at his table, drank his beer, slept on his feet through winter nights. Good, simple life.

But now the cap. When the dog was shot at Silver Veil Falls, Cairns put everyone on it. Had Olivos figure out the trajectory, had men and women scour the ridge line above. Again, they didn't find shell casings—the shooter took them with him. But near a ledge they did find a Dodgers cap. Cairns sent it special to the FBI lab in San Francisco and they found no clean fingerprints, no hairs. Just a report about some conditioner residue—an expensive brand, probably European.

Just before the cap went out, Lars made his mistake. He could kick himself. He had told Cairns to let his two best dogs, Blackie and Buck, get a good sniff of it. That way, they could track the bastard the next time he killed. Cairns grinned, brightened up to the idea, and at that second Lars knew he let his pride sink him. Right away, Cairns ordered him, Blackie, and Buck to set up in the tent city—be on call 24 hours. So Lars sat there, staring at the radio, looking at his two dogs. He fed them plates from the Valley cafeteria, he stroked their hair with his big, thick hands. He gave them his food, because the longer he sat outside the tent the more his appetite disappeared.

The cap had come back, rested on a shelf in the tent next to the radio. Wrapped in clear plastic. Lars wished he could ditch it. Eli and Karol had come by the night before, the Park socialites, tried to cheer him up a little. But all he could tell them was that he sunk himself. Worse, he put his dogs in real danger.

Blackie and Buck were labs, two brothers, the pick of a once-in-a-decade litter. Lying now in the late afternoon shade at his feet, side by side, sleeping. Lars watched their slick black hair rise up and down with their gentle breathing. Buck kicked gently in a dream.

"We've got him, Lars," the radio blurted again. "Why don't you answer? Come in!"

It was the second call, and Lars had no choice but to respond.

He lifted his huge, heavy frame, picked up the transmitter as he watched Blackie and Buck lift their heads.

"Lars here."

"Get out to the meadow." Cairns's voice, upbeat, his plan working. "A chopper will rendezvous."

"Copy." He could already hear the helicopter coming in. He picked up the cap. "Damn," he muttered, pulling it out of the plastic. He checked his gun in the holster, said damn one more time, and ran out of the tent. "Up boys," he called. But they were already with him.

Blackie and Buck galloped ahead, jumping up into the helicopter that had just touched down in the meadow. Tourists were crowding around, taking videos, walking all over a meadow that had been roped off to preserve the fragile highland grass. Lars pulled himself in and up they went.

"Don't look so glum," Olivos smiled at him. "It's all going according to schedule. Just fifteen minutes ago the shooter blows an old woman's Pekinese practically off her lap, just a few hundred feet outside the Muir parking lot. She's all right. But the dog—another shot to the head. Very clean."

"Great," Lars grunted.

"Almost identical to the last one. Late in the afternoon, from the top of a cliff wall. He's working into a pattern." Olivos patted Blackie on the head. "I found the slug dug in the road. Pretty sure he fired down from the Albright trail, or damn near it. We're setting down at the flats up there, should be on him in no time. Lenahan and Heinze were walking the trail when it happened; they'll meet us."

"Sure." He wished Olivos would keep his hands off Blackie.

"C'mon, Lars. We've got this prick. They never count on tracking dogs, right?"

"This one kills dogs."

When the helicopter landed on the flats the men and dogs jumped off, then the chopper went back down the Valley to be ready to place more personnel as needed. Olivos handed Lenahan and Heinze M-16s; he had one himself.

"Cairns's gone all out, eh?" Heinze checked his weapon.

"Damn straight," Olivos said.

Lars fitted the tracking units on the dogs, antennas sticking up from their heads like arrow shafts. He tested the tracking receiver.

"You ready?" Olivos was walking toward the trail.

"Yeah," Lars said. "Just the scent." He slowly pulled the cap out of the bag and let the dogs sniff it. "Go boys."

They worked slowly up the trail for a half mile, and then Buck lurched to the right.

"Off trail," Olivos said.

The dogs went into the woods, noses raised and then to the ground, until they came to a cliff overlooking the Muir. Then they started off in a trot.

"Hold!" Lars yelled. The dogs stopped.

"What's the matter?" Olivos asked.

"I don't want them to get ahead of me."

"C'mon, Lars."

"No, damn it." He looked at his dogs, saw they were nervous, pawing, ready to go. "These are SAR dogs, all right? They're not used to tracking criminals."

"What about the bust at the Muir?"

"I mean tracking killers." Lars looked at the ground; just a few pine needles scattered. "The shooter did it from here. Didn't leave much of a trace, no shell casings again. He's smart. I'm staying with the dogs."

"That will slow them down."

"That's right, Olivos." He turned to Blackie and Buck. "At a trot, boys."

The dogs worked through the woods, crossed the trail, started toward a ridge, the men jogging behind. Nearly a mile later they crossed a small swampy meadow, mosquitoes rising in clouds as the rangers plunged through. Although the sun was low, and the evening breeze cold, the men sweated, running, packing their guns.

"Up pace," Olivos puffed. "We'll lose him in the dark."

"Give me a break," Heinze gasped.

"Run, boys."

They all ran at a climb through a redwood grove, then plunged down into a small valley. Lenahan slipped and fell. Saw the men going ahead. Got up and ran after them. Reminded him of his chubby days when he was back in the boy scouts, always lagging behind.

The dogs stopped at a stream.

"Break," Olivos said.

"It'll be a short one," Lars rested, hands on his knees, but looking at his dogs. Blackie went upstream, Buck down. Blackie yelped, charged into the woods, and Buck followed. Lars saw the dogs were smiling, panting, tails erect. "They think this is a game."

"What?" Olivos said from behind.

"Nothing."

In less than a quarter of a mile they came to the Muir Trail, the foot highway of the Sierra. The dogs slowed, looking for a thread of a scent among hundreds buried up and down the trail.

"I think he knows we're after him," Lars said, heart beating in his ears.

"Why?" Olivos caught up.

"First the stream. Now he goes for the Muir Trail. Trying to throw them off."

"It's not working," Lenahan said, just ahead of Heinze now.

The dogs headed up trail.

"He's going toward Anderson's Pass," Olivos said. "Once over he might try to duck us at Farrah's Lake. Lars, how far ahead do you think he is?"

"Two miles at most." Then he started after the dogs, which had nearly run out of sight.

Olivos radioed to send the second team by chopper to the lake. They'd close on the shooter there.

Without an M-16 to carry, and with his dogs at stake, Lars pulled ahead of the men. He kept those black tails in sight, watched them wave to him in the gathering dark as the sun set.

He pushed himself beyond all thought to keep up—had to stay with his dogs. Despite the tracking device, he could not let them out of his sight. They stayed on the Muir, and it was late enough that no one was hiking the trail. Lars knew a campsite less than a mile ahead—if the shooter made it there, the scent of all the backpackers and their cooking would slow the dogs. But not for long. Still, they were racing against the dark. Lars did not want his dogs out chasing this killer in the night. Besides, it was the night of the new moon—perfect for this shooter to slip away. As if he had planned it that way.

Lars ran and ran, and fell into a stupor on the trail, his eyes falling to the grey earth at his feet. At a clearing, with his chest and legs aching, unable to catch his breath, he looked up. Buck was lying down on the trail, legs out like he did when he relaxed on cool grass in a hot summer sun. His head was down.

"Hold!" Lars screamed to Blackie.

Blackie, ahead, had already stopped. He looked back at Lars, then stumbled forward, tripped, and fell.

A pool of blood, black in the cold evening light, soaked into the grey earth near Buck's head. One look and Lars knew the dog was gone; he touched its side, and trotted on.

But Blackie twitched, with some life left.

He knelt by his dog. Lars, breathing hard, looked up into the woods, knowing from where the man must have made his shot. He stared but the view went out of focus as he choked and tears blurred everything. He saw nothing.

"Lars!" Olivos' voice boomed somewhere behind, deep in the woods.

"Get back here, Lars!"

The handler looked into Blackie's eye and watched all recognition seep away from it. The dog wagged its tail once, convulsively, and became stiff. Lars looked back at Buck, then touched the thick blood soaking Blackie's fur. He sat down in the dirt.

"Shit, boys," he wept. "I was so proud of you, eh? Oh, damn!"

Olivos and the other men almost made the clearing.

"Get back with us!" Olivos screamed into the woods with all the breath he had left. He unshouldered his M-16 and carried it before him, his strained back, legs, and arms sharp with pain. Olivos knew the plan was unraveling. "Get back here now!"

Lars never heard him.

XXI

"On this expedition," Spell paused, looking directly into Doug Evers' eyes—testing him. "I'm having trouble with dogs."

"What do you mean?" Evers came around the counter, whispering, looking anxiously back toward the stairs hoping fervently that his wife would not come down. He did not know why.

Spell stared, looking down, just two feet from Evers' face. He had set claws and teeth into this man, worked him harder than any fool on the trading floor. Much more than money was being bought and sold now. Spell had used money, of course, had invested in Larry's small shop like a multinational invests in a third world country. Puts so much money into it that all traditional ways and morals are forfeited for more investment. And Spell could see that Evers was forming other attachments that the poor man himself probably didn't understand. Still, no man is perfectly predictable. And there was his wife.

"I'm not sure what you mean, Jake," Evers looked up at him.

"Well," Spell put his arm on the man's shoulder; a necessary gesture for the moment, however uncomfortable. "I'm on a peculiar expedition."

"I know," Doug smiled, heart beating fast. He had lain awake in the old house, listening to his wife gently snore, and he thought of Spell, wondered about his expedition. Often added up all the equipment bought again and again. Nearly forty thousand dollars in a month and a half. All cash.

"Where I go, I can't have dogs." Spell squeezed Doug's shoulder and let go. "I've been followed by dogs."

"Tracked?" Evers whispered again, and understood why now. The thought thumped him roundly in the chest: this is the man in the Park! The killer, the one they tried to track down two days ago! Made the headlines of the Monterey *Herald* for a week. God, he thought, I'm glad no one is in. Glad my wife has never met him, hardly anyone has seen him. And the cash! Evers didn't know if it had been his greed or just dumb instinct, but he had not been keeping the big sales on his books. He'd have to destroy any receipts he had left, make damn sure no one ever saw this man in his shop again. But— Oh my God! But—

"Why?" Evers shook.

Spell enjoyed watching him struggle, liked the color of fear in the man's ashen face, liked the fact that Evers was the kind of man who would follow along. Spell breathed in deep; he had read Doug perfectly.

"What do you think of the Park," Spell leaned closer. "How do you like it?"

"I don't go there anymore."

"Of course not. Twenty thousand people crowd into it every day. Everyone wants a piece of it. They come in caravans of RVs, tenements on wheels, fill the place up with smog, trash, crimes." Spell realized he had not spoken about this to anyone, and it made him feel more alive, reaffirmed what he was doing. For the last two days he had needed that feeling—perhaps that was why he felt like giving it all away to Evers.

"It's a mess," Doug said.

"And I've come to clean it up." Spell looked up at the posters on the wall, spoke to the air. Feeling very good now. "Imagine what that Valley would be like without any people and all that comes with the crowd. What would that be like? Clear for the first time in one hundred and fifty years."

"God."

"Yes."

"But why the dogs?"

"A beginning," Spell said. "But it didn't keep them from rushing in. Didn't even seem to keep them from bringing dogs."

"So now—"

"The expedition becomes longer," Spell turned to Doug again. "I have more work. But I can't be tracked down."

Evers heard his daughter giggle from the top of the stair. Past closing time. Someone might come down. "I'm not sure what I can do."

"You know people who can help."

"Well—"

"You've been on your own little expeditions."

Evers remembered going with the others to spike the trees, moving from one trunk to another in the dim moonlight, hammers muffled in canvas. Yes, he knew people. They had planned for dogs, though none came. But they had been ready.

"I can get something that will help," Doug said. That evening he could make a run up to Palo Alto—Suko Egusa would have what Spell needed. "Come back tomorrow, after I close." He remembered when Maggie would be away, and he could plug his daughter into the TV upstairs for a little while—she was an addict already. "Come at 6:30."

Spell shook Doug's hand with a warmth he did not really feel. "I knew I could count on you. I will pay you very well."

"Yes," Evers pulled his hand out of the hot grasp. "You sure will."

Spell left The Vantage Point, driving his own Jaguar out of Carmel—he needed to drive something familiar and had felt reckless in the last two days. He turned onto the 17-Mile Drive, paid the fee, sank back into the leather of the Jag, and followed the curves of the road. Took the trail, in and out of hills, coming up at a mansion on the cliff, then an open stretch of white beach cut like a scar in the ocean. He tried to focus on those houses, estimated the cost of a small castle near The Lone Cypress, even thought how easy it would have been for him to buy a house in cash and live in seclusion. But he had his ambitions.

Evers will find something for the dogs, Spell thought, and then everything broke in on him again. Already he had made a mistake, in the first week. Lost that damn cap. Had not foreseen the dogs, and the trap the rangers set for him. He had no idea they would take the death of a few pets so seriously. The tourists didn't seem to.

So I have to go all the way now, he thought as he pushed the accelerator down and screeched through a blind curve. Eased up and coasted down a hill.

After he had blown away the old woman's dog, a difficult shot not to hit her too, he watched the panic for a moment and then started up to the high country again. Perhaps that had been his second mistake, after losing the cap: he had slipped into a predictable pattern. Repeated his M.O. Like the cap, that would not happen again.

He had started for the high country, cutting across two trails, heading through thick forest. Walking through the woods, smelling the sharp pine, feeling that wonderful sense that this was his land. A growing belief that the Valley was his to protect from all comers. He was creating the place that Ellen had searched for, and that gave him a stronger sense of purpose.

Then he had heard it: the faint reverberation of chopper blades echoing off the canyon walls. This made him more alert, tensed against something that was coming. As the sound beat closer, he ran to a high clearing, stopped, saw the helicopter in his binoculars. When it landed he could see the men coming out of it and then two small specks running much faster than the men. Dogs. He had come within a half mile of the cache where he had planned to store his Dragunov, but now he knew he needed it. Carrying it made him powerful but also easy to identify and therefore vulnerable, too.

Spell had run down the mountain; the gun felt heavy in his pack. He had not thought of the dogs but had thought many times of ambush. He crossed creeks, across a boggy meadow he knew. Back up a hill to a clearing, breathless, he waited.

They came to the bog, led by the dogs, tromped across it right on his trail.

Spell had doubled back to the Muir Trail. Ran along it, stopping once to avoid one weary group of backpackers crossing the Muir on an intersecting trail. Spell knew exactly where he had to go, to a pile of granite slabs just above an exposed curve of the Muir Trail. He had just assembled the gun, and set his sights where the rangers would have to come out, when the dogs appeared. He took the larger one to the back first, then the closest dog. The animals went down slowly, peacefully. And then the man had come out of the woods after them, screaming.

Spell concentrated on the traffic. He left the 17-Mile Drive and headed into Fisherman's Wharf. Cars jammed together in lines, piling toward the small, over built bit of coast. He lost a lot of them in the vast parking lots by the wharf, cars nosing for spaces. He drove on toward Cannery Row, slowing for the careless pedestrians, bicyclers, and roller bladers. Came to a quieter road and pulled onto the oval drive of the Spyglass Inn. Left the keys with a valet and walked into the cool, darkened lobby. He had checked in earlier, at the peak of the day, a faceless guest among a crowd of conventioneers. Paid cash, used a different name.

Now the lobby was quiet. Walking across the dark green carpet, taking in the crystal windows, the walls of imported black walnut, the amber lighting, original paintings, and the exotic flowering plants in large brass planters—he felt hungry. For the first time in two days he wanted to eat. Perhaps the peace and the faint smell of grilled fish put him at ease. He passed through large French doors onto a wide veranda overlooking the bay. Sat at a small table, its single candle brightening in the falling light of day. Seals called from the breakwater, and a jazz combo played a slow conga rhythm that seemed to move with the pulse of small waves on the sand below.

He hadn't had a drink since that first night at the Muir Hotel but he ordered a bottle of Chardonnay from a wine captain he hardly saw. Kept his gaze on the darkening sea, followed the line of a sail boarder far out. Later he had his waitress bring out the grilled swordfish in capers and garlic butter. And in time he noticed a woman sitting at a table nearby. The only other person on the veranda. When Spell saw that she too looked out at the horizon, ordered wine without noticing the waitress, he looked at her closely.

A tall woman, long-limbed and fine, in a white dress and white hat. She stretched her dark legs out, kicked off her shoes, put one foot on the low rail of the veranda. The light silk of her dress hung from her leg, nearly touched the floor. Her profile cut sharp against the air, long breasts coming full to a point under the thin fabric just above her middle, and above, her sharp chin and nose. Black eyes and hair. Probably Latino and something else. Finally, slowly, she looked over in his direction and just stared.

Spell turned away. Another time he would have enjoyed the wine, the fish, and the woman. But he could not touch any of these now, and the jazz buzzed flatly in his ear.

He had seen the man run to the dogs, and for a second Spell thought he could escape. But the man had looked up, stared directly at him, and Spell ducked behind a rock. He knew he had been seen. In seconds he thought, how far to go? Hadn't they pushed this thing to the next level, come with dogs, helicopters, M-16s? Nothing to do but go through with it all—he had been seen and he had a plan to finish. And now he could not wait. So he sighted on the man quickly, cross hairs on the back of the head bowed over the dead lead dog. Spell stopped. Then heard another man's sharp call from the woods. With no time, he pulled the trigger, and had seen the man fall silently across the dog.

So Eldred Spell watched the chill fall off his wine bottle, the butter congeal over his swordfish steak. And by the time he stood up to go, glancing in the direction of the woman, he saw that she had gone.

XXII

Eli walked from headquarters, heading home, gun on hip, thinking how the Park was changing. With the first two dogs, the changes were unnoticeable. A few more rangers walking the trails, some in protection doing double shifts, Cairns becoming more official and uptight. All nothing someone walking across the Valley would notice. But with Lars killed, everyone did extra shifts, any ranger certified wore a gun, and more patrol cars went up and down the roads. Tourism began to fall, and cancellations for the tent city and even the Muir Hotel were coming so quickly people in reservations could hardly keep up. Just a few dogs in the Park now, and none of them loose—Eli saw them panting in cars, or straining against short leashes.

She had just left a general meeting Cairns had called, with nearly every ranger attending. The superintendent had paced about in front, absolutely no smiles, his face grey. Olivos looked the same way—pale, and no sleep. Eli had never seen them this way; no matter how tough the rescue or difficult the drug bust, those two men never lost their macho swagger. But that had been blown away now. She heard that the secretary of the interior had called Cairns, read off some newspaper headlines to him, questioned him closely on the botched attempt to catch the shooter, questioned his judgment. Then, she knew, Cairns called in Olivos and did the same to him.

At the meeting, Cairns had introduced agents from the FBI, and looked away from the group as he explained that he would share interdiction with an agent who had not yet arrived. Shirley Weaver, the tall, gaunt executive manager of all Heston Company operations in the Park, had stared intensely at Cairns. She gave a very brief report on the cancellations, and asked Cairns if he planned to question her employees. He simply nodded.

An FBI agent reported all they knew: the killer used a European conditioner, bought a Dodgers cap available from retailers throughout the country. He announced that all of the slugs had been analyzed very carefully, and he felt certain that the high-powered rifle was an exotic from the old Soviet Union, perhaps a customized version of the Snayperskaya Vintovka Dragunova, or an advanced prototype. The agent added that the weapon was excellent for the kind of operation the killer seemed to be mounting.

"We have no notes from him, no communications," Cairns concluded the meeting. "His motive is not clear. Lars might have seen the man; that may be why he's dead. But now that this shooter has killed one man, we can expect he won't settle for dogs anymore."

Shirley Weaver added that with each success, he would feel free to be more bold.

Eli thought it interesting that everyone assumed the shooter was a man.

After the meeting broke up, Cairns had walked up to her and said simply, "you're in protection now, under Olivos. Sandra will do all of your interpretations." Before she could answer he walked to his office, head down, followed by Shirley Weaver. She'd give him hell, on behalf of Heston, for the falling concessioner's profits. All the bad P.R.

Pressure from all sides, Eli thought as she walked through the meadow near her house. For once he has to take it. Some other time she might have felt good about his squirming, saying let the manipulative bastard see how he likes it. Some rangers felt that way, even now. Most personnel in the Park had wanted to see him go for years, and despite the tragedy of Lars, some couldn't help but read the disaster as a mark by which his days were numbered.

Eli couldn't see it that way. To see Cairns on the run, taking Olivos with him, meant that they were all in trouble. The Park had always been the rangers'; they owned it in the sense that they knew it better than anyone else. Anything that happened within it quickly came under their control. A drug ring at the Muir, a lost child, a body found in the woods—all these things soon came under the rangers' order and organization. Twenty thousand people in the Park came and went every day, tourists and criminals alike, but none of them really knew the Park. Rangers answered questions, gave directions, interpreted the wildlife—this was their world.

Now something was loose in it. Eli could tell by the look in Cairns's eyes that this shooter was something new to him; she felt that he held back what he really thought: that this well-equipped, hard-to-stop creature would roam the Park, operate on unclear motives, know things the rangers could not, and, in that way, begin to take the Park from them.

Eli stopped in the middle of the South Meadow, took in the still air, noticed that on this calm evening, with the grass glowing, the granite wall cutting into the golden sky, that no one was out walking. No couples in the meadow, no photographers bent to their cameras and tripods, catching sunset shots. The meadow was a quiet part of the Valley, Eli knew, but for the first week of June this was unusually quiet. Already patterns in the Valley, the way the people acted, the shifts of the rangers and their jobs, all of these things were changing. The Park was becoming someone else's creation. That, Eli thought, is what makes Cairns and Olivos so nervous beneath everything else. The chance that they are losing control, losing ownership. And that was why she could not enjoy their squirming, even in secret deep down.

"You make a great target." Her father had crept up behind her. "Standing out here like this, daydreaming. How was the powwow at headquarters? Aren't you all at war?"

"Something like that." She looked slightly down at him, as she stood a few inches taller. He had always said she took her height from her mother, and strength from him.

"You going to make war with that pussy .38 of yours?"

"It's standard issue."

"Oh, hell, come with me."

As they walked to his cabin, she followed his marching step. Sarah's laugh came lightly over the meadow, from far away, and Eli squinted toward a line of pines at the south end. Karol and Sarah darted in and out of the trees, running. He fell flat and Sarah pounced on him.

"Your husband's been drinking today," Jack said. "Been grab-assin' around with your daughter. Why don't he get a job?"

"He has one."

"Poet. Yeah, right."

"I was thinking his job as a father."

"Bullshit." Jack stamped his boots on the porch and threw open the door. "He makes a good mother, anyways."

"Yeah," she glanced back, saw he was up and running again, with Sarah in the lead. "He does."

"Sit down, daughter."

She sat at the table while he went into his room and came out again, a gun and holster in his hand, the belt rolled up. He set it beside her. "Now you take off that rig of yours, and put this on."

She touched the black handle of his gun. "I'll try it later."

"Always an argument," he smiled. "All right. But you put that thing of yours away and keep mine until someone catches your bastard in the woods."

She pulled the gun out of its holster: a Colt .45 from her father's Korean service. Jack claimed he had taken it off a dead lieutenant. Although he had started her with the .22 rifle when she was eight, he put her on the firing range with his .45 when she turned 13, and that was the pistol with which she learned to hit targets. Sometimes he had taken her deep into the woods, on hikes far out of the Valley, to shoot it. He never let her hit birds or wildlife with it, taught her that only assholes did that.

"I cleaned and oiled it today for you. How about a drink?"

"No." She slid the gun back into its holster.

"Don't need a snort to settle your nerves a bit? C'mon."

"None of us are to drink now; we're on call 24-hours a day."

"That so?" He took down the bottle and poured one for himself into a fruit jar. "I suppose that's good thinking. Damn, I'd hate to be a ranger now."

"I know." She knew a lecture was coming and tried to change the subject. "Lars' funeral is tomorrow."

"Can't believe it," he drained his glass. "Here's Lars, a good man, blown away. In thirty years I worked for the Park, we never had a man shot. Oh, came close with the riots in 1970, all those damned hippies in the Park high on LSD and shit. I knew we were losing it then—that's what you get when you open up the gates, let all these assholes in, trample the Valley. Too many bastards running around this Park; getting to be like a slum. After 1970, I counted the days for my retirement. Never felt like that until the riots."

"I don't want to talk about it."

"Why the hell not? Wasn't Lars your friend?"

"Of course." She closed her eyes, surprised how her throat suddenly squeezed as if she would cry; she hadn't felt that coming. "But," Eli opened her eyes, "I don't retire for twenty years."

"You got a long way to go," he tossed back another glass, looked at her carefully. "By the time you retire you'll be driving an armored vehicle—"

"Dad."

"Okay." He looked out the window, and they were quiet for a long time. "But you wear my gun. I got it all ready."

"I will."

"That's a good girl." He squinted into the window. "Oh, no—"

Karol knocked loudly on the door, opened it, and Sarah ran in. He poked his head in, but did not go any further. Karol smiled, his face flushed, looking at Eli.

"Daddy says you have to come home now." Sarah pulled at Eli's hand. "He's made dinner."

"Sounds great." She picked up the gun and holster, looked at her father. "Thank you."

"Sure." He held out an arm to Sarah and she hugged him. "And what are you having, my dear?"

"Beef Burgundy. Salad with fresh greens we picked from the meadow. And homemade baguettes."

"Your daddy is a fine cook."

"The best." Sarah went back to her mother, took Eli's free hand, and led her to the door.

"You're welcome to eat with us," Karol said.

"Good God," Jack grinned. "How much of that Burgundy missed the skillet and went into you?"

"A good deal."

"I thought so," he stood up. "Now, Karol, what the hell would you do if I accepted your kind invitation?"

Karol shrugged.

"Shit a brick, right?"

Karol ushered Eli and Sarah out the door. "Probably two." He winked, and slammed the door behind him.

"What a pussy whip." Jack walked to the cabinet, looked in at a row of Kraft Macaroni and Cheese boxes. "But the bastard can cook."

Outside, Karol asked Sarah to run ahead and set the table. He took the gun and holster Eli had been carrying. Looked at it carefully, walking very slowly.

"Eli," he said, "we're in trouble, aren't we."

"Yes." She hugged him around the waist, smelled his breath. "While this is going on, would you please not drink? We all need to be alert now."

He stopped, looking down at the gun in his hand. "How bad do you think this is going to get?"

"I don't know." They started walking again. "It's been bad enough already."

As they came to their cabin, Eli looked up at the Valley walls. Saw them darken. Heard faintly the siren of a patrol car. Noticed the stillness of the South Meadow. She hugged Karol tightly again. People and rhythms in the Park were changing quickly. The Valley felt different, unsafe, and for the first time in Eli's life she felt there was a chance she would no longer own the place she called home. Even more than the loss of Lars, this bigger loss made her angry, made her want to weep.

XXIII

Spell came into Mammoth Lakes on the Greyhound bus, stopped at Schatt's Bakery, drank coffee, ate a Napoleon, and read the local paper. The shootings in the Valley, a story over a week old with nothing new, still made the bottom of the front page. The article had to do with a shift in tourism, hundreds of people were rescheduling vacations from the west to the east of the Sierra. The inns at Mammoth were completely full, with no vacancies in sight. A ski resort that had closed for the season reopened to take advantage of the overflow. The story quoted a Shirley Weaver, who said tourism in the Valley was a bit off, but few had actually canceled their reservations. The Park superintendent, a man named Cairns, assured readers that everything was being done to make the Valley safe.

The bottom line was becoming money, and the undercurrent was that the Valley's loss was Mammoth's boon. Spell smiled; it reminded him of New York. He did not care if Mammoth filled up; to his mind the place had already been ruined, with its bare mountain like a strip mine above the town, whole patches of pine trees dying on the slopes. As he shouldered his pack and walked up the crowded highway through Mammoth, in clouds of exhaust and the clatter of construction, Spell felt better. The paper said tourism in the Park had fallen twenty percent. That meant more of the mess he walked through had come to Mammoth, and left the Valley. Twenty percent wasn't enough, however. He would have to get to work.

He took the trail from the Devil's Postpile, but to get in he had to pay a fee for a tram; so many people came into the area that an attempt had been made to regulate the traffic. From there he hiked toward the Minarets: tall, jagged mountains near the border of the Park. At dusk he camped beneath them, on the bank of a crystal lake, and listened to the bump and grind reverberating from a boom box playing across the water. Watched the sharp Minarets become black at sunset, cutting like teeth into a rose-colored sky crisscrossed by the vapor trails of transcontinental flights.

That night, like many nights, he did not sleep well. His mind filled with plans, how he would pick up his gun, how he would avoid being detected. On the edge of unconsciousness, the numbered zones he had made of the Park blurred with stock figures, all on a screen, merging into white. And then a loud pop in his head, jerking him awake. When he finally settled on a dream, he saw white rock rising from the Valley like a forehead, and a cliff wrinkled with grey lines of age. Saw himself climbing the back of the bald, a speck crawling up a tremendous skull; he saw the image over and over until the quickness of his thumping heart and the sweaty suffocation in his close tent woke him. He did not recall the dream. By dawn he had packed, eaten, and returned to the trail.

In the Park he roamed through the dark woods, cutting across zones, making his way to the Dome. A tremendous bulb of granite, it rose like a half moon; its backside was a half globe protruding out of the forest and its front made the northern wall of the Valley, a great face of rock long ago sheered away by a glacier. By late afternoon Spell had reached the cache where he left the Dragunov, slipped the gun into his pack, and came to the base of the trail. He hid in the trees as a late party departed the Dome and headed down into the Valley. When they were gone he heard nothing but the hiss of wind shaking the pines, heard the creak of timber groaning from the strain, like creaking masts in tall ships.

The Dome trail was actually a steel cable held in place by poles drilled into the rock, spaced ten feet apart. Like a miniature telephone wire with poles, it went up the smooth rock and disappeared over the Dome's horizon. One had to climb the trail, hand over hand, walking up the bare granite. The cable ran up over a thousand feet. At the base were several notices, advertising the dangers of the trail and emphatic that the Park service could not be responsible for those who fall off. A special sign etched in steel warned of lightning and wind—a bolt could hit the cable, send a charge down—in past summers people had died that way. Some who attempted the Dome in high wind could be blown off.

Spell heard a distant boom of thunder, though he could not see clouds. He felt the wind blow pumice dust at his feet, and he shifted the pack on his back with its extra weight of the rifle. He had told himself he could not afford any more mistakes, and he knew that going up the Dome was foolish. With no trees and only one route of escape, a helicopter could pick him out. All the rangers would have to do is wait for him to come down. He should at least put the gun away, so nothing could happen.

But the thunder boomed again, closer, and the sunlight fell away. No one else would be up there now, he knew, and he had to answer a call from somewhere inside him, something strongly telling him that he should go up. Spell did not know how, but making the trip had something to do with his greater plan for the Valley. He started up the cable, hand over hand. The grey steel felt slick in his dry hands, and the wind pushed him from side to side. Thunder groaned, but when he dared to look up and away from his hands, he still saw no clouds. At one point on the trail he rested on the curve of the great rock, and saw only dim granite with black veins running to horizons above and below. He could see no bottom nor top nor sides, and everything seemed very clean and clear, with the wind blowing through his spirit. For a moment he thought this was all he needed, that this solitude, this washing out, was what the day meant for him, and he could go down. But something, almost a voice, urged him up.

Walking along the bone-white top of the dome he soon arrived at the edge, and the flat gave way to the Valley nearly a mile below. Half the sun peered above a line of thunder heads on the western side of the Valley, and the peaks to the east were gold. The top side of the Dome, as much as he could see of it peering down, glowed brightly. Spell walked along the edge until he saw a lip of rock, a small outcropping slanting downward. He put his pack aside, sliding out on his belly, holding tightly against the angle of rock and the gravity that wanted to propel him forward over the edge. He put his chin over the side.

After a boom of thunder echoed across the Valley, he heard voices. Spell crawled to the side of the outcropping and looked down at two climbers, near the end of their ascent, just twenty feet from the upper edge of the cliff. Fitting hexagon chocks into crevices, clipping rope on and off, the men spoke to each other tensely, all sinew and muscle in lycra body suits. They had almost conquered the rock. He watched them working on the cliff, sorry and angry that they were there. They did not notice him.

Spell slid back from the outcropping, marched to his pack, and assembled his gun. At the edge, looking over the Valley, he had felt some relief, some completeness, that all he had to do on the Dome was to take stock. To breathe in the beauty of the darkening Valley and feel more fully that it was all his to know. The climbers would serve his purposes well, he could see, for the way they would die would be spectacular and have much more effect than several simpler, conventional deaths. These climbers would help kill tourism and empty the Valley. But as he locked the barrel into place, he felt angry at them because they were an interruption, in the way of something greater he wanted to feel. Now back to business. He put aside the scope; he would not need it at close range.

Creeping back to the edge of the outcropping, the weight of the gun ahead of him pulled him forward. Spell locked the toes of his boots in a crevice and slid to the edge. The climbers had made nearly five feet since he last saw them. Very close to the top, they were illuminated in a last narrowing band of sunlight—the granite darkened below them. Even in the wind and distant thunder, he could hear them very clearly now as they climbed less than fifteen feet from his position.

Pausing to pull up a rope, the lead climber noticed Spell first. His face was buried in a beard and helmet, but Spell could see that their eyes met, and knew that the climber saw the sleek black barrel pointed at him.

"Horton," the lead climber called down, nervous. "There's some guy up there with a gun."

The lower man, the belayer, did not look away from the rock, nor from the aluminum block he was slipping out of a crack.

"Horton!" The man spoke through his teeth, believing that Spell could not hear him. "It's the sniper."

Horton finished his work and looked up.

"There," the lead man pointed quickly with his free hand.

Spell liked the way Horton slowly looked up at him, the way his face did not change expression. The upper man had already become jittery.

After a moment of staring, Horton asked calmly, "Are you the sniper?"

"Horton! Don't ask him that!"

"Yes," Spell said, keeping his aim on the lead man.

"You planning to kill us?"

Spell liked the way this Horton came to a point. "Yes," he said.

"No fucking way," the lead man cried out. "I mean, why kill us?"

"Because you are here," Spell said, irritated again. He did not want to talk with this man.

"Listen," Horton said, looking away as he quickly clipped to a fixed bolt. Horton did not believe in the bolts—he was one of those who felt a string of them polluted a mountain face and took the adventure out of a climb—but now he was glad to clip his rope onto this more secure protection. He could not be sure the blocks would hold the abrupt fall that was probably coming. The dead weight. "We've worked hard on this climb. Working hard to get up before dark. Can't you let us make it?"

"Yeah," the lead climber said with desperate enthusiasm. "Listen to Horton, we can talk—"

Spell fired twice into the man's chest, heard the gentle smack of the suppressor and the thwack of the shells cutting through flesh. The upper man let go, slid down ten feet, caught in the rope, and flipped over just a few feet above Horton. With his back to the cliff, the lead climber hung lifeless upside down as blood from his chest spilled over his face, a trail of it splattering down past Horton and out of the band of sunlight.

Horton did not move, the rope taking the lower man's weight at a block several feet above. He looked down.

"I thought you'd fall with him," Spell said.

"I secured myself; tied off independently of him," Horton studied his ropes. Focused on them in order to keep absolutely calm. For a split second, as he saw Thomas shot, panic traveled down through him like an electric flash. But as he watched Thomas sway above him, he knew exactly how a show of fear would affect the man pointing the gun. "You don't know much about climbing, do you?"

"No."

"I'll tell you this," Horton eased his rope up to another fixed bolt. "I can be at the top in a few minutes."

"No," Spell said with the same casual voice that Horton had managed. "You can't."

Horton clipped his rope on the bolt anyway.

Spell fired a round into the rock, pieces of granite shattering into Horton's upper hand. Several fragments imbedded in his knuckles and he pulled his hand back quickly. Quietly, sucking in breath, Horton tried to open and close the hand but the pain was too much. The rock cut like shrapnel; he figured two knuckles were crushed.

"So," Horton tried to keep his voice even as he held his hand against his chest. "That does it."

"Yes," Spell said. "If I had let you up, you might struggle, and neither of us would like that much."

"I might."

Spell liked his answer, and the calm delivery. Something about the man, perhaps his apparent relentlessness, appealed.

Horton looked down. "I'm a financial planner in Los Angeles. Quite successful. Have a wife—" He stopped, waiting with Spell as the last ray of sunlight winked out, covered by the approaching storm.

"Children?" Spell asked.

"No." Horton thought hard, through the pain in his hand, because he figured as long as he spoke calmly he might have a chance. But he also knew absolutely that he had no chance. "She loved me in a way that I could not quite feel.

Didn't want to risk children yet, although neither of us said that."

"How long have you known that man above you?"

"A year or so. This was our third climb together; his first as the lead climber. Thomas was doing well today—don't judge him by that last little panic there." Horton thought this note would appeal to the man with the gun.

"I could understand it."

"You can't imagine how he'll be missed. He had a son and daughter—the girl starts kindergarten this fall." Horton looked up at Spell. "You really have no idea what you've done."

"Will you be missed?"

"Rebecca will miss me." Horton looked ahead into the rock, biting his lip hard. The pain had traveled up his arm and shoulder now and was becoming enormous. He could not hold out much longer. "But he's the real loss. You won't hurt as many by killing me."

Spell had aimed the rifle at Horton's head but he could not pull the trigger. He did not want to, and he felt ill. But the storm was coming, and it would soon be too dark to safely climb down the Dome. He wished he could pull back. But that was not the way of the world when combatants were face to face. Something like gravity compelled them to fight, to get it over with. It was a major and a young boy in the woods, the father who left his mother when she declared war, or two opposing armies ready for war in such a way that diplomacy is mere pretext. People killing each other was something preconfigured in the universe, the darkest and most inescapable truth. "Time is running out for us."

"You mean for me."

"I'll give you a choice," Spell lowered the Dragunov. "I can just shoot and you can hang there, or I'll let you jump. If you push off, you might land in the lake down there."

"You don't know much about falling either." But, given the situation, the idea appealed to Horton. Jumping was not a new thought for him. On several climbs, especially lately, the thought of letting go and falling had become a fascinating notion. So much so that he considered giving up climbing—it was true that some climbers feared falling, while others feared wanting to fall. He had said nothing about this to Rebecca, but he could tell by the look on her face when he told her about his climbs that something worried her. And even on this trip, at a number of turns, he thought of pushing off the cliff, letting free the lines. Sometimes he thought it was every climber's secret dream, the thing that attracted them to the sport in the first place. But to actually do it—

"That's some choice," Horton said. He looked down at the slate color of the lake below, measuring his thirty-five years. Not many years, really.

"You'll have to hurry." Spell saw that the clouds were pouring over the Valley, tall black thunder heads with licks of lightning gobbling up the sky closer and closer to the Dome.

Horton also saw the clouds, but he searched for helicopters or any sign that someone was coming. He listened for any other voices. No cavalry, he thought, that's not the way it's ever worked. He slowly unhooked his clip from the rope, now was unattached to the line and the fixed bolts. With his good hand he gripped a small ledge in the rock. Pulled up his legs, turned so that he was facing the sky with his knees out and his feet hard against the rock. He moved very slowly.

"Ever shoot off the side of the pool when you were a kid?" Horton asked. "Fire yourself into the deep water?" It was a last stab at familiarity; Horton still hoped that if the conversation could be casual, without the shadow of fear or death, then somehow they'd make a connection. The body twisting on the rope just above reminded him of the reality, however.

"Yes."

"That's how this will be."

Although his one hand was straining, and he was convincing himself that the jump was the thing to do, Horton could not let go yet. He entertained the wild idea that he could make the lake, might survive; he rarely gave into such daydreams, but now was a good time.

"What's your name?" Horton asked. Still no rescuers.

"Eldred Spell." He had not spoken the name in several months.

"Why are you doing this, Spell?" Horton's voice trembled, either from the pain of his hand or something else that he refused to think about now.

"To clear the Valley."

"Get rid of the people, eh?" Horton's leg muscles, bunched up as they were, began to cramp. His good arm shook. "That's a stupid idea."

Spell watched.

"Soon this will be you." His good hand was cramping up now; he couldn't believe he would finally let go. No time left. "I'll see you later."

Horton let go, pushed out from the cliff with his legs as hard as he could, and dove out into the Valley. He cleared the face of the Dome, and let the growing lake and the rush of air fill his head. Slowly he rotated until his feet went below him. He looked down beyond his boots, his eyes tearing quickly, the pain gone from his hand now, and he made no sound as he went down.

XXIV

Strike Team Alpha scrambled out of two Naval Air Station helicopters in a clearing near the base of the Dome trail at dawn, just before the sun started over the Valley rim. FBI agents, an ATF weapons specialist, and handpicked Park rangers. And two dog handlers from Virginia, with four bloodhounds specially trained to track dangerous human beings. Eli leapt from one of the choppers with Olivos by her side. She had spoken little to him during the trip across the Valley, but had looked out the window at the Channel 5 TV crew hovering by the face of the Dome in their helicopter, recording footage of the dead man hanging from the cliff's face. She thought of

Sarah still sleeping in the cabin, of Karol sitting on the porch, quietly sipping coffee, as he had watched her go.

She hit the ground with the .45 at her hip and an M-16 on her shoulder. Olivos had spent the last week training her on the rifle, amazed at her proficiency. He did not have to urge Cairns to put her on Team Alpha; she knew the Valley better than any of them, she was an excellent shot, and could be counted on. All of this appealed to Cairns. Working out of the worst PR mess in his career, he also needed her to do some interviews. Eli Ware would look good for the cameras, and for him.

The FBI continued to let Cairns have much say in the operation; they expanded his plan to use dogs, although they would use their dogs and handlers now. Cairns argued that the team could not be set down before dawn—the killer had already ambushed a group before, and following him on a moonless night, during a violent lightning storm, in high country terrain, which several members of the team did not know, would be unthinkable. Still, setting down a well-armed team at the point of the trail where the killer had been and following his trail would reveal his escape route. At the very least they would better understand his movements.

Once the team was down, the Navy helicopters hovered above and forward of the group, a position they would maintain along the trail in order to spot anyone ahead. Eli and the others moved out of the clearing to allow the Sheriff's helicopter to land, so the coroner and his group could bring up the dangling body. As they moved off, the dogs immediately went to work. Big red hounds, noisier than Lars' dogs, they shoved their noses in the trail and sniffed up the dirt until they picked up a distinct scent. Then all at once they began to bark and pull at the leashes.

"That was quick," a handler said.

The group moved forward into the woods, with FBI agents in camouflage gear flanking the trail on either side. Eli was behind Olivos, on the trail, at the front. The two rangers, Lenahan and Heinze, stayed at the rear. The group moved at a trot just behind the handler and dogs, a tight phalanx, with Olivos on the radio constantly to the two helicopters above. Once he felt they had a definite fix on the killer's direction, he could call for Teams Bravo and Charlie to land on trails miles ahead. Others would be set on trails further out, setting up temporary checkpoints.

Every hundred feet or so the dogs stopped, breathing up the trail, hot on the scent.

"His trail seems very fresh," the handler noted. "He may be closer than we think."

"I'm surprised he stayed on this trail so long," Olivos said to Eli. "I thought he preferred to stay off trail."

"He was in a hurry," she said.

"Then how come his trail is so fresh?"

They passed through a small, wet meadow, where a wide creek meandered in the tall grass.

"He didn't try to duck us here," the handler said. "Just stomped right through."

"Bravo command," Olivos spoke into the radio. "His scent continues to be very strong—he may be traveling slower than we thought. We'll check this a few minutes longer. If we stay course then you should fly over Illouette Pass; maybe we'll box him in there."

Eli began to perspire in the stiff new cloth of her camouflage gear, and the butt of the M-16 banged her hip as they trotted along. They came to Cade's Meadow, which spread out in several acres like a lake of green flung with the pinks of shooting stars and the white blossoms of pussy toes. Peering from under the brim of her black cap, Eli saw that the cool of the morning would quickly give way to one of the first warm days. Mid-June, any other year, and she could be planning for the first swim of the summer down in the river, teach Sarah to dive off Adam's Rock into the Big Pool. Karol would prepare the first batch of North Carolina barbecue. Any other summer.

The meadow was empty. No tents, no one fishing the creek. Perhaps a few day hikers would wander out by noon, but even the hikers were staying out of the high country. Just some diehard backpackers. Eli had never seen the meadow empty in season, and she wished she could stay and enjoy it, see and hear a stillness which had never been possible before. If the meadow stayed clear of people all summer, she wondered what the wildlife would do. After awhile, if one sat still in the quiet meadow, what might venture down? And what would a colony of wild flowers look like without trails worn through, or groups tramping over and plucking them up?

As they passed out of the meadow, up on a dry pumice trail that wound through an old grove of lodgepole pines, the dogs began to slow. Eli noticed that they had stopped barking, just letting out a whimper or a howl, becoming as quiet as Lars' dogs. She figured they were losing the killer's trail.

"Hold, Bravo," Olivos spoke into the radio. "Dogs are slowing—we may have a shift in direction here."

Olivos ordered the rangers to put M-16s in ready position. The FBI agents fanned out, running from tree to tree, while the helicopters came in closer, the noise of their blades clattering down through the tall columns of trees. One of the dogs made a high-pitched groan, then a shrill sound that bounced Eli's heart. With the others, she looked around at the trees, between the trunks, ready at the trigger.

"I don't think we need to worry," the handler said. "They wouldn't act this way if he were here."

The group stopped, and they looked at the dogs. One hound, breathing heavily, lay on the ground. Another, also panting quickly, circled the hound that was down. One walked lazily ahead and another drifted, wobbling, off the trail.

"Dogs halt!" The handler bent over the dog on the ground. The circling hound lay on a patch of grass nearby. The other two kept walking.

"Dogs halt!" The handler repeated.

The hound nearest him started convulsing, its eyes becoming white as they rolled into its skull.

"Fuck!" The handler stood up, yelled to the FBI agents by the trees. "Bring in those two!"

The wobbly dog fell, the lead dog strained feebly to go ahead until an agent forcibly stopped him. Now the hound on the patch of grass convulsed, too.

Eli ran forward to the dog, putting her hand on its quaking side. "What is it?"

"They're dying," the handler said tonelessly. "And I don't think there's much we can do."

"What's going on?" Olivos towered over the handler, gun still at the ready.

"You might cancel this operation." The handler saw the wobbly dog begin convulsing. "The man's probably long gone, and I think he left a present behind for the dogs."

The handler carried the one conscious dog but they left the others behind. Olivos did not want the team burdened with the animals while the killer might still be waiting in the trees somewhere. They stayed at the edge of the meadow until the choppers landed. Eli sat quietly with Olivos in their chopper as they waited on three FBI agents who volunteered to go back for the dogs. The handler left first, rushing the conscious dog to a vet waiting in Wawona. When the agents returned, they dumped the dead dogs in the back of the Huey, and then Strike Team Alpha left.

As they flew into the Valley, hearing on radio how Teams Bravo and Charlie found nothing, Olivos turned to Eli. "Well, we don't know how he left the Park, or even if he did. We just have three dead dogs."

Eli rubbed the tense muscles in Olivos' shoulders with one hand. "This is going to be harder than any of us thought."

Olivos looked at Eli, into her brown eyes, felt the softness of her hand on his aching shoulder. "Thank you." He looked down at the skid of the chopper as it hit earth.

He hopped out, looked back, saying loudly, "I'm glad you're on the team." Then Eli watched a group of reporters engulf him; she walked around the chopper and headed in the other direction. Something went right for once, because no reporter noticed her as she walked the back road toward headquarters.

Late that night she had just begun to doze in bed, her around Karol, when she heard the phone ring. She left the room, carrying her silk nightshirt, and padded across the cold wooden floor to the kitchen. She slipped the nightshirt over her head, let it fall, then picked up the receiver.

"Yeah?"

"Hi, Olivos here."

"It's late." She could not see the clock, but guessed it to be past midnight. "Has something happened?"

"I just came back from headquarters."

"So?"

"Well, we know what killed the dogs today."

"You mean yesterday." The kitchen was very dark, and as she looked out the window Eli saw a cloud of stars above, brightening as her eyes adjusted.

"Right." Throat clearing. "Should I call tomorrow?"

"I'm up," she half smiled in the dark. "Tell me what happened, Olivos."

"He made up some kind of powder, very fine. We'll go up to the Dome tomorrow to see if we can collect any on the trail. An FBI toxins expert in San Francisco says he must have worked up a sweat, mixed his scent in a powdered poison, and cut it with some anti-caking agent. He put it on the trail, and as the dogs inhaled it, the poison soaked through the membranes in their noses. The level of it in the blood was very high. Those dogs were trained to sniff out the usual things–this stuff was something new. They are not sure yet what it was."

"What about that lead dog?"

"Oh, he's a tough boy. He'll make it."

"I'm glad."

"Eli?"

"What?" She just made out Karol's outline as he stepped into the kitchen.

"Cairns didn't ream me out today."

"He's been sensible lately." She watched Karol open the refrigerator, look for a bottle of chardonnay that wasn't there, and close it again.

"Eli, you were a big help today, I mean—you know what I mean?"

"Thanks." She could feel Karol watching her. "I'm tired."

"Yeah."

"I'm going back to bed."

"Check."

"Good night."

"Okay."

She hung up, wondering what was the matter with Olivos. Sitting by the phone late at night, calling her, looking for assurance. He was a handsome man, very solid, and ought to have someone of his own.

"Was that Olivos?" Karol lit his pipe, opening the screen door. "One of his weird late night calls?"

"Yeah." She followed him out.

They sat on the back steps, feeling the cold, looking out at the black outline of her father's cabin. Any night the air was remotely warm enough, they did their serious talking on the steps of the porch, sitting in the dark, watching the constellations move and the rogue shooting stars arc the sky. She saw the glow of his pipe, felt his warm hand slide over the silk, over her shoulder and down to the side of her left breast.

"I took a walk with Sarah from the Muir on down to Tent City," Karol said. "We saw as many reporters as tourists. Sarah looked at them for awhile, and decided they were worse than tourists. She used the word obnoxious for the first time."

"Smart girl." Eli settled her hand on his thigh.

He took a long puff on his pipe, breathed deep. "My mother called again, campaigning for us to flee to the Smoky Mountains."

"Oh God."

"She really wants Sarah to come, at least." Another puff on the pipe. "She says it's not safe here."

"She's right about that." Eli crossed her legs and folded her arms. Karol's hand fell away. She hated that Meredith had any point at all; she was a soft southern woman who wouldn't leave her mountains but expected her son's family to leave the Sierra. The best thing about Jack was that he kept Karol's mother from visiting. But Meredith for once made sense—Sarah should go to her grandmother's big, comfortable, soft house. Eli stood up abruptly.

"You're mad," Karol said.

"Your mother is right."

"But you want Sarah here."

"Of course I do." She threw open the screen door. "You and Sarah can just spend the summer in North Carolina but I'm stuck here. You and Sarah—that's always the way. How would you like it?"

"I'm in no rush to spend the summer in North Carolina." Karol stood up, and knocked the pipe out against his hand. "I can keep an eye on Sarah here."

"Sure you can." She slammed the screen door shut behind her.

XXV

VICTIM: "HE WANTS TO CLEAR THE VALLEY"

Spell read the headline set in large red letters on the cover of *Newsweek.* The head ran across the top of the cover photo: a shot of the dead man hanging from the face of the Dome. The quote came from Horton. He had fallen nearly five thousand feet, carried out by a strong undercurrent of air from the approaching storm, and he sailed feet first into the lake. Herb Parish, the trout fisherman, saw an explosion just ten feet in front of him—thought a rock had fallen from the cliff—until he saw a hand surface from the water. Overcoming fear, Herb waded in and pulled the broken body out. The autopsy later would show that Horton had shattered nearly every bone in his lower body. But Horton had a few seconds left; staring up at Herb, choking on blood and losing consciousness, he whispered one last line before he died. After some time and questioning, Herb was able to put together what the line was: "He wants to clear the Valley."

Spell turned the magazine over and set it down on his table. Pushing aside his shrimp, he looked out from the veranda of the Spyglass Inn at the bay and thought about Horton. Admired his relentlessness, the strength it must have taken to get out that last line. Now they have a motive, Spell thought, and as their confusion fades I will have a much tougher time. Damn Horton. Good Horton. He shouldn't have been up there.

The chill was coming off his bottle of wine, so Spell poured himself a glass. He picked it up, thought of drinking to Horton. Played the jump in his mind, heard Horton say "this will be you" once again. Spell put the glass down without taking a sip. The front page article in the Monterey *Herald* that he had read that morning, about the death of the tracking dogs, had been better. Park and FBI officials agreed that dogs would no longer be used, but denied that a protest by Animal Rights activists at Park Headquarters had anything to do with the decision.

He closed his eyes, leaned back in his chair, listening. The jazz bar at the Spyglass Inn had opened for the evening, beginning with a golden riff from a saxophone soloist. Now a bass and the undertone of a slow rhythm, bringing Spell back to the clubs in Manhattan. Saw himself with other brokers, the select artistic group, loners who gathered in the Village after a hard day. Loosened ties, talking loose. Spell saw himself in these places, saw himself watching his colleagues from the edge of the group. Perhaps a woman with him, usually a woman with him, and hadn't he enjoyed them? Did he have friends among the brokers, weren't those nights a pleasure before they disappeared as he became more relentless and more successful? When you excel at what you do, his mother had told him, then you pull ahead of the group. In college, in New York, now in California, he always pulled ahead. Left them behind, and by that time they were all glad to see him go.

He had seen the look in Horton. A man who pulled ahead, isolated in success. Would become the greatest financial planner in Los Angeles, would climb so well that he would have had to go solo in the end. He had taken that last dive too easily, not much protest there, not quite relentless enough to pay the price of perfect success. Entered the competition and leveled them all, rose too high, did what hard mothers and the American dream challenge you to do. Then you get there, then what?

It occurred to Spell that he had risen above them all, from private grade school, Jackson Military, to Harvard, to the Exchange—outstripped every runner and ran alone. And would run alone in the Valley, in another field of people to beat, in a bigger thing to own. And then: "soon this will be you." The higher you climb, the farther you fall.

"You don't seem to like the food."

Spell opened his eyes, expecting to see his waitress. But he straightened up, saw in the evening glow that it was the woman he had seen on the veranda the last time he had stayed at the Spyglass Inn. That she recognized him was reason to worry, but not enough to make him leave.

"Is there something wrong with it?" She smiled, sitting at the one other chair at his table.

"No."

"Then why aren't you eating again?"

"Does this concern you?"

"Of course. I own this hotel."

He looked at her carefully. Perfect evening gown, designed for her dark color and long features, probably Halston. By the tiny crows feet at her eyes, the tightness of her long neck, about thirty-five years old. Too young to build a multimillion dollar hotel like the Spyglass, too at ease as an owner. Had someone else running it, he thought, inherited the whole thing from some spent father or lover, probably some old man blown away by a failed heart.

"You look tired." She had been studying him, too. "And very strong, I'd say, but too thin. Recently lost that weight, by the way your clothes are hanging there." She reached out and pulled at his sleeve. "Do you run marathons or something?"

"Yes." The smart thing to do would be to get up and leave. Check out right away and never come back. But as she watched him, smiling and waiting for him to speak, Spell could not leave. Some of the ruined part of him, the piece that had come to Manhattan with enthusiasm, was still alive. It questioned his mission in the Valley, and urged him to stay now. The stronger voice within him could be ignored for the moment.

"So?"

"Yes, I've been running."

"Then take care of yourself." She looked up and the waitress came immediately. "Maria, take this away. Have Ramon put together something with red meat—tell him to do his filet with the bearnaise."

The waitress took the plates away, grinned at Spell, and left without a word.

"And bring a bottle of Cabernet—a good one," the woman called out.

Then she turned to Spell. She kept eye contact, so they looked into each other's eyes, because both of them had been taught that was the way to dominate. And they waited a long time for the other to speak, very calmly, because they both knew that the talkers were the weak ones. They listened to the music, and the old New York man in Spell made him feel at ease for the first time in months, perhaps years.

The steak came, laid on the hot plate in garnish, parsley, and sizzling butter. Grilled red potatoes and asparagus, endive salad, a bottle of 1982 Napa Valley.

"Well—" Spell said at last.

"No," she said. "I'm paying for this, so I'll tell you how to eat. With no talk. That's the order from my father."

"Is he—"

"Deceased." She turned away, profile dark gold from the lights of the jazz bar inside. "You eat. I'll listen to Sheryl on the keyboard, and we'll talk when you're up to it."

He obeyed her order, and ate the entire meal very slowly. Spell drank several glasses of wine, which she poured, and after a time all he saw of her was her hand at the bottle. The blood of the beef ran into his veins, mingled with the wine, and let the old New York man flicker to life. The waitress had removed his *Newsweek* from the table, and then he could ease into the self-hallucination he allowed himself. Or that this woman allowed him.

"So you run?," she said at last.

"Yes."

"For a living?"

"It's what I do now."

"Do they pay runners enough to dress as you do?"

"No. I don't get paid for running."

"Then what?"

"I get by eating free meals. Thank you."

"I'm glad you enjoyed it."

She kept her black eyes on his, without varying once, and he found her gaze both unnerving and familiar. He hadn't been watched like that since he left his mother's house. Spell wondered how long people could stand to be with this woman who owned the Spyglass Inn.

"So how did you come to possess this hotel?"

That turned her eyes, and she looked out to sea again. "My father built it. And he built the restaurants on the end of the Wharf, the ones you think compete against each other. But I own them all. He started out as a good Portuguese fisherman, then went to his own boat, then climbed over the rest of them to build his empire. Sold his boat for a restaurant. Sold that restaurant for one on the wharf. Then bought two, three. Papa bought inns and had this place built. He died just before it opened."

"How?"

"That's not a polite question," she stared at him again. "Are you interested in the way people die?"

"I like to know the end of a story."

"You're looking at the end of his story."

"A wonderful ending." Spell raised his glass.

"As you'll see, I think."

When the band in the jazz bar took a break, they left. She took him to the Steinbeck Suite at the top of the hotel, where she lived, and they stood on the private balcony. She made him quiet, kept the conversation minimal, long silences they both enjoyed. And in time she took him to her great open bath, washed him by hand, learned him by sinew, muscle, and bone. All the pieces of Spell sunk in the warm, bubbling water, like whiskey in the low amber light. He rose from the waters, picked her up, rose up into her as she straddled his legs, and they clawed and twisted in the dark rooms, moved in strength and rhythm, in tandem. Water running to sweat. Spell exploded many times, so much pent up, tight lines loosed at last, and she took everything that he gave.

Back at the balcony, the jazz bar long closed, the music had given way to the lap of waves and the clang of a buoy far out in the harbor. They felt the bite of cold salt air on their slick wet skin, legs and backs beginning to feel the night chill. Spell propped his head on his elbow, let his leg slide off hers, and looked down into a dark face he could not see in a night nearly black, illuminated by the faintest sliver of moon.

"I already have a man," she said. "But if I know you'll be back, I'll let him go."

"I will be back."

"Then it's worth it."

"Worth what?"

"To know your name."

"Oh, yes." He laughed. "Eldred—" Stopped, and the new man with the new mission came screaming in. His heart thumped. Everything about this was foolish: giving names, coming back. But he knew he would stay at the Spyglass again. "Eldred Wright."

"Ah, Mr. Right." She put her hand on his chest, misinterpreted the pounding she felt there. "You are a strong one."

"And you?"

"Andrea Giari."

He stood up and leaned on the balcony rail. One hundred yards out in the water the kelp bed was lit by underwater beams; he saw the black silhouette of a diver caught in the light. A party of divers, and above them several more in a dive boat rocking in the gentle waves, their backs to the glow of a small cabin and the red running lights.

"Those are the experts," Andrea said, standing at his side.

"They come when everyone else has gone," Spell said, recoiling from her cool skin. "They want the harbor to themselves, when it has been cleared out."

XXVI

Karol sat under a pine on the edge of the South Meadow, with a pencil and the yellow pad he used to catch words for his poems. He spent time looking at the line of trees across the way, watching the dark blue light of late afternoon fall on the meadow, shadows lengthening. In the last hour a few hikers had come by, but otherwise he worked alone under his tree. Most of the noise came from stellar jays chattering. He saw a pine martin weave a cautious trail through the tall grass—he had never seen one down in the meadow before. Lately, in these unusually quiet afternoons on South Meadow, words grew quickly into lines on his yellow pad.

It was July 2. The killer had not struck in two weeks, the media played up the story enough to keep the scare on, tourism had fallen to numbers not seen since the 1930s, and Eli Ware stayed on alert 24 hours a day, seven days a week. Karol had plans for his wife.

At last she came through the trees. Walking with her head down, hair hidden in the brim of her hat, all boots and uniform. Jack's gun still at her hip. She marched toward the cabin.

"Hey," Karol called out.

She looked up, smiled, and walked slowly to his tree.

"The reporters are really bored," she said, looking down at him. "One from the *Chronicle* got around to interviewing me."

"Oh, God," Karol stood up. "The Park Service Princess."

"Yeah." She put her arm around his waist. "That's the angle, I think. Cairns put her on to me."

"He's been through enough interviews."

"Through enough of everything. How's poetry?" She pulled gently, starting him toward their cabin.

"I feel a little guilty, but in the midst of crisis, poetry is doing well. Called my editor at Ecco and told him the book would be ready by Christmas. Has something to do with the peace we're getting now."

"Peace for you, anyway." She walked ahead of him up the steps and into the cabin. "Where's Sarah?"

"Gone with Gramps for the evening."

"Really?" She shook her hair out from under the hat. "Is he—"

"Sober as a judge. They're catching dinner and a movie down in Coarsegold—my idea."

"Oh." She looked in the refrigerator.

"Put on a bright summer dress," Karol walked up behind her, put his arms around her middle. "And forget the leftovers. I've made reservations at the Muir—Stan's doing something special for us."

"I wish you would've told me, Karol." She turned to him, kissed him on the cheek, and twisted out of his grasp. "Sandra's sick, and I volunteered to take part of her shift tonight."

"No," he said, closing the refrigerator door.

"I can't say no," she headed out the room.

"Wait." He caught up with her.

"I'm sorry—really."

"What happens if you just tell them you have other plans?" His voice was already rising—he had enough of the little war in the Valley. She came home tired, lifeless, from working on searches and patrols that always turned up nothing. Some on the FBI team were beginning to theorize that the killer had left, might move on to another park. And he had been setting up this plan for nearly a week, even went so far as to negotiate some babysitting from Jack.

"I can't." She started to walk away.

"Stay here, sit on the couch."

She could see the way his lower lip had turned down, a kind of pouting look that meant he was angry and one that she rarely saw. She was tired, and depended on him not to be angry. She could feel her muscles tense up with his order, given in a tone that sounded like her father. She would not take it from Karol, and never had. But she sat down.

"Don't lecture me," she warned.

"Have no intention of that." He paced the room. "Won't talk about how tired you are, how sick I am of seeing your daddy's gun there, the joke I have with people that my wife is doing a tour in 'Nam this summer." He could see her jaw clench, that she was ready to let go. "No, I just have one question."

"What?"

"How can I take you out to dinner tonight? What's the procedure?"

"There isn't one." She looked down at her boots, too tired to fight him. "I'm stuck tonight."

"I won't accept that."

"That's it, Karol."

"You can't call the boss?"

"No. He's wound up. A mess right now."

"So are you." He went to the wall, picked up the phone, dialed headquarters.

"What are you doing?"

"Getting permission to have my wife tonight. What can the boss do with the local poet?"

She settled back in the couch, weary, and relaxed, because maybe Karol could get away with it. His resolve as he waited on hold for Cairns amused her, woke her up from the tension of the past days. All right, she thought, let the man deal with it.

"Cairns," Karol said tersely. "Eli's off shift tonight, by order of her husband." He waited, smiling wickedly, then added, "You can't talk to her. It's my turn to abuse her tonight. Yes, I've had it. She'll be in tomorrow, on time. But she's mine tonight so screw you." Karol paused, winked at Eli, then added, "Thank you, sir." He hung up.

"Am I fired?"

"No," Karol held out his hand for her. "He says you are overworked. He told me to have fun abusing you."

"Sometimes," she stood up, "he surprises me."

"And me?"

"*Muy macho*."

They started for the bedroom. "Did you think to iron my white blouse and cotton skirt?"

"I did."

She saw it lying on the bed.

Eventually she put the dress on, and Karol wore his coat and tie, and they still had some time to walk to the Muir Hotel because he had wisely made the reservations for nine. The Salon, a huge room illuminated by candlelight, had a dozen people among nearly one hundred round tables. Although they had laid off waiters, the pianist played the grand in the corner, notes reverberating softly against the walls of wood and glass. Shirley Weaver had found that she had to cut some corners, but she spared the Muir its evening piano.

They sat at a small table in the corner, at the apex of two tall clerestory windows. Carl, the headwaiter, blew out the candles on the empty tables around them, darkening their part of the room enough so that the stars outside were visible. Stan came out in his whites and chef's hat, and had enough extra time in the kitchen that every dish he brought them was a specialty not on the menu. "Enjoy," he said, "you've just about got the place to yourselves."

Across the room Eli could see that the remaining guests were either old couples, people bent on keeping an annual tradition despite the terrorist, or groups of reporters from the papers and TV stations, attracted by the terrorist. The piano sounded miles away, the tinkling of silver and glasses remote, and the occasional eruption of laughter from a group of reporters seemed eerie. Eli was used to the people, to the crowd in the Muir that would be there so close to the Fourth of July. In the quiet salon, Karol drank a good deal of the wine and pointed out what constellations had spun into view, and eventually Eli fell in with his drift. She could almost enjoy the comfort of her cotton dress, the glow of her blouse in his eyes, the slow courses of the meal.

From far away, just before Eli completely slipped away with Karol, came the distant crash of glass. Followed by a sudden hush, the abrupt freeze of the piano keys, a quick wave of fear coming in, then the sharp cries, a rush of reporters at the tables, people running in the hotel. Disturbance in the lobby beyond. Eli stood up, and Karol woke to the end of his perfect evening.

FBI agents ran across the lobby with rangers. Already the choppers in the meadow near headquarters were revving up. Through the window above them, they could see a helicopter swoop in low, its spotlight touching the glass before it swept the back of the hotel. Sirens wailed in the distance, patrol cars converging on the parking lot behind the hotel.

"It's on the east side," Eli followed the chopper with her eyes. "All this—it has to be him."

"Well, damn." Karol followed her to the lobby. He took in the sirens' wail and the sudden crush of people pouring in, tourists with questions, reporters rounding up their teams, agents and officers running back and forth with the loud static of their radios—the clash of disaster against the elegance of the Muir. He felt dizzy, like the lobby was listing, in the panic of a sinking grand liner. "Shit," he said to himself, "great time for a night on the town."

Cairns ran across the lobby, pointed to Eli, and Olivos approached at a trot. He was about to say something, stopped, looked at her dress and Karol, and started again.

"Listen," Olivos said. "I'm going to figure the angle of his shots and then we'll meet in the back lot. Team Alpha in Chopper One—I've got some gear in there, might be big for you, but just throw it on."

"What happened?"

"He shot up windows on the east side and hit some trucks in the lot. Went after media vehicles and nailed their suites—knew where they were staying, I think. Gotta go." He sprinted off.

"Anyone hurt?" She yelled over the noisy crowd.

Olivos ran up the stairs and did not turn back.

"I just love his fucking timing," Karol's lip had turned down sourly.

"Look after Sarah." She kissed him on the cheek and started away.

"Honey," he grabbed her arm. "North Carolina is looking a lot better suddenly."

"We'll talk later."

"Damn straight." He let her go. As she pushed through people to get to the back of the lobby, he called out after her, "Be careful." But he could tell she could not hear him, and he slowly went in her direction, shoved by people, adrift in the growing panic. The list of the room seemed to increase. Seeing her go, he felt completely useless.

Eli ran to the waiting chopper in the parking lot, while two others swooped overhead. Someone flashed her picture. She ran in and out of the spotlight of a TV camera crew setting up on the lot. Someone on a bullhorn was ordering the reporters to vacate the area, but they ignored the voice. She thought every patrol car in the Park had arrived, a storm of flashing light bars, spinning blue lights, and sirens.

She knew the pilot, and he waved her to the back of the helicopter. The crew was already assembling there, and they looked up briefly from their preparations when Eli came in wearing her dress.

"Don't look back here," she said as she found Olivos' extra outfit. Looking at them, she kicked off her heels and shoved her skirt down. Pulled up the baggy camouflage pants, tucked her white blouse in them. Put on heavy woolen socks so the oversize boots fit. There was a bulletproof vest, a dirty camouflage jacket, and a greasy black cap. Eli felt smothered in Olivos' big, filthy clothes. She rolled up her skirt and set it next to her dress shoes.

"Ready?" Olivos hopped into the chopper, yelling to the group. "We've got searchlights on the Rim Trail; shots look like he fired from there. He broke a lot of glass, scared a lot of media people. But no one was hurt." He glanced at Eli. "Every team is on this. We'll get the bastard tonight."

The helicopter's blades revved, flailed noisily at the night air. As they rose into the sky, Eli looked down at the parking lot. Karol had walked close to the chopper, and he stood squinting up into the sky. He had taken off his jacket, and it flapped in the wind on his arm. Eli saw him become smaller and smaller as the group of agents and officers checked weapons, maps, communications, tactics, plans. Someone put an M-16 in her hand but she kept her eye on Karol, until the chopper sped away and the sharp spears of the tall pines cut into the illuminated lot, closing in on her husband like the lower half of a black jaw.

XXVII

Once Spell had come into the Park from a difficult trail from the north, across the Sierra crest from Mono Lake, he forgot about Monterey and Andrea Giari. The two rangers he saw checking back country passes on the trail reminded him that he was there for survival, do or die. He ducked off trail, cut across sectors, found his Dragunov carefully stored in a cache. He spent the late afternoon in a deep grove, meticulously cleaning the gun. Loaded ammo and night-vision goggles in a black day pack and set out. Put on his new, special outfit. Spell moved toward the Valley carefully, had read in the papers and magazines how many agents and officers were put all over the Park to catch him. But he doubted they figured he would strike in the heart of the Valley.

Coming close to the Muir Trail after dark, not far from where he had shot the dog handler, he suddenly stopped. Felt something wrong in the air, a tingling signal in his nerves, like the sense he used to have when a sure stock was about to fall. He waited silently. Two figures passed close by, quietly walking the trail, and in his night-vision goggles he saw the guns they carried. Spell thought of picking them off, but knew that several more were close by. Besides, he had a particular target in his mind, something more important that would advance his cause.

When they were gone, and he moved forward through the trees, the pleasure of what he was doing came back to him. Something very elemental: a feeling that the Valley had become an extension of himself, that he knew its movements like an animal natural to the terrain, and he almost rejoiced in the simplicity of the hunt, the coming success. But as he searched the woods in the green night-vision goggles, sizing up the artificially enhanced world of the forest floor, he wondered if the joy he felt was illuminated by the stifled remembrance of Andrea, of a place to return to when he had finished.

At the cliff's edge, hugging the rock as a helicopter swooped by, all he knew was the twitch in his nerves, the tightening of muscle and tendon throughout his lean body. The Muir Hotel stood below him, lit so well in the building and parking lot that he took off the night goggles. He unshouldered his rifle. Roamed the lot and the windows with the cross hairs. Readied on the trigger, recalled his escape route foot by foot.

The week before he had sat on the veranda of the Spyglass Inn, breakfasting with Andrea, reading *USA Today*. Nothing much was happening with the story of the Park, so naturally reporters began to write about themselves. While tourism had drastically fallen off, they wrote, the numbers were propped up by the army of media personnel in the Valley. Spell saw photos of a parking lot crammed full of TV vans, photos of media crews during a lull, sitting in the salon of the Muir. He decided the reporters had to go. The idea was confirmed when he slipped into the Park on a tourist bus, walked among the reporters in the Muir, saw them crowding the bar that evening, taking over accommodations where others had canceled. Panic sale. Cheap rates. Waiting for the big story. No more.

Through the glow of windows in the Muir, he could not see them in their rooms. No kill could be sure now, and perhaps none would be needed. Pulling rapidly at the trigger, he blew out window after window. Then he hit the TV vans, shattering windshields and blowing out tires. A patrol car stopped abruptly in the lot, idling uselessly. In less than a minute he was finished, had kicked the ant hill, and now the scrambling would begin.

He planned to go for the Mammoth side, because once he crossed the Park boundary, he would be in the company of backpackers who did not need special permits for the Valley. Once over, he could blend in well. But that was eighteen miles away, across the Illouette Pass, and he knew things would be harder now. Even at night, even without the dogs. He shouldered his gun, would keep it with him almost to the edge of the boundary, and he ran through the woods.

They were ready this time. He could almost feel the Park moving, and he did hear the thunder of several helicopters rising from the Valley floor. He figured in five minutes they would know the point from which he had fired, and would converge all around him. Tighten the net. His plan was to head for the pass, cross several of his sectors, come near a cache with a different gun if he needed it. But he had to cross one open meadow, where the small valley he would run up narrowed—an open place with sheer walls on either side. He could make it in twenty minutes, but if they were fast and smart they would be waiting for him there. And that's when the clothes he wore, supplied at a high price from Doug Evers, might work for him.

His heart pounded and his legs ached. Just two weeks of easy living in Monterey had softened him. He could not maintain top speed. As he leaned against a tree, breathing heavily and too loudly, he saw a glow in the woods behind him. Heard the roar of helicopters; already they had spotlights on the place where he had come from. They were better organized than he had imagined. Now Spell had to push himself, ignore the sharp pain in one cramping thigh.

As he started to move again, he abruptly stopped. In a dark cavern of manzanita, not far from a trail crossing, he thought he saw something move. Slowly, he slipped the night-vision goggles over his eyes. There, on the edge, four figures were waiting for him. Radio silence. Very clever. Spell moved back and around them. The gathering noise of the helicopters helped deafen them to his movements. The illuminated spot of woods was at his back, less than a quarter of a mile away. And now a party was behind him, loud, beating the woods with chopper blades above and the loud bark of their radios. The plan was to flush him out, like some rogue animal.

Spell moved too quickly, without the necessary care now, because the trees just behind him were glowing—sickly white and electric blue. Somehow, without any method he could think of, they were right on his trail. The open meadow was just ahead. He had trapped himself. He could not turn back, and saw that they had landed several crews out in the meadow. It crawled with black figures and roving flashlights and spotlights from above. He ducked in the hollow of a moist creek bed, unsettling a cloud of stinging mosquitoes, as a Huey roared overhead. It landed fifty yards in front of him, disgorging another crew with rifles. He adjusted his cap, took his chance.

Before the chopper lifted off he sprinted into the open and followed the group, hanging back just enough, but looking like a part of their ragged formation. He could hear their chatter, calling names back and forth. The man running just ahead of him, Lenahan, puffed loudly, following the group to the edge of the wood on the other side—just the place Spell wanted to go. An engine thundered just above, almost blew Spell's cap off; he believed he could feel the heat of the great encircling spotlight on the back of his Park uniform. Just one hundred yards to go. The spotlight stayed on them, did not roll off them as it had the other group. Someone in the chopper above was studying them. Fifty yards to go.

"Team Alpha," a voice screamed over the helicopter's P.A. "Halt!"

Just at the edge of the wood, the team stopped. Spell kept going, slipping out of the light. He dove into the woods, running as fast as he could, heart in his ears so that he could not hear the orders coming furiously from the helicopter.

The spotlight followed and then almost caught him in its beam. He veered toward the ridge, heading directly for a cache he had there. Into a rocky creek bed, where the woods formed a thicker canopy. The beam scattered in the trees but it always stayed with him.

"Stop now or we'll fire!" The P.A. yelled.

Spell heard the zip of a bullet, felt a rock shatter near his leg. Shooting at him, and he had never been under fire before in his life, and he flared with rage. He jumped to a large tree, kept in the shadow of the trunk, out of the beam. Heard the thunk of shells slamming into the old redwood. Spell grabbed his Dragunov, peered around the edge of the tree, set his sight rapidly on the windshield of the Huey hovering just above the tree line, and fired. Heard a tink against metal and then his shells found the windscreen. The chopper veered up and away. But now he heard voices on the ground, on all but one side. He ran, banging his shin violently against a rock as he scrambled up out of the creek.

Two choppers came down low again, illuminating the ground just behind him. He moved ahead quickly, taking full advantage of the fact that these men did not know the terrain as he did, and that they were slowed in a momentary haze of confusion.

Spell led them by an eighth of a mile, not much. Already the sound of helicopters ahead told him they were landing another group in his path. No way to go now. But he came to his cache, searching for the markers, the little yellow patches he made on the trees. He found the one he was looking for. Pulled out his knife, had to run his hand along the trunk until he found the line painted the color of the bark. He cut it quickly and a small bag fell from the tree in a thud. The men ahead were closer than those behind. Trees lit up around him as if he were on Central Park West on Saturday night.

With the Dragunov banging on his shoulder, he savagely ripped at the dark plastic, and pulled out his Hungarian machine gun. Loaded it quickly and expertly. Like the forest service drab he wore that had fooled them for a precious moment, this new firepower would take them by surprise. But they would find the bag, the food, the remnants of his cache. He had no time to do anything about that. There was nothing in there that would identify him or Doug Evers. No fingerprints. Everything was clean. Later, if they somehow missed them, he would get these things outside the Park.

Just ahead he knew there was a very small clearing, the last before the steep climb up the ridge. He had to get there before the others. Spell made it in seconds. He slipped on his goggles, readied his weapon, and ignored the sound of the others closing in from behind. Holding his breath, with the feel of men just at his back, he looked ahead. Waited for the group in front to come out into the clearing, on the run, incautious as they closed in for the kill.

They came out of the trees into the clearing. He opened fire, swept them with bullets, heard them scream, heard someone cry out for Team Bravo, and then he sprinted across the small opening. Stopped at the other side, turned, and fired back without taking aim. Those behind screamed orders to each other. The small clearing filled with light.

The wounded would slow them down.

Spell started up the ridge, crossed a trail, climbing painfully hand over hand up the rocks. He slipped several times, scratched his legs and pounded his gloved hands, beaten by the jagged granite face. The choppers followed the trail, for the moment kept the beam on the grey line that any sane man would follow. And as he moved up the ridge, the beams scattered in their search, while the vast dark expanse of the steep woods swallowed him up.

They had kept him off the pass, pushed him off his escape route, so Spell moved toward a hiding place. The cave. Like Ellen, they were tracking him to the cave. He came to the edge of the trees, looked out over the open tumble of rocks at the base of Illouette Ridge. Now he had to sprint into the open, with no cover, and for the next quarter mile if the helicopters found him then Spell was finished. He looked below, and the helicopters were doubling back, looking for signals from the people on the ground, the tangle of flashlights searching for any sign of the new direction. Spell stopped, wheezing, amazed that the wounded had not slowed his pursuers at all.

Once, as he came close to the small crevice in the rock he looked for, a sheriff's helicopter, beam down, hovered at his elevation. Spell could actually see the outline of the pilot in the cockpit. Then the beams below converged, homing in on his trail. They would soon be on the rock face. He had no time.

Spell passed the pile of rocks he was looking for, had to go back again, feeling desperately with his hands. Then a large boulder moved and he felt the cool breath of air from the crevice below—his cave. The slope just below him filled with light. They would be on him in seconds. Jamming himself into the crevice he pulled some rocks back over the entrance, slicing his forearms as he moved quickly and recklessly. With these in place as best he could get them, he slipped back and down into the belly of the mountain. The small opening ten feet from his head exploded with light, a thin beam thrust in and caught his forehead. Spell did not move. Then, finally, the light passed away.

For a long time he rested, regaining his breath, gathering strength. As he did, the pain of all the cuts and bruises on his hands, legs, and face entered his brain like a shrill chorus. After a time, these diminished and gave way to a dull headache. He took off his black day pack, took several long swigs from a water bottle. He set the machine gun down, but kept the Dragunov shouldered. Listening for voices, hearing none.

Spell had meant to explore the depths of the cave, but Ellen always held him back. She liked to hide in there with him, but she would never stray too far from daylight. Now he stood, felt the descending angle of the rock below him. He wanted to go ahead a few feet further, to be completely out of sight in daylight if he had to wait that long. Sliding his right foot forward a few more inches it met empty air. His left foot slipped on a loose rock and it felt like the mountain inhaled, sucked him down, and he fell through a crack. He stopped, caught painfully in the vise of the crevice, then moved, and slipped again. Then he was wedged, his feet dangling. He lifted his arms to reach up for a handhold and slipped further. Then gave way completely, the sharp rocks tearing at his arms, the back of his neck and head, as he fell through. He did not go far, and hit a patch of moist earth and gravel. Shaking his head, in pitch black.

Slowly he stood, putting his hands up, and he could feel nothing. He recalled that he had left his pack and machine gun above, including his flashlight; he almost chuckled at the absurdity of falling into a hole he probably could not climb out of. Where the rangers had failed to trap him, the mountain had not.

"My God," Spell said to himself. Already his mouth felt dry. At least the Dragunov had slipped through with him; he hoped it had not been damaged. Cautiously, he turned and stepped forward. He found he could walk, but going deeper into the black cave with no light would be insane. After making what seemed to be a turn into a chamber filled with damp, musty air, he stopped. Filled his lungs with a rank smell. Froze as he heard a rattling noise ahead of him. Something just in front of him hissing, alarmed.

He stepped to the side and kicked a mat of fur. Something seized his leg just below the knee, tooth and claw, hissing fury. He jumped forward and it slashed him, tore his pant leg, took a bloody chunk out of his calf with its mouth. He ran ahead, feeling empty air in his outstretched hand as the creature growled just behind him. He hit his forehead on a hanging rock and staggered.

Spell fell back, the hiss of the beast amplified, until he met a sharp blow, hot, blinding.

XXVIII

By 2 a.m. some of them pulled out; the one wounded ranger had been removed and all the members of the teams counted themselves lucky. But they had lost him again. His trail disappeared somewhere near Illouette Ridge, trampled out by the troops, faded away in the confusion and the night. Helicopter crews scanning the ridge carefully found nothing; their lights spotted a camp off-trail and a father and eight-year-old boy were raided by a team, checked out, and then whisked away. But they clearly had nothing do to with the killer. Olivos found the ripped plastic bag and carefully sealed food and water—aside from confirming the killer had caches, he doubted it would reveal anything important. The man they were after would not be sloppy. Olivos decided to stay in the woods, hopeless as it seemed now, but Eli came in with part of the team. She wanted to go home.

She looked down out of the Huey and saw the Muir parking lot below, filled with reporters and flashing lights just as she had left it four hours before. As they lowered into the lights, she took off Olivos' old jacket and noticed a splash of Lenahan's blood on the collar of her blouse. Still some on her hands. Despite the spray of machine gun fire, which seemed to come from both sides of the meadow where the teams had tried to converge, only Lenahan had been hit. He had gone down just next to her, clipped in the thigh, a hot slash. She had stopped to check on him, had refused to leave—disobeyed Olivos. Others came up to help, but Lenahan knew her and wanted her to stay by. He had been medivaced to the hospital in Fresno, and she guessed by the look of his wound that he would be fine.

What talk she heard from the others in the helicopter, most of them people she did not know, spun out a theory that there was more than one shooter. Some grumbled that they had been caught in a crossfire. But she had been there, stepped into the meadow just after the first burst and before the second round had been fired. Thinking about it she thought she saw a man running ahead—just a dim outline of shoulder and head from the glow in the trees. And the lapse between bursts was just enough for him to get across. None of them were dead because he had not tried to aim—just fired off rounds to startle them. That had certainly worked. No one expected a machine gun.

When the helicopter touched down she let the others go out first, and she threw off as much gear as she could. A ranger from another park agreed to take her M-16 away. Eli wanted to slip around the back of the helicopter, duck all the people, and head home to the cabin. But she knew Cairns would want an immediate report, so she plunged ahead, straight for the Muir Hotel. Cairns was surrounded by reporters on the lot; he winced at the TV lights, and strained to make the latest failure seem less than a failure. Most of the reporters stayed with the cluster around Cairns, but a few cruised the lot, hitting members of the teams who struggled across.

Before she could reach the lobby, Eli had been spotted. A reporter broke away from Cairns and intercepted her. She recognized him, a short man with wire rim glasses who had interviewed her before. She figured he was fresh out of journalism school, hot to get a different angle, and he had zeroed in on her as human interest. But she saw as he approached that he had noticed the blood on her blouse, that he watched that, biting his lip, anxious for the story.

"Excuse me," he began, trotting to keep pace with her. "Eli Ware?"

"Yes." She looked down on him, saw him work to keep pace, so she took longer strides.

"You were just out there?"

"Yes."

"Is that your blood?"

"No."

"Whose?"

"Another officer."

Other reporters had noticed, and were moving in on her.

"Look," she said, coming close to the Muir, "as soon as I'm in the hotel I'm not talking. I'm tired. So ask one intelligent question, because that's all you get."

"Why are you wearing that white blouse?"

"That's a good question." She was at the door, turning away from him.

"Then why?" He grabbed her arm lightly and let go as soon as she looked at him.

"Because my husband and I were having dinner when all this started. We're getting sick of my uniform, the killer, and all of you."

"Can I call later?" The short man stopped at the door.

"Call away." Eli went across the lobby, glanced back, and saw the little man already hustling back to the group around Cairns. The big room was surprisingly dead as she walked through.

At the front of the Muir she hitched a ride to headquarters in an unmarked car with two FBI agents. They were silent, probably thinking about the latest fiasco, but when she stepped out of their car one asked why she was wearing a blouse. She didn't answer, but went to her tiny office, turned on the Mac, and typed out a draft of her report. Let the facts wash across the screen while they were still very fresh in her mind.

By 3:30 she had done enough, and stared at the computer in a stupor for several minutes. Her eyes felt dry and tired; she looked at the walls of her silent office with the buzz of helicopters, gunfire, yelling still in her head. When she closed her eyes she became dizzy, the exhaustion settling on her as if she had been boxed in the ears.

"Eli?"

Cairns had come by, leaning against the door frame. He usually stood erect, never leaned on anything, but lately Eli noticed that Cairns did many things he had not done before. Spoke in quieter tones. Sometimes didn't look people in the eye. Above all else, his eyes were bloodshot, rarely clear, and he often seemed distracted. And he never came down to her office as he did now; if he needed her, he always called to tell her to come up.

"I finished a draft of my report."

"Fine." His eyes drifted to the posters on her wall—pictures of other parks—he could not recall seeing them before. Cairns noticed the pictures of her husband and daughter on the desk. He had no pictures of his wife in his office.

"I'm going home now." Eli stood up.

"Oh." He paused, looking down. "An FBI agent on your team says you disobeyed an order by Olivos to follow the others just after the shooting. The agent seems to think the delay might have let the killer move ahead at a crucial moment."

"Olivos did order me to go, but I stayed with Lenahan. He'd been hit."

"I know." Cairns pulled himself erect and looked straight at her. "I'm on my way to the hospital in Fresno to see him." He stood silently, watching her, and his mind wandered again. In his haze of exhaustion, he thought how fine it would feel to be away in Fresno when the secretary of the interior called in the morning.

"Well," Eli stopped in front of him as he blocked the door. "I need to get home; I'm sure Karol's worried." And suddenly she remembered that she had not called him.

"Yeah." Cairns backed out of the way. "I just wanted you to know that I spoke with Olivos on the radio."

"He's still out there?"

"Finding nothing." Cairns smiled weakly. "Anyhow, he says he made a mistake, got caught up in the chase. You were right to stay with Lenahan, of course. I think you were right."

"That's good to hear." She looked at his smile, and it was painted with defeat, something she had never seen in his expression before. He was so quiet, not in any hurry to fill the air with his voice. "Thank you," she added.

He kept walking with her as she went down the hall, and Eli wondered why. Normally, he said what he had to and went on his way.

"You know, Eli, I think they'll want me to close the Park tomorrow. Shut the whole thing down."

"Really?" Eli could not think of anything intelligent to say. He had never talked of his situation so openly; he was a man who kept everything but essential knowledge to himself—she always figured controlling information was a big part of his management style.

"Can you imagine closing the Valley at the peak of the summer season?"

"No," she said, trying to be polite. But lately she thought that closing it was the best thing to do, and she found herself agreeing with the editorials that called for him to shut it down. But then there was the other side to the question—the economics. "The Heston Company would have a fit."

"Serve my head on a platter at the Muir." And he smiled that weak smile again. "Can I drive you home?"

"No." She stopped. "But thank you. I need a walk right now, tired as I am."

"I wish I could walk to Fresno."

"Maybe you should check in with your wife."

"I'll put that off. I have enough shit to walk through already."

He opened the main entrance door of headquarters for her, and then followed her out.

"Goodnight," she said as she started down the road.

"Eli," he called out over the dark lot; she could see his dim outline. "We're the federal government. If we can't protect people in our own Park . . ."

She waited for him to finish, but he didn't. "Right," she said.

"Right," he answered. His voice barely carried.

When Eli came to the edge of the South Meadow, she left the road and cut across the field. Here the Valley was silent, without the echo of a party in the camps, nor teen lovers to chase out of the meadow. At times she had secretly enjoyed the strange quiet that had come over her home, but now it bothered her. As she thought of Cairns, on his way to Fresno and too tired to drive, the feeling of sorrow she had for him came as a surprise. Not too long ago she would have liked to see him suffer, take what he gave out. Not now. And she felt the same about the peace and quiet in the Valley that at times, in the middle of a normal season, she had often longed for.

As Eli walked in the open meadow, under the light of the half-moon, a few scattered bright stars, and the blue cliffs, she looked at her shadow, weaving on the tall grass. A feeling came over her such as she had not felt since she was a little girl, out with her father on a late night hike. The feeling that something was watching her, a fear of being alone in the dark. She knew the killer was nowhere near, had to be on his way out of the Valley by now, but she felt exposed. She fought the sudden urge to run to the cabin, and walked toward it with determination. The picture of the head and shoulder in the light—definitely a man, she thought now—swam in front of her in the moonlight. She walked fast, faster as she came to the porch. The fear made her hate the killer intensely, brought her back to how she felt worrying over Lenahan, checking his wound.

At the porch she saw a man sitting on the steps, head bowed, bottle in hand. Karol. Eli stopped, looking at him, wondering if he were awake, and the fear and hatred drained away. She felt too tired to hold it long. She sat down next to him.

"What's the deal, darlin'?" He dropped the empty bottle, and they listened to it bounce down the three steps.

"Where'd you get that?" she asked.

"Your daddy came by with Sarah. Remember her?" He looked out over the meadow and would not turn to Eli. Hell with Eli, he thought. Hell with her old man, too. "Your daddy brought this with him, figured a pussy whip like me could use it. Well, darlin', I took a drink with him. We put Sarah to bed. Then me and that bastard sat on the porch and had a little talk."

"What about?" She did not like the sound of his voice, sour on Wild Turkey, in a tone that he rarely directed at her. "Listen, I'm sorry I didn't call earlier. Things happened out there tonight—"

"Sarah enjoyed the Disney cartoon," Karol ignored her. "But your daddy thought it sucked, of course. Well, he brought the bottle and so we sat out here and drank."

"Karol, I think I'm going to bed." She started to get up but he held her arm. His grip was tight, nearly hurt, reminding her that he was a thin, wiry, but strong man. A characteristic she usually admired in him. She sat down heavily. When he was mad at her, he usually talked about her father. Firing oblique arrows—that was his way. The Southern Way, he once told her.

"Well, darlin', what we tried to do was wait for you." He looked at the rims of the blue cliffs, lines in the moonlight, not at all clear to him. "While you were out there shooting it up in the hills. You know, your daddy and me could agree on something, yes we could. Actually agreed." His voice trailed off.

"On what?" She felt just tired and guilty enough to let him go on for awhile. Then she would get up whether he liked it or not.

"Yeah, darlin'." Karol looked down at his bare feet, pale and silver in the light, which was easier than staring at the hard cliffs. "We like the peace and quiet. We like the lack of tourists. The Valley is so fucking beautiful, don't you think? I say you're fighting the wrong battle. Let your crazy man have his way, clear the Valley out, right?"

"That's enough." She stood up. "You're drunk and I'm going to bed. I've got to work tomorrow."

"Ouch." He fell against the porch post as if he had been shot. "Got to work, unlike me. Well, hell."

She opened the screen door.

"Wait," he said, not turning around. "We did have a fight, as you might 'spect. I said I was worried for you out there. Thought you could get killed by our eco-terrorist, you know?" He slurred the word, terrorist. "Said I was worried."

She looked at his back, watched him blur in her tears.

"Worried." Karol looked at his feet, putting words together in his head. "Now, daddy thought that was silly. Yes, he did. Said I didn't know the girl he raised, no sir. Said I didn't have faith in you. You could take care of yourself."

She let the screen door shut, tears hot on her cheeks. "I'm working very hard, Karol. I'm doing the best I can."

"Yeah, you are, keeping your daddy and everyone safe in the Valley. Doin' your damnedest. I don't need to worry about a thing, shouldn't sit like some scared old woman by the phone when you're off on night tactics."

"Would you just hold me, Karol," she said through the screen. "Would you just shut up and hold me?"

"No, darlin'." He waited a long time to speak again, uncertain if she were even there. "No, I don't think I will hold you tonight."

XXIX

In the dark of the cave, Spell had lost track of time and direction, and without a sign of day or night, without sounds except those he made himself, he was no longer sure if he were asleep or awake. But he seemed to become conscious, for in the dark the pain in the back of his leg deepened as if he had just been hit in the calf with a baseball bat. Then the compression on his chest, tight from being caught between rocks, closed in on him again. Spell tried to wriggle, could not move, and strained to find a way to fight the panic. Certain he was awake now.

For some time he had been trapped, after a long slow crawl, to where the sides of the cave had narrowed. He had kept pushing forward, pointing the Dragunov ahead, always afraid it would hit granite—a blunt dead end. And then he became wedged in the rock, pushed hard despite his throbbing leg, got in deeper and tighter. Squeezed by the ancient mountain. Once again he picked up the rifle and tapped the walls ahead, side to side, over and over. Ahead the fissure opened. The walls absorbed the click of the barrel on the stone so he stopped. He shoved wildly, surged forward, scratched his ribs and moved an inch forward. The rock closed tighter, with the darkness like thick felt over his mouth, suffocating him. The earth in the Valley was unstable, he knew, one tremor would be enough to pinch him in half.

He screamed, or he thought of screaming—the boundary between what was in his head and what was out had faded away.

He pushed in other thoughts. Tried to measure how far he had come. Shut his eyes enough to feel the little muscles strain—eyes screwed tight so that they made a yellow color under the lids. This was becoming habit, shutting his eyes tightly until there were patterns of yellow, with the dull blue orbs of his eyes at the center. Thought of how far he came, hundreds of yards, walking and crawling for hours, perhaps a day. Maybe two. Put figures in his head, saw them swimming there like stock figures on a screen, added them up. He must have come at least a mile, two, three. What worried him most was the fact that he was going down, could feel the pull of gravity on his head and shoulders. Down into the mountain until he hit rock, and then nowhere.

What was he doing here? The thought had come to him several times. Could have been in the Tower, he thought. He pictured white walls, saw himself walking across the carpet and looking out over Manhattan. A commanding view bought by a command of the numbers, a place completely artificial and completely controllable. What was wrong with being comfortable? Nothing was comfortable for him, never had been.

He struggled against the rock. Stopped.

He opened his eyes to a picture long ago, an image of a hill and white wooden steps going up. The sound of waves breaking behind. And up ahead, that woman in a white sun dress, long legs pumping, moving quickly up the stair. Long rigid back, spine up to the coral white nape of the neck, and hair done in a tight black bun.

"Get up," she had said.

"I can't."

"I'm not waiting."

And the part of the memory he saw that never seemed real was the dark brown hands that took him up. The strong arms that held him and carried him up the stair from the beach. But never to the woman, his mother, and then always the reality came back that no one had helped him. No man was there, no father, just the servant who was not allowed to help.

"Get up."

Spell curled his legs, let go of the gun and brought his arms back. The rock cut his chest.

"Get up."

"I can't do it."

He pushed against the ground, ripped his side on a jagged outcropping, and suddenly slid up into the open. He had been trapped in a trench. Crawling through, he came to the other side, slanting down, where it was wide open. He ran his hand back along the V-shaped floor and found the gun.

When he laughed the picture of his mother exploded, and he returned to the black.

"I'm getting out of here," he said. And he could stand up on his feet, and walk along slowly in a crouched position. Ignoring the bite in his leg, the way pain slithered up to his inner thigh, he kept moving further down hill.

In time he thought he felt a breath of air coming up the throat of the mountain; cold, damp. His heart came to life, beat hard, though he knew his forehead had become hot and dry. Awake, but ahead he saw shapes moving against the black—things jumping out of the corner of his eye, like those brown phantoms that moved across the empty highway when he had been driving too long. Now, sometimes, they had the shape of an animal, hissed sharply, and several times he stopped, raised his gun, and found the trigger. But before he fired he would realize nothing was there.

Sometimes the breath of air felt cool, like he was coming closer to the source. Then he might pick up his pace, stumble forward for a time.

"Get up," she had always told him. "Keep moving."

As Spell grew, he had understood that she tried to rob him of his father, had him convinced the man wasn't real, and that his name was hers to repeal. For years he could not resist her; he had become like the trained attack dog, forged to beat those who were weaker, yet unable to rush the master. Until that last day at home.

"You can go to hell," he had told her.

But that brought on a rare smile. "What I've given you is more than the mother's love you look for. You'll serve no one, and you'll succeed." In the last argument, years, since he last spoken to her. He had spit in her face and she relished it.

"The soft flesh is weak," she had told him. "But its your spine that holds you up. Makes you different."

"Damn you."

"Then damn your father," she had said.

Eldred could not believe that she spoke of him and he had stood at the door open mouthed.

"I've only cultivated what was in you all the time, what you have from him. Who do you think made me the way I am?"

He ran down the hill, the big white house floating higher and higher above him.

"You're his vengeance on the world," she had called after him. "Not mine."

"Well, I'm done! Finished!" he yelled into the rock walls, blew out what seemed the last of his breath, from a mouth as dry as the inside of a skull. The ground caught his legs, came up abruptly to his knees, kicked sharp pain into them. He threw the gun away, heard it clatter ahead of him.

The cave filled with images, of the people he had shot, of Horton on the rock, of the unseen men he had cut down with his machine gun. He had no count of them, how many he killed.

What was it all for, really? That thing in him he had been so proud of, that kept him one step ahead of the others, kept him alive when he should have been caught long ago, where did it bring him?

Here, a voice said from deep inside.

He winced, clenched his eyes shut until they hurt. Spell stepped into the air above the Valley. Somehow the mountain had parted, fallen away, while the sun burned strong and yellow—a huge circle in the center of his vision. From below, he heard the song of trees, pines bent in a sharp wind. The Valley filled with blue light, clear as water, clean. The roads were empty, the tents without tenants, with the sound of canvas flapping idly in the breeze.

It has not been this way in over a century, the deep voice said. Only one man could do it. Only one man has the strength to cut himself loose from the web of human need, to clear what could not be cleared. You.

The voice came to him as large, strong hands.

"But I'm through," Spell said.

Open your eyes.

He opened them and the Valley faded away sharply, and the black loomed up, filled his sight. The dark breath of the cave blew away, disappeared. He had been walking. And he slipped on a sharp rock, which jabbed rods of pain up his wounded leg, raked the cuts over his ribs. He sprawled flat on the ground, scattering chips of granite.

"I'll never get out," he called out, his voice dry and cracking.

Look up.

Spell turned over, rolled on his back slowly and painfully. He stared up for a long time until the points of light above began to sink into his mind. Stars.

The moon was not up, but as his eyes had long been searching for any light, the stars seemed very bright to him. He thought he saw the dim reflected light of stars against rock as he faced the mountain, but it was not the cliff face he had crawled into. The mountain sloped down until it opened to a small, dark gully. Spell thought he saw a crack in the rock ten or twenty feet above where he lay.

Slowly he sat up, and not far from his feet, across the ghostly rock, he saw a small dark line. Something lying there. Free from the cave, his mind awoke, and he thought of the voice. He had remembered it before, when he had run drunken and foolish through the Valley on his first night—he had dismissed it as a delusion. Yet ideas and visions had come before, and he had learned to obey them.

Spell realized he had been scared, asleep, exhausted in the cave. He ran a hand on his forehead. Probably running a fever. The voice was in his head, a part of him. Speaking to himself in a dream. Yet, as he stood up, shaky on his feet, he could not be sure where the deep voice really came from.

It didn't matter, he thought as he reached for the dark line, picked up his gun, checking it. The Dragunov had come through with him. Whether real or in a dream, what the voice said was all that was important.

What mattered most was that an army had tried to kill him and failed—the people who pushed Ellen into an avalanche were now being pushed by her brother. What mattered was all that Spell had planned for his Valley was coming true. He would not stop now. He had tumbled out of the mountain, weak but alive, and despite the fever he felt, the crippling wound in his calf, he would keep the pressure on them.

Spell started for the black trees below and discovered he had come out on the other side of the ridge. He must have followed the fissure at least two miles until it opened on this side. He recognized where he was, and began to see ahead to what he would do.

Limping, he shouldered the Dragunov. They thought he was gone or dead. But there would be no easing off. Part of him spoke up inside very clearly: he would hit them harder now. But another part of him felt beyond the pain, felt the silence and the embracing air of the dark wood, fell in love with the Valley as it was becoming, this a part of him that was simply glad to be alive, that looked forward to seeing Andrea again. A part of him that had come out of the cave less sure, more passive, yet hearing the stronger voice in his head that said over and over relentlessly: hit them.

XXX

Sarah Ware wanted a puppy, and as she looked across the living room at her father she was thinking about how to reel him in. Karol sat in the big chair, bare feet tapping the floor, listening to an old recording of Gershwin's "I'll Build A Stairway To Paradise" as he read a book. Sarah knew by the sunlight streaming into the cabin, by the quiet meadow outside, and by his tapping feet that Karol did not want to stay inside. She knew that if she could get him out in the South Meadow that he would soften, hear out her puppy proposal again, and she would win him over. Getting him outside was the key.

Sarah had figured out early on that her father was the easy one in the house. As far as she could remember he had never raised his voice to her, and every punishment he devised for her occasional misbehavior always collapsed. She could blow him away by crying, or by pulling out the words, "you don't love me anymore." Grandpa said he was a southern boy with no resolve, but then Sarah could get Jack Hattan to do just about anything she asked, too. Sometimes she played them off each other. Most of all, though, she played her father off her mother. Eli was a brick wall, what she said was law, and sometimes she backed it with a sharp word or a quick slap to the back of the head.

But Sarah rarely disobeyed her father. What she only half understood was that his easy way had wrapped itself around her soul enough that if he gave even the slightest look of disappointment, anything that she read as "you don't love me anymore," she was devastated. Far worse than a harsh word from Eli. Lately, her mother had been so angry most of the time that it didn't take much for her to fly off. If the house was messy when she came home, Karol and Sarah would both get it. Sarah recognized Karol as the buffer from her mother; he had a way of calming her down, of making Eli laugh at herself—something Sarah could never do.

Eli had ordered them to stay inside, and Karol agreed. Sarah was worried about her mother, hunting down the man who shot dogs and people. More worried because she could see that Karol was quieter, even more thoughtful than usual, afraid—she knew what was on his mind. Sarah had to cheer him up, but when she reminded him how great it would be that the two of them were going to spend time at Grandma's in North Carolina, he'd smile but become even more quiet. Her mother would not say much about it, just that they had to go as soon as possible, and would tell them when they could come back. Kind of a vacation, she had said, and Karol had that funny smile on his face when she said it. Sarah worried about him—wanted to see his spirits climb up again.

She depended on him. Growing up in the Valley she had learned quickly that friends came and went. Some rangers had kids but it seemed they always moved on soon. Sometimes she made friends with a boy or girl in the tent camp, part of a family staying a month or so, exchanged addresses when they left—and never wrote nor received a letter. She had friends in the school down in Wawona, but she didn't see them much in the summer. She always had Karol. Taking a walk with her mother was something like a march, always had to keep up—Eli couldn't stand to wait. But her father had the long, slow easy pace that she liked. He kind of drifted across a meadow or wood, was just as apt to follow Sarah as go in his own direction. Her mother pointed everything out, catalogued a flower or lizard and described its habits—just like school—but Karol didn't talk too much. He answered her questions, yes, but he also asked her what she thought. Sometimes they made up stories about the way the plants and animals lived in the Valley that would have made her mother mad. At least that's what Sarah thought. She and her father kept a lot of secrets. Eli didn't believe in secrets.

Sarah quietly put down her book and sat up on the couch. She saw him look out the windows again, for a good long time. He wanted to go out as badly as she did. She could work him, have him out in the meadow in no time, and talk up the puppy again. Her father was being stubborn about it; she knew he had his back up against a wall: his faith in conservation. He kept saying a dog would just wreck the ecology, trample the flowers, chase the wildlife. No Miss, he had told her, he would not have that. But she could tell that he was slipping from his position, and he never told her to stop asking. He was about to say yes, she thought, and once he did they could bring it up to Eli. Sarah didn't know what she would say, most likely it would be no, but once Karol was behind it he could get her to agree. Sarah could ask, and it would be no—but Karol could sway her. Almost always he could do it. Most times Sarah asked her mother through her father. That always worked better.

"What are you reading?" Sarah asked.

"It's a new volume of poems out from Princeton," he looked at the cover of the book and frowned. "Called *Love Is Biodegradable*—good ideas, but the author ain't got no rhythm. You interested?" He pitched the book at her and she laughed.

"How are your Ray Bradbury stories? *R Is For Rocket*, right?"

"Good." They were too, but she did her best to look very bored.

"We could play a game," he said.

"I would if it were raining. But it doesn't seem right to play indoor games on a morning like this, does it?"

"I'd have to agree." He looked out the window again.

She watched the sun on his face. She liked that he was thin and long, liked the natural tan color of his skin. Smoothest I've touched, Eli once said. Sarah often looked in the mirror for the part of her that looked like him; she was a bit short and stubby now, but she hoped to grow up and look like him, long and slim. Was glad that her skin was like his. Maybe her yellow hair would grow dark brown like his. The most important compliment in her life, the one she looked for in people, was that she was the spitting image of her father. Only Grandpa said she looked like her mother, but Sarah knew that was just his wishful thinking.

"I want to go outside," she said.

"Of course," he looked at her on the couch, her boots on, ready for a hike. "But I don't see how we can. Might take a stroll when it's dark."

"We're missing a great morning, sitting in here."

Karol sat up, still tapping to the Gershwin—"It Ain't Necessarily So"—and looked at his shoes. Those were the words he always used on her to coax her out on a hike. Great morning. And it was; how could he be stuck in the house when the South Meadow, the whole Valley in fact, was almost clear of people the morning after the Fourth of July? About this time the Park should be full of the roar of buses, straining under a diesel haze, as the holiday crowd got one last wallow in the river before they went back to the city.

He felt Sarah's soft brown eyes on him; she was working him over. He pulled out his pocket watch, glanced at the time—Eli would not be back until noon, finishing an early shift on patrol in the woods. She would never know if they took a quick look around the South Meadow.

"C'mon." Sarah could almost read his mind.

"Your mother said we should stay indoors, at least during the day. We've got just two days before we fly out of here to Grandma's. We can stay in for two days."

"I can't."

"I know, but I happen to agree with your mother."

"No you don't. You want to get out of here as bad as I do."

"Well." He watched a new hatching of butterflies meander across patches of cow parsnip and milkweed. He had felt bad about telling Eli off three nights before, especially since he had promised not to drink. But her damned father. Last night Eli managed to get home early, and insisted on cooking dinner—apparently she had felt as bad about that night as he did. She tortured Sarah, bossed her around the kitchen, but the two of them had managed to come up with a pretty fine meal. Her usual—chili and cornbread, although she had added cheese and jalapenos to the bread. Sarah couldn't eat it, but they had all managed to laugh about Eli's Hell Bread.

So he did not want to push his wife now. They were on the right course, in full agreement that they had to get Sarah to North Carolina and out of the Valley. He'd usually slip around Eli's orders; staying indoors felt cowardly and ridiculous after all. But she was having a hard time and didn't need him to be screwing around.

Sarah watched Karol. She knew he was struggling with it and so waited for him to come around.

What bothered Karol most was that he would never see the Valley like it was now. Soon enough the siege would be off and the crowds would come pouring back. Already Heston was planning some big discounts and enticements to pull the tourists in. The Valley would be a mess again, people tromping all over the meadow. It would never be so clear, so much like his own, again. Out in the meadow now, hushed but for the wind in the pines and the hum of insects, Karol could feel dozens of poems. The music out there, the sound of centuries, would be sunk forever once the people came back.

He heard the screen door bang. Sarah had quit waiting, so she ran out into the meadow, giggling.

"Undisciplined child." He smiled and pulled on his Rockports. He shoved a pencil and notepad into his pocket, turned off the old phonograph, and stuck on his old straw hat. He stepped out onto the porch.

"Sarah," he called to her. "We're staying out for a half hour. No more." She waited. He walked to her, thinking that Eli would never know. But he did wonder if Jack were around; if so, he'd report everything to his daughter and that would be hell. The old man would love it, and that was the worst thing. Karol was taking a chance.

"Maybe just twenty minutes," he said.

"Okay." But Sarah knew she could keep him out most of the day if she wanted to.

He took her hand and they walked to the center of the South Meadow, and then he stopped them. He motioned for her to sit.

"I want you to listen to this," he said.

"What?"

"Be quiet. Absolutely still."

He thought he could hear everything, straining his ears. He heard the stellar jays in the woods, the drone of a bee flying heavily by, and things slithering down low, causing the tall grass to hiss. He believed he could hear the wind come over the edge of the cliffs, believed he could hear the occasional rock fall and clatter to the bottom of the wall, and the soft hum of the Valley waterfalls in deep chorus. Nothing polluted this clear, ancient music. "That's the sound no one has heard in this Valley for years. It takes you away to another time, and it will never be like this again." He closed his eyes, leaned back, and let the sun slip in under the rim of his hat.

"Dad?" Sarah was ready to make her move. She could see how the meadow had softened him.

"What?"

"I really need a puppy—you know, a dog."

"Now why would I want to have this all messed up by the barking of some animal?"

"I get lonely," she said. It wasn't really true most of the time, but she knew what worked on him.

"Really?"

"I don't have a lot of friends."

Well, he thought, I suppose there's a point.

"Didn't you have a dog when you were a boy?" She knew perfectly well that he had, and she was hitting home. "Wasn't a dog your best friend?"

"My dear, I believe you're putting the bite on me."

"Didn't you have a dog?"

"Of course." Karol opened his eyes, stroked his daughter's long blonde hair, and stood up. They walked across the meadow, toward the dark edge of trees, while she asked him about the dog. Soon she had him going on Sam, his Walker hound and Saint Bernard mix, the ridge runner that stuck by him as a boy. She brought him back to his long walks in the mountains of North Carolina, hikes on Savannah Ridge, and she made him remember how important the companionship of a dog had been.

They walked through a stand of ponderosa pines and went back toward the meadow, keeping clear of the road. He did not want any of Eli's friends spotting them while on patrol; she would no doubt hear about it. All the while Sarah kept on about Sam, even wondered if there could be that kind of dog in

California. She made him stop and show just how tall Sam had been, and he held out his hands to demonstrate the size of the dog's white paws.

As they came back to the edge of the meadow, Sarah hit home. "I wish I could have a dog like Sam."

"I suppose you do." Karol smiled; she was slick.

"We could train him not to mess up the Valley," she reached for his hand again.

"No doubt." Come to think of it, he thought, Sam wasn't much of a hunter anyway.

"So can I have a dog?"

"We'll see."

But they both knew that with Karol, that was the same as saying yes. As she gave him a hug around the waist, Karol saw something move ahead in the grass. He stiffened.

"My God," he whispered.

"What?"

"There he is again." He pointed it out, the pine martin, a sleek, ferret-like animal that he had seen only once before in the meadow. He had tried to get close to it then, but it shot back into the woods, about where they were standing. For a martin to come down into the Valley in broad daylight was rare indeed. He hoped Sarah could get a closer look, and had an idea.

"Listen," he told her, crouching down. "I'll circle around the martin, staying wide of him, and then I'll slowly come at him from behind. If you just stay back, real quiet, I'll bet he'll practically run up into your lap."

"Do they bite?" she asked.

"Don't worry," he rubbed the top of her head. "He won't come that close, but you might get a good look."

He crept forward into the open meadow, moving slowly as if he were on the hunt. Once the martin, fur glossy and amber bright in the morning sun, rose up on a dead long and looked around. Karol became still, and the martin went back down to look for mice.

He finally came around to the back of the animal, and peered up to see where Sarah was. He looked hard but could not see her; she had hidden well. He stepped forward carefully, eyes on the glistening back of the martin, when he heard an odd zip in the air.

Sarah watched him carefully, eyes to him and then the martin. She saw the animal abruptly leap away, to the side instead of toward her. The flash of her father's white hat caught her eye, but when she looked up she could not see him. The pine martin had scampered out of view, disappearing in the grass.

Sarah waited, but when she still could not find Karol she walked out into the meadow, following a straight line toward where she had seen him last. Perhaps he was playing a game, hiding in the tall grass, but she was surprised he had given up on the martin. She caught sight of his hat, hanging on a tall weed. As she walked toward it he came into view, lying flat on the ground, still. Something about it bothered her and she ran to him. And when she saw the blood on the grass by his chest, more blood than she had ever seen in her life, and the way his head was twisted around on the ground, and the white look in his eye as he stared up at her out of the dirt, she stopped.

At first Karol had felt a sharp blow to his chest, like a fist passing through it, and he fell to the ground. But the pain gave way to the realization that he could not breathe, as if he had forgotten how. He had been on his side, but when he felt the blood spurting from his chest, hot and sticky, he rolled over, so she would not see. He turned to look for Sarah—his head suddenly became very heavy.

When she came, after what seemed a very long time, he was losing his sight. He wanted to tell her to run away, but had no breath for his voice. The last thing he did see was the way she looked down at him, completely confused, and above all the pain and panic of dying he knew that they had lost each other forever. I am so sorry, he thought at last, so, sorry Sarah.

Eldred Spell lowered his gun. He had not expected the girl. He had seen the man stalking some kind of animal in the meadow and decided to blow him away and hit them hard, right near the heart of the Valley. Spell had been walking by, just in the trees, looking for someone, and here was this man out in the meadow. A perfect shot. But after he went down she ran out to him. It was not the way she looked at him now, stone still, staring, that bothered Spell. It was the way she had looked for him, smiling, as if her father had been playing some kind of game. Hide and seek.

He could not look at her anymore. He wiped his brow, hot with fever. Spell limped through the woods, following a route he had planned. Going for the river. He did not know what the girl would do, how long it would take for someone to find out. They seemed alone. She seemed very young. He stopped occasionally, briefly, to wipe his eyes. They stung him.

At a dark bend of the river, overhung with thick pines, he came out. He saw no one. Spell had lost his pack in the cave, and he had no way to hide the gun. None of his caches were anywhere nearby, and he did not have the time nor strength to reach one. All of his energy, everything he had left, went into the discipline of being invisible that McCrimmon had taught him. Spell came to a deep pool at the river, a place where a large boulder loomed over swirling white water. Very deep. He looked at the Dragunov. And when he waded out to the edge of the pool, he pitched it into the water. It sank down out of sight. Sometime he might come back for his once-treasured rifle, but he did not think so. He wanted to be as far away from it as possible.

His wound had become dark and ugly. In the woods he rebound it in a filthy handkerchief and covered it over with his pant leg. The river water had washed off most of the blood. The pain shot up his leg every time he put weight on it, but under the cover of the forest he practiced walking normally for a few minutes. He then left the river—he had little time.

On the road out of the Park he looked carefully for patrol cars. He found none; in fact, there were few cars at all. At a pull-off ahead he saw an old van, with a bunch of young campers, college types. All men. Perfect, as if they had been waiting to pick him up. He fought the lightheadedness of the fever and ignored the pain of his leg as he walked on it. He fought something else, screaming from somewhere inside, and the pain actually helped him ignore it.

They were on the way out of the Valley, headed to San Francisco State, and they gave him a ride to Fresno. One of them offered him a hit from the joint they fired up, but he said he was just too tired. He pretended to sleep until they drove out the Park gate. Then he slept. Less than a half hour after shooting the man, he had escaped again. The little girl must have been slow to alert anyone.

They dropped him off at the Fresno Regional Airport overnight parking lot, as he had asked them to do. They were happy to take the fifty dollars he offered. He limped heavily to his Jaguar. He had not planned on being gone so long. For a moment he was afraid that his keys were in his pack, lost in the cave, but they were still in his pocket.

He settled into his car, his leg stiffening quickly. Spell looked briefly at himself in the rearview mirror, and then he turned away. The little girl had broken something in that voice that drove him, and for now he could not hear it at all. He wished that he could. Perhaps he had come close to the very picture that he had been seeking, the father and child in the meadow—that clean image, a picture he had erased.

"What now?" His voice sounded dry, without force, and very hollow.

The deep voice had no answer.

THREE

XXXI

Eli and Sarah took the train east, because they both knew that was the way Karol would have wanted his ashes carried. He had not believed in air travel, and planned to fly with Sarah only because Eli had insisted on the practicality of it. He thought that people should move slower, live closer to the earth. So the small box that contained his remains traveled on Amtrak. The closest railhead to Jackson County, where Karol's mother lived, was south of the North Carolina border, in Toccoa, Georgia. They had not slept well in the three nights on the train, and found little of interest in the scenery that passed by. The journey was almost at an end, the next stop Toccoa, and they sat quietly in coach, bags ready at their feet.

Sarah had cried hard and often, but Eli did not. That was one of the things that made a widening gap between them. They needed Karol to bridge this space, and had not known how wide it was until he was gone. Eli sat in her blue jeans, dark near Sarah's yellow cotton summer dress. It had already collected a tea and jelly stain from breakfast, but Sarah was adamant she wear the dress for Grandma, since Karol had brought it home a month before.

No one could be sure how long Sarah had stood transfixed over her father. Olivos thought it might have been an hour, based on the time of death determined by the county coroner. Olivos himself had caught a glimpse of Sarah standing alone from a gap in the trees along the road north of the meadow. He had pulled over, walked into the meadow, and began to trot when he noticed how she was staring down and would not answer his call. He knew she was not supposed to be out, especially as a standing target almost dead center in the South Meadow. Then he found Karol.

Eli had been walking with a team on the Muir trail when she was called in. Cairns himself radioed, but would not say what he wanted. When they sent out a helicopter to bring her in, she started to worry. When she met Cairns at headquarters, and all the other people seemed to have been cleared away for the meeting, she felt worse. He told her, looking everywhere but at her, in the same odd soft voice she remembered he had used for the avalanche victim's lover months before. She cut him off in mid-sentence, didn't want to hear any condolences from him, and told him she wanted to go home. Eli had to move.

When they had come to the meadow and she saw the people standing around, looking down, she did not wait for Cairns's truck to come to a stop. She leapt out and ran, broke through Olivos, who lamely tried to stop her, and she knelt by Karol. Could only touch a spot of flesh exposed above his sock, confirmed that the skin was cool and already seemed stiff. Ever since, even on the train, she felt that cool skin on her fingertips.

Then she had jumped up. Olivos wisely kept the reporters far back when she sprinted to the cabin. In the living room she found Sarah, bent down, crying hard, in the arms of a woman doctor. The woman moved away and Eli put her arm around her daughter. She did not know what to do, but it seemed that Olivos, Cairns, the strange doctor, all looked at her as if they waited for her to break down. Eli searched for her father, who stood in the corner of the living room, hemmed in between two windows. He nodded to her stiffly, could not seem to take her looking at him. He fidgeted with his hands, rubbing them, nodded once more, and then walked out of the cabin.

Eli could not cry.

She had seen little grief in her life. No one close to her or her father had died. Her mother had left long ago, and that felt like a wound that would never quite heal. But there was not the sharp blow of death. Once, Rex Murdoch, an old friend of her father's—a man he praised as one of the true old-timers—had died in an accident. Though about 70 years old, the man had been fond of hiking to the higher country and challenging the deep pools of the river during the spring runoff. A circular pool he especially enjoyed had a natural whirlpool and he liked to test his strength against it. One day they found him sunk in the center, shirt off—he had jumped in and not made it out. Some said he must have suffered from a heart attack, or that year's unusually high spring water, to lose against the current.

Her father drank a lot as a remembrance, and told Eli the more likely story was that Rex felt weakness and age creeping in, and took the plunge to get it over with sooner than later. Suicide from a position of strength, he had called it. As Rex had no family, Eli watched her father settle the man's affairs. Jack Hattan liked to take death from the business end, he had said. When the few possessions were disseminated and Rex's old cabin was signed over to the Park in eminent domain, Jack said that was that. He never shed a tear, nor seemed sad. He just went into action. And that was Eli's model for grief, the only encounter she had with it.

So she was not surprised that her father had walked out, although she did not like it. But he did leave her to handle the business alone; Eli saw that the autopsy and reports were done quickly. She made the call to Meredith Ware, Karol's mother, and insisted the old woman not try to come out to the Valley. Eli wanted to put off seeing her, did not need Grandma sharing Sarah's crying jags, moments that made Eli feel uncomfortable and inadequate. There would be enough crying in North Carolina. She managed to get the cremation done quickly; she stood stiffly at the Park memorial service, which Olivos had done a lot to arrange. Jack neglected to come.

They had gathered at the outdoor chapel, sitting on rows of crude split logs under a canopy of pine branches. The nondenominational minister said a few words while patrols up in the hills defended the listeners. Reporters stood at the outer edge of the mourners. It seemed everyone waited for Eli to cry. Her daughter most of all. But Sarah did enough sobbing for them both.

Eli had already made mistakes with Sarah. Without Karol, she knew that she and her daughter would need to work into a new relationship, a closer one that Eli had always wanted but did not quite know how to go about. But Eli had begun wrong.

There had been that first clear space the morning after Karol's death, when for a time the two of them were alone in the cabin. They sat at the table, staring at bowls of granola soaking in milk. The silence and the fact that Sarah would not look up began to irritate Eli. A reporter had gotten through, called them on the phone, and Eli told him to go to hell. The outburst gave some relief to her, for she felt as if her soul had been coiling up inside all the long sleepless night. Muscles tightening on the bone—she had been hit and her reaction was to move, fight or flight. With Eli that meant fight.

After slamming the phone down she went back to the table and stared at her daughter. The silence tightened on Eli, and the ticking antique wall clock that Karol once bought felt like a ratchet, winding her up.

"Sarah," she said, trying her softest voice.

The girl looked up, eyes watering and red, a sickly look that irritated Eli more.

"Sarah." Slightly louder this time.

The girl stared silently.

"Can you tell me why—" Eli stopped, could not ask that question, even though it had been on her mind for nearly 24 hours. She tried another. "Can you tell me how long you stood by your father?"

Sarah shook her head.

"Did it seem like a half hour? Maybe an hour?" She wanted to reach out and touch Sarah's hand, started to, and stopped. It was difficult. Eli caught herself instinctively looking for Karol. Back to business. "Sarah, it's important. If you have any idea. It might help us figure out how the, how he got out. We want to stop him."

"Can't stop him," Sarah whispered, looking down. "We should have left, like Daddy said."

"You were leaving, just as fast as could be."

"We could have left sooner, like Daddy wanted."

"That's not true." Then the coil in Eli unwound a bit more and she spat the words out. "What I really want to know, Sarah, was why you two were out in the meadow at all. I told you not to go out there."

Sarah slapped the cereal bowl off the table, turned and ran out of the room. Later, Eli had gone to her door, listened to her cry, and cursed herself for not being more careful. She could not handle it all as smoothly as Karol would have; Eli figured she never could go as deep as he could. He had always been one to be in touch with his feelings, and she had been raised to think being in touch was a load of bullshit for whiners. As she stood outside that door, emotions jangled inside her, feelings she did not like.

On the train, alone together, Eli felt a bit more in control of herself. Hoped that the long gash that Karol's death had left in her was beginning to heal. She focused on her daughter, tried to make conversation and ignored the frustration when she couldn't reach her. She had only the slightest, secondhand idea of the things Sarah and Karol had talked about.

By the train window, though, with their reflections together in the glass, Eli thought she could interest Sarah in the new scenery. Eli talked, sometimes fast and desperate, about the change in the land outside. The ecology, climatology, geology in the movement east, as the earth went from tan to red, as the trees thickened, lowland rivers stayed full even in late July, and the humidity of muddy waters gathered in the air. She tried to hold back on the long lectures, tried not to bury Sarah in the information, and sometimes a conversation would blow up like a fitful fire in a breeze.

Then Eli had made another mistake. For three days she had been averting her eyes from the papers and magazines spread open in coach and the diner car. Once she saw a photograph of Karol in the meadow, captured by a *Time* photographer. She looked away, and felt Sarah squeeze her hand harder. The wire inside Eli tightened, tugged her inside so that it almost was a physical pain.

During the last dinner in the dining car, while they had rattled through Mississippi, a conversation from another table drifted over their silent meal. A young couple, seemed just married, talked over the man's open magazine. He spoke pointedly about the failure in the Park, said that bunch of rangers should been cleared out of there—let the FBI and maybe the National Guard move in. How hard could it be to catch a band of eco-terrorists? Eli took it, until she saw Sarah turn and listen.

"C'mon," Eli said in a low voice to her daughter.

She tried to walk by the couple's table, but he kept on about the Park Service's ineptitude, and she stopped when he said something about letting another death in the Valley just slip by.

"You don't know much about the Park Service, do you?" Eli looked down at the man and his magazine.

"Excuse me?" He looked up, curious. But the woman with him saw the look in Eli's face, and she felt nervous.

Sarah had let go of her mother's hand, moving away.

"What the hell do you know about what's going on there?"

"I'm not sure what you mean." The man closed his periodical and looked at his wife. Sometimes he spoke too loud, people said he was opinionated, so he really had a sense of what she meant.

Eli grabbed the magazine in one snatch, threw it down in the narrow aisle. His coffee cup had spilled, and somehow that made Eli angrier.

"Listen, asshole." She hissed at him, put her face in his, made him back up in his seat. "I work for the Park Service. I'm a ranger in that fucking Valley. Lived there all my life. And that dead man you've been reading about is my husband. Got his ashes in this train right now, in a box. My daughter saw it happen, stood over him in shock while the bastard got clean away. Stood over him for a long time, wouldn't you?"

He had nothing to say, but looked around for a steward, for someone to help. He was frightened by the way she clenched her fists and leaned over him, and believed she was going to hit him. Get hit by a strange woman in front of his new young wife—he had no idea what to do.

His silence enraged Eli. "You bastard," she yelled. "What do you know about it, sitting here, two thousand miles from it?"

She saw that everyone in the car was looking at her now, noticed that two stewards stared at her from one end of the car. They looked frozen, helpless.

"What the fuck do you know?" she yelled again, but this time not just at the man but at the entire car. And then she saw that Sarah had gone.

So, the morning Eli and Sarah pulled in to Toccoa, they sat in the coach seat and had nothing to say to each other. Though she had been dreading Meredith Ware, did not want to see any new displays of grief, she realized the grandmother would be some relief. Eli would have time to get some distance from her daughter, take a breather, and try again. Worst of all, though, she felt that wire tightening in her when the brakes of the train screeched and they came to a stop. She had hoped that the outburst in the dining car would make her feel better, as long as it had happened, but it did not.

Meredith Ware waited at the station in Toccoa, standing on a bare cement platform near a small Amtrak office that rarely housed an employee. Across the tracks the vacant lot was high with weeds and stunted locust trees. When Eli stepped off the train behind Sarah, the air felt thick and heavy. Already the light morning sky had faded to a greasy brown color as the humid air choked the sun.

Sarah ran ahead, into the arms of her grandmother. As much to commiserate as to get away from me, Eli thought. She walked slowly, in no hurry, watching them both sob. Karol's height had come from his father, long gone from pancreatic cancer, but the leanness had come from Meredith. Though a short woman, she had the figure of a girl when seen from behind in a dress. Until one saw the bun of white hair gathered tight in the back. Soft as Meredith was inside, Eli always admired how sharp and neat she kept herself. And now, when the old woman looked up at last from Sarah, Eli recalled where Karol's large soft brown eyes had come from. And the long nose. Meredith's narrow face, browned in the sun, brownest against the white of her hair, seemed a miniature of Karol's face. Eli had not remembered that, for it had been years since she had seen the woman.

Meredith opened her arms, but Eli held out her hand. They shook awkwardly, and Eli felt her daughter's eyes.

"I'm very sorry." Eli did not use her name, always had trouble with what to call her—Karol had told her that she expected "mother," but Eli just could not say it. So she never called Meredith anything.

"I know you are."

They stood quietly for a moment until Eli could not pause any longer.

"I'll get the bags from the porter." She needed to get to business. That's what her father would do.

"The porter can carry them to the car—it's that old white Lincoln there."

"I can carry the bags." Eli saw the porter place the bags down by the tracks, the few people who were getting off were already in the little parking lot. The train would soon go. Next to Eli's two suitcases and overnight bag was a carefully wrapped tan box.

She managed the suitcases and the overnight bag. Without a word, Meredith picked up the box. With everything in the trunk, they began the two hour drive to Jackson County. Sarah sat up front, and the grandmother drove. The old woman wisely kept the subject to the train trip, other things would come later, at a proper time. Eli sat in back, soon falling asleep in the air conditioning and relief of not having to make conversation.

That afternoon, as they settled into the large old Ware house on Savannah Ridge, Meredith insisted Sarah go down for a nap after the long trip. Eli sat on the porch, noticing the fresh wood of a new deck that expanded from the front of the house. Beyond, past the steep slope of a large lawn, was a view of the Blue Ridge Mountains. Eli had a glass of iced tea in her hand, though she did not drink it. She heard the old woman upstairs, heard her come down slowly.

Meredith stepped out the front door, holding Jack's .45 in her hand. The heavy gun hung from where she held it by the barrel. She looked hard at Eli, tan face flushed red.

"Where did you find that?" Eli asked, standing up from the rocker. She put her iced tea on a small round table.

"Had to get Sarah's teeth brushed before the nap." The woman's voice shook. "I found this in your overnight bag."

"Lately—" Eli stopped. She had kept a gun with her for the last several weeks, and it just seemed natural to stay armed. She had put it in the overnight bag without a second thought.

"My Karol was shot," Meredith said.

Eli saw the heavy gun swing slightly in her hand.

"Can't you imagine how I would feel about this now?" She shook the gun. "I won't have it."

And she did something that surprised Eli. The old woman pitched the gun into the front yard, straining in a long underhand throw. Eli watched her father's gun skid down the grass slope a few feet.

Looking straight into Eli's eyes, Meredith said slowly, very clearly: "I am angry."

"Well," Eli exhaled, looking at the gun. "At last you and I have something in common."

XXXII

Spell had no idea what had awakened him from the comfortable cotton stupor he had fallen into. Then his mind recalled a sensation, rewound through his senses, of a sharp pin in his arm. But he felt something more now, much more acute and lasting, like a blade slicing his flesh. He abruptly opened his eyes, looked into the white sheet, saw that he was face down on a bed. Hard mattress. Voices.

"Hold his leg here."

"Are you sure?"

"Yes. He's awake, and he won't like this."

The hands were cold and tight on his left leg. Then the blade came down again, picked at his open wound. Spell flinched, the hands gripped harder, and he could barely move anyway. Muscles slow, squirming in cement. But the cutting shot clean through to his mind, nothing muddled the pain.

"What is this?" Words came slowly out of his mouth, in thick bubbles of saliva. "What?"

"It's all right."

He recognized the voice, had to think: it was Doug Evers.

"Ah," he breathed out. Not more than a whisper. The probing knife on his infected flesh, cutting away. It stopped. Spell turned his head, saw a room, very white, something like his old office and not a hospital room. White table, orchid floating in a crystal bowl, mirror above, redwood shutters pulled open, and a bank of dark blue fog out the window. Haze of a distant streetlight.

The fear of pain stuck like a needle puncturing his brain, alerting him, waking him further. He remembered little of the drive, it seemed the Jaguar had led the way. Followed lines and signs, and somewhere down the coast, close to Monterey, just past Fort Ord—very clear now—an image from the trip more vivid. The highway in the late afternoon at times had jumped without warning, skipped like a film off the track in a projector. He had worried about stopping, kept going, knew that to stop would attract a highway patrolman. Knew that if he stopped he might just fall asleep, while the fear of running off the road held him together just a little longer.

Spell had wanted to go straight to the Spyglass, to Andrea, but the deep voice in him said that his body was failing. He could not go to a doctor, and passed the exit for the hospital. Stopped across the street from The Vantage Point. The store had just closed. Pounded on the door, and a woman—Mrs. Evers—answered. He had never seen her before, and remembered no more than a tangle of black hair now. Evers came, she disappeared, and Spell found himself in Doug's truck. Spell waited. Then Evers drove, said he had made some calls.

Here. The blade cut again, deeper. Spell tried to move his leg, but the muscles were sluggish, felt overheated. Sweat dripped into his eye. He turned his head, looked back, saw the small woman raise the little knife, looked at the small triangular blade in the light, a smear of blood. Then she bent to work again.

"God." Spell bit his lower lip hard, screwed his eyes shut, and saw the yellow shapes he had come to depend on in the cave.

"She's almost finished," Evers said. "She just needs to cut the rest of the dead skin away. You, you have a pretty bad hole in your calf, right here."

"Shut up, Mr. Evers," the woman said, in a quiet, delicate voice. "I'm working."

"Oh, God."

Finally he heard the blade clink as it hit the bottom of a metal dish.

"I'm done," she said.

A long breath emptied him, and the fog rolled in thick and warm, filling his eyes and ears. As Spell slipped away, he felt movement, hands moving his legs, helping him down the long dark slide.

When he awoke again, staring around the room, he realized he had been in the bed for some time: wrinkled sheets wet with sweat, his heavily bandaged calf exposed, lifted slightly by a pillow. He lay on his back. The lower end of the sun hung from the top of the window, the sky clear, and he heard the screech of a distant sea gull. Another day.

Once again Spell worked to recall how he had arrived, and the images came to him a little quicker and clearer this time. Still, he had no idea where he was.

The sun had climbed out of view by the time she came into the room. A dark Asian woman, a face of lines cut by sun, and darker spots on her cheeks burned in by the days. Skeletal round head, bony hands, and a thin, erect frame under a plain light grey dress. Wide streaks of grey in long black hair that hung thick around her shoulders; that seemed out of place, the thick healthy hair loose like a young woman's. She gently lifted his calf, observed the bandage, and set it back down.

"Lift your arm," she said, and shoved a thermometer under it. They looked at each other quietly for some time while she waited. Then she pulled it out, looked, nodded, and set it on the small white table.

Spell discovered that he was naked under the sheet.

"Who are you?" he asked.

"The more important question concerns who you are." She pulled up a small cane chair to his bedside.

Spell looked at her closely; there was no curiosity in the way she looked at him. Very calm, placid.

"Doug Evers told you about me."

"He did," she smiled briefly. "You are quite an eco-terrorist."

Spell had read the theories about eco-terrorists in the Park and he felt odd being described that way. They were part of a group, and he had no interest in them. What he was doing in the Park was entirely his own, and not of any larger organization. Then he remembered the little girl in the field, suddenly, recalled that she had been swimming through his mind waking and sleeping, somehow part of the pain he felt, the throbbing that shook his body. But that pain was easing off, he hoped.

"I'm not an eco-terrorist," he said.

"Not in the traditional sense." She continued to stare at him. "If so, I would have known of you by now."

"Are you an eco-terrorist?"

"I am a professor emeritus of Stanford."

"A doctor?"

"Yes." She laughed. "But in chemistry. You, of all people, should know by now that I am no M.D. I'm surprised you're still alive."

"How am I?"

"Good, actually. You had quite an infection, but fairly localized. No doubt you have a strong constitution." She leaned closer. "Do you know what attacked you?"

"I didn't see it."

Spell felt strange talking to anyone about what he did in the Park. Almost embarrassed. He had Andrea completely convinced that he had taken a leave from his job as a stockbroker—in Chicago, he had told her—to train as a marathon runner. Told her he was fulfilling a dream that had consumed him, and she seemed to admire him for it. No doubt his thin, sinewy body had the look of a runner, and he had indeed done quite a bit of scrambling in the last few months. He told Doug Evers almost nothing, kept things to business, although Doug often seemed anxious to get to know him. Spell used the money and Doug's hope of a certain kind of relationship as leverage; it had worked well, for Doug had brought him to this woman. But Spell did not know her, and wanted to tell her as little as possible.

"Who are you?" Spell asked again.

"Suko Egusa. The one who supplied the rather complex derivative that kept the tracking dogs out of the Park."

"So you are an eco-terrorist."

"I serve quite a few causes. Needs for sophisticated chemistry are various." She stood up. "I'd rather not be put into a category."

"You've helped Doug in the past. Is he involved in a group?"

She laughed again, short and quiet. "He would like to be. He's a sheep who runs with the wolves—he admires you very much."

Egusa left him and went to the kitchen. She heated up a soup rich in beef blood, stirring in long strips of meat. Water on the gas stove came to a boil, and she poured it through an ornate silver strainer of green tea leaves; the steam smelled like fresh-cut grass.

Mr. Spell had been in her house for three days, and she was glad that he was well, that his temperature was down and he would be able to take care of himself. She would have Doug pick him up this afternoon. The man was an interesting specimen, shot through with the kind of relentlessness only possible in the most violent society she had known. His kind was why she came to the United States, to a people capable of the most single-minded action. Rugged, bloody individualism. Always interesting when they turned it on themselves; this man had them on their knees.

Egusa inhaled the steam and looked out toward the Pacific. She had worked in an air power plant factory in Kobe during the war. A girl only 16 years old. Her father, a plant manager with a degree from the University of Chicago, had secretly been appalled at the destructive turn of Imperial Japan. The war in the Pacific had dismayed him—the massive conflict between two merciless cultures. He had become completely unstrung by the nighttime fire bombings in March 1945, while she had been the only one in the family who adjusted to the city wastelands created by the war, who took the struggle in quiet perspective.

After the factory she worked in had been destroyed, she toiled with a group of women attempting to salvage bolts of cloth from the tangled heap of a textile warehouse near the shore. Air raid sirens went off one afternoon when a group of B-29s passed high overhead like a formation of silver ghosts. She and dozens of other workers ran out toward the beach–bombs did not fall, as Suko learned much later the planes came to drop mines in the harbor. But a squadron of P-51 Mustangs roared in from the sky as if they would strafe the people. She ran with the others into the water. Suko stood in waist deep, completely exposed with no place to hide. The water seemed very transparent to her that day. As the last of the planes flew over without firing, she felt the insulation of Imperial Japan fade around her. She watched the victors quickly disappear in the sky, and Egusa knew she would leave Japan.

That day had changed her life, although there were many more like it to follow. After the war, she came to the United States, where as a young Japanese woman in the American universities she became tougher. Began her research and teaching career in small colleges in the east, but had such successes that at last she came west and settled in Stanford on the junior faculty in 1968. Never married, never went that soft. She observed that the Americans actually grew in violence, sharpening against themselves in urban riots, rural militias, drug wars. When she visited Japan, walking the Rapongi in Tokyo, with all the prettily dressed boy-men and girl-women of fat prosperity, she knew she had made the right choice. Life was actually safer and always more interesting within the walls of the United States than outside.

She looked at the white strip of coast from her picture window; that day of 1945 was one she thought of often. The soup was ready, as was the tea, so she brought these in a tray to Spell. She watched him eat; he was hungry, and he finished very efficiently.

"Do you really plan to clear the Valley?" she asked him.

Spell just looked at her; it was something he would not talk about.

"But they have not closed it yet, have they?" She left the room and came back with a copy of *Time*. "You may have closed the trails around the Valley, and you've just about shut down the Muir Hotel, but the Park superintendent vows in this issue that he will not close the Park. They're still getting a few thousand tourists a day. What do you think of that?"

"I think I'd like to try to put on my clothes," Spell said. He did wonder why the Park had not closed; he thought it would have long ago, but he said nothing.

"The fact is, you can't get what you want with a few random deaths, a dead dog here or there, some shot-out windows."

Spell watched her roll the magazine up and hold it tightly in her bony hands. He sipped the last of his bitter tea; he knew green tea, and she had made it too strong.

"You need some chemistry." She nodded to him. "If you have the resolve."

"What do you mean?"

"Forget the shootings. I've studied the situation. To close the Park, you destroy the water source. There's a water tank at the north end of the river."

"I know of it." She had a point; he recalled that he no longer had his long rifle. And he knew that he had been lucky; in a visit or two, they would surely catch him.

"Of course you do." This man was perfect, she thought, few could go as far. What she could do through him would be amazing. "It would take a thimble full of a variety of sarin, dumped in the tank, and that would be the end of the Park. The Valley would be clear."

"Poison them all?" Spell saw the hairline crack running through one of her long incisors as she smiled broadly. He wished she would give him his clothes.

"I could provide it. In one visit, your job would be done."

Spell looked at her, could tell she was serious. He pulled his sheet up a bit as she took away his tray suddenly. Suko Egusa was a frightening old woman. But her idea about the water tank at Happy Isles made perfect sense.

XXXIII

Eli watched a four-foot-long black snake slowly navigate the lawn and slither into the shade of a row of tomato plants. Across the valley the Blue Ridge mountains were buried in a thick hedge of thunderclouds. The leaves in the big red oak that sheltered one end of the deck rustled lightly, telling Eli that an August storm was probably building behind her, pouring over Savannah ridge. The grass still glistened in the orange sun, wet from the squall that had passed over and on to the mountains across the valley. Eli drained off the last of her raspberry iced tea, a sweet drink she never would have touched when she arrived in Jackson County nearly a month before.

Nothing had happened in the Park, except for one bit of good news. A week after Eli had left with Sarah, a gun was found in the river. A prototype of a sophisticated Soviet gun, a kind of Dragunov rifle that few in the world knew anything about. A hiker had walked far down the river one day, felt hot, and dove into a deep pool. His leg touched something cold and metallic, and he went back down for a closer look. The hiker pulled it out of the water, and headed back for his car. Before he made it to his Nissan in the parking lot, he found himself surrounded by a cloud of unmarked patrol cars and nervous men in suits. He was ordered to drop the gun, and then he had been taken into headquarters for some hard questioning. The condition of the gun, already grown over with a thin coat of algae, and the fact that his alibis checked out, meant the hiker was soon released. The young man swore that all he had planned to do was take the Dragunov to headquarters. He did say he had never seen such an attractive rifle.

Eli received a call from Olivos, who wanted to tell her that the gun was definitely the murder weapon—used in every shooting except the one that hit Lenahan. But there were no prints on it. Then, after the news, Olivos hung on the line, trying to drag out the conversation, asking several times when Eli would be back. Soon, she told him.

But, to her surprise, she felt content to continue her leave of absence. In her last phone conversation with Cairns, he did not seem to care when she came back. Eli figured he did not want to see her, to be face to face with another reminder of failure. And with Eli and Sarah in North Carolina, there would be less chance of an embarrassing interview. The last time Cairns called her, he was so hopeful with the discovery of the gun that he did not seem interested in her at all—preoccupied with a victory at last. One unnamed FBI agent said the gun was so rare, tracking the owner would be easier—if Russian officials cooperated. The agent said that once the FBI had an I.D., the killer would be finished.

Lately, with no other news, the media pushed the story with theories about the killer's retirement or death. He had left his precious gun, and since then nothing had happened in the Valley. Interest in the story waned, and it dropped off the front pages and the nightly broadcasts. Heston Company representatives even had the confidence to predict numbers for the coming Labor Day Weekend would be good. Not normal, but the Valley would not be so empty either. Heavy snowfall had been predicted for the year, Shirley Weaver said, and with no other incidents, and some substantial new discounts, the cross-country ski season in the Park would be spectacular.

When Eli had first come to Meredith's house, the Valley and its problem seemed close, a hot breath on the back of her neck that kept her tossing and turning at night. But scattering Karol's ashes had changed that.

The church ceremony had been very simple, arranged by Meredith. The old woman had left the box of ashes at home, and represented Karol with a large bouquet of flowers cut from her garden. Early that morning, Eli had watched Meredith and Sarah go out into the garden, and even into the surrounding woods for greens and ferns. She watched the two of them come back, working over the sink in the kitchen, discussing how to make an arrangement Karol would have liked. Eli had no idea what that would be, but Sarah and Meredith did, and easily came to agreement. In the back of the Lincoln, Sarah had sat alone, carefully balancing the large, fanlike bouquet on the way to the church.

Most of the people at the Methodist church that Meredith attended were her friends. Eli did meet a plump woman Meredith introduced as Karol's old high school girlfriend, and the old girlfriend cried and shook Eli's hand several times. Eli felt the little congregation of people, as well as Meredith and Sarah, watch her eyes. But she still did not cry, and the minister's voice and the people seemed to float farther and farther away as the service went on.

To Eli, the scattering of ashes had seemed the only memorial that really mattered–the reason they had come to North Carolina. Meredith made sure that the three of them came home alone, and they quietly changed. When they were wearing hiking boots and jeans, Eli felt much more comfortable. The old woman said she did not care much for a hike at all, and did not care for the way the blue jeans chafed, but she carried the plastic box herself and led the way. The narrow trail switch backed up the side of Savannah, cutting through a deep hardwood forest, until it reached the crest of the ridge. Meredith puffed quietly, said nothing, and kept going. From the back, in her jeans and hair tucked under a broad hat, Eli thought she looked younger than ever. She could imagine what Meredith might have been like fifty years before.

They had come to a clearing on the ridge, a large patch that had been logged years before, where for some reason many of the old grey logs had been left, toppled down the steep slope. Some shrubs and poison ivy had sprung up, but the dead wood choked out any chance of new forest for a time. They had stood in a small clear field of knee-high grass, looking over the crumbled ridge out into a wide view of the Great Smoky

Mountains and the Blue Ridge closer in. Eli had been to the spot years before, on a hike just after Karol brought her to meet Meredith for the first time.

Without warning, the old woman reached out and took Eli's and Sarah's hands, and they formed a circle around the box. Meredith prayed in a halting voice that finally trailed away into tears. Sarah trembled. And carefully, Eli eased out of their hands and broke the circle. After a time, Meredith opened the box. She made Eli pick up a handful of grey, powdery ash, and offered the box to Sarah, who took some in her fingers. Abruptly, the old woman shook the box of ash into the breeze, and Eli and Sarah threw theirs into the air, and Karol floated off over the dead logs in a fine cloud.

They looked over the edge, and Sarah wiped her tears, making a faint grey streak under one eye.

Turning from the horizon, Meredith said to Eli, "Couldn't you find the strength to cry?"

"Couldn't you find the strength not to?" Eli said. As they went back down the trail, Sarah and Meredith some ways ahead of her, Eli realized that had been her father talking. She regretted the remark.

The little ceremony had broken the urgency of the Valley for Eli, had broken the hold of her job. She settled back on the deck, drank her tea in the sun, and retreated to watch the summer storms pass over. The wedge between her and Sarah had grown, but Eli was content to see it filled by the grandmother. Meredith and Sarah gardened, made up the dinners together, went to the store together. On Sunday mornings they went to church while Eli just stayed in bed, pretending to be asleep, but listening to them getting dressed. Sometimes the girl crawled into the grandmother's tiny lap and they both cried without warning, without a word. Eli would walk out of the house then, feeling awkward, as if Sarah were the older one.

Eli thought about going in for another glass of raspberry tea. Getting addicted to it, she thought. Coleslaw almost every night, made sweet, and grandmother's vinegar pie. Fried fish with sweet homemade tartar sauce. All things she had never liked before, but which she ate now. She would just sit on the porch, sliding along, and maybe learn how Karol had grown up. A postcard had come that day from her father, and it sat on the little table, a picture of Illouette Pass on one side, on the other a note scrawled in thick black pencil: "When the hell you getting back here? I miss my women." It jarred with the late summer days, the highland cool air, the growing tint of yellow in the trees, and the dull sunshine parted by curtains of warm rain showers.

Meredith and Sarah had been in the house for some time after a stint of gardening, and Eli heard the faucet run, the bang of a closet door. Then they came outside, both in bright dresses, and Sarah with a little of grandmother's makeup on.

"We're going to the mall," Meredith said, smiling.

"In Asheville," Sarah said. "We've got some special shopping and we want you to come with us."

"Thanks," Eli said, not getting up from the chair. "You go. I'll keep an eye on the garden—I saw a black snake crawl in there that I might chase away."

"No," Meredith said. "You have to come."

"Yeah, mom." Sarah reached out and pulled at her arm.

"Why?" She did like the feel of Sarah's warm hand.

"Because I'm sick of seeing you in those awful jeans," Meredith said. Eli made sure the woman was smiling when she said it, and she was.

"Grandma says she's going to buy us dresses."

"Us?"

"I'm curious to find out what you look like in a dress." Meredith started for the Lincoln. "I'm willing to pay top dollar for the privilege. And if we can get you into one, why, I'll pay for dinner as a kind of victory celebration."

"C'mon," Sarah pulled at her.

So Eli sat in the back of the Lincoln, and as the car wound down the hill toward Asheville, and Sarah chattered at her grandmother, Eli fell asleep. More and more, she stayed up at night and napped during the day, which had never been her way before.

Eli jerked awake when they stopped, and she blinked against the afternoon sun as they all walked across the large parking lot of the Biltmore Square Mall. Once in the huge air conditioned corridor, filled with little neon signs and flashy displays, where all the indoor trees were manicured and the floor was shiny tile, Eli recalled how infrequently she and Karol would go to a mall. Both preferred to shop by mail-order catalog when they had to buy clothes. Sarah skipped up and down, cheered by the fluorescent light and the weak sun filtering through the skylights. I'll bet Karol's wondering where we went wrong, Eli thought.

They went into Dillard's, the store Meredith said would be the only place to find a decent dress and proper help. Eli drifted over to the men's cosmetics, and picked up a bottle of a cologne by Bill Blass. She thought about buying it for Jack, make him wear it, just to see him sweat a little. She sniffed it, instinctively wondered how it might smell on Karol's skin, and she put the small bottle down.

At the children's department Meredith let Sarah try on one dress after another, and Eli could think of little to do but smile each time the girl paraded out of the dressing rooms. Grandma had all the right adjectives. Sarah picked out a green and gold print dress, and when Eli glanced at the tag, she was pleased she was not the one paying for it. Sarah wore it, putting her old clothes into a bag.

"Now you," she said happily—as happy as Eli had seen her in a month.

"Grandma has spent enough already."

"No," Meredith said. "Let's see what you look like in a dress, then maybe we can bring you to church Sunday."

"Don't bet on it."

"I'll take my chances."

In the women's department, which seemed to be endless from Eli's point of view, they searched for a dress. She shook her head when they pulled one from the rack for her.

"Being difficult," Meredith said to her, out of Sarah's hearing.

"Don't waste your money."

Eli almost won; the old woman was about to give up because the saleslady seemed to be watching them with amused curiosity. Meredith did not like the embarrassment. Eli was a barbarian, rough stock from her animalistic father. Hatched in the wild woods. What had Karol seen in her?

Sarah found a green and gold dress on a rack and pulled it out. "Here," she said. "It's like mine!"

"Not my size," Eli handed it back to her.

"Here's one that is, I bet." Meredith smiled grimly. "Try it on and don't disappoint her."

"Fine."

In the dressing room, Eli threw off her jeans and T-shirt. The dress was difficult, good on the hips and waist, but a little tight on the bust and too short in the leg. Typical. And it buttoned from the back. She could never understand why women's clothes had to button in the back. But she got it on at last, and stepped out of the dressing room.

"Well, my God," Meredith said.

Her amazement seemed to mock a bit, Eli thought.

"I love it," Sarah said. She pulled Eli over to the mirror.

"Well . . ." Eli stopped.

She looked at herself, in three different angles, in the big three-paneled mirror. Just behind, in three ways, her daughter seemed an echo of herself, in gold and green. The dress made Eli look at her reflection more carefully, study the length of her long blonde hair, the brown in her eyes, her dark tan, the good shape of her figure. She looked for a long time, and saw herself through someone else's eyes. The dress made her feel strange, and then she felt one of the jangled lines in her tug suddenly. It made her wince with pain.

She went back into the dressing room, slammed the door, and shoved her old pants off a bench. Eli sat down heavily, doubled over, beat her forehead savagely with her hands.

Sarah stepped in quietly, shut the door, and latched it. She touched her mother on the head, cautiously.

Eli felt the hand on her head, and though small, its gentleness reminded her of someone else. She put her own hands down. The tears came hard, pushed their way out of her so that her eyes hurt. And she felt she could hardly breathe in the little room.

"I miss him, Sarah." Eli looked up at her daughter, saw the tears pouring over her face, and saw that she too had a face twisted up in pain. She pulled the girl close.

"I made him go out in the meadow," Sarah said hoarsely, so loud that Eli jumped. "I made him go out there."

"No, you didn't," Eli said, struggling to smile. "He was a man who never did anything he didn't want to."

"He was good," Sarah said simply.

"He was." Eli found her daughter's chin, and pulled it up so Sarah looked at her. "I want to talk to you about him. I know a lot, and I need someone I can talk to about him."

"I do too."

"I need you, Sarah." And Eli felt the tears push out fast and hot. She did not know when they would stop. "I need you very much now."

Meredith stood outside the dressing room door, listening. Eli and Sarah stayed inside a long time, and the grandmother kept the customers and saleswomen away.

Finally, a middle-aged woman, wearing a grey suit dress, walked up to Meredith. "Excuse me, but do you know what's going on in there?"

"Yes," Meredith said. "It's private."

"But I—" The woman began.

"Not to worry," Meredith said, feeling good for the first time in a long while. Amazing what a good trip to the mall can do, she thought. "I'm sure she'll take the dress."

XXXIV

He walked on the trails that led up the eastern crest of the Sierras, his new backpack heavier with the things Egusa had given him. As nothing had happened in the Park for over three months, backpacking was open again on the east side. In the Valley itself and the surrounding mountains, backpacking was still forbidden. When he came to the Valley border, feeling but not seeing personnel ahead, he walked off trail. The late afternoon fog, a low cloud colliding with the mountain, made the red trunks of tall trees seem out of focus. The blur hid him. Late October in the Park, and he was returning. Eldred Spell had recovered physically.

On his way to Johnson Pass, taking the long way around so as to approach from the west, Spell tried to concentrate on what he had planned for the next twenty-four hours. By dusk, in the portal of the pass, up at 11,000 feet, he watched the clouds blow through the stunted white bark pines, watched until nightfall as the blue and purple phantoms stretched against the black trees. At the rim of the Valley now, he felt dangerously unfocused. With what Egusa had given him, he knew the Valley would no longer remain open; his work would be done. He had grown tired of it. The feeling reminded him of New York, where once he retained his high position, the life there began to die. As he leaned against a tree, out of breath and weak from being away for so long, the urgency of his mission seemed diminished.

Yet he still loved the Valley, and what it had become. Even if only for a summer, or perhaps into the winter if he were successful, he had given Nature back to itself. Something for Ellen that only he could do. A silence had come over the woods, and the animals had a chance to live in a way they had not for over a century, a way they would never have again. As he watched the darkness settle, feeling the cold, damp autumn air blow through his coat, he tried not to think of the costs. The man with the dogs, Horton on the cliff, the girl in the meadow had chipped away at his sharp focus. And Andrea, with the soft days of recovery in Monterey, splintered his focus even more. One life was dissolving behind him, and a new one coming into shape. The old New York part of Spell tried again to seduce him to a new easy-out lifestyle.

He started down, navigating by the dim green light of his night compass, until suddenly the fog blew open in patches and let the full moon come through. The forest swam with moving grey light and he felt like he walked down the quiet floor of a deepening lake. When he would stop to rest, troubled by how weak he had become in fifteen weeks, he listened for others in the forest.

Occasionally he put out his hand, closed his eyes, and imagined he could feel through the forest. Imagining himself feeling so close to the earth, so much a part of the land he had saved for a time, that he could second guess where they would be waiting for him. He believed it worked. In New York, when his sense of purpose became vague, he pressed his hand against the plate glass window of his office and found what he should do next. The city told him. Not the people—they were unreliable—but the buildings, streets, roads, and all wires leading in and out. But now he had something much cleaner, a voice from the land itself. Spell subscribed to no religion nor cult, none suited him, but he had constructed one for himself.

By midnight the clouds had blown away and the Valley filled with bright silver moonlight. Spell saw his shadow clearly against the ground as he walked and the sharpness of the light reminded him of his vulnerability. He could be seen. But he had chosen the full-moon night on purpose; he had things to do that would require light by which to see, and any flashlight would make him a clearer target. Survival focused his mind again, put him in keener touch with the land he walked upon.

He believed the vigilance of rangers and FBI had slackened; too much time had gone by with no attack in the Valley. The story played itself out and dropped from press coverage. Once, as he came into a narrow gap where two trails crossed, he stopped suddenly. Three figures walked silently along the trail, hunting him, and he did not move until they had gone. The hunters had been perfectly silent, and Spell admired their prowess after so many days with nothing to do.

The momentary tension gave him strength, and he hiked toward the Illouette Ridge with fewer rest stops. Almost as strong as he had once been. The great cliff glowed grey, and Spell looked up at the moon, seeing the steam from his breath pass across it. For a moment he lapsed, thinking of Andrea and the new possibility she might provide for him. When he had become well enough, they made love often. A kind of violent, clawing, muscle against muscle as they rolled across the floor of her room. They attacked each other, and sex seemed an act of harmless violence. She challenged him at all times, kept a tension between them that he enjoyed; both struggling for domination in the relationship and neither were able to attain it. That suited them both well. The struggle kept the relationship alive to Spell, and satisfied both the part of him that wanted some kind of normal life, and the part that craved purpose, challenge, war.

What he sought, Andrea taught him, was something that he could not conquer. Perhaps that would be her. He told her that he needed a new career, and could invest nearly three million dollars in the Spyglass Inn. He hoped she and the partnership would be enough. Once he triumphed in a relationship or a career, the thing he won slowly died. What made the Valley alive to him tonight was that it was not yet won. What split his focus was that another thing, Andrea, was not won either. Spell felt good.

He pushed himself and found the cave quickly. He rolled the boulders aside, and crept into the mountain. Using a dim amber flashlight he searched the cave and soon found his Hungarian machine gun against a rock, its barrel already growing a small spot of rust. He took his pack off, and pulled out a German Maschinenpistol 5SD, a small machine gun with a short barrel and sound suppressor. He had brought it along, taken from a cache buried near the outer boundary of the Park, because it weighed less than seven pounds and would be easy to use in the narrow cave.

Carefully he slipped down into the deeper level of the cave, and as soon as he dropped to solid ground he pointed the gun ahead and turned on the dim light. The beam found a huge raccoon, standing on it haunches with forepaws raised, its back up against a cave wall. Much of the fur had gone grey, and it hissed at him and shook with fury at the intruder.

"I thought you might be down here, you bastard." Spell spoke to it because he was in a good mood.

He fired a quick burst into the raccoon's chest, pressing it against the rock until the animal collapsed. The small cave room filled with the sour odor of musk and blood. He took the raccoon by a hind leg and pulled it down deeper into the cave. When he came to a narrow place with large broken pieces of granite, he wrapped the animal in plastic and buried it under a mound of rocks.

"Sorry, new occupant," he said as he left the narrow place. He could still feel some weakness in the calf that had been bitten.

Soon Spell moved most of the contents of the backpack down into the cave room. The cave would be another cache—a base if he needed one. For some time the place had given him nightmares, and so he decided he would make it his own. His mother had once taught him to bite off the head of any fear; when she discovered his horror of the grey ticks that swelled off Buddy's ears, she made him remove them—again and again—until he had overcome his fear of ticks.

He kept the things Egusa had given him, but left behind her homemade trip wires with the transmitters. He might need them later for the cave, if he ever came back. Sometimes he knew he would come back, the deep voice within him told him so, but at times in Monterey, lying awake by Andrea's side, he hoped once the work was done this day he could leave the Valley forever. A very faint hope. Still, as long as no one could identify him, he could quit. The FBI and ATF had examined the Dragunov carefully and tried to track it to its present owner—this was the one deadly link to him—but they were stalled by the chaos of the recent collapse of the Soviet Union. No one in Russia seemed to know about such prototypes; the officials there were reluctant to help.

Once Spell had everything in place and was outside, he passed his dim light into the cave to see it was clear of any evidence of him. He put the small boulders back in place and started toward the Valley floor. Within a few hours, still plenty of time before the sunrise, he came to Happy Isles. Through the trees he saw the white water tank, sitting on its four wooden legs. A small automatic device that measured water levels of the river hummed nearby. Sure that no one was near, he worked quickly on the water tower, following Egusa's instructions exactly. Within an hour he finished, just as the light of the moon disappeared behind a ridge and the early glow of the rising sun exchanged the silver light for a grey that would grow into the new day.

Spell hid in a thick clump of incense cedar seedlings, and could just see two of the charges: small white rectangles taped to the tower's legs. Two others were out of view, as was the timer and the white wires, hanging between the legs, that connected the charges. Egusa had been clearly disappointed in him when he insisted on blowing the tower up, instead of poisoning the water. Before he left her house they had argued about it very quietly, and when he suggested that she probably could not devise an adequate plastic explosive to do the job, he won her over. A month later she gave him more of the material than he would need; she said it would be a bit less powerful than other plastic explosives, but could certainly blow the wooden legs off a water tank. She smiled, saying the explosion might be bigger than he would expect, that he should move some distance from it. You might find yourself full of wooden missiles, she had said. Like General Custer. She had laughed at the joke, and seemed most amused that Spell and Doug Evers did not even smile.

Spell had his German machine gun at his shoulder, the empty pack on his back, and his escape plan in mind. He had fifteen minutes before the explosion, if Egusa's clumsy-looking timer—made with a travel alarm clock—was accurate. He stopped, heard a noise. Someone humming tunelessly, coming closer.

In the gathering light of the morning, Spell saw a tall, heavy man stumble out of the woods and walk to a spot just underneath the water tower. The man looked up at the tank, and seemed to notice the wires as he hummed a string of low, meaningless notes. If the charges went off while the man stood there, he would be filled with wooden shrapnel before a steel tank with at least a thousand gallons of water fell on him. Spell watched, thinking.

The man walked in little circles under the tank, still humming, in what appeared to be a dance as meaningless as his tune. Just as he appeared to be ready to leave, he got down on all fours and stuck his face in the ground, and began grunting like a pig. Then he fell over on his side, as if he were going to sleep.

With ten minutes left, Spell decided he had to go down. Clearly the man was drunk or unstable, and he could disconnect the wires—they were within easy reach of his hands if he stood up again. Pink streaked against the eastern sky, the yellow and red Indian hemp along the river began to find color. The sun would be up soon. Rolling abruptly to his knees, the man stood up again, humming and staring. He seemed to notice the wire hanging a few feet in front of his face, but he did not go toward it.

"This is a problem," Spell said. He listened carefully, but no one else was nearby. Just the gentle gurgle of the river in the early morning. And the tuneless humming.

"Hello," he said as he approached the man.

"Hi," the man looked at him, smiling broadly. Well built, thick chest and large biceps bulging under a white T-shirt, the man seemed no older than twenty. He stood solidly, blue eyes bright and clear, and Spell became certain he was not drunk nor drugged. He seemed perfectly normal, handsome and alert.

"Do you play golf?" The man asked; the flesh between his wide set eyes furled as if he struggled to put the question together. His forehead was just a few inches from a hanging wire.

"I used to," Spell answered. He looked around for any sign of another person. No one. Eight minutes to go. "Why don't you come out from under this water tank?"

"Oh," the man looked up, as if noticing the tank for the first time. "Okay." He stepped forward, hit the wire, backed up.

"Duck under it," Spell said. He saw the wire had held.

"Okay." The man crouched down, then crawled, looking up at the tank as he passed under it. He kept crawling, on past Spell.

"You can get up now."

"Okay." The man stood up. "You play golf?"

"No." Seven minutes.

"I like to play golf."

"That's fine." Spell figured he had to get the man at least a hundred yards away, around the bend in the trail. Probably not that far, really, if the wires were still a concern. But the man himself was a concern, and Spell felt that odd lack of focus again. "Let's walk down the trail here."

"For golf?" The man seemed planted in the ground, his thick legs visibly shivering in the gentle breeze. Wearing shorts in air no warmer than forty degrees.

"I would say for fishing."

"I don't like fishing."

"What do you like, besides golf?"

"I . . ." The man looked back around at the tank, and Spell was afraid he would start back toward it. "I play football."

"Really?" Five minutes. Spell walked a few steps down the river, hoping the man would follow. "Are you on a team?"

"High school team." He followed slowly, carefully putting one foot in front of the other. He was proud of his big legs. He flexed his chest muscles and his arms, liking the feeling. "I was on a high school team."

"Which team?" Spell picked up his pace, hating being on the trail, exposed. Above the sky flashed with bright orange as the top rim of the sun started up over a ridge. The man followed, but they were only ten yards from the tower.

"Coach was mad at me." The man stopped, thinking, seeing himself stretched flat out on the ground. Looking up, with the coach red-faced and waving his arms. And all the people. It was a picture in his mind that he liked to replay. "I made a bonehead move."

"Come on." Spell smiled, beckoning. "You tell me about golf." Maybe that would get the man moving again.

"I play golf." The man grinned, the lines on his forehead flattened. "Do you play?" As he jogged to catch up, Spell quickened his pace. The man kept jogging. "Do you play?"

"Yes, I like to play a lot." Maybe twenty yards from the tower, not far from the bend in the trail. Still nothing ahead, but Spell began to dread the sound of a radio, expected to hear a bullhorn, a voice telling him to get his hands up.

"You play? I like to shoot the windmills, and there's this big pink castle, and the little hole you got to get that ball—"

The timer was inaccurate, and the legs of the tower exploded three minutes early. The two legs facing Spell disintegrated first, and the tank tipped forward, going down in a flash of orange flame that disappeared in a cloud of smoke and dust. Spell tried to turn away but a wave of hot air, rocks, and splinters of wood caught him, lifting him briefly, piling him into the ground ahead. The dark cloud of dust enveloped him, and the hot, gritty air filled his lungs. A boom hit his ears, followed immediately by another, and it felt as if he were being punched in both sides of his head.

He stood up quickly, steadying himself in the thick cloud, when a cold wave of water slammed into his shins and knocked him down again. But soon he was running, ignoring the cuts and one big tear in his knee, ignoring the mind-numbing ring in his ears, putting both hands out as he stumbled forward. Hit the river and sloshed into it, falling twice before he got across. Breathing hard, shaking from the chill of the water and the adrenaline, he went up into the woods.

Spell turned, waiting for his heart to slow enough so he could stop gasping, and he saw that the water tank had been completely destroyed, the legs shattered and the tank flattened, lying on its side like a crushed tin can. Below, the man walked unsteadily, becoming clearer as the dust and smoke drifted away. He stopped, bent down, and picked something up.

Spell looked at his hands, saw his gloves were intact, and watched the man stumble down the trail with the black German MP5SD in his hands. For a moment, Spell felt like running down, taking the gun away, and chancing capture. Now they would have two of his guns. But then his mind cleared as he watched the man begin to trot down the trail, machine gun in hand, finally disappearing around the bend.

"Perfect," Eldred Spell said. And then he ran deep into the woods.

XXXV

When he first stepped into the shower, Nick Cairns heard a dull boom beyond the splattering hot water. He had not bothered to see about the weather, but thunder so early in the morning and this late into fall mildly surprised him. He turned up the hot water; the mornings seemed to be colder than usual for October. 6:15 a.m. He planned to spend a long time in the shower, and even longer alone in the kitchen with a cup of coffee. For the first time in his life since college, he found waking up harder and harder, each morning a bit tougher to face. He did not sleep well. Even in college, even on nights when he was wound up about some terrible ROTC drill, Cairns had never been troubled by insomnia.

His difficulty sleeping meant he spent more hours awake in the house with Claudia. Except in the last few months, his sleep cycle and his wife's had continued to diverge. For the first years of their marriage, they had made an attempt to sleep and wake together. He had struggled to stay up past ten, and she tossed and turned in bed while he gently snored. Then no children came along, and his job became a wave that he rode high while she looked on, while she sat in government housing—or lately the superintendent's house—wherever they may be. She grew chunky, then fat, then obese sitting in those places. Cut her thin red hair short, rarely washed it, just pushed the oily strands out of her face. Took tranquilizers. Did not go out, and lost whatever direction she may have had.

Claudia stayed up until two or three in the morning, woke up in the afternoon, while Nick kept to the sun—rose with it and tried to go down with it as well. He spent most of those hours at work, so he and his wife had succeeded in rarely encountering each other. But now that he could not sleep, that system failed, and they faced each other in the house at night, near strangers walking around, wondering how in the hell they had wound up with each other.

The phone rang, but he had no interest in trying to dry off and reach it. Claudia would sleep right through it, although an extension was just a foot or two from her ear.

He let the hot water hit his tiny bald spot, not quite scalding, running over his lowered face. Often he focused on a picture of her when they had first met in his senior year at Humboldt State: pleasant round face then, always a smile among the freckles, long straight red hair done in the style of '73. She always had wide hips, smallish breasts, but that long straight hair was what caught him, and the thought of it could make him feel good. Sometimes he wished he could force her to lose weight, get a perm, somehow resurrect herself.

The phone kept ringing.

He wondered what happened to her—a question he thought of often to take his mind off the mess in the Valley. Claudia was almost a comforting problem, a private one that was his alone, and although it was something he could never solve, thinking about it he fell into one of the deepest grooves of his life. He liked to go back, analyze where the relationship had begun to unravel. His second assignment: Big Bend National Park in southwest Texas. She hated that one. That's when she started missing parties with the rangers, began to keep home, refused to hike in the godforsaken country with him. For twenty years she wanted to be back in Northern California, be near her family and the woods she loved, but every opportune move he could make, each promotion, took them farther and farther away. By the time they came to the Valley, as close to her home as they had been in decades, it was too late. She did not want to see her relatives. He thought she felt shame for what she was, or maybe what he was, or probably that they were ugly and childless. Yeah, he thought again, that first hot, empty summer in Big Bend was where she started to sour.

He stood, repeating the thought mindlessly, as the water grew cold. Eventually it would go cold enough to chase him out of the shower and push him into another day. Then the water pressure suddenly fell to a trickle. Cairns heard that someone was pounding on the front door, and the phone still rang.

"Coming," he screamed, a bit too loudly he supposed. He toweled himself off quickly, drops still flying as he trotted into the bedroom. He dressed, feeling the back of his uniform shirt get wet. All the time he watched the big pile of covers in the bed, and saw that one heavy arm had snaked out of the blankets, as if she had made a grab at the phone. It still rang, but he'd be damned if he would get it or the door before he put his clothes on. No doubt this day was going south already, slipping into the valley of recent days that was the worst slump in his life.

He decided to go for the door first, swinging it open with a jerk, catching Pickering in mid-knock. Pickering looked tall, gangly, and stupid to Cairns.

"What is it?" Cairns noticed Pickering's truck, lights spinning.

"There's been an explosion." Pickering sucked in his breath. "A bomb. Heinze's up there, with others now, FBI too, and they've caught some guy walking down the trail with a fancy machine gun."

"Damn!"

Pickering suddenly looked a lot better. Cairns put his hand on the holster of his .38, relieved it was there. Things were in order. Maybe they caught the bastard. His heart raced, blood pumping free and clear in him for the first time in months.

"Let's go."

They ran to Pickering's truck, jumping in, slamming doors. Pickering hit the siren and punched the accelerator. Cairns rolled down his window and the cold wind blew through the wet bristle of his short graying hair.

"Olivos there?" Cairns grabbed the radio and looked at Pickering.

"By now."

"Olivos, this is Cairns," he yelled into the transmitter over the siren. "You with the suspect?"

"I'm looking at him." Olivos coming over, very excited but controlled. Good man, Cairns thought.

"Is he still armed?"

"Yes," Olivos said. "We're less than a quarter mile down the trail from Happy Isles. Chopper overhead reports that the water tower has been blown up. We have a white male, approximately six four, machine gun with a sound suppressor in his hands. He seems confused. We're trying to talk him down."

"Copy that. My ETA—" Cairns checked Pickering's speedometer. "Under four minutes."

"We're behind cars. Under cover. Cochran's talking to him. Suspect is not responding."

Cochran, Cairns thought. Of course he's there first, finding himself in the spotlight. Senior FBI man trying to take over things as it is, already counting reporter's flashbulbs.

"Punch it, Pickering."

Past the Muir parking lot, half empty, and on through to Tent City. The explosion had been close, and the few remaining campers were up, heading after the speeding cars and sirens. Pickering had to warn some people away with his P.A. as he slowed on the Happy Isles road. He hit the brakes hard when they stopped behind the trucks and unmarked cars cramming the narrow gravel road by the river.

"There," Pickering said, squinting.

Cairns hopped out, left the door open, and crouched low as he ran up to Olivos. They smiled at each other, and then Cairns nodded to Cochran, who crouched behind the door in the car next to Olivos' truck.

Olivos handed Cairns a bullhorn, switching it on for him. Cairns nodded to Cochran again, who lowered his own horn. Cairns peered over the door—Olivos had lowered the window. The suspect was a big man, with very powerful, muscular legs—he had the superhuman body that Cairns had pictured the killer to have during sleepless nights.

The man's big soft face, half smiling now, was a surprise. If not for the black machine gun that hung from one of the man's big hands, he would not seem dangerous at all. Cairns had pictured a leaner, tougher face, maybe an ex-commando or a Middle Eastern terrorist. But this man, with a huge black-and-blue welt on the side of his face, grinning stupidly as he looked at the flashing rollbars, did not quite fit the expectations of Cairns' imagination.

"What do you think, Olivos?"

"His explosive went off early, and he's dazed. Cochran's been telling him to put down his weapon, but the man doesn't seem to understand. He's made no move to get his finger on the trigger or raise the gun. If he had, he'd be dead by now."

"Yeah." Cairns looked at the rifles and pistols pointed at the suspect. Heinze, nearby, seemed very anxious to shoot as he aimed his 30-06 at the suspect's head. A county sheriff's helicopter hovered high above, ordered farther up by Cochran, who did not want the noise to obscure his dialogue with the killer.

"Put down your weapon," Cairns said over the bullhorn. "We don't want to hurt you."

The man turned in the direction of the bullhorn. His brows came together and he stopped smiling, as if he were straining to understand. He took a step toward the sound.

"Halt!" Cairns yelled. "We'll fire!"

He took another step forward.

"Stop!"

"We ought to just shoot the bastard," Olivos muttered.

The man stopped.

"I want to hear his story," Cairns said. Then he spoke through the bullhorn again. "Drop your weapon."

"What?" The man asked.

"That's the first word he's spoken," Olivos said. "He seems to be waking up."

"Drop the gun," Cairns ordered again.

"What?" The man squinted up at the sun, and the black-and-blue welt on the side of his face was clearer to the onlookers.

"Drop your—" Cairns looked at the welt, and thought the man may be suffering from a serious concussion. He spoke slowly, "Drop that thing in your hands."

The man looked down. "This?"

"He's really out of it," Olivos said.

"Yes, drop that."

The man let the machine gun fall. He smiled.

"Get him," Cairns said to Olivos.

Olivos sprinted, gun pointed forward in his right hand.

The man suddenly grimaced and crouched down, ready for the attack.

Olivos knocked the man back onto the dusty road. When he started to scramble up, Olivos hit him behind the ear with the butt of his pistol. He hit him hard, and the suspect rolled face first into the ground. An FBI agent cuffed him.

Cairns stood up, and turned to Cochran. "We got him."

"We'll see," Cochran said, pistol still in hand.

Typical FBI caution, Cairns thought.

The medic could not wake the suspect, so he was thrown onto a stretcher and taken to the Park infirmary. Cairns rode with him in the ambulance, and watched the reporters as the ambulance drove through them. Cairns was anxious for the man to wake up, to have the interview with him that he had been dreaming of for so long. Finally, Cairns thought, he would have something definitive for the media. For once, he could shut up the secretary of the interior, who had fallen into the habit of calling. He could satisfy Shirley Weaver and The Heston Company that sales would soon return to normal. He might even be in the position to tell his wife to beat the pills, get off her butt, and appreciate her position as a Park superintendent's wife. As the sun rose higher in a bright blue sky, Cairns saw that things had suddenly turned.

But waking the man had become a problem. In a small white room in the infirmary building, Cairns watched Carter, the Park doctor, check the man's vitals over and over. In the lobby of what was really an oversize cabin from the 1920s, the reporters and TV crews filled the room like a flood ready to breach a dam. Weeks of frustration seemed at an end. Here was a story. But the suspect carried no ID; the superintendent needed a name. Cairns shook his right leg nervously as he sat in a small folding chair. Walking back and forth in the room, Cochran kept pulling at one end of his walrus mustache. His eyes seemed small, hard, and red to Cairns.

"Olivos gave this man quite a wallop," Carter said. "This welt looks to be from a piece of board that hit him in the blast. His vital signs are stable, but if we can't rouse him in ten minutes or so, I'd say we better airlift him to Fresno. We have a serious concussion here, I'm afraid."

"Shit," Cochran said.

Cairns had never heard the man swear, and took pleasure from his discomfort. He planned to keep cool. But his leg shook vigorously at the thought of the man leaving the Park before he could get in a preliminary interview.

Olivos knocked at the door, came in, and bent to Cairns' ear. "We've lost all water pressure in the Park. With the tank gone, no one will have water."

"I'll deal with that later."

"Shirley Weaver is already here. She's out in the lobby, says people are complaining, and wants to know what you'll do."

"What can we do?" Cairns looked up, irritated that Cochran was just standing there, in his freshly pressed field outfit, hearing all of this.

"No water?" Olivos pursed his lips and blew out some air. He didn't want to say it, especially with Cairns just about to lose his temper.

"I know what we have to do," Cairns said between his teeth, looking at the man in the bed. "And as soon as I have some news, as soon as I've talked to this suspect, we'll get on it." He clenched his fists and suddenly had the completely unreasonable urge to strangle the man in that bed. They may have caught him, yes, but his last act had really screwed the Park. Damn him.

"Weaver wants to speak to you now," Olivos hated to go on.

Cairns stood up abruptly. "Just tell her—" He stopped, feeling Cochran watching them carefully. "I will see her as soon as I've interviewed this man."

"Yes sir." Olivos rarely used "sir" with Cairns, but now seemed a good time. He left quickly.

"What's that about the water?" Cochran asked.

"It's out."

To Cairns' immediate relief, the suspect opened his eyes. The young man gently put one hand on his forehead and looked at the doctor.

"I took a hit," he told Carter.

"Yes, you did." Carter checked the pupils for dilation, and they were fairly coordinated. Perhaps the concussion was not so bad after all, but he was surprised it had taken so long to bring the man around.

"I took a hit," the man said again.

"What's your name?," Carter asked, trying his best to smile kindly. "You didn't have any I.D."

"Huh?"

"What's your name?" Cairns asked, by Carter's side.

"He's still disoriented," the doctor said.

"Right," Cairns crowded Carter out of the way. He felt Cochran at his side, practically breathing on his neck. "I need your name."

"Smerve," the man blinked at Cairns. "My head hurts."

"I'll bet it does. What's your full name?"

"Smerve, I said." He seemed gently irritated, and then smiled. "Do you fish?"

"Sometimes." The question surprised Cairns. "But what I want now is your name."

"I fish," the man started to sit up and then slid back down. "Boy, does my head hurt. I took a hit. Took a big hit."

"My God!" Cairns looked up.

"Shit," Cochran said again, in a matter-of-fact tone.

"I told you he's very disoriented, although I don't believe his concussion is serious," Carter added.

Cairns could feel the media outside, The Heston Company, the secretary of the interior, the FBI, the very personally unpleasant announcement he would have to make soon—all of it hitting his head like several blows. His chest felt congested with the tense, unsprung desire to kill the man in the bed. He took a deep breath and tried once more.

"What is your name?"

"Smerve." Then he mentioned, as if it helped, "And I do like to fish."

"That's it," Cairns spat out.

"Perhaps if I try," Cochran said calmly.

"You couldn't get him to drop the damn machine gun," Cairns stared at Smerve. "At least I brought him in without shooting him to pieces."

"Calm down," Cochran said mildly, very close to Cairns now.

Cairns stepped away from Cochran, trying to ignore him, and bent over Smerve. "Listen," he hissed at the man. "You tell me your full, complete name right now." He felt he was losing control, letting his anger run ahead of him, but he no longer cared. "Tell me now," he yelled in the man's face.

"Wait a minute," Cochran said, his voice rising. He put a hand on Cairns' shoulder.

"Keep your fucking hand off of me," Cairns pulled away from Cochran. And then he noticed that Olivos was back in the room, standing with a bearded man wearing shorts and a Braves T-shirt. The man's prolapsed belly hung out under the shirt. Seeing the look in the man's eyes, and the panic in Olivos' face, brought Cairns back down. He felt the blood rush to his cheeks.

"This is Ray Craddock," Olivos said. He felt ill; he had never seen his superintendent so out of control. The only relief was that Cairns, though still shaking, seemed to come back to reality.

"So?" Cairns asked.

"So that's my brother you got banged up there," Craddock said. "He's not your killer." He spat on the floor.

"And while we're at it, I don't like the way you're yelling in his face. What kind of officer are you, anyways?"

"I'm the superintendent of this Park," Cairns said, his throat and chest tightening. All he wanted to do was get out of the room for a few seconds to catch his breath. Get some fresh air. "We found this man with a machine gun in his hand, walking away from a bombing."

"I know that," Craddock said. "But he just got away from us, is all."

"Mr. Craddock is from Atlanta," Olivos said, trying to fill up some space to let his boss regain control. "He and some friends are touring the west, and were having a party last night. Mr. Craddock is rather hungover."

"You can say that again," he looked down at the floor. "I guess I should of watched Smerve more carefully."

"His name is Mervin Craddock," Olivos said. "His brother had some I.D., including a driver's license."

"That's a few years old." Craddock walked over to his brother as Cairns backed out of the way. "He used to drive. But then my little brother had an accident on the high school football team. He's in a permanent state of confusion." He looked back at Cairns and then Olivos. "I suppose after what you've done to his head, he'll be worse off now."

"Hey, Ray, do you like to fish?" Smerve asked.

"Yeah, Smerve, and I like golf too." Ray spoke like it was a line he repeated often. "And I don't like football."

"No, we don't like it." Smerve tried to sit up again, and slid back down. "I took a hit."

"Looks like you did," Ray agreed.

Cairns looked at Cochran and knew what he was thinking: shit. Then he looked at the clock on the wall. They had given the real killer an hour to get away, if he had been nearby at all. Then Cairns had an idea, saw some chance, and looked down at Smerve.

"Who gave you that gun?" Cairns asked.

"Huh?"

"That gun you had in your hands?"

"Do you like to play golf?"

"Well," Ray said, stroking his brother's arm. "I guess he won't talk to you until we get a lawyer."

"I doubt that will be necessary." Cochran walked out of the room.

After the Craddocks left the Park in an ambulance, headed for Fresno, Cairns bypassed the media and called a meeting of the rangers. He gave them the evacuation plan for the Park, the one he had devised some weeks before from scratch, because the Park had never been evacuated before. He then told Shirley Weaver, in private, to shut down all the Heston operations. She lectured him on his incompetence. But Cairns ignored her as he looked out his office window, watching the remaining campers drive in a long line up the road and out of the Park. Evacuation will take less than four hours, he thought. All very efficient, as my people have been rehearsing it in their minds for weeks. Later he had a long talk with the secretary of the interior on the phone. And then Nick Cairns walked home.

Alone, he picked at a lukewarm TV dinner tray in the kitchen. Claudia watched the 6:30 news and said nothing to him. For hours they avoided each other in the house. Normally, stuck with her at such close quarters, he would go out for a long, comforting walk in the Park. There, in the fresh air and the relative quiet of the meadows, he could remember why he had become a ranger in the first place. Could look beyond her unhappiness, and the pollution, and the drug busts, and the paperwork, and even the terrorism. But that night he did not want to go out. He tried to go to bed, but he lay there in his pajamas and he listened to his name repeated several times on the eleven o'clock news. He had even been called by *Nightline*; Ted Koppel could set him up via satellite relay. Cairns had refused.

Finally, he rolled out of bed, and he padded into the living room, looking over his wife's heavy shoulder as she watched Ted Koppel speak his name again and again.

"Do you have to watch that, Claudia?"

"It's the only way I can find out how badly you screwed up," she said through the crackle of a handful of vinegar and salt potato chips. "You'd never tell me."

"I'll tell you one thing," he said.

"What?" She never turned away from the TV.

"I'll bet if I request an assignment in Big Bend National Park, I'd get it." That should nail her, he thought. He locked himself in the bathroom, quickly undressed, and stood for a moment under the dry shower head.

XXXVI

Most of the leaves had blown off the trees by the end of October; wind knocked the yellows and reds to the ground, where the papery, sweet-smelling colors piled up around the trunks of hemlocks, poplar, and hickory. Eli stopped raking, cooling off quickly in the sharp autumn breeze, growing colder as nightfall neared. She breathed in the smoky air. Meredith had another fire going, and blue smoke peeled off the top of the chimney.

Sarah kept raking industriously, piling up the leaves, because she looked forward to burning them soon. With the breeze coming up, Eli knew that would have to wait. But as long as Sarah worked hard, Eli would let her think they were going to do the burning right away. She liked to watch her daughter work, but as Eli stood with the rake in her hand, she realized that for weeks she herself had been doing very little. Shopping. Cooking. Planting bulbs. Tilling the garden under after the first frost. Meredith and Sarah enjoyed the time.

"Get to work, Mom." Sarah glanced up at her as she raked, blowing her bangs up to get a better look. "I'm doing everything."

"That's fine. I'm just resting."

"Are you tired again?"

"I'm tired of raking." They had raked the leaves from the edge of the house, down the slope of the lawn, into six large piles along the edge of the forest. Eli figured they had six more piles to make.

"Always tired." Sarah started raking again. "C'mon, I want to fire up one of these piles before it gets dark."

"You sound like grandpa." Eli raked slowly, looking into the darkening woods. Now that the leaves were gone, and the woods were a field of long brown and grey trunks, she could see further into them. Fall deepened the forest here.

"What about Halloween?" Sarah asked as she raked quickly against the waning light.

"I don't know." Eli stopped. "Grandma says we'll carve jack'o lanterns and then go to the Pumpkin Walk in Sylva. Hard to say what we'll do."

"I wish we had a plan. Halloween's just two days away."

"Well, grandma will make the plan. She knows this place."

The girl stopped raking and looked at her mother.

Eli looked back. Watched Sarah's long blonde hair, uncut since the spring. Maybe she had grown taller, Eli thought, and a bit wider with all of her grandmother's sugary, fried cooking. But her color was good, for Meredith had a way of coaxing a lot of work out of Sarah, and had practically put her in charge of the yard. Eli had learned that Sarah liked being in charge of something. But as she saw her daughter now, quietly standing apart, Halloween troubled her. Troubled them both. It was the first major holiday without Karol, and reminded them that the first strange Christmas was not too far off.

"Maybe we can go on a midnight hike," Eli offered. That had been Karol's tradition; he took his daughter on long dark walks and told frightening stories. Sarah usually did not sleep well when they came back, but it was something she would never give up. It was one of those things she did with him—the walk made her Halloween complete.

"Maybe." Sarah set her rake down and kicked gently at a big pile of leaves. "I don't know where we'd go." She did not sound enthusiastic.

They both stood quietly for a long time, watching the night come, thinking hard. Whenever their conversations bordered on the subject of Karol, they dropped off into silence.

The porch light came on and Meredith stepped out the door. "Eli, there's someone on the phone for you."

"If it's a reporter, just take a message." She had squeezed them off that way; when they called, Meredith took a name and number and Eli did not call back. Two reporters came to the house shortly after Karol's death, and Eli had refused to see them. Lately, they had given up, but Eli still made it a policy never to answer the phone.

"No, it's that man, Olivos."

"All right." She turned to Sarah. "Are you coming in?"

"No."

"It's getting cold."

"That's okay."

Eli walked in, felt the warmth of the house on her face and enjoyed the smell of Meredith's bread from the kitchen. The old woman had already gone back in to finish making dinner. Eli picked up the phone in the living room, from where she could just make out Sarah's outline near the woods.

"Hello, Eli?" Olivos' voice, he sounded eager to talk with her.

"Yes."

"How are you doing out there?"

"Just the same as when you called a few days ago." Olivos had fallen into the habit of calling regularly, and clumsily stumbled around the question of when she was coming back nearly every time. The question crossed her mind more and more frequently, but she did not let him know. She felt amused and a little disgusted by his strong desire to have her back in the Valley. Without Karol, Olivos would be something to deal with.

"The shit has hit the fan here; I mean—" He corrected himself. "We're in trouble. Have you heard?"

"I don't hear much, except what you tell me." Meredith did not have a television, and took no magazine nor newspaper. Eli tried not to hear what was happening in the Valley, and certainly did not want to know if her or Karol's name came up in the news, but Olivos kept her informed anyway.

"The son of a bitch blew up the water tank at Happy Isles, so Cairns had to evacuate the Park. What water we get is trucked in."

Eli felt struck by that odd feeling again, the one she had felt in the South Meadow, that the Valley—her home—was lost. "I don't suppose they caught him?"

"No. Some guy with a machine gun came walking out of the blast. We thought we had our man, but it turns out that this guy was some nut—I mean really mentally ill—who just happened along and really caused us to screw up. From what anyone can get from him, somebody led him away from the explosion. You should see what the media's done with that—killer leads disabled man from blast and shit like that, if you'll pardon me. They're making him look like some damned Samaritan."

"Do we have a description?"

Eli noticed a flame about the size of a hand begin to dance outside. She could hardly see Sarah, bent over the fire. The girl was not supposed to start the fire, and should not have matches, but Eli decided to see how she would do with the burn now that she started it.

"A police artist came up with a sketch from the retard's description. It looks just like Mr. Potato Head. Totally useless. Everyone wants to kill the retard, man."

"Olivos?"

"Huh?"

"Have you been drinking?" Outside, the fire grew quickly, and Sarah stepped back from it.

"Well, I've been keeping your dad company. We look like a bunch of assholes down here—you know what I mean? The FBI took over everything today."

"What about Cairns?"

"He's out. That guy Cochran took over the investigation. There's talk of calling in the National Guard. And an interim superintendent—a woman, of course, very damned P.C. if you know what I mean—well, the secretary's installing her tomorrow. I know you didn't like Cairns, I know a lot of people didn't, but he got a raw deal. It wasn't his fault. Not our fault either. But we still look like a bunch of assholes."

"How about your job?" As the chief of protection, second in command, Eli knew that Olivos might be transferred out as well.

"I'll probably go. Maybe this woman will fire my ass and replace me with—" He shut up.

"Some woman like me?"

The fire covered one side of a pile, pressed toward the trees by the wind, long flames throwing out burning leaves. Sarah ran toward the house.

"Hell, Eli, I'm just a little drunk, a little mad, you know?" He sounded crestfallen, and desperate to impress. "We've been working so hard, we should have won by now."

"I know."

Sarah burst into the house, and the fire outside had blown up like the tail of a meteor crash in the yard.

"Mom!" Sarah yelled.

"Olivos, I've got to go. My daughter's burning down the forest here."

"Hey, Eli—"

She hung up. Before Meredith could speak, Eli ran to the shed, pulling Sarah after her. She threw a shovel at her daughter and she grabbed the one with the shorter handle.

"Pile leaves on the fire!" Eli yelled as she ran around to stand between the flames and the woods.

"What?"

"It's all we've got to smother it." Eli dug under the pile and folded a bank of leaves over the fire. They were just damp enough to slow it down. She stood on the black leaves, tamping them under her boot, as she advanced on the flame. It licked her face, and the smoke came thicker than Eli would have believed, as if they were burning tires rather than leaves. Her eyes filled with stinging tears and she could hardly see. But the fire smoked more and grew smaller. Fewer burning leaves flew into the woods.

"Get the hose out here!" she ordered Sarah.

But Meredith had rolled it out and was already dousing the flames. The stinging smoke gave way to clouds of steam. The fire went out, smothered in grey hissing plumes, and Eli staggered out of it. Wiping her eyes, she could see again, and she walked around to where her daughter stood. Sarah had dropped her shovel.

"Great move," Eli said. She reached out with her boot, hooked the girl's leg, and tripped her. Sarah went down on her rear with a thud.

"Mom!"

Eli knelt down by her, seeing the outline of Sarah's face in the porch light. The girl looked wild-eyed and angry; Eli laughed out loud. In time, seeing that her mother was amused, Sarah could smile.

"I don't think that was so funny," Meredith threw down the hose. "I rather like my woods." She stomped back toward the house, calling back, "don't burn leaves in my yard again."

"Hand over those matches," Eli said. They laughed.

Dinner was quiet until Sarah worked up a formal apology for her grandmother. Everyone agreed that she should go to bed early, a light punishment that actually relieved Sarah once she saw that Meredith was angry. After putting Sarah to bed with a ranger lecture on fire safety, Eli sat down by the phone and looked out the window. The little speech reminded her of how it felt to be an interpreter, and she thought of her old job. She sat alone for a long time.

Meredith brought two cups of tea, quietly handing her one. She sat down in the easy chair across from Eli. The fire needed more wood; the room grew cold while the wind picked up outside.

"Did you see her start it?" The dark lines in Meredith's face cut against her skin, shadows accentuated by the glow of the dying fire.

"Yes." Eli knew she was in trouble with this woman, but she had grown used to it.

"So why did you let it go on?"

"I wanted to see if she could handle what she started."

"She could have burned up my woods." Meredith set her cup down and looked at the fire. "All this acreage around, and those trees just out there, have been in my family for over a century. Part of me, part of my family. I take a fire seriously."

"I know how you feel." Eli looked in her eyes. "I am sorry."

"Your idea of mothering is peculiar to me."

"It reflects how I grew up." Eli looked out the window again, seeing the dim reflection of her face in the black glass.

"I expect that's true." Meredith had read the few postcards Jack Hattan sent, and she felt very pleased to have met him only once, at the wedding—he was an ass, staggering through that day in a haze of alcohol. Meredith saw enough of his work in Eli, the tall, masculine woman sitting in front of her. Built well, and pretty in a wild, out west kind of way—no question how Karol had fallen for her. But she hardly knew how to buy a dress for herself, could barely cook a meal, could not cry at his funeral. A young woman brought up too hard.

"What was that phone call about?" Meredith asked. She wondered why the same man, Olivos, kept calling. She had her ideas, but did not say anything.

"Things are worse in the Valley." Eli ran her hands through her hair, bit her lip, stared at herself in the window. Miles beyond her reflection she saw a light, another house on another ridge—she wondered how far away.

"What are you going to do about it?"

"Go back to work."

"What about Sarah?"

"I'd like her to stay with you."

"Of course." Thank God, Meredith thought. She had been worried that sooner or later Eli would go back, and might be foolish enough to take her daughter along.

"Until the Valley is safe, anyway," Eli added.

"Oh, yes." Meredith had no intention of going west for even a visit, and had not made the trip when Karol was alive. But she felt afraid that Eli would take Sarah away, with no desire to come back, and then what would she do? She was 72 years old, the last of her family now that Karol had died, and she did not want to live alone on her mountain. Having Sarah had become too comfortable, and she did not like to think of her granddaughter gone for good. Meredith could see she was having some positive influence on the girl; God knows what Sarah would be like living with her mother and grandfather as role models. Probably a lot like Eli.

"I'm leaving as soon as possible."

"I don't see why."

"I feel the same about my land as you do yours."

"You intend to track that man down, don't you?" Meredith looked at Eli, trying to catch her eye. "Maybe kill him?"

"I want to help." Eli stood up; the old woman's gaze bothered her. Three months with Meredith was enough. "He should be stopped."

"Let someone else do it. You belong here, with your daughter. You're not a policeman."

"Yes, I am." Eli picked up the empty tea cups. "That's the damn shame. I feel useless here. For awhile I felt numb, but not anymore."

"I don't—"

"He took Karol." Eli looked for that light again, and saw her reflection had faded by the failing light of the fire, saw just the glint of her hair in the black window. "I want him stopped, and I feel that more strongly every day. I need to go home."

Eli turned and walked toward the kitchen, bothered by the feeling that she might cry again. She did not want to, felt that she no longer should have a need to.

"Eli," Meredith called.

She turned, and the old woman looked bent, even tiny, wrapped in a blanket and looking into the fire.

"Of course I want this man stopped." Meredith thought for a moment, watching a blue flame crawl up a log. "No, what I really want is for him to be killed. Just shot. No long trial. No book or movie deals. Nothing." As Meredith thought about Eli going, and felt her standing by the kitchen with the teacups, something else came to her mind. Something stronger than her irritation at her rough daughter-in-law, at the profession that Eli should never have practiced. Stronger even than the fact that Eli kept Karol in her Valley, and put him in a place where he never should have been anyway, where he had been killed. Meredith was surprised by what she felt.

"Eli," she said. "I have very little family left. You're important to me now, much more than before."

"I thought you didn't like me."

"I hardly do, to tell the truth." Meredith smiled. "But I need you, and needing leads to liking, I'm afraid."

Eli returned the tea cups to the kitchen.

XXXVII

When the sheriff, the ATF agents, and the FBI came for him, they would come in a line of cars down the gravel road. That's what he figured. He had, maybe, twenty minutes before he would be captured.

Well, fuck, Clyde Bumber thought, they're already coming.

From the attic of his Ohio farm house, he looked out the small window and far across the rolling field, about a mile away, the headlights winked as the cars bounced up and down, the lights coming through bare trees. Just a hint of violet and purple lit the lower sky, but already enough to make the thin coating of November snow a sickly grey. The old family farm looked like the surface of the moon, and felt just as cold and dead to Bumber as he saw the cars claw their way over the broken road that led right to his door.

He had made mistakes, no doubt. When Mr. Spell had left him naked in the field, waiting to be shot, that was mistake number one. He waited and waited, but when he had finally turned around, freezing anyway so a shot in the forehead wouldn't matter, the man had quietly, expertly walked away.

Number two mistake was employing Rex and Briggs. Two simpleminded custodians. Rex had been working over the dead deer and let Mr. Spell just walk on by with the best gun Bumber had ever scored. Mistake number three was continuing the CB Gun Company. But the orders kept coming from Manhattan, his brother in Budapest shipped interesting weapons, prices soared. The money made it so easy to forget the screw-ups. That's probably what led to mistake number four. The big one.

The night before word came down from the Ore Car that someone was looking for the CB Company. When Briggs called about it, and said there was some guy in town all right, Bumber decided to let them handle it. He asked Thelma to get ready at the motel to play with a newcomer—maybe someone she'd like to screw like Mr. Spell. His little girl never could get over Mr. Spell. Let them handle things for once, Bumber had thought. He just hadn't wanted to touch the situation.

Then Rex' wife called; Mayra said he was not home and wondered if he was at the farm drinking? That was 1 a.m. Then Sal called about Briggs, said he was busted, said that Briggs and Rex got the shit beat out of them by some guy, turns out he worked for the FBI—turns out there was a bunch of agents ready to rush in. But, Sal said, the way Briggs looked it seemed the G-man didn't need any help. That was 3 a.m.

Here it was a little after 6 a.m. It took awhile for Briggs and Rex to talk; maybe they'd been unconscious. Yeah, Bumber thought, maybe mistake number one was keeping Briggs and Rex in the game. One-dimensional guys. You didn't want to run with one-dimensional guys if you wanted a fourth-dimensional operation. He should have known. Especially after Mr. Spell.

Tired of looking at cars, feeling too much like the rabbit caught in the headlights, Bumber turned inward. In the dim early morning, there wasn't much to see in the attic, but his old Flexible Flyer, unmoved for years—maybe since Thelma last gave it a try. It reminded him of other days in the attic, with his brothers, messing with granddad's stuff, or when he came up by himself sometimes just to watch dust motes float down in the afternoon rays. Letting his ma, grandma, and granddad all holler until he finally decided to come down for supper. And that teenage girl he called his wife sometimes, the same girl Thelma would have called mother had she known, didn't they first sneak up here to make love? Wasn't that the old musty, stained mattress propped up against a shadow over there?

As he heard the cars now, engines humming like an ill wind, the thing that bothered him was what would happen to the farm. He had been the caretaker of the Bumber place, the eldest son put in charge of it in his father's will, there to hold it into the next century. And now here came the federal government, raiding the place, probably going to seize the whole thing. And his great-grandfather, and granddad—the moody old bastard—everything they put together probably was coming to an end. Clyde told himself that he set up the CB Gun Company to pay the taxes, to keep the place. That was the noble thing. Of course, he pocketed the money for other uses, but still he had found a better way to keep the place in the family than kicking dirt clods. Guns were a crop that did not put you at the mercy of the weather, or the banker, or the department of agriculture. And guns were a lot more popular in America than corn.

Well, fuck, and here he was losing the place, counting the last seconds the Bumbers might be able to call the land their own. If the Feds didn't seize it outright, the fines and absentee ownership while he sat in jail would put an end to everything. Losing the farm, that was the tough part.

Clyde tried to be cool since he knew Briggs and Rex were in jail; he wasn't going to panic or run. He could think his way out. The only thing he had done was move some guns from the shed and plant them in the field. But now that he looked through the window and saw the cars fan out in front of the house, saw each one hit the brakes, his heart beat a little faster. Somewhere in the back of his mind he had the urge to run. So he looked out the back window, and could see the men running across the snow, black little figures scrambling for position behind the house. Some surrounded the shed. They got here before the cars even arrived, Bumber thought, now how the hell did they do that? Must have just snuck over on foot from Wade's place.

He could hear boots on the porch, could almost feel the men encircling the house. Then the sheriff, old Rudy himself—old high school buddy they probably figured would be a good bet to ease the suspect into arrest—Rudy came to the door. A lot of men with rifles came with him, dressed dark, military-like. They were right; Clyde did feel comforted by the sight of Rudy, with his unassuming light brown uniform.

"Clyde?" Rudy knocked on the door. "Your truck's out here, Clyde, so I know you're in there. C'mon out."

"We have a federal warrant to search your farm, Mr. Bumber." That was a stranger's voice, punched up by a bullhorn.

"Better come out, Clyde. This is pretty damn serious."

They didn't hesitate for long.

Bumber sat in the corner of the attic and waited for them to find him. He heard them crash in, and figured his mother's prize mahogany door had been splintered. They broke open the back door, too. Something crashed in the kitchen as the boots came through, most likely the old salt and pepper silver set on the dining table. They rushed the second floor, kicked some things around in his bedroom. Some men spent a lot of time in Thelma's room; sounded like they were ransacking it. Bumber wondered where she might be; most likely they nailed her at the motel where he had told her to wait. She could take care of herself, no doubt. But the old house, from the sound of things, was being kicked to pieces. He hated to listen to them, violating the place, stomping heirlooms and memories to shit.

The boots came up the stairs. He could make out a rifle poking into the attic, hard to see in the light, but probably the nose of an M-16. Then a man leapt in, wearing a black cap, black clothes, flak jacket, moving smooth and quiet, a silhouette sliding forward. Two others followed. The lead man spotted him.

"Don't move," he said.

Clyde blinked at the bright light in his eyes and before he could say a word they pinned him, cuffed him, searched him, went over his rights, and hustled him down the stairs, keeping that light in his eyes the entire time. Out the door into the cold morning air, lifted off his porch, off his land forever.

And before he knew exactly what hit him or how he should feel about it, Clyde Bumber sat in the back of a sedan with two men in suits riding up front.

"Are you all right, Mr. Bumber?" The man in the passenger's side turned, grinning wide. Pleasant looking Oriental fellow, Clyde thought, so slick and at ease. Bumber felt a little better.

"Sure." But he didn't feel that fine.

"Now you know you don't have to say a word to us until you have a lawyer present, right?"

"Yeah."

"I suppose you know you will be arraigned on several violations of federal law concerning trafficking arms and munitions? And other charges, but you'll know soon at the arraignment."

"Munitions?"

"Our metal detectors turned up quite a few things buried near your shed."

"You found the 20 millimeter shells?" That made him wonder how long they had been searching his place. He thought he had those buried deep.

"I haven't heard about those yet, Mr. Bumber."

"Shit." This guy is pretty good, he thought. Better shut up until I see a lawyer. The other man looked into the rearview mirror. Some clean-cut white guy. Both men were young, maybe just in their thirties.

"You FBI?" Bumber asked. He wanted to talk to them. He couldn't help it, chatting was part of his nature.

"Yes, we are. I'm agent Chang."

"I'm agent Wallace." He smiled and waved into the rearview mirror.

Bumber looked ahead; Rudy's car led the way. Behind, another unmarked car. His farm was out of view. Most of the cars and men he had seen were still back at his home. God knows what they would uncover. The white countryside whizzed by in a blur, and the car bounced violently until they hit pavement. They were driving fast, and Clyde figured they would be in Brulingham in a few minutes.

He took a deep breath. Time to work fourth dimensionally, he thought. Not much time. Clyde had no doubt that Briggs and Rex had screwed him over completely; the whole operation was blown. They'd find everything on his farm and all the stuff in the maintenance closets at Agassiz College. Might as well plead guilty. No, he thought, might as well cooperate, maybe work out a deal. He had seen it enough on TV, sometimes a deal could take a person far.

Then Bumber smiled. He had something that the FBI agents would drop down and die for. Clyde knew the number one man they wanted, the eco-terrorist who made assholes out of all of them and controlled an entire National Park. Eldred Spell. In the first reports of shootings, there had been talk that the killer used a fancy Soviet weapon. *Guns and Ammo* made a big deal out of it; the expert rifleman in the Park had some kind of sophisticated Dragunov, and they ran a special sidebar on the gun. Bumber figured it out quick, then, that the man who left him naked in the field, the man who stole his gun and then raped the Park Service—that was Mr. Spell. They would die to have the identification of that man. Since Mr. Spell stole the Dragunov from him, and money never changed hands on that weapon, they probably would not come down on Bumber for the transaction.

Briggs and Rex did not know. Each had a head like a box of rocks. And Bumber had thought ahead just enough so that he did not let on that the eco-terrorist was Mr. Spell. He had been smart enough to keep that secret as a little insurance policy. He could cash that one in now, big time.

"I had quite an operation," Bumber said, easing back in his seat. He could get in good with these guys.

"That so?" Chang had a pleasant smile.

"Probably like nothing you or the ATF ever saw."

"It was unusual," Wallace said.

"Sorry that your man got roughed up."

"Oh, he was fine," Chang said. "Really."

"Well, you know, with an operation like mine, with international connections, I had to have a system for checking people out. Couldn't let people like you just infiltrate us."

"Of course not."

"So when we knew a stranger was asking for us, we'd work him over a bit."

"Why?"

"Think about it." Bumber could see that Chang was fascinated, and that made him want to talk even more. "If we beat an agent up, we figured people would come looking for him. We'd put the fella up in a motel and watch. If unmarked cars came by, if suits like you checked in, bingo—we disappear."

"I see."

"But if you were really clever and were willing to wait, well, I had a back up plan."

"Back up?"

"Yeah. Thelma would kind of bait the guy, you know? If he went for her, no doubt the guy wasn't a professional."

"Who's Thelma?" Wallace asked.

"Let's just say she's a hot one." Bumber chuckled. She was every bit as hot as her mother was, and he knew that from personal experience. Some kind of woman. "Real jail bait, or used to be anyway."

"Did you ever try this out on anyone before last night?"

"Hell, yes." Bumber saw that they were in town now, just a few blocks from the county courthouse. He had to get these agents very interested, and in a hurry. Chang already seemed to be licking his lips for information.

"Twice. Some guy a couple years back—we made a monkey out of him before he scampered out of town." Bumber leaned forward and lowered his voice. "Then a second man. Someone you might find real interesting."

"Oh?" Chang smiled wide.

"I can't talk about it," Bumber sat back again. "I'd like to see my lawyer first, have my people talk to your people. Work out a little deal, right?"

"Mr. Bumber, you are an original." Chang turned around, talking to Wallace. "In my career I have never encountered anyone like this man."

"Indeed," Wallace said.

They laughed heartily, and didn't stop until they pulled in to the courthouse parking lot.

The idiots, Bumber thought, they have no idea what I'm offering here. He folded his arms and decided he would wait until he had a lawyer and could rustle up someone of more intelligence. He did not think Chang and Wallace were very professional at all.

They led him gently into the courthouse, and they did not smile, as they were walking with other agents now. Rudy, leading the way, would not look back at Clyde.

As they rounded a corner, heading down the hall toward the county corrections wing, he saw two men leading Thelma in his direction. She smiled at him, which struck Bumber as odd. Thelma had not smiled at him in years, it seemed. And now she was, even though he could see she was in deep shit too.

"Wait," Bumber said. "That's my daughter."

The agents stopped, and he stood face to face with her.

"Are you all right, Daddy?" she asked.

When was the last time she called him "Daddy" instead of "Shithead"? Bumber figured she was playing some kind of act, working her own angle to get out. Her hair seemed a little cleaner than usual, and she had it out of her eyes. She wore a turtle neck sweater, nothing cut low to show her sharp cleavage or big jugs. Even in cold weather, that was unusual. She had on a skirt, tight enough, because it was the only one she had, and one that she had not worn since she was fifteen. Definitely playing sweet, Bumber thought.

"Daddy?"

"What, my dear." He could play along.

"Daddy, I told them all about Eldred Spell on certain conditions that they've agreed to."

Bumber said nothing, but noticed that they did not have any cuffs on her. He had told her nothing; Thelma figured out Spell all on her own.

She leaned as close to him as the agents would allow, speaking to him softly, pursing her lips sensuously as if she were about to give him a wet kiss. Like he had taught her to do when she came of age.

"I walked in voluntarily."

"How long has she been here?" Bumber looked away from her to Chang, and then he veered his eyes away from the man's irritating smile. Rudy gave him a sour look, lips curled down, and Clyde knew then that he would have to get used to such looks.

"She turned herself in just before four," Chang said.

"And I've got a lawyer already. A good one. He's coming down from Columbus this morning. I'm going to tell him everything. People around here say he's quite a thinker, and I bet we press charges against you for molestation, maybe other things. Isn't that what you'd call fourth dimensional, Daddy?"

Bumber could think of nothing to say. Chang and Wallace seemed anxious to move him along, and they went down the hall toward county corrections. Clyde looked back once, catching a glimpse of the back of Thelma's muscular legs as she walked away. Then Chang opened the door for Bumber.

Damn that Mr. Spell, Clyde thought, if he would have had the guts to shoot me none of this would have happened.

XXXVIII

They were silk sheets, the only kind Andrea said she would sleep in, and when he awoke and slid his hand over them, Spell liked the cool, slick feel of the fabric. she had left, so he thought it must be late, but his Rolex on the night stand read just 8 a.m. Odd that she wasn't there. He lay back and thought for a moment, wondering how the day would go. she had drawn the curtains over the French doors that led to the balcony, so he could not see the weather. But enough grey light filtered through the curtain that he knew the morning fog was still in; he hoped it would blow away soon, for he looked forward to a clear, cold day.

Eldred could picture how it would be, another morning in the cafe, talking with her over a lobster crepe, Hawaiian coffee, perhaps the paper. Lately he had lost his interest in reading the papers, however. He preferred to talk to her. Sometimes he had the notion that his mother would like her, that Andrea might be one who would measure up. Andrea, tall and dark, was tough physically and mentally. The kind of person his mother had made of him. He had not seen his mother in years, did not call nor write. Just that one e-mail was all the communication between them for a long time. she would probably admire his resolve; the last time he saw her in the big white house, he screamed that she would never hear from him again. Embarrassed them both, with that screaming. So, better that he kept his promise to her. Still, he'd almost like to see Andrea and his mother in the same room, maybe square off right away while he watched.

What would come after breakfast would be a jog along the beach on the other side of the bay. They raced, always underdressed against the cold, both believing they could be sharpened by it. They pushed each other in speed and stamina, and Spell had to work hard to stay ahead. Later she would show him more of her business, for they had agreed quietly while he recovered from his wounds–a terrible running fall, he had said—that he could come in as a partner. she needed capital to remodel; the Spyglass Inn required a facelift to survive the competition of a new hotel going up a block away. He transferred almost all he had, three million dollars, into her accounts. Now that the announcement of his partnership was a few days away, they argued about what his role would be. Discussed who would be in charge—both enjoyed the debate immensely.

Late at night, when her work was done, they wrestled in her room. Opened the French doors to the cold air but still working at each other in a sweat, each demanding more and more of the other, fighting as much as making love. Sometimes, when she would ride his thighs and he would slam her into the wall, he wondered if he could hurt her. He came very close to it a few times. she came back at him harder, biting his ear or running a long slender nail down his back. she took advantage of the lingering tenderness and weakness in his wounded leg. They tore clothes and broke things in the room, but somehow came just short of hurting each other. No cuts nor bruises in the morning. But the intensity increased, and it seemed that both of them were coming closer to real pain on those nights, and that they both craved it. The nights satisfied that deep, relentless voice within him.

Yet this life with Andrea also suited the New York man still alive within him, the one who had searched in the past for a stable, civilized life. That part of him could imagine the years ahead as a prominent businessman in Monterey, and he already had plans to expand the hotel, to capitalize on tourist trends, and perhaps seize other businesses. Like New York, Monterey had been ruined long before—he felt no grief contributing to the next layer of development. It would take a lot of time and work to beat the competition, to rule this place.

Occasionally, when he walked idly about Monterey or went shopping with her in Carmel, he'd think about the Valley. For the most part, he had cleared it. Tried to convince himself that he had worked out that desire. His life there became more and more detached from this new one with Andrea. But without another visit, he knew that soon people would return to the Park. The Heston Company already worked on installing another tank, would soon have the water on line, and was offering incredible discounts on the ski season to bring people back once the Park opened.

Sooner or later he would lose what he had created. That made the stronger part of him stir, flex its muscles, and so he poured himself more fervently into Andrea. When he felt drawn to the Valley, to walk through the new land that he had created, the urge came strongly over him. Eldred Spell wanted to go back. If he learned his new land was fading away, and the people were filling the Valley again, he did not know if he could silence the insistent, deep voice. Sometimes at night, feeling what he did, he wanted to clutch Andrea, lift her up violently, beat her head against the wall. He had come close. she did not seem to mind, and could hurt him as well. Spell just did not know, when he would admit it to himself, how long the pleasurable tension of his new life in Monterey would hold.

Getting out of bed, he felt his heart begin to beat hard. Something about the morning, his thoughts, the drawn curtains, and her absence made him feel uneasy. Spell showered quickly, toweled off, threw open the French doors and let the cold, foggy breeze bite his wet skin. Somehow, the hotel sounded unusually quiet, and the clang of the outer buoy in the bay seemed muffled and much farther away than a mile. He put his hand in the air, closed his eyes, while his heart raced. Spell waited, and flinched when he heard the door open and shut behind him.

"What is it?" he whispered to himself.

"Put on your clothes," Andrea said. Her voice seemed flat, unusually passionless.

"Why?" He turned, seeing that she already attacked his clothes in her closet, throwing them mechanically on the unmade bed.

"You're leaving." She grunted as she threw his suits, hangers and all, onto the bed. "Get in here and close those doors behind you."

"What's the matter?" He did as she ordered, looking at the thong he had left on the floor the night before.

"Check the night stand."

She had thrown the copy of *USA Today* upon it, knocking off the small lamp and his Rolex. Spell picked it up, saw his name and photo on the top of the front page. He looked grim in the picture, one of the bad portraits Whitston Harris had taken of him when he had been hired. His hair was shorter; he looked much younger. Part of himself collapsed inside, and he felt momentarily weak and dizzy as he looked at the paper. The other voice rose up, already recognized that the photo made him look different enough that he might have a chance on the streets.

He let the paper fall, and pulled on his thong. He dressed slowly in jeans and the shabbiest shirt he had—anything to appear different from the clean cut, three-piece suit look that he had in that picture. Andrea watched him.

"You don't have a suitcase, do you?" she asked.

"Not anymore. I bought most of these clothes here."

She wore sweats, her hair tousled. Her eyes set black and hard against him, but the red showed she had been crying.

"Keep the clothes," he said, avoiding her look.

"I'll throw them away."

"Fine." He picked up his watch and his wallet. "I won't need them." He stood looking down at the pile, recalling his apartment in Manhattan. This was another evacuation from another lifestyle that suddenly exploded. Life in Manhattan had already died, and it was not so hard to leave. But this one had been beginning. The movement from one life to another seemed to be accelerating. He knew where he had to go now, already his muscles tensed and the old voice in him spoke. He would probably not last long in the Valley. But he could give them hell for a time, could keep his new land for a bit longer. That was where he belonged, the voice said, anything less was an illusion. He was following Ellen's tracks and they would soon be after him; it was all so inevitable. Looking up at Andrea, who had managed to strangle most of the emotion from her face now, Spell's New York man died away. He had little to say. Put on his dark sunglasses.

"Do you have everything you want to take with you?"

"The rest is in my car."

"Then go." She went to the door but did not open it. "You don't have much time. The night manager recognized you, came up here to get me an hour ago. I told him not to call the police or I would fire him. My hotel doesn't need the publicity."

"Exactly," Spell said.

She handed him his car keys. "I parked it up the street, by the Sheraton lot. Go out the fire exit. Stay out of the lobby."

"All right."

They looked at each other, pausing at the door. Her face had set hard, paled slightly, and she stared at him as if he were a stranger who had just intruded. The look came strong enough, so vehemently, that he suddenly wanted to get away.

She cut him off quickly, relentlessly. Just the woman he could have brought home to his mother. A rare one.

"My money—" he began, almost stammering.

"I'm keeping it." She broke into a tight triumphant smile. "You ran up a monstrous bill here."

"I paid my way."

"No, you didn't come close." She opened the door, peered out, and motioned him through.

"Good bye," he said, searching for anything to say. The kind of words he might have had for her just a few minutes before were gone. Nothing like love could come to his lips, and he could see that nothing in her would receive him. He just felt slightly amused and amazed at how quickly they could run back to what they naturally were.

She shut the door and locked it.

The day he had hoped to have had dissolved. As he walked quickly to the fire escape exit at the end of the hall, Spell felt the razor edge of the days ahead. Life or death, with not long to go. The way now would be hard, keeping a heartbeat ahead of everyone in the country. With his identity out there, he would have to take everyone on.

As he jogged down the stairs, he wanted to believe he preferred things that way. That he really wanted to go back to his Valley. And wait for them all to come after him.

XXXIX

Just outside of Concord, Massachusetts, Agent George Tinker pulled his tan, government issue Crown Victoria onto the Cheltingham estate. All the leaves had fallen from the huge sugar maples that lined the one-lane drive, but the fields on either side held a bright green hue under the small but brilliant November sun. Though cold, the sky was lit with such a deep blue and the rolling land so beautiful, that from the warmth of his car Tinker could pretend winter was still far off. When he rounded a curve he caught a glimpse of the house through the trees, a mansion starkly white in the morning sun.

Tinker had spent the last two days conducting interviews, faxing reports as he went, compiling a picture of Eldred Spell. He had put together criminal profiles for the agency for years, concentrating on field interviews in particular. And he had never come across someone like Spell. Even with his experience, Tinker still had some trouble picturing this wealthy stockbroker, silver spoon in mouth, running up and down the mountains of California fighting like the kind of crazed veteran the public loved to watch in movie theaters. What had given this man such a hard edge, he wondered. Revenge for his dead sister might be the motive, but that could not have prepared him to do what he had done.

The previous day at the offices of Whitston Harris in New York, Tinker interviewed the owning partners themselves and everyone on down the hierarchy who knew Eldred Spell. Of course, with his identity out and all the hype in the media, most everyone there knew he was a killer from the start. But after awhile they admitted that he had done nothing violent while he worked there. Mr. Whitston said that Spell was the most brilliant stockbroker he had ever seen, a man who could predict trends in the market with uncanny accuracy—a fabulous asset for the firm. Others on down, even grudgingly, confirmed this—explaining why Spell was known as the Voodoo Broker. From a business sense, they hated to see him go.

Some confusion about what happened to Spell on the day of the World Trade Center bombing. Clearly he had snapped. Kerry Womack, the man who took over Spell's office once they were sure he was not coming back, said that Spell was violent. Womack paced the office during the interview, waving his arms, explaining how Spell nearly pushed him out of a window during the evacuation. "A very, very scary person," he had exclaimed. But Spell's secretary, Tereza Limon, presented him as a courageous man who took charge and led them safely out the building. He even saved two children who were nearly trampled by people fleeing down the stairwell.

People in his home at The Towers did not know him, but the doorman identified his latest lover. Alanis was straightforward, and described that the man could be fantastic in bed and was good company; though she had moved on to other men, she did miss him.

Clearly, Tinker thought as he stopped in front of the big white house, clearly I'm working up two distinct profiles out of one man. An intelligent stockbroker who appreciates fine food, music, and women. Another who's nothing short of a commando, who lives some kind of Spartan life on the run, doing battle with the federal government and winning. That side of him took over when his building had been bombed. The day he discovered his sister had died in the Park. Violence begat violence. It was odd, though, in a man who grew up in a mansion and never did a day of military service in his life. A high school career at a military prep school could not account for it; what leads to anything unusual there stopped at the last commandant, McCrimmon—a man who had put a gun to his head many years ago.

The Cheltingham house looked like a federal building, with a heavy portico supported by colossal columns; all white, blazingly white, so that the shadowed recesses of the house glowed blue, like shadows on snow. It reminded Tinker of the supreme court building, just smaller. He walked up the wide stone steps to a huge, intricately carved set of teak doors and rang the chimes.

"Are you with the Federal Bureau of Investigation?" A slim middle-aged woman, dressed in a dark blue pantsuit, opened the door. Grey hair pulled back, she looked him over with tiny eyes sunk behind thick wire-rimmed glasses.

"Yes." He knew the look, so he showed her his identification. "I'm Agent George Tinker. I have a ten o'clock appointment to see Ms. Cheltingham."

"You're the one who called us yesterday?"

"I am."

"We may have a problem, Mr. Tinker."

"How so?"

"I'm afraid your voice misrepresents you."

"What do you mean?" But he knew; he had heard this before.

"Wait here." She closed the door.

Tinker stood looking at the large white columns, feeling the cold work through his suit. On the far end of the great lawn in front of the house, he saw a crew vacuuming maple leaves. After a few minutes, he checked his watch.

Abruptly, the woman opened the door. "I'm sorry, Mr. Tinker, but you'll have to leave."

"Why?" But he knew why, and tried to stifle his growing irritation. He could not afford the time of sending out another agent, so he had to stay calm.

"Perhaps if you send someone else."

"Who isn't black?"

"Precisely." She began to close the door.

"Wait," Tinker put his hand on the brass knob, stopping her. "Would you please explain to Ms. Cheltingham that the best I can do is come back with, say, four black agents? We could inform reporters of our visit as well. You know how difficult they can be." He smiled, watching her frown. "Probably be some black reporters as well, after some racial angle."

"The reporters have come and gone," she said.

"If they hear a carload of FBI agents are coming—"

"Of course." She looked at his hand on the door, waited for him to remove it. "Wait here."

Ten minutes later she came back, opened the door without a word, and ushered him in. "Follow me, Mr. Tinker."

The inside reminded him of a federal building as well, marble floors and oversized halls—he felt like he was taking a tour through the capitol building. Except that inside it was hot; he already felt uncomfortable, cold as he had been, and wondered if the interior was kept in the eighties. He could not imagine the expense of maintaining that heat.

"Mr. Tinker," the woman announced simply as she opened French doors that led to a large sun room. She stood at the door as he went through.

Tinker walked over the great green and purple Persian rug, keeping his eye on the old woman breakfasting by the window. She took tea and croissants, sitting in a plush chair with her back to him, looking out one of the large windows. He noticed there were no other chairs nearby, so he stood at her side, looking down at her small head, white hair pulled back in the same fashion of the woman who let him in.

"Thank you for seeing me," Tinker said. Play it cool, he thought, just pump the old lady for information.

"You'll forgive me if I don't shake your hand," she said. "You have found me at breakfast."

"I understand."

Her voice struck him as much younger than she looked; tense, low, and rather powerful. She wore a white dress, with a button-up collar, and looked like she had just stepped out of a turn-of-the-century Impressionist painting. Bathed in the sun as she was, he wished he could put on sunglasses to look at her. The blue veins clearly stood up on the tops of her hands; he guessed she was in her seventies.

"Why did they send you, Mr. Tinker?"

"I interview people, and the government feels I am quite qualified for what I do."

"Why is that?"

"I have a degree in journalism from Columbia, graduate degrees in criminal psychology and clinical psychiatry from Johns Hopkins. I have been interviewing people for the agency for twenty-three years. They send me to help with the background of important suspects."

"Dangerous criminals?"

"Most often, yes."

"Who have you interviewed about Eldred Spell?"

"Workers, associates in New York." He paused. "Lovers." He shouldn't have said that, he knew, but he could not resist the great temptation to anger her.

"Then you probably know more about him than I do." She looked up at him, smiling, as if she had just won something. "So I'll give you five minutes of my time and no more. Ask away."

She pulled a large gold pocket watch out of her dress pocket, flipped open the lid, and looked down at it, squinting as it glistened in the sunlight. He noticed it was a man's watch, and figured it to be very old.

"All right." The sun room seemed very hot, possibly in the nineties. Looking at how thin she was, and seeing that she still had a blanket draped over her lap, he guessed she had heart trouble. Looking more carefully, he saw what he thought to be a small bottle of nitro pills just behind the silver tea set on the table nearby. This was out of Cheltingham's reach, so that the woman in the blue pantsuit would have to serve her. Probably one of the reasons why she stood by the door, watching and listening.

"Has your son had any military training?"

"None that I'm aware of."

"What about the Jackson Military Academy?"

"That was a high school, Mr. Tinker."

"Does he have an interest in exotic weapons?"

"I wouldn't know."

He stopped, thought a moment, and asked, "how long has it been since you've seen your son?"

"Ten years or more, I should think." She sipped her tea.

"Do you have any photos of your son that I could look at?"

"None readily available, no. Perhaps in a trunk somewhere, if we had the time to look. Do you really need a picture? I think the ones in the newspapers are adequate likenesses." She set down her cup, and rubbed the crystal of the watch with her long, thin thumb.

If she had any normal feeling for her son, Tinker thought, she's clever at hiding it. Although he was running out of time for now, he thought carefully about the next question. What could he ask in this short time that would be useful?

"Ms. Cheltingham, do you believe your son is the eco-terrorist?"

"I don't think he'd concur with that term." She reached for the tea cup again, her hand shaking this time. "He was never a joiner. But, yes, I imagine he's the one you want to hunt down."

"You think he's guilty?"

"I think he is active." She set the cup back down, without taking a sip, and let her hand rest on the arm of her chair as if the effort of moving tired her immensely. Turning to her watch, she said, "you are almost out of time."

"Why do you suppose he's doing this? Revenge for his sister?"

"For Ellen? Perhaps. But more for his father." She rubbed the watch again. "His father left us all when Eldred was four, and died not long after that. Don't ask me where or how. But, yes, his father is much of the cause."

"Why?"

"Eldred is a stubborn person; he became fixed upon the fantasy that his father took him out west, to that Valley. All his father did was tell the boy stories, romantic tales that his blood was Indian, that California would call him one day. He described the Valley, and Eldred came to believe he had been there. Something I could not shake out of him—the one foolishness that worked its way into the boy's blood. And from there to his sister. Eldred's father was quite destructive."

"Was he Native American? I did not see that in his record."

"An Indian? Of course not." She raised her voice slightly.

Tinker was cheered that she seemed bothered.

"His skin was dark—tan, I mean, nothing like yours. He made a lot of it. So did other people." She closed the lid, and slid the watch back in her pocket. "Eldred is dark—in mind, I mean. I suppose he believes he has some stake, some kinship in that land. Some part of his father working in him. Maybe something he owes his sister." She paused, squinting into the window. "Rather disturbed children. But now your time is up."

"Do you think we'll catch him?" He knew this would be a question she would want to answer.

"No." She let out a short, brittle laugh. "He will always be one step ahead of you—that's in his blood, too."

"From you?"

"From his father." Very slowly, she stood, her back to Tinker. "But his strength comes from me." She turned to him. "He might be killed, but you won't subdue him." Cheltingham's large blue eyes widened, and her smile pulled back over her porcelain teeth. "I raised him, and he's a hard man. You have no idea."

"Ms. Cheltingham—"

"Miss Brace." She turned to the woman in the pantsuit. Cheltingham began to breathe in short puffs. "Show him out."

As Tinker drove away, he glanced back at the large, cold white house in his rearview mirror. He imagined what childhood would have been like out here, with her as a mother. Tinker began to see why Eldred Spell was such a tough case—wealth did not always breed softness.

When he pulled onto the highway off the Cheltingham estate, Tinker thought of the profile he was putting together. No wonder the Park Service had been in such trouble. With Spell, they would all be in trouble until the man was dead. That last part was Tinker's private opinion, and he did not plan to put it that way in the official report.

XXXX

Eli sat on her porch and watched the heavy snow. Over two feet on the ground, grey under the thick ceiling of listless clouds. Building up for another storm. The pine trees were black in the dull twilight, with the limbs of the nearby apple trees thrown up like withered veins. She knew the Valley well, and an evening this cold with snow on the ground in early November probably meant that they were in for a brutal winter. Heavy powder on the ridges, which would please The Heston Company if any skier were allowed into the Park. Following the willowy steam of her breath, her eyes scanned the South meadow, the cliffs above. For the first time she could remember, Eli saw no beauty in the land.

Her fourth day home from North Carolina, and she thought she never should have come. At least with Meredith and Sarah she could slip into some kind of emotional underwater, drift with whatever currents they made for her, and pretend there was nothing she could do. Forget her anger. But since she had come home, Eli had been breaking things. At first she thought she simply dropped a dish or accidentally overturned a chair when passing by. But now she tossed the cookware around, regularly attacked cups and plates. She tended to kick anything in her path, and she let the mess grow. The cabin was in disarray, as if someone had been searching for something important but could not find it.

Between her cabin and her father's a dividing line had been made, hardening every day. She could not see him, and he made no effort to see her. Eli expected that he would come by once she was back in the cabin, but he did not. She could understand how he had avoided her when Karol had died—he did not like the face of grief—but she did not know why he avoided her now. Since she had been the one who suffered, and the one to return home, Eli decided she would be damned if she would go to his place. Olivos came by, of course, acting the go-between, urging her to see him. But Eli suspected Olivos made things his concern as an excuse to see her as often as possible. She kept him away when she could, made sure she gave no encouragement.

Olivos had another campaign: to get Eli back to work. She had postponed an appointment with the new Park superintendent, squeezing out the last of the leave Cairns had granted her. Soon, though, she would have to start back. Out on patrols, under the direction of the FBI. They had effectively taken over the Park. She had no desire to answer to any of them, or anyone. She did not think she was fit to take any orders.

More and more she thought of Eldred Spell. Olivos had brought a pile of newspapers, magazines, and official reports concerning Spell. He believed the information would help, pull her into the spirit of the investigation and the guard duty in the Park. But all she could see was the picture of the man who had killed Karol, and felt somehow cheated that Spell was not some kind of professional killer—a terrorist or ex-army ranger. Merely some kind of super weekend warrior, a stockbroker kicked loose from New York, come to their Valley to clear it out, to take over. Along the way he happened to kill Karol Ensley Ware.

The evening before, she read that Spell's Jaguar had been found stripped in Compton. Spell's prints were all over the vehicle, and an FBI agent found a brochure from the Mexican Tourism Bureau on the ground nearby. No one in the neighborhood would say anything about the car, how it got there, or who left it. Thousands of dollars of expensive parts and equipment had been pulled off it; no one had anything of value to tell the police. Some commentators theorized that with his car left as it was, where it was, the man might already be dead. A trace of his blood was found on the upholstery and steering wheel. The brochure suggested Mexico, and the border was on high alert to look for him. Authorities in Tijuana, Tecate, and Mexicali were also informed about Spell. Some in the media speculated that the man, as clever and rich as he was, had already gone far—possibly to South America by this time. Experts on Nightline and CNN agreed that he had probably fled the country the moment his identification was known, if not before. They all noted how long it had been since his attack on the water tank.

Eli did not think he had gone. She knew how he felt about the Valley; like her, he was someone who had a stake in it, felt he was an owner. Like her, however painful it might be, he would be back.

She stood up, looking at the cold rock walls towering over the meadow, smelled a trace of wood smoke from her father's chimney. Somewhere, up in the ridges, maybe as close as a mile or two, Eldred Spell waited. Once someone felt in control of the Valley, close to it in that way, he or she could no more leave it than throw out a piece of soul. Her father liked to talk about the families that came back to the Valley, carved their own two weeks out of it, year after year. "It has that effect on all of us," he had said. "We all want a part of it—that's why we're wrecking the Park."

Walking along the porch, Eli stopped at the edge. The snow in the meadow lay like a sheet of dull paper—perfect, except the tracks across it. Where someone stepped in the layer of snow, they left a hole, a black track. She stared at the tracks, almost losing them in the quick autumn nightfall. Eli stood frozen for a long time, while the night settled into black, until the buzz of a distant helicopter broke her thoughts.

Eli had been imagining what she would do if she were up there, hiding. Picturing him had kept her up nights; Spell stayed in her mind, always leading to the question of what she could do about him. Deep inside, she hoped he was still in the Park because she wanted to be the one to do something about him, ever since Karol had been killed. The thoughts were bloodthirsty, ridiculous, and easy to keep back while she counted fireflies with Sarah or raked up the fallen leaves. But alone, back in the Valley, with the killer named and pictured on every form of media, Spell and her feelings became inescapable. Didn't he own a part of her now? Bagged his claim when he shot Karol, compelled her to throw dishes into walls. What could she do?

The tracks in the snow were out of sight, except for a few under the glow of her father's porch light. He usually left it off, but he had it on every night since she had returned—as close as he would come to a formal invitation to her. She realized she had been walking slowly, was halfway to his cabin. Following tracks in the snow.

Another helicopter flew overhead.

Spell would not be fool enough to travel with the snow on the ground, she thought. Even at night. If he moved, leaving black footprints, the patrols, the chopper pilots, the trackers would pick up his location easily. And the snow had been a surprise; this storm was supposed to miss them. So he would be trapped, and now he had to wait and see what would happen, when he could find a break. Had to wait in some hiding spot. But he would know his escape would be as soon as—

"It snows again," Eli said to herself. "He'll move when the snow comes again, when his tracks can be covered, when visibility is low."

The snow on the ground was left by a series of freak squalls; but the first real storm was on its way. By the next afternoon it would be on the Valley, laying down at least another two feet, in one heavy blow. He'll know that, she thought. And he'll move, maybe move out for awhile.

"But where in the hell is he?"

Eli shivered. She had a plan at last. Now all she needed was a destination. Anyone could guess he would be on the move in a raging storm; he would have to try it. But where? If she could not predict where, out of hundreds of square miles, she would have no chance of catching him—especially with visibility so reduced. At best, up on the ridges, she'd be lucky to see a dozen feet around.

She ran up the porch steps of her father's cabin and beat on his door, feeling something like real, active pleasure for the first time in months. Most likely she'd get hypothermia out there, but at least she could finally do something.

"Come in!" her father yelled. He sounded belligerent.

She walked in and saw him at his heavy oak table, a bottle of JD in reach. A single bulb on above his head, dishes piled by the sink. The fire dying, the cabin cold. And his eyes the color of the fading embers. Dead drunk again.

"So," he said, leaning back in his chair. "Why don't you shut the damned door? It's cold." He watched her take a chair. Her hair had grown longer, seemed dirty, and she had gained some weight. Grief is the best excuse to do nothing, he thought.

"Been sittin' on your ass for a few months, I'd say."

"Just like you," she said.

"How about a drink?"

"No. I want to talk to you about something."

"Talk over a drink."

"I need your advice."

"You?" He saw her lean close, a glint of the fire in her eyes. She seemed serious. "My advice?"

"Listen—" She stopped, looked into his face. He was drunk all right, but not too far gone. He could still help. "Where's your topo map of the Park?"

"What you need that for? Don't you got one?"

"Yes." She looked on the wall, saw the green and white survey map tacked up. Eli pulled it off the nails, and laid it on the table in front of him.

"What the hell?" He stood up, felt a little dizzy, waited for his eyes to focus. "Why are you tearing up things? I haven't seen you in a long time, and you just run in here and tear up my damned place."

"This is important."

"So's my place. What in the hell you doing?"

"Give me a chance to say." She paused, looked him over again. Yes, he might still be sober enough, and she knew how to calm him. "You know this Park better than anyone else, right?"

"Huh."

She saw his scowl, the gathering storm as he had been working up his temper, fade away. Jack Hattan looked down at the map.

"Yeah," he said.

"I want to find Eldred Spell," she said. She figured how he would take this: he'd think she was a fool. That was always how he reacted to her plans. But he would also help; she knew what worked with him.

"You want to die? What the hell can you do about Spell?" His temper flared up, and his cheeks reddened while his eyes narrowed and became grey. "That man's dead or somewhere in Rio by now. They lost him. Let him go, I say. Let's just get on with our lives here, I say. What the fuck's the matter with you, little girl?"

She waited. If she were quiet, and let his rage pass over her like a wave, he would come around. If she spoke, that would give him something to push against. But if she were silent, he would settle down.

"What are you up to?" He sounded calmer.

"I think he's here."

"Why?" He took a gulp from his bottle and set it down, keeping an eye on her.

"If you were him, would you leave?"

"If I were him—" His voice started to rise.

"Would you leave?"

He stared at her, breathing heavily, head rocking from side to side with the palsy of drink.

"If you chased everyone out of the Park, single-handed, would you leave?"

"Of course not."

"Neither would I." Eli could see she had his full attention now, skipped him out of his anger. That was easy to do when he drank too much. But he would soon find something else to pick on.

"He's here," she said. "But I'll bet he didn't expect this snow. He can't move."

"So?"

"He'll move tomorrow, in the storm. That's how I'll find him."

"You're an asshole, Eli." He could see she meant it, as ridiculous as the notion was, and that bothered him. She could be stubborn, no matter how foolish her idea. More than that, he didn't like to talk about it, or have to look at the map, because it just reminded him of something he had been trying to forget. Something he wanted to hold back from her. Jack wished that his head was clear. "You won't find a remarkable killer bastard like that in a big blow, in gale force winds. You'll just die out there. I don't even want to talk about it."

"I can handle storms." She drove into his soft spot, his ego. "You taught me how to weather them."

"Yeah, but I don't recall we hiked in storms to find dangerous killers." He looked down at his bottle. "Now, why don't you tell me about something you really know—how's my Sarah?"

"I want to find him."

"Shit," he spat out the word. Why wouldn't she let this thing go? It conjured images in his mind, made him twist with regret painfully—remorse was an emotion that usually lay dormant in him. Now it worked inside, grated like a rusted coil. He had been waiting a long time to see her, but now he wanted her to go. "No one's authorized you to chase after him, I'll bet. You want to lose your job?"

"When did lack of authorization stop you? I can find him."

"What for?" he yelled, exasperated. "Let the man be. Let things run their fuckin' course."

"Don't you want him caught?"

"Why don't you just get the hell out of here? I don't recall inviting you over tonight." He sat down, breathing rapidly, caught hold of his bottle.

"You admire him, don't you?" Now she was mad, with the blood rushing to her head, thumping white hot inside of her. She might have believed it before Karol was killed, but not now. She clutched her fists, and almost hoped he would give the wrong answer, help push her over the edge somewhere, because that's what she wanted.

"No." He took another gulp. Damn girl, he thought, just clear on out.

"Yes, you do."

"He's a bastard. But I admire what he's done." Jack stood up, steadied himself on the table with both hands. He did not look at her, but focused on the map. "He's given the Valley a breather. I have never seen it so beautiful." He looked up at her. "Last summer, last fall, it's how I dreamed it could be. I've taken walks, through the meadows, by the falls, up the ridges, and I don't see any people. I don't hear any fucking people. Taken a lot of walks." He was coming close to telling her, damn it, and he didn't care. No sense in sneaking around with it. She was just his daughter, after all, and she would have to live with it. Like he did. Why couldn't she just clear out? Give him a chance to cool his head. He looked at her, saw her clenched fists, and shut up.

"You admire all of this?"

"So do you. Admit it. You want this Valley to yourself as much as anyone."

"You don't know me," she said evenly.

"Maybe not. Why don't you get the fuck out of my house?"

"I will." She pointed to the map. "After you tell me where he would be. Give me a chance out there."

"I know exactly where he is." He was coming close now. She put him on the spot, and he wanted to tell her. Just to cut her for making him feel so bad in his own house.

"How?" It wasn't just that he was boasting—he acted as if he were certain. "How could you know for sure?"

"Because the day after he got away—that time you all came close, but lost him—I had an idea about how he did it. I took a hike, felt along the base of Illouette Ridge for a little cave I know about. Then I found it, just a tiny opening, but I looked in." He stopped, looking at her. Eli stared at him, lowered her head slightly, looking up at him through her brows. A look of hatred she had learned when she was a little girl. Used to make him laugh when she gave it to him. It wasn't funny on her face now.

"You found something?"

"Saw something down in the rock." He could not look at her anymore. She had him mumbling; he felt whipped. But he would have had to tell her sooner or later. "Maybe the muzzle of a gun, something he left behind. It was dark down there. I'm not sure. Now, why don't you get out?"

"You found this before he shot Karol."

"Just go, Eli."

"You wanted to let him keep on, right?" She moved close to him now, screaming. "You shit! You wanted to see if he could really clear the Valley, is that right?"

"I let things run their course," he looked her in the eye. Wasn't going to let Eli think she had him on the run. He'd be damned if he would back down to his own daughter.

"He killed Karol!" Eli picked up his bottle, looked at it, and then did something she had been dreaming of for most of her life. She hurled it into the wall, watching the glass shatter.

Jack stared at the mess, saw the dark stain on his floor and the flames dance in the shards of glass. He felt cold and his mind blanked out with rage. "You little bitch!"

The old man swung and hit her in the jaw.

The punch felt weak to Eli, nothing like they used to feel years ago, and she quickly shook it off. Standing a little taller, she looked down on him, saw him sway. Eli grabbed him by the hair at the top of his head with two hands, and pulled his face into her knee with all the strength she had. He tried to stand, but she threw him onto the table, so that he bent over it, face down. She pulled his arm behind his back, in a tight lock.

"This how you drove her out?" She screamed, losing sight of him in her tears, but pushing his arm up as hard as she could as the rage of months, years, unwound inside her. "Now I know why I grew up without a mother."

"Talk to the man she run off with."

"I'd have done the same."

"I bet you would. You got some whore in you." The blood from Jack's nose collected in the back of his throat and he spat on the map. If he hadn't been so damned drunk, he could take her. "Let me go."

"Show me the cave." Seeing the blood, Eli relaxed her hold on him, but not too much. She did not know what he would do once he was free.

"About there, damn it." He pointed to the spot with his left hand. "Now let me go or I'll give you a real fight."

She released him. Jack turned, looking at her, letting the blood run quickly down his face, dripping off his beard. They both stared, breathing heavily, he more than she. Something between them had just changed, and they both knew it.

"God," Eli said, "did I break your nose?"

"Damn near." He touched it gently. Jack felt relieved to have gotten it out at last, thought the price he paid wasn't really that high. She'd feel guilty enough about the wound, he could tell. Her strength amused him, cut into his anger some. "You're some piece of work. What kind of woman are you?"

"The kind you raised."

"Get out of my house," he said.

She turned, shaking, and walked quickly to the door. When her hand was on the old brass knob, he spoke.

"Hey," Jack sighed softly. "Come back later. I got some things you'll need for your fool expedition."

Eli looked back at him, and he sat heavily in his chair, watching her carefully, gently wiping the blood from under his nose. Grinning.

XXXXI

Eldred Spell knew that someone was coming for him, and he sat at the mouth of the cave, looking out through a hole just twice the size of his head. A single person, coming despite the winds and the heavy snow. He did not see the person, nor hear one coming, but his other sense told him that someone was close. He could almost see what would happen when he closed his eyes; never before had his sense of things to come been so clear. Still, he could not see exactly what he would do.

Spell believed that this part of him, what he now hoped to be the most worthy, had grown stronger because everything else in him had died in the last few days. Little by little he disconnected himself from the rest of the world, and now he saw that everything he had done in the Park had been to prepare for this time in his life. To give him a place to go. To make that place, he had forced himself to retire from the world. Some kind of circle that he was coming to the end of, and as he watched the storm grow stronger outside, felt the gale force winds and the ice cut into his exposed face, Eldred Spell wondered where the circle had begun. Perhaps when his father had taken him to the Valley so many years before, planting the driving images in his mind, so that everything else had been a diversion, or a way to gather resources to come to these days at the end.

Andrea had receded down the hoop out of sight, along with all of his money. Followed by his Jaguar, a car he had kept against all reason because it tethered him to that other life in New York City. He had driven down Highway 1, all the way to

Los Angeles, because he knew that from Carmel, down to Big Sur, Santa Barbara, Malibu Colony, Santa Monica, he would be running with the other Jaguars. An expensive car would not stand out. He took a chance, of course—one passing highway patrolman might have finished him. But his vision was clear; he knew they would not catch him on the highway. He never saw a patrol car.

He drove into Compton, finally pulled onto a quiet vacant lot, rolled over the dry weeds and broken beer bottles. The ground was hard, trampled. Dry, brown palm trees lined the road. He had collected brochures about Mexico, and scattered a few in the lot as he left. Took the key, and locked the doors. No one saw him, and he looked back at the Jag, sitting in the lot, with the dirty stucco wall of a liquor store in the background. The car would last a few hours at most.

Walking along the street—sun out but still somewhat chilly at noon—he took in the people who passed by. Smelled the gritty air as he hiked inside the great brown mountain of smog. In his backpack, he had as many MREs as he could hold, along with the last submachine gun he owned—a trusty 9 mm Sterling, a weapon he could depend on in adverse weather. People, mostly women and children, looked at him with his backpack. They tended to look at the backpack more than at him. If anyone appeared to recognize him, which he doubted in that neighborhood, he would be ready. He had his gun.

Within fifteen minutes he found the kind of situation he had been looking for: an older man standing by a beat-up car. They spoke little. The man readily understood what Spell wanted, as if he had been waiting for a man like Spell to show up all along. Spell took the keys, turned the ignition; the old Ford LTD idled poorly and blew some smoke, but it would do. He handed the old man a thousand dollars in cash, close to the last of his money, and drove away. Spell left the car in the parking garage at LAX, and he walked to the Greyhound bus station in Santa Monica. Took the bus to Mammoth Lakes, timed it so he arrived late at night. He walked through a residential area, and at the edge of the woods he found a trail.

By the next morning, when he had hiked to the cave, the clouds had poured in and the wind picked up. He had just enough time to check the trip wires he had set some time before—thin wires the same shade of grey as the cliff rock—and he noted the faint circuit had not been broken. He checked the batteries, the small radio transmitters that would send a signal if the wires were tripped, and he went to the cave just as the snow began. Everything had been perfect, as if he were walking through a memory, so that each step he made had the outcome he had already seen. Except the snow. No one had predicted it, and he could not see the squall coming until just an hour before the snow fell. He wondered at that; nature seemed less predictable than the human world, lacking the lockstep systems of artificiality.

Spell had plenty of food collected inside but he did not feel hungry. With a black tarpaulin flap he had rigged, he could be warm, out of the wind. As he stood at the cave entrance, he did not feel the cold, the loss of Andrea, the money, the car, nor any dread at what he believed was coming. He had the Sterling under his thick coat. Eldred Spell simply looked at the heavy snow, driving straight into him now that the wind had shifted, columns of flakes coming out of the white like great hands and fingers, reaching. He had followed Ellen's tracks to the end. And he watched until his eyes stung, trying to picture the one who was coming after him.

Eli stopped at the base of the Mist Trail, could hear the roar of the falls, and could just make out the sign: TRAIL CLOSED—ICE DANGER. She could feel the rock under the snow vibrate with the thunder of the falls, and felt unnerved that she could not see the water, but just a wall of snow falling. She had to sit on the ice to pull off her snowshoes, tying them to her pack and tucking everything under the white canvas cover her father had given her. She pulled on boots with long sharp cleats, made for biting into ice. Sitting down, with visibility so low, she felt vulnerable. He could come down any second.

Eli stood up, tested the boots in the ice, and walked around the sign. The trail was over a thousand stone steps, with a rock wall on one side and a cliff on the other. The steps, slick with ice from the waterfall mist and a new coating of slippery snow, seemed to slant toward the cliff side. If she lost her footing once, she would slide into the huge hole the falls had carved out of the rock. Two hundred feet down at least. Several times she, or her father before her, had gone on SAR teams to find people who had tried to do what she was attempting now. They found them, bodies eviscerated, caught on the jagged rocks below, in what she and others called the teeth of the Merced River.

Starting, there were many things she tried not to think about. Falling. The possibility of meeting Eldred Spell when she was not ready. Being fired for making the attempt to go after him alone. Her father, who would not look her in the eye when she had come back to the cabin for equipment. But above all, she tried to keep Sarah out of her mind. What kind of woman are you, her father had asked. What kind of mother, Eli asked herself. One slip, or if Spell jumped her, or if the wet snow came down from the ridges in an avalanche, or if she simply became lost and froze to death—there were many ways to leave Sarah a ward of Meredith. Maybe the way I am, she thought bitterly, it may be for the best.

That was self-pity, though, and she would not allow such indulgence. Soon enough, she did not have the time. At each step, she brushed the snow aside, set her left leg down firmly so she dug in, and slowly hoisted herself up. The better she became as she caught the rhythm, the faster Eli moved. Wind increased, and the snow fell more heavily. Wearing the old white ski coveralls, with white gloves and cap, she could hardly see her own body against the white landscape. As if she were a ghost, an invisible figure, climbing up the trail. When the snow grew denser, and her goggles clouded, she seemed to fade away completely. Once she slipped, and her leg slid away as if independent of her. After that, she paid more attention to the roar of the falls, deep against the howl of the wind. Finally she came to the backside of another ice warning sign; she had made the top, but realized coming down would be much harder.

Cold seeping in through her thick clothing, Eli put her hands on her knees, waiting to catch her breath. Although she had left at sunrise, it was noon and she had several miles to cover. The wind already blew hard, but she knew it would be far worse up at the base of Illouette Ridge. Her plan had been to get to the Ridge, check it out, and come back down so she could bivouac at a lower elevation, in the shelter of trees. At the pace she made, Eli realized she could be stuck on the ridge at night. If the storm continued to blow, she would very likely freeze to death.

Putting her snowshoes back on, she started walking. The trail had been obliterated, but she used the sound of the river, her illuminated compass, and occasional tree markers to find her way. The trail to the ridge cut off to the left and required a river crossing. Eli had walked nearly a mile beyond the cutoff before she saw a sign for the Seaver Lake trail. She backtracked until she found the sign for Illouette, which she had missed. She crossed on the trail bridge, the water so high it shook the timbers. Wood slippery and heavily glazed with ice and snow. The storm continued to grow worse, shaking the trees and pushing against her, and she had just lost another hour.

On the Illouette trail, he felt closer. The afternoon had grown dark, and the shadows in the swirling snow would startle her—they looked like a man running. She did not drink nor eat, for fear that she would have to relieve herself, spending even a minute or two off-guard and defenseless. Hoping that the storm would abate as she climbed; it didn't. Made her feel like the Valley had something against her, trying to push her down the mountain. Despite her layers of clothing, by the time she had climbed to 10,000 feet, the cold cut through. Now she had to keep moving to stay warm, for the cold moved in very quickly the moment she was still. The uphill climb and the weather drained her energy, and once she relented and ate a chocolate bar.

By four the trail began a steep descent and Eli almost slipped. Stopping, she realized that she had gone off the trail, and was heading down Illouette Ridge. Had she kept going, she would have walked into the forest, where, she began to think, she should be anyway. But Eli started up, looking for the cliff wall. An hour later, she found it, and she came to a great vertical groove in the cliff where there was some protection from the wind. By then the snow, flying through clouds settled on the ridge, had become dark grey in the last light of the afternoon. She kept a map deep in her heavy wool sock just below the knee. Unzipping the coveralls, she pulled up her ski pants. Everything seemed hard now. Tired. At least the map was dry.

Goggles raised, she looked at the folded square in her gloves. She could guess where she was on the map; the cave might be no more than fifty yards away. Eli felt certain that meant fifty yards ahead, although she might have bypassed it when she drifted off the trail. Her hands no longer shook, numb even under her layered gloves. She thought she should go down to the woods, find some shelter in the grove, and eat. Down there she could brace against the storm and survive the night. Caught up here, things would be rougher. Already the temperature plummeted and still the wind became stronger. Upgrading to something like a blizzard, she thought. At least like one up here.

Yet her nature directed that as she was so close, she could not go down without one pass by the cave. Besides, if she waited for the next day, the storm could well have passed, when it would be impossible to approach the cave without being seen half a mile away. And if the sun came out, all of the snow piled above would become very unstable. She would also be quickly found walking around the ridge—a helicopter would come by, they'd have her over at headquarters, and she'd have to explain to a new superintendent why she was searching for a killer without even reporting in from her leave. Spell might not even be up there; she could be throwing away a career, risking her life, for nothing at all.

Pulling her pack off, struggling painfully with its weight, she set it down. Taking out her father's .45, she checked it carefully. Then Eli realized she could not even shoot it with the heavy gloves she wore. Despite the cold, she stripped down to one layer for her right hand. Then she packed up and readied herself for the final walk. She decided to give it a half hour, and then start straight down. From the cave, the slope was steep but not impossible; she might have to go a few hundred yards before she hit the tree line.

Walking ahead, she could see almost nothing. All was a dark grey, except for the gun, a small black hole in her palm. She stayed close to the cliff wall to keep her direction and to check for the cave. There might be a light or some indication if he were inside. She doubted he would be out now. Only a fool would travel in this, she thought.

Now that Eli came so close, she had to confront herself with what she would do if she found him. Almost night, with her strength spent, she could not subdue him. Even if she could, where would they go? She had a radio and could call in, but no helicopter or team would be able to come out. Taking him alive would be extremely dangerous. But, she admitted to herself, that had not really been what she pictured. Yet Eli could not see him sprawled dead before her—she had never shot anyone. Even her father had never been compelled to do that. She stopped again. He had been right to call it a foolish expedition; she had no idea what she would do if she found him. She had not expected the storm to become so intense. A few steps farther, and she would have to go down. If she were lucky, no one would learn what she had done.

The thing was to get out of the cold; the thought began to overcome all others. She had taken winter hikes before, sometimes in brutal weather, but nothing like this. And those other times, she had been with someone. Her father had taken her, trained her in heavy winter storms, but he had been there. Even now, she felt he knew more about it than she did. And really, neither of them knew anything about tracking down killers. Thoughts of Sarah crowded into her head, and the weight of what she was doing, the insanity of it, came down on her.

She looked away from the cliff, which was nothing but a dark blur anyhow, and she stared down into the snow wall, imagining the line of the slope she would go down. Surely no more than three hundred yards. With her compass, she would not drift. She could make it in time, before the night set completely.

As she started down, one of the shadows in the snow swirled in front of her. It did not pass by, but kept coming, and when she saw that it took the form of a man, a black figure swimming out of the grey, there was no time. Eli did not even raise the gun. A painful bright glare filled her eyes completely and she saw nothing else.

XXXXII

Eldred Spell had not thought about what he would have to do if the person who crumpled in the snow did not die. He should have fired; instead, he slammed into the side of the attacker's head with the steel butt of his submachine gun. A simple burst from the Sterling would have been better. After all, he was certain the person was alone, so no one would have heard the gun, no one would have come running out of the storm. This person came to him just as he had expected. He was seeing things very clearly now. Still, he hoped he had a dead body to bring down into the cave, probably stuff it in one of the small fissures, seal it up with loose rocks. Like the raccoon. The smell would not be too bad, especially with the cold.

By the time summer warmed up the cave, and bodies would more quickly putrefy, he expected to be dead anyhow.

Spell picked up the .45 and put it in his jacket pouch. Then he leaned down, put his arms under the shoulders of the body, set his boots against the sloping snow, and pulled. At the mouth of the cave he dug away the ice, managed to move a boulder back, so he could stuff the body inside. It slid to the narrow cave floor. He crawled inside, set the boulder back in place, and looked out at the storm. Night had come, the snow black. But he could hear the wind, roaring at some fifty miles an hour, so he could picture the merciless, pounding ice—tons of frozen water shooting across the Valley. No one else would be out there. That cheered him; though there would be trouble when the sun came again.

Dropping the tarp, weighing it down with rocks, he secured the cave. The black canvas hardly moved, for little wind touched it. He pulled off his gloves and pushed his hood back; his nose was numb. Stepping over the body, he turned on all four of the small battery-powered heaters. His low-energy halogen lantern cast an amber light on sharp grey walls. The canvas on the other end of the little room, which shut out the rest of the cave, was also secure. He waited as the air warmed.

When Spell had rested, and felt he could waste no more time, he knelt down next to the body, turned it right side up. All white coveralls; tall, rather thin person. Streaks of blood from the head wound ran down the right side of the hood. The plastic goggles were cracked but still on, so he pulled them off, and pushed the hood back. Blood mixed in the blonde hair. He had not expected a woman. But that should make no difference, Spell told himself. He could simply hold his glove over her nose and mouth, suffocating her—that would be a neat way to finish this. Could just shoot her now, he thought, kill her with her own .45. But Spell recognized her from the media photos.

He shifted her onto the pallet he slept on, covered her with his blankets, and moved the heaters closer. In their soft glow, her face seemed golden, and the blood on the side of her head and hood dark brown. Although he felt compelled to do the sensible thing and kill her before she woke, he decided to wait. He would see if she did stir, if she could talk, and he might as well find out how she came. As he looked at her face, certain who she was, he knew why Eli Ware had come for him alone. He could be sure that no one authorized this trip. But she could not go through with it, apparently. She had not even raised the gun.

It would be easier to do away with a man, he thought, some clean-cut military type. Even a man like Horton. Still, he thought, such consideration is quite out of date.

Spell sat down, leaned back against a rock, and waited. Within two hours she began to move very slightly, head rocking back and forth, lips twitching, eyebrows knitting, like a young child coming out of a bad dream. She opened her eyes a long time but did not seem to record anything. Eventually, recognition crept into them. He found the process fascinating, and was glad he had waited to kill her. Plenty of time for that, he thought, always time for that.

Coming out of unconsciousness, the first thing Eli Ware's brain recorded was the pain. A dull ache spread across the right side of her head, as if someone had slammed her with a heavy iron pan that still clung to her skull. When she moved, the pain stayed imbedded on that right side. Beyond the head, came lesser pain; small cuts and bruises along her backside. And her right knee had been banged. But she could move, she could breathe, she could hear faintly the wind blowing.

Looking straight up, her right eye seemed clouded. Swelling on that side. But she saw the outline of narrow cave walls, moving up, toward each other, until they met far above somewhere in a fissure of darkness. Saw the dim lights of the heaters, and the stronger light of the lamp. It hurt to look at that. On the other side she saw him, sitting, staring at her.

Abruptly, she recalled what had happened.

She looked at him for a long time; a tall, thin man. Dark. Angular. Older than he appeared in the newspaper photos. But no doubt, it was Eldred Spell. She tried to sit up, but with the slight elevation her head throbbed, as if the heavy pan dropped, finding new pain centers. Eli slid back down, still looking at Spell.

"How are you?" he asked. His voice was flat, lacking any tone of concern.

"Fine."

"I've been sitting here, trying to figure out why I didn't just shoot you." He looked away, the underside of his long chin lit up against the black fissure above. "I should kill you."

"What can I say to that?" she asked wearily, trying to blow away the fog in her head, control the pain, so she could think clearly enough to find the words to talk herself away from Spell, out of his cave. But then she remembered the storm outside, the night, the miles from home.

"I hear the storm," she said.

"Yes, it's still out there."

"Is it night?"

"Only nine. There's a long way to go."

"I feel warmer."

"The heaters." He looked at her again. "Extremely efficient solar-powered cells; their batteries collect sunlight, so tonight we have heat. I suppose they're worth what I paid for them." Toward the end, he had discovered that Doug Evers was marking up his prices substantially. He had made a lot of money off Spell. Not that it mattered. As Spell fled Monterey, he made a quick stop at Evers' for the MREs. The man trembled at the door, wouldn't let Spell in, and begged him to leave. The FBI had been by several times. Evers will cave in, Spell thought, he'll be ruined. At least Suko Egusa had been smarter; Evers said she had already left the country, even before Spell had been identified. Turned out her house and furniture were rented; although she had told Evers she would be on vacation, Spell knew she would not be back. They would never catch her. A relentless, admirable woman.

"Are you hungry?" Spell asked. "Thirsty?"

"No." So far, she had been spared the urge to relieve herself. If it had been a problem before, it would be a nightmare now. She did notice that Spell seem relaxed, and appeared to be thinking of something that made him smile slightly. Eli wondered if she could talk, get to know him—it might make killing her off more difficult. But with the pain and fatigue, she had trouble with conversation. If she could stay alive until the storm abated and daylight came, she might have a chance— she must stay awake and keep talking. Her eyes were heavy, however, and she wanted to sleep. Eli reminded herself that with a concussion, which she probably had, sleep would be dangerous. Sleep would also make her that much easier to kill.

"I think I have a concussion," she said.

"Yes," he said, looking at how the flesh on her cheek and around her eye had swollen. "I've had recent experience with concussions."

"I shouldn't sleep," she said.

"You might not wake up."

The way he said that, with the slight grin still on his face, roused her. Made her angry, brought the blood up—no matter how much that hurt her, it was what she needed.

"Was this all for revenge?" she asked. "For your sister?"

"That was part of it."

"It wasn't all?"

"I've been thinking about that." He looked away from her again, stared at the rock. There was plenty of time to ponder on this question and other things, time to discover himself, or at least what was left. Take stock of the damage.

"So why?"

"To give this land back to itself. I should think the answer is obvious to you."

"Me?"

"You're with the Park Service."

"I'm a ranger." Her eyes closed, and she began to drift away.

"Don't sleep," he said. He knelt closer to her, touched her shoulder. Despite the swelling, he could see she was a beautiful woman, and for a moment he did not want her to fall asleep. Not that the beauty mattered. No. But she was a ranger, and it occurred to him that the way things would go he would not have a chance to talk with any of them. Something pleasant about chatting with the adversary. This was a rare chance. Surprised, he realized that he did not want her to die. If that were to happen, it would be on his terms. "Get up."

"All right." She focused on him again. "You keep me awake."

"I will." He took in a deep breath, looked at the wall again. "I wanted to simply clear the Park out. Like the line the media made so much of."

"What they got from that man," she said, coaxing out her anger, hoping to draw on some energy there. She tried to remember his name, but could not focus.

"Yes." He paused. Did not want to think about Horton now, but instead pictured the Valley, how it appeared, clean and empty. Quiet. "Can't you appreciate what I've done?"

"No."

"Be honest." He came closer to her face, wishing she was not so misshapen by the swelling. He had hit her far too hard. "Some part of you, as a ranger, as someone who appreciates this Valley, wanted it emptied out, too."

"All right." She wanted to find the argument here, but felt too weak and unfocused. Falling asleep. Yes, there had been a part of her that enjoyed seeing the Valley quiet, beautiful, like everyone who lived there hoped it would be. Yes, if she admitted it, there had been plenty of days that she wanted all the damned tourists to get out and give the land a chance to heal.

"There," he said. "I've done what many people, even you, would do."

"No." And something tore through her, brought her to life for a moment, and she struggled to get up despite the pain that wanted her to lie down and give in. "I wouldn't do it. No one I know would do it. Think of what you've done. The people you killed."

"Had to." He admired how she fought the pain; looking at the way she sweated, the yellowing on the side of her face, the thickness of her voice—he wondered if she were dying. Once she fell asleep, and that would be soon, she probably would die. "There's always a cost. That's a fact of economics, the thing that drives everything we do in this country."

"Human life is too high." She thought of Karol, her heart raced now, pumping so that the iron pan swung into the side of her head again and again.

"No, not really." Spell actually enjoyed the conversation, for he felt like he was talking to some extension of himself. A part of him that he had put away somewhere. Sometimes, as he had moved through the Valley at nights and had time to think, he had this conversation with himself. He knew where it would go.

"We all know human life is cheap. It's a common fact. A few lives, against the restoration of the entire Valley and all that lives in it, is nothing. There are too many of us. Since you and I were born, the population has gone from three to six billion. What is a few lives? Really, as a country, we won't say it aloud, but we all know."

"Life is sacred." She wanted to say something more profound, for the point seemed too obvious. He would laugh such a statement off. Most people would find such a cliche simplistic. It had nothing to do with reality. But, tired as she was, already slipping away again, she could think of nothing better.

"That's nice," he said. The thought had occurred to him. An easy one to talk down. "Nothing important gets done without the human cost. Movements roll better on blood. Look at our country: wars and riots, crime, the death penalty, euthanasia, abortion."

"Human life is sacred. You should hold that up to everything you do. The real test." Eli was not sure she believed it herself, for she had never told herself before that human life was sacred, and had not considered it a test for her values. It was simple, basic, but also uncommon. Hadn't she been taught instead that there were many things worth killing and dying for? Would the Valley be one of those things?

"A man once told me—," Spell started.

Her eyes drooped, and he shook her gently, more and more anxious to keep her awake.

"He said, `America is a violent country.' He had a point. At the time, I could have shot him. Instead, I let him go. Now because of that mistake I'm here."

"You're here because you're stupid." Eli's words were slurred as she closed her eyes. The warmth enveloped her, pain faded away. She could hear her voice, but it seemed that someone else was talking.

"Stupid?" He felt irritated suddenly, amazed that she would say that. Many of the things Spell had done made him reexamine himself, the killings at times made him feel like a bad person, but never in his life could he consider himself stupid. "How can you say that? I've beaten the entire government; took the land from them, from you. How am I stupid?"

"Killing is the fool's way out." Her voice seemed completely independent of her now, somewhere in a blank space while she spiraled down to a comfortable dream. "We believed you were smart. But you're a stupid, fucking terrorist."

"I am not a terrorist." She bothered him now, but he still hoped she would not fall asleep. He shook her harder. "That label was pinned on me."

"Just a killer who wanted control. You'll lose it. Like all the other assholes who kill to own the land."

"I wanted—"

"Control." Her voice floated somewhere far above; Eli could hardly hear it anymore. "This winter you'll be dead, the lodges will be packed. My husband will still be dead. Your stupidity."

"I am not stupid." But he felt like a child for having to say it. The execution of everything he had done was brilliant; even paramilitary experts on television praised his tactics. Couldn't imagine how a stockbroker had learned so much. State militias across the country praised his abilities, admired his resolve. Radical environmental groups condemned the violence but lauded the effect. He had been relentless. He had done something that was incredibly hard; harder than mastering Wall Street. Took a very hard person to accomplish it all. For her to say it was stupid. The thought struck him, and he was bothered that in all the long conversations he had with himself, where he balanced the costs and the morality of what he was doing, he had never considered the possibility that his was a stupid action.

Eli fell asleep. Spell shook her violently but she did not respond. He wished he could wake her to find out exactly how she believed what he had done was stupid. The fool's way out, as she put it. Now, while she slept, he would have to work it out in his own mind, turn her words in on himself and see what the outcome would be.

Spell stared at her for a long time. Her breathing was regular, but she might have slipped into a coma. Kept telling himself that he had hit her too hard. Or that he should have shot her right off. Then it occurred to him that she should have been killed another way. Something was wrong with the damn circuit he set up. Feeling irritated, he became angry at the notion that he was irritated. He had to get out of the cave.

Spell opened the flap and saw a wall of snow; he dug out with his gloved hands, then wriggled out of the hole. The wind had died and the flakes fell gently on his upturned face. But the snow was too deep to walk in, and he had forgotten his snowshoes. Going back to get them, he checked on her. No change. Still breathing. Then he went out.

Exactly one hundred feet to the left of the cave entrance, Spell dug carefully into the snow, searching with a dim flashlight. At last, he found the trip wire. It had been buried deep in the snow, and he realized she had probably walked right over it. Switching off the circuit, he raised the wire two feet and reset it. He would have to do the same with the wire one hundred feet to the right of the entrance. An elephant could walk over that one, buried as deep as it was, and Spell would never know it. For all the hard, dangerous work he had done, the remaining charges Egusa had given him would never go off with the trip wires buried. He stood in the dark, thinking about how he had not considered the impact of the rising snow level.

"Stupid," he said to himself.

XXXXIII

In the center of the dark was a very bright patch of light, and Eli had no idea what it was until something snapped, synapses registered as in an old damaged machine. Winding up in the jangled lines, under the flatness of a heavy ache, she awakened. Focusing, looking through the pulsing veins in her eyes, she recognized the entrance to the cave—dug out of the snow. Sunlight so bright she had to blink, so bright that everything else in the cave had gone black against that screaming yellow patch. Etched in the light, a line between sun and shadow: Spell. Still, as if he had been there, in that position, for a long time. Slowly, he turned his head, the edge of a smile in the sun.

"You're awake."

"Yeah." Her head and jaw ached. The inside of her mouth was gritty and dry, as if she were waking from a bad bout of anaesthesia.

"There's a water bottle by your hand."

"Thanks," she said mechanically. Slowly, Eli sat up, testing her limbs. Everything worked, coordination seemed to fall into place. Turned the lid on the bottle, opened it, and drank. Becoming slowly, painfully alert. She noticed the barrel of the submachine gun pointing into the sun, where the black polished steel rode up his back from the shoulder strap. She had no idea where her gun was.

Sometime after dawn Spell had knelt down and put his hand carefully over her chest. Felt the strong regular beating of her heart, counted the breaths, the little steam that rose into the cold air from her lips. He went through all of the power in his solar batteries, turned what might have been a few day's power loose. He figured she would live, and waited hours for her to awaken.

Finally he had opened the flap, looked outside, saw the thin layer of snow that had fallen on the tunnel he had dug. The sun had risen strong over the Valley, lit up the thick covering of snow sharp and harsh. Reflections bore upon reflections and the air heated up quickly. By 9 a.m. he took off his heavy jacket. Looked through the binoculars, saw no one down below. A helicopter flew across his view a mile out, flying straight—nothing that looked like a search pattern. She had come alone. He pondered what to do with her. Often, he looked at the trip wires; they were hard to see, thin grey lines against the white.

The thing to do, he thought, was to let the wire decide it. Wait until she could walk, let her go. If that did not work, he could shoot her. That would be much harder, he admitted. The other way, if he stayed in the cave, his tracks would be covered, and her tracks as well. He could go through the mountain again, if he wanted to escape.

He did not eat. That no longer mattered, he felt more and more certain as he watched the sun climb higher. Eldred Spell did not know the outcome, could not quite feel it, but did believe this was his last day. Probably hers, too. So for the morning, he could just sit and enjoy the silence of all the slopes without skiers.

"I need a bathroom," she said.

"Last night I fashioned something for you. That plastic jug cut in half, by your hand, might work."

"Oh," she picked it up. "You use this?"

"I prefer a full jug." He smiled, still watching ahead. "Don't worry, I won't look. My mother raised me to be a master of self-control."

As quietly as possible, looking at him when she could, she stripped down the layers of her pants. Hard to balance herself over the damn jug. Cold. And now the pain, worse than in her head. All the signs of a bladder infection. She put aside the jug and dressed. Sat down for a moment while the cave spun. Then perceptions aligned again, as her brain struggled with all of its tangled, swollen messages.

He had not turned.

"I'm sick," she said. "I need to leave."

"I've been thinking about that. Can I turn around?"

"Yes."

"Now, you came here to kill me?"

"To stop you."

"That would mean kill. How else would I be stopped?"

"I don't know."

"You meant to kill me."

"I'm too tired for this," she said.

"Just admit what you came here for."

"Yes, probably. I suppose I pictured you dead." She had wanted to kill him, down in the Valley, while she twisted alone in her bed, hands reaching out for a man who was no longer there. Yes, she had wanted to kill him. But now, the thought added to the nausea that she had awakened with. That memory, of wanting to blow his brains out in a scene right off the movie screen, that was now just another pain.

"No one knows you're here."

"My father does."

"So we have little time."

More time than you think, she thought. I doubt he's even awake right now. "So what do we do?" she asked.

"We've been very civil to each other, considering."

"That you killed my husband in front of my daughter, yes."

"That you came to shoot me, yes." He did not want to think of her daughter. The picture of her in the field that day reeled, tore through his mind the entire night as soon as he matched her swollen face to the one in the newspapers and magazines. He knew the names: Eli Ware, and Sarah, and Karol.

"I think you are a strong person," his eyes narrowed on her. "Hard person, aren't you? But something softer, too. I believe I watched you dance once for some Japanese men, back at your cabin."

"You watched us?"

"Only that evening."

"Did you pick out my husband? Plan it?"

"Random chance. But I don't want to discuss it."

Eli had no desire to push him. He looked at her harshly, and he had pulled the machine gun around, set it on his lap. She thought he was screwing up the courage to shoot her, and was amazed that a man so accomplished in killing delayed at all. Tensing, she drew as much strength into herself as she could, readying to attack him if he pointed the gun at her. Pictured clawing him—she had slipped her gloves off. Could bang his head against the side of the cave. But the thoughts brought on the nausea again, even stronger than before.

"Thinking of killing me?" He saw how she balanced herself on her thighs, legs tucked under, ready to spring. But she was wobbly, like an angry beast hit by a car. Trying to stand on the road. The grotesque swelling on the side of her head added to the effect. She seemed the kind of wild, wounded animal one does well to pump a few rounds into. That's a nice picture, he thought, if I could just be convinced by it.

"Let me leave."

"And if you survive the walk home, you'll send an army after me." Actually, he did not care. But he found it amusing to test her.

She exhaled slowly and sat back. Eli found her gloves and pulled them on. "I'm tired. I'm going."

"All right."

He stepped back out of the way of the hole. "When you're ready, go ahead." She looked wary, curious, face upturned like a child. The fact that he had her off balance gave him a curious pleasure, and he wished he could have met her in a different time. Alanis and Andrea both had been tough, both good players of a mental game. But neither could have sought him in a gale, nor had the grit to come out and off him.

"Do you have everything?" he asked.

"Yes." She tried to put up her hood, but it had stuck to her matted hair, her dry blood acting like epoxy. She had no desire to move it.

"Then go ahead."

Eli did not believe him. Figured as soon as she passed he would shoot her, or plunge a knife into her back, and throw her body back somewhere down in the cave. She moved to the entrance, watching his eyes. Very green in the reflection of the sun, they told her nothing. She looked away—wriggling through the entrance felt like moving through to the abyss; at any moment he would stop her heart. But she came out into the bright light, watching her white canvas coverall disappear into the landscape except for the blood stains. Standing was not easy, and she discovered her right knee was weak, causing pain when she put weight on it.

Immediately he was up behind her, right next to her back, taller. She strained her eyes to see someone below. Strained to hear the hum of a chopper's engine. But only a muffled wind, like static in a microphone, came to her ears.

"I didn't think you'd let me through."

"I could have killed you in the cave."

She took a step forward and sank to her thigh in the snow. Forgot her snowshoes.

"I'll get them," he said.

He did, and she put them on. Then she looked at Spell. She could not read the expression on his face, but he seemed slightly amused.

"You still think I'm a stupid man?"

"Did I say that?"

"Last night."

"What I think—." She stopped, too tired to be angry. Trying to kill him had been more than enough, all rage and blood had drained into the pain she felt. "I want to go home to my daughter. You remember her?"

"Go."

The picture of her daughter in the field came up in his mind and he tried to overpower it, set it aside. That almost dead part of him, threshing about. He picked up the Sterling, sighted on her back.

She staggered off in the direction she had come, but this time the wire was in place, where it should be. But if she could get past it, he had the gun. If he timed his shot correctly, he could make her fall across the wire. He studied the way she struggled rigidly to keep herself upright. Perhaps her concussion was worse than his had been. He had hit her very hard, after all.

Eli refused to look at him. There was a tightness in her back, as if she could feel the very point where he was aiming. She wanted to close her eyes, or even to get on her knees and plead, or simply to pretend that she had passed out. But she knew better than to look back. She narrowed her eyes, set them straight ahead, and concentrated on walking. Just that required enough of her mind. Pick up one shoe, set it down, follow with the other.

Her left shoe stuck on something, and she had to push it down.

"Stop!" he screamed. "If you move, I will shoot you!"

Here it comes, she thought. If she had more strength, she could throw herself down the slope, roll down three hundred yards. Maybe she'd make it. But he stood beside her by the time she resolved to give it a try. He put the gun in her side.

"Don't move your left foot," he said.

For the first time, she could sense in his voice that he was angry. His voice had become low, strained, and she believed he was putting himself up to shooting her.

"Lift your right foot and put it ahead. Move your left, and I'll kill you."

She lifted her right foot, and in her dizziness nearly fell. But Spell stood next to her, bracing her so she could not fall.

"Now what?" she asked. The barrel felt hard in her side; she could imagine how the burst of bullets would feel. By the pain in her head, it was easy to imagine.

"You're going to run, precisely when I say. You should run down, diagonally, toward the trees."

"Why?"

"So I won't have to shoot you." He sounded enraged.

But she began to sense that his anger was not directed at her. He did not look at her at all, but instead he stared down at the ground.

She looked at the trees. If he did not shoot, she could find some cover. As she felt now, she could not outrun him. But she would find a place to hide.

"Your daughter's name is Sarah." His voice suddenly softened. Compared to the harsh tone he had spoken before, he almost sounded like another man. Relaxed. Even relieved.

"And you're Eli Ware."

She turned away from the trees, looking at him. The taut lines in his brown face were gone. He smiled broadly, as if they had just met at an important business meeting. Eli could not figure him out at all.

"You have no idea what's going to happen, do you Eli?"

"No."

"I do. That's my gift. Do you know what's going on here?" He looked down again.

Eli saw that her left snowshoe was on a wire, as was his.

"What?" she asked.

He took the gun from her side, pointing the barrel away.

"Something intelligent, Eli." Then his smile fell, and he said very quietly, "Now, run."

She ran as he told her to, starting down the slope toward the trees, running as best she could, struggling not to fall.

He heard a gentle click as she started away.

"I'll be damned," Eldred Spell said to himself.

Eli had not gone far when she heard a loud pop from above. She stopped, turned, and saw a large puff of snow billow out from the overhang of the cliff, where there was a thick bank of snow, hanging like a blue lower lip. A second later she saw the second pop. Two small explosions. She saw Spell was looking up as well. For a moment the little pops faded into silence.

And then came the huge boom, a sound like cannon fire, that Eli had heard before. The great lower lip of snow, all across Illouette Ridge, began to fall. She knew that it would be backed by tons of snow pack sloping down on the bald granite dome above the cliff. She turned and ran toward the trees, diagonally away, as one would ski from an avalanche.

Spell looked up at the crashing snow, saw it collect force and open into a huge spray as it shot over the cliff like a great falls. He had positioned the charges perfectly. And the white wall filled his eyes, blinding. "Ellen," he said softly. "This is why we came."

Before the ice hit, his body filled with thunder.

Olivos, exhausted from his quick march, stood about where the trail should be, where he had a good view of Illouette Ridge. Jack Hattan had phoned him before daybreak; the old man had called in every favor Olivos owed him, to go out and find Eli without letting the superintendent know.

Olivos had not scanned the ridge long with his binoculars when he saw the tiny figure of a man, holding something. And then Olivos saw the faint outline of someone in white, running, just a smear of blonde hair in his lense. The explosions distracted him. He looked up; the entire cliff seemed to come down. Desperately he tried to refocus on the people below but they were lost in a roaring, white cloud. Olivos ran hard, heading down, trying to figure where the bodies would go, calling into his radio as he went, all fast enough that when he reached the base of the avalanche tiny crystals of ice were still floating gently down to the ground. He cut through a rainbow as he left the forest and stepped into the bright sun.

Eli turned and ran over the slope, but her gait was slow and her shoes heavy, as if she were running in a nightmare where everything moved quickly but her. She fell, tumbled, struggled to get up. Heard the snow coming down the mountain, like a wave, like a tornado rolling on its side. It picked her up, threw her around end over end, caught her in the boiling white curl. She thought of the trees ahead. Imagined the rocks she could hit as she tumbled. She drew up into a ball, held her arms in front of her face to make a pocket of air when the snow settled. Fluid as water when it moved, the moment the ice stopped it quick froze, hard as cement. No escape. The crushing roar, pounding movement, blew all the insignificant pain from her mind, blew all thoughts away.

Until Eli stopped. Opening her eyes, she saw snow. But when she took a breath, she found free air. Her right arm was pinned, but she could raise her left hand to her face and wipe away the crust on her eyes. Above, a line of pine trees, still rocking from the impact. Her right arm, chest, and head were above the snow. But she was trapped, could not move her legs. She felt no pain, but that meant nothing in the cold. If she could get out, God knows what she would find. Split muscles, shattered bone.

For a long time she listened to her breathing, watched the sun cut through swaying branches, and the world began to spin. It began to spin away into a hole, and black edges began to grow thicker, the colored center narrowing. A face swam into view, someone she recognized, and it pushed away some of the black.

"Olivos," she said faintly.

"I've got help coming."

"Olivos," she said again as the black overtook her. "It's always Olivos."

"Absolutely, Eli. Every time."

XXXXIV

Eli looked across the South Meadow, waiting for her daughter to come home. Bright morning sun, no wind, but still very cold, with snow piled upon snow—early December now, and the meadow had not been clear of ice all November. Sarah had not been out more than an hour, but Eli waited, watched. Had brushed away the snow from the top step of the porch, settled back, and let her right leg and its brace lay upon the cold powder. The freeze eased some of the pain.

She kept looking ahead even as she heard her father tramp over from his cabin.

"Saw you sitting out here," he said as he kicked the snow off the porch and made himself a seat. "You seem to be bent on getting hypothermia this morning, but I thought you might take a cup of coffee anyway."

"Thank you." She took a sip, surprised at the flavor. "What is this?"

"Good, eh?" He smiled at her. She had received his smiles for some time, his special look where he nodded at nothing, watched her eyes, and mutely pleaded for redemption. Jack did not say a word to her, never asked for any forgiveness nor indicated any grace was needed. Except in that look.

"I never knew you to go in for cafe mocha."

"Oh, I wouldn't." He took a sip and looked at the rim. "This is Sarah's recipe."

"So you give her coffee when she goes over in the morning?"

"Why not?"

"You want to stunt her growth?"

"You drank coffee since you could stand up." He grunted, looking her up and down. "I don't see where it stunted your growth any." He pinched his nose, rubbing its side conspicuously. "Wish to hell it would have."

"How about the rum?"

"Just a drop." He smiled. "That's my part."

"You don't give any to Sarah, I hope."

"You think I'd waste my good liquor like that?" Vigorous nose rubbing now, even blew something into a kerchief. "Don't you like it?"

"Yes, I do."

"Then shut up and drink." He gulped his down, though it boiled against the back of his throat. Jack didn't like cafe mocha much, anyhow. Straight and black was always best. "Where the hell is Sarah?"

"She's out taking a hike."

"You shouldn't let a little girl go out there alone."

"Are you kidding?" Eli said, amused. "I remember having to go out there alone just to track you down."

"Wasn't so dangerous then. Now we have all these assholes in the Valley."

"There's hardly anyone out here now."

The silence in the Valley she listened to that morning reminded Eli of Spell. People had not come back in the numbers The Heston Company had anticipated. Perhaps, Shirley Weaver explained to the local press, the ski reservations had already been made elsewhere before Spell had been killed. Colorado, Utah, and Montana were packed. Eli thought it had more to do with the blood on the Valley; people had to let that sink into the ground for a time before they were ready to come and play. Spell would have been pleased by the residue of his work.

Many things, like the lack of four-wheel drives on the road or the emptiness of the Muir's dining salon near the peak of the ski season, reminded her of him. At night, alone in her room, she might hear the wind fall down the ridges, and she might even go out on the porch, watching the clouds of fresh snow blow over the cliff, fans of silver in the clear moonlight.

Jack could see Eli had faded away, into some dark thought or another, as she looked over the meadow. He did not like this moodiness in his daughter, this pensiveness, and that was not the way he raised her. He couldn't wait for the leg brace to come off, so he could get her out on the trail and put her mind right. And his, as well.

"What's the matter with Sarah, anyway?" he asked.

"Huh?"

"It's not like her to go out on these hikes alone."

"She doesn't feel alone when she goes out there."

He gave her a look out of the corner of his eye. Wanted to say that's a load of crap. But instead, he stood, picked up the cups, and started back. "I've got to get going."

"Thanks for the coffee."

"Yeah." He took a few steps out, turned. "By the way, Olivos said he was going to come out today after his shift and check on you."

"Would you please tell him not to bother? Just say I'm not seeing people right now. I'll call him some day."

"Tell him that yourself." He wanted her to get together with Olivos—that's what should have happened anyway if not for Karol coming into the Valley. All right, maybe not Olivos, but some man like him. Someone like his daughter was built for.

But he saw that look in her face, like a part of her had gone out and was searching for someone. Jack Hattan had seen a look like that in the mirror, years before, when his wife left him. The thought reminded him of those first days, with his raging toddler in the throes of being two and suddenly without a mother. Days and days of trying to figure out how he was going to go about raising her. Standing there, looking down at Eli, he could recall her struggling up the same porch, waist deep in a foot and a half of snow, quietly fighting to come to him. All of it had been a lonely business, but they made out all right.

"I'll tell Olivos to lay off for awhile," he said. Then, quickly as he could, Jack tramped back into his cabin and slammed the door to seal it tight against the cold.

When he left, Eli studied where the trees met the meadow. Looked for just the spot where Sarah should come out. At times, alone, she often measured the costs of last summer and fall against some gains. Every time she did, the results came out differently.

She had lost Karol, but gained his poetry. While he had been alive, she'd let him read a few new poems to her and she'd admire with him the graphic design of a new book when it came out. But she had not read his work. Now, she studied the books propped up against each other on the top shelf of the bookcase, she took the little volumes down. Read them. Ran her finger over the print, the thick paper, down the spine, searching for the man who wrote the words. At night she read his poems to Sarah, or Sarah read them back, and for awhile they could live the illusion that he was in the room, his words everywhere, in conversation. The poems fell off the pages like chameleons, colors changing with the mood of mother and daughter. The words were never the same, for the ears that heard them differed every day. Karol's books, spoken in the great room of the cabin, brought him back in. Left a trail by which to find him.

But at night, as she lay in bed, or during the day, when she passed a couple going down the road, the words became words only. She could not feel her way through the lines on a page and touch the flesh and blood.

Eli had gained a daughter, for she fell against Sarah now. Pulled her into her arms in a way that she would never have before, took pleasure in feeling the heartbeat, the warmth in hand, the smooth skin above brows. Sarah knew better than Eli, had learned ways from Karol to go into the woods and see more than ice, dormant shrubs, dark cliff sides. He had started speculations, conversations in her that she picked up on her own, to keep going. When Eli walked with Sarah now, hobbling at her side, leaning on the girl's shoulder slightly, she listened to her daughter, heard Karol in the rhythm and cadence of Sarah's voice. As Eli held on and listened more than ever before, she heard more than Karol. At last, Eli was hearing Sarah.

The phone rang. A voice on the answering machine, pleading into the empty cabin. Eli made no move to go inside.

Eldred Spell had given her more attention in the press. After the media's initial delight in his death—the fascination of his body, pressed up against a rock, with the lower half of his face ripped away, eyes open and screwed steadfastly toward the ridge top—after that faded from view the press looked for her. She had found him out, they wrote, pushed him to the brink, until he finally made a fatal mistake as he tried to kill her.

Cochran and others figured that his plan was to let Eli die in the avalanche while he slipped back into the cave. They had found that it went through, discovered how the man had escaped that night when they thought he would be caught for sure. With Eli dead and the entrance covered, he would have crept out the other side. But, the media went on, this woman, bent on revenge for her husband, came out in a near blizzard and forced the most resilient criminal of the century to come too far, coaxed him out to destruction. She made the cover of *Newsweek*.

None of that was important to Eli. What was, however, was the place the spotlight gave her in the Park Service. She had become a fixture in the Valley, the media associated her with it. Eli had expected a reprimand for her solo adventure from the superintendent and none came. Just more interviews. Only Cairns, featured in sidebar articles, exclaimed from his outpost in southwest Texas that she had been a fool, had not been a team member, and was lucky the man had not simply shot her. Eli had to agree. But the result was that Eli had better terms now, and she could reclaim her old job as an interpreter. No one would transfer her out of the Park.

What she could recall of her conversation with Spell in the cave made her give up Protection. What she thought she saw in his face just before he told her to run, the resolution of that struggle inside him, so strong that it enveloped her life and everyone else's in the Park, what that was she wanted to know. A kind of intelligence he may have had in the end, a line of thought that she might not learn and breathe of while she packed a gun and did drug busts. She had gone up the mountain to kill him, and had come down half alive, certified in a subject other than corrections protocol or firearms expertise.

Slowly, she stood up, leaned on the knotty, twisted blackthorn that her father had lent her. Saw a flash of movement between two distant tree trunks. Here, she had the time to learn the Valley, see the play of shadows in trees, know how the sunlight lit up the darkest clearing. And here, trotting quick and steady across the snow, came her daughter into the South Meadow, with stories to tell and things to pass on. Coming fast.

Eli started to walk ahead, pictured herself and Sarah together in the meadow and could feel the warmth of her daughter's hand. That, Eli Ware thought, that is something.

Acknowledgments and Notes

I am grateful to my family, my wife Sandra, my sons Travis and Justin, and my daughter Cadence for patience, inspiration, and love. I am grateful for the advice of Great Readers: Ed Allen, Rick Boyer, Charles Campbell, Steve Eberly, Denise Heinze, Matthew Nichols, and especially Jim Pearce (a man of vision). I am grateful for the experts who helped me (the fictionalization of facts are mine alone): Ginger Burley (ranger/naturalist), Christine Peatross (ski patroller and avalanche survivor), Dave Panebaker (protection ranger and chief), Ben Tholkes (wilderness expert). I am grateful to John Gist, who allowed my troubled characters to live, and to Jodie Rhodes, who never gave up. And many thanks to Eldred Spell, who lent me his name but nothing of his character.

And two notes. One, people familiar with the Yosemite Valley will recognize that the Park of this novel is only an approximation of the real thing. In this novel, the Park is a representation of many parks across the United States. Two, I drafted this novel before the second World Trade Center bombing and I am very sorry that the frightening predictions of one of my characters became too true on September 11, 2001. Too often reality overshadows our darkest fictions.